# THE LAST CHAPTER

# THE LAST CHAPTER

*A Novel*

Antonio Casale

iUniverse, Inc.

New York Bloomington Shanghai

# THE LAST CHAPTER

iUniverse books may be ordered through booksellers or by contacting:

iUniverse
1663 Liberty Drive
Bloomington, IN 47403
www.iuniverse.com
1-800-Authors (1-800-288-4677)

Because of the dynamic nature of the Internet, any Web addresses or links contained in this book may have changed since publication and may no longer be valid.

This is a work of fiction. All of the characters, names, incidents, organizations, and dialogue in this novel are either the products of the author's imagination or are used fictitiously.

ISBN: 978-0-595-49856-7 (pbk)
ISBN: 978-0-595-61277-2 (ebk)

Printed in the United States of America

# Acknowledgements

My nephew Peppino walks with crutches. Polio struck in his childhood.

I work as a volunteer in a health institution. I started before retiring from teaching. I can't even begin to mention the diseases that affect them.

Each year, I developed a newer mentality, a softer disposition toward the sick, a more humble attitude toward the unfortunate. This evolution of thought helped me tremendously in my relationship with others and with God.

I met people of all ages, but mainly senior citizens. Some could no longer hear or see; others could move little; and still others lay in a vegetative state.

It was not easy for one to like dealing with them. The sight of blood, the smell of urine, the sound of lamentations, the sight of their internal agony were sufficient to discourage me and to resign.

This novel is a tribute to them, especially to the bedridden, to those relegated to wheelchairs, and to the ones who scream inside seeking help. I'm immensely indebted to them both on a human and literary level. They have been inspirational to me and I hope that you, too, my dear reader, will be touched by their daily struggle in a world theater where the main actors are the diseases, pains and solitude. These victims are our brothers and sisters.

Changing our lifestyle may avert or allay some physical or emotional ailments or even postpone our encounter with death. Within this context, very sick people are confronted with the euthanasia dilemma.

Parallel to the human demise, there is the affective aspect of human life, which touches everyone of us, clergy included. The Church struggles to understand human suffering and give it a just interpretation; however, unless we look at it within the realm of original sin, it will always remain a mystery.

Additionally, the Church is being confronted with another issue that touches the human heart of her own members. Traditions are sacred. In this book, we will see how a priest will react in his highest level of responsibility.

This is a work of fiction. All of the characters, names, incidents, organizations and dialogue in this novel are either the product of the author's imagination or are used fictitiously.

Dina

# THE CALL

"Hello!"

"Hello! Who is this?"

"Hi, Massimo, this is Fania." (For security reasons, and not to confuse the readers, we leave the names as they are now.)

"What a sweet surprise! What's going on in Toronto?"

"A lot of commotion! But, tell me: how's your love life?"

"It could be better."

"What do you mean? Is there something wrong?"

"No. The memory of that wonderful girl I met in Lugano, Switzerland, has been haunting me for three years."

"What was her name?"

"Ariadna, Arian, for short."

"What happened?"

"I lost track of her. All these years, and I can't find her phone number. I'm sick over it."

"I have no magic wand to help you, but never stop dreaming. One of these days, you may run into her."

"Yeah, when I'm old ..."

"Don't despair."

"I'm on the verge."

"Don't be silly. Are you still living at Rue Christoph Colomb?"

"No, we moved to Boulevar Cartier on the other side of the Riviere des Prairies, in Montreal."

"Do you like the new place better?"

"I'm not too thrilled."

"Well, it's only temporary. Tell me about your job."

"I'm writing political reports for the Montreal French newspaper, Le Soleile. The pay isn't spectacular. A novice has no choice but to wait his turn."

"How would you like to be on a million dollar mission?"

"What …? Did I hear you right?"

"Yes, you did."

"What is it all about?"

"You have to write the last chapter of a manuscript." A call came in on the other line. Fania looked at the number and copied it down. Then, it rang again and she did the same. "Massimo, I have to go. It's Mitango Africanus."

"Who is he?"

She laughed on the other side. When the laughter subsided, she whispered, "Extremely important to your literary adventure. Without him, there is no Last Chapter. I'll call you in the next few days. Stay put! And by the way, sweet dreams!"

"Don't be sarcastic." He paused a moment and added slowly, "Adventure? Wait …"

It was too late. Fania had already hung up.

Ching's Last Breath

Dear reader, I apologize if Fania didn't help me give you a detailed account of the protagonists. Don't worry! I won't disappoint you. Just follow me. I need your company during this trip.

The phone rang. "Hello, Hospital St. Vincent."

"Hello, this is San Lazarus. Send an ambulance immediately. Someone is dying outside the main gate."

The sirens screamed the entire fifteen minutes from the hospital to the hospice. When the paramedics arrived at the scene, the man had already expired.

Ching Yen was born in Shanghai in 1970 to a poor family of fourteen children, ten of them girls. His father was a farmer. His mother had her hands full at home and had to stand for hours in line to get the food provision for the week. There was an insistent rumor spreading, according to which Ching was not the boy's real name and that he was adopted from an orphanage. A more consistent and believable story had the child abandoned in a church. A custodian, during his morning cleaning routine, heard some cries and looked apprehensively in the direction of a pillar. He approached it cautiously and found an infant wrapped in a wool blanket. The same anonymous source, even though he got paid for the information, made an additional revelation. Ching's mother put a tattoo under the heel of the baby's right foot. She disappeared from circulation after the Muslim community, of which she was part, got news that she had turned Catholic while serving as a secretary of a priest. According to their religion, whoever abandons Islam for Catholicism deserves death, even though there is no such provision in the Koran. An analogous situation happened later in Afghanistan. To avoid the people's anger and international protests, President Barzai took a middle of road decision. He accepted the mediation of the Italian government and sent the converted young man into exile in Italy.

The truth is that Ching's mother was never seen again in the area. Maybe she left for an unknown region of the vast country where no one knew her. After a couple of months, the priest took the child from the Catholic orphanage and arranged an adoption by a family in Shanghai. Each month, the new parents received a monthly allowance from an undisclosed benefactor. We are not in a position to confirm if the child support came through a foreign embassy or other undisclosed source. When the authorities found out about the baby, they expelled the priest with the accusation of conducting subversive activities.

As the child grew older and attended elementary school, he became irritated by his classmates' continuous scrutiny. They whispered that Ching's mother had him out of wedlock by a stranger from a distant land. Some mothers told their sons, instead, that Ching's father was an exchange student from Angola. The wildest rumors flew around, but none of them was close to the truth. The only incontrovertible evidence was the boy's somatic features, half Chinese and half African, that made him feel uncomfortable. His hair was curly and the nose a bit flat. The skin was clearly darker than others.

His own sisters and brothers looked at him as if he landed from another planet. In the streets and around the school perimeter, boys and girls often lobbed racial slurs at him that left him feeling disoriented, embarrassed, and guilty. During those moments, the burden of those looks was too heavy to bear and he ran outside in the open field to cry.

The Chinese political system didn't admit distraction or the wasting of time in the life of youth. After school, military vans picked up the youngsters and transported them to farming areas, where they helped the older folks in menial labor.

The situation ameliorated somewhat in the eighties, as the government, under Deng, sought a more liberal and aggressive economic policy that relied heavily on technology. Western investments were no longer considered an evil. The new industrial approach eased the peasants' hard work in rural areas and students were required to assist only during the summer months. By the new millennium,

China was beginning to assume the role of a world power in all its dimensions. Factories mushroomed and commerce flourished. Even Yen's family started to taste the fruits of the economic upturn.

Ching Yen was a bright student and after graduating from high school at the age of sixteen, the Communist Party sent him to Beijing University. He had a vocation for International Journalism and pursued it very seriously. Soon after graduation, they found employment for him with the Red Star, the major editorial publication of the capital.

As mentioned earlier, body-wise, Ching was short and with a propensity toward obesity. His hair was loosely curly, and greasy so it gave him an almost a gypsy look, which he tried to camouflage by his genuine smile. He had dark eyes and wore contact lenses. His clothes were typically Chinese, unpretentious and casual. He used a necktie only in official meetings. He made up for the lack of a refined taste in clothes with a gentle demeanor and a soft, almost feminine voice, which caused his friends to doubt his manliness. He kept a big handkerchief in the top left pocket of his jacket to wipe his brow when he sweated profusely, especially during the summer period.

Professionally, he was impeccable. His colleagues were the first to recognize his natural writing ability. His articles focused on political and social issues and he loved to investigate political intrigues and corruption at every level of society. He was single and hardly went out with girls; to close friends he confided that he didn't have time, but the self-imposed isolation gave rise to gossip.

In his new position, Ching tried to gain some knowledge of his ancestry and checked the state's archives or whatever he could get his hands on. His colleagues shook their heads.

On June 24, 1995, fearing that Ching might create some problems among the politicians, the Party dispatched him to New Delhi as a foreign correspondent. He packed his suitcase and left for the new destination. He spent ten years of his life there, traveling the countryside and reporting on unemployment, illiteracy and drug traffic. He enjoyed tiger hunting and, on one occasion, even killed one which had terrorized the villagers. He attended most of the Parliament sessions and was an avid note-taker. He even interviewed Sonja Gandhi, after her refusal to become the First Lady. He was stunned at the racial discrimination that the opposition leveled against her. India, one of the most democratic countries in the world, was not ready to accept a lady from Italian lineage to become its Prime Minister. To avoid internal tension and possible bloodshed, she renounced the highest office. She made such a pleasant impression on him that he wrote articles in her favor.

On January of 2005, Ching met a man in his forties who helped a minister unmask one of the most serious health violations in Indian history. The man always wore his sunglasses. The two shook hands. Ching dropped something in the man's hand. The Indian perused the corner of a bill and twisted his lips. Ching looked around. He slipped other bills in the man's hand. The man checked again the numbers on the bills and nodded. Disguised as contractors, the following day they penetrated a cavernous complex in the east side of New Delhi, where over five hundred children were being employed illegally in heavy, dangerous and underpaid work. The Chinese Mafia was managing the factory's operations with the cooperation of local notorious outcast bosses.

After that experience, he wrote:

The managers buy children from derelict and impoverished, deeply indebted families. They bring them here and force them into hard labor. When the financial deal falls short, the bosses resort to extortions and abductions.

The working conditions are absolutely inhumane. The children can't go to the bathroom, except at noon; they can't converse with other; they work without lights—the only one comes from outside through circular openings—they wear no masks in dusty places, and are exposed to dangerous chemicals. The working space is like prison cells. Medical benefits don't exist. The pay is ridiculously low, and the children have no rights. These types of illegalities are mostly common in areas like New Delhi and Mobutu.

The report, like others that followed, was announced on a private Indian TV station and caused great havoc among the population.

A Parliamentary commission urgently nominated an 'ad hoc' investigation committee. In a hasty scheduled meeting, the pro-temp president called on Ching to provide evidence of his charges.

After the opening remarks, the president addressed the issue, "It would be unfair to refer to India as a country that doesn't protect children. The government passed the Child Labor Act in 1948 according to which only youngsters fourteen years of age can work." He said he appreciated Ching's concern in the matter, and declared that the matter needed full attention from all political forces and the cooperation of the industrial sector. Then, he asked Ching how reliable his sources were.

"Mr. president, I must confess that I penetrated the outlaws' impregnable fortress with the cooperation of a businessman."

"Why did you put your life at risk? Why so much interest for the children's sake? Is it a quest for fame?"

"Sir, I have no intention of becoming famous."

"Did you have any intent to discredit your guest country?"

"No, sir! Nothing of that sort ran through my mind."

"Did you act under the order of your country?"

"Mr. President, I have, have … a debt with children. I mean, my conscience can't be idle in the face of the barbarian exploitation of children. There is no justification for mistreating children, for dehumanizing them, for destroying their bodies and minds, for preventing them to construct an honorable future for themselves."

The President looked at this man with dismay. There was a long pause; then he dismissed the journalist.

Ching's report stirred emotions in a large segment of the population. The Human Rights Movement initiated street protests that culminated in additional Parliamentary inquiries. During the first session, the resentment of the Nationalist Movement exploded into an open rage against the Communist Party, which accused the National Security Office of being too credulous and lenient on foreign journalists who divulged the news without thinking about the national consequences. At that very moment, scuffles erupted and chairs flew on both sides of the aisle engulfing the whole Parliament. It took a good hour before the custodians could restore calm and the session coud resume. Despite the good will of many of them to continue on more moderate terms, the majority voted to adjourn the session and the meeting came abruptly to an end.

For Ching, peace was not in sight. In fact, there were also unconfirmed reports in the capital that the Chinese mob was looking for him.

Ching met again with the man in sunglasses and again they shook hands. The man realized that his hand was not curved enough and shook his head. Ching dropped something else in the man's hand. The man noticed the knuckles of his hand protruding and withdrew it. The two stared at each other and bowed their heads.

Three days later, the man showed up again, this time with two friends. They drove to the village of Malana in the district of Kull, in the Northern part of India of Himachal Pradesh for a fact-finding mission. They spent three days there; then Ching picked up the phone and called his newspaper editor. "Great place to be! The peasants are enjoying a tremendous economic boom never seen before. The pay is so high that it attracts laborers from neighboring countries."

"So, what's the scoop," replied the editor.

"In this desolate land, one can see royal palaces like those of ancient Babylon, or houses with roofs made of golden tiles. It reminds me of the mythic El Dorado, where the king bathed in gold. The Spanish Conquistadores pursued to the end the search for that legendary city ..."

"You mean ... somebody found it?"

"Evidently ..."

"Where do they get the gold?"

"The primary source of income is a flourishing business of hashish."

"Is that all? We heard similar accounts before from Colombia and Bolivia."

"Well, the peace here is being disturbed by a government's plan to burn the farmland and run a road across it."

"Is it news to you?"

"No, but the local community is opposed to it."

"They're always opposed to it. Look in Afghanistan! Where have you been?"

"Listen! The government is trying to sell a proposal that would create meaningful jobs, modernize the area with new roads, bring in more traffic and transport all sorts of goods to the rural areas creating an unprecedented economic boom."

"I guarantee you that they won't budge. How can they?"

"You have to understand that the drug lords have dominated the economic and political activities here for decades. The farmers have been conditioned to this sort of living. They enjoy complete freedom in a lawless land. The pay is competitive with even that of New York. There is no crime and no one steals. Lastly, no one smokes marijuana. It's forbidden. When the workers go home, they are searched from head to toe."

"O.K., O.K., and the police have not been able to quell the protests?"

"Are you joking? This is their livelihood, their only source of income."

"They could be malleable if it weren't for the collusion of some corrupt pol ..."

"It's possible, but I have my doubts. The government's goodwill and the police efforts have failed so far. In the meantime, the project remains inoperable because of lack of trafficable roads. Yesterday, the President of Internal Affairs dispatched his representative to engage in a fruitful discussion with the local population. He addressed the crowd in this way, 'Dear Indian brothers, I came to inform you that New Delhi is very much concerned about the situation here and wishes to promote a better understanding between us.'

"A fat man, who appeared to be a ringleader, took the large Panama hat off his head and said, 'Sir, Minister, we don't bother anyone. We are good people. We cause no problem to the government. We don't even ask for jobs. We take good care of ourselves. The politicians owe us appreciation because we don't bother anyone and are happy with our lives. We don't steal or cheat; we don't have crimes; we don't cheat on our wives; we don't ask for any police protection and we keep money in circulation.

Now, you come and you want to take away from us our livelihood and our happiness. Is this the government's role? To meddle in individual freedom?' He turned to the crowd for assent and a loud shout followed, 'Yeaahh!' The same speaker continued, 'Why don't you leave us alone. No one is complaining here.'

'My good friend, the government wants to help you. We offer incentives to the farmers, who wish to return to the traditional agricultural products, such as, potatoes, beans and wheat.'

'That's not an incentive. That's a buyout.'

'Why do you say that, sir?'

'We need no grant. Unemployment doesn't exist here. We are an asset to the government. We are honest people doing our thing. We even employ foreigners and pay them well. They can attest to it.' The workers shouted, 'Yeeees!'

'Sir, the law of this land has decided to shift emphasis onto agricultural products. Our people are starving. The whole world needs vegetables, grains, and fruit, not grass.'

'If the grass keeps us wealthy, why not grow it? We can't give up our independence, our peace, and the high standard of living just because you bureaucrats want to change our lifestyle by driving machines on our property,' responded the man in a visible state of excitement.

"The crowd got unruly, yelled epithets against the commissioner and wanted to stone him. When he realized his effort to conduct a civil exchange of ideas was unsuccessful, he decided to return to the capital. The issue was stalled in the Parliament and the situation in that region has remained stagnant."

The editor sank on his chair and remained silent for a while. Finally, he asked, "What do you want me to do?"

"Run the article! What else!"

Ching returned to his office and the editor called for a meeting to keep everybody abreast of the situation. One by one they spoke in Ching's favor, but one colleague expressed concern that too much exposure in that country's internal affairs could have political ramifications between China and India. One even feared for Ching's own safety, asking him "What did you go there for? You are jeopardizing your life among those people. Not to mention our security here."

"A reporter's main objective is to reveal the truth to the world. In this case, we are being confronted with a degrading and depressing educational reality. Most of the population is illiterate. They are too busy producing hashish. Never has a drug lord even remotely considered the possibility of building a school for the children."

"Again, with the children! What are you trying to do? Remember that your article is a double edge weapon." He looked down to the floor and added, "You are getting in between two fires. The drug traffickers have already made attempts on your life, and the politicians of both branches are beginning to frown when they see your name on the newspaper. They see it as an intrusion in their internal affairs."

"I brought to their attention a sore spot of their society, touching the most vulnerable members, the children."

"I realize that India's image is deteriorating. I value your professional conduct, but be careful!"

Ching stood pensive for a while. He couldn't understand the reason for so much indifference among the Indian authorities. Only the Communist Party was throwing some support to him. The other political factions were keeping a distance.

One month passed and he made news again. He visited the community of Rajahmundry, in the central part of the country. This time, he reported on a positive action taken by some citizens, on a new tax conscience evolving in that part of the nation. He wrote, "If someone doesn't square off his revenue status with the IRA, a group of people from the same department, armed only with drums, surrounds the house of the tax delinquent and plays music day and night until he decides to pay off his debt. This behavior is unknown in China because people are imbued with a deep sense of honesty from childhood." The Interior Minister reacted acidly to those comments. In a brief letter of rebuttal, he said, "This noble and democratic nation doesn't need any lesson on morality, especially when it comes from a Chinese citizen."

This was only the tip of the iceberg; the rest was only postponed. It came when Ching wrote an article on Kashmir, a region hotly disputed by both India and Pakistan. The Prime Minister attributed to the report a malicious intention of interference in the internal affairs of India and a malignant and misguided depiction of its territorial integrity. After various high-level consultations, the government declared Ching persona non grata and gave him three days to leave the country.

The Chinese government vehemently rejected the accusations leveled against the newsman, and expelled the Indian diplomatic attaché from Beijing.

Ching's superiors made him pack his suitcase in haste and dispatched him to Malawi, Africa.

Three weeks later, Mitango traveled to Malawi to attend a conference on poverty.

Ching was in attendance with many foreign newsmen. During a news conference, after being recognized, he rose to his feet and began, "Mr. Chairman, you may appreciate knowing that in some villages, whoever has a few pennies or a bunch of bananas, whoever has meat or rice is considered well off." The audience approved by stamping their feet. The prelates whispered to each other. Ching continued.

The chairman nodded.

Ching continued, "Sir, what's more deplorable is that extreme poverty is pushing parents to do unthinkable acts. They are giving their little girls—ten, twelve years old—in marriage to old, decrepit rich men. Regretfully so, this shameful phenomenon is no longer circumscribed locally, but it's spread to the whole African continent. That's why we would like to know what you intend to do about it."

"That's why we are here, to discuss, learn and solicit the governments' resources, whatever they may be, and with the help of the richest countries in the world, put an end to this barbarous activity."

"But this isn't all," added Ching. "Mr. Chairman, besides poverty, there is a plague here that is disseminating death."

The chairman looked at him quizzically.

"Mr. Chairman, AIDS is a deadly monster that's spreading its tentacles all over the continent. The percentage of people with HIV in Malawi is about 40% among adults. I refrain from mentioning the statistics available about the young girls. These are the sacrificial lambs predestined to the altar of sexual infamy. There are wolves on every street corner.

"I gather we must launch a massive educational campaign."

"Exactly! The people are completely ignorant of preventive measures. They need to be educated, but it's not enough to preach and solicit financial and medical assistance from the wealthiest countries on earth. We all need to make a change and the Church has to come to terms with this reality. I envision a day when Africa may be in a position to help the world, but right now it's moribund and needs urgent attention." The prelates looked at each other and exchanged brief comments.

Ching didn't wait for the chairman to invite someone else to speak and continued, "As a reporter, I'm doing my report even more due to my personal experience. Traveling here, I saw village after village disappear, like being sucked up by arid, bloodthirsty land. You can't imagine the fear that one feels when returning to a hamlet after a day or two and finding everybody dead. The richest country on earth can't ignore this tragic reality. Poverty, ignorance and AIDS offer the Church the opportunity to be a model of Christ on earth and for rich people to rise to the occasion to assist their fellow men."

Mitango pulled the microphone toward him and replied, "I can assure the gentleman from China that we are well aware of the problem. The Catholic Church, as you may know, is poised to begin a project of prevention and healing, but we lack the necessary funds to undertake and carry on such gigantic tasks. We are wholeheartedly committed to educate people and raise worldwide sensitivity to the problems." He returned the microphone to the chairman and remained silent staring at Ching.

The chairman said, "Africa needs the world's attention. There is no doubt about it. Everyone has to do his part."

Ching was not paying attention anymore. His eyes met Mitango's.

The chairman announced that he had time only for one last question. The reporters raised their hands to be recognized, but Ching raised his voice, "Mr. chairman, I don't mean to be discourteous."

"Well, you have been all along," responded one of his colleagues. Another added with evident resentment, "You have acted as if the floor belonged to you. It's pure egocentricity."

Ching smiled and apologized, but kept on without skipping a beat, "Are you doing anything for the orphans? As I emphasized previously, without guidance, except their grandparents', who, in some cases, give them in marriage to old, wealthy people with no teeth, they have no future. Starvation is their companion and uncertainty marks every day of their lives," he asked. The audience, upon hearing, "with no teeth," erupted into resounding laughter.

Eventually, the noise subsided and the chairman had the opportunity to respond, "Of course, the Church condemns and discourages these marriage arrangements. Their justification is that the whole family benefits from the conjugal knot."

Once again, the audience applauded in its own fashion.

The chairman wrapped up the conference with these final remarks: "We appreciate your sincere and deep concern for the people of Africa. I agree with you that we must put the world's conscience on the alert, and I extend the invitation to everyone not to succumb to the forces of evil. Your concerns are our concerns. We hope and pray that at our next conference we will be able to fit on the agenda all these issues and be able to provide some answers to them. As you all know, the globe is engulfed in the flames of terror and war. In the end, love will prevail. Thank you."

Ching shouted, "We are waging wars against the wrong enemy. Our enemies are drug lords, mafia, cancer, AIDS, hunger and hatred. If we want to grow, we can't tolerate this genocide. Instead of dropping bombs, let's drop medicine and food. Instead of holding a gun in our arms, let's hold a flower. Instead of building nuclear bombs, let's build bonds of love. Instead of building walls of hatred, let us open the doors of friendship. No one should go hungry or without medical care. We take pride in killing ourselves and others, but we are the most pitiful creatures on earth!"

Everyone rose to their feet and applauded. The chairman looked around confused and attempted to get up. When he realized that the ovation was unanimous, he decided to stand up all the way.

A bishop asked Mitango, "That reporter should be a preacher or maybe a politician. No, he would not make it. They would corrupt him." He looked at Mitango and waited for an answer that never came. "All of a sudden you lost your voice?" He paused a moment and continued, "You know what? I noticed in him some of your oratorical qualities and the same powerful voice."

Mitango left the building without releasing any comment to the press. As he was walking out, Ching followed him with his eyes and then decided to run after him.

Mitango noticed a long shadow behind him. He slowed down and so did the shadow. He turned back in a slow motion. Neither one of them would take the next step.

It was terribly hot. Mitango wiped his brows with a white handkerchief. On his ring finger, he wore the bishop's ring. The shadow moved toward him. The distance got shorter and shorter. The shadow stopped again. The men were now facing each other. They were drawn together, but only for an instant. A car briskly stopped, raising a cloud of dust. Both men were unable to see. As soon as the dust settled, the driver invited Mitango to jump in. A prelate wearing a red biretta reminded him that there was no time to waste, "The plane for Rome will depart in twenty minutes." The driver nodded. Mitango showed signs of hesitation. The voice from the car said, "Hurry!"

Mitango gave a last glance to Ching. The chauffer was holding the back door open. Ching opened his mouth half way. The syllables got lost in his throat.

Mitango took the back seat and the car sped away, raising a bigger cloud of dust. Ching remained immobile for a minute or so trying to follow the car as far as he could with his eyes, while pondering the missed opportunity. He took the handkerchief from his pocket and cleared the dust off his face and glasses. He kept looking in the direction of the car even though the traffic had already swallowed it up. A fellow reporter nearby called him. but he didn't hear. It took a second call to grab his attention. He turned and joined him.

The reader may be disappointed that we didn't introduce Mitango, but we urge you not to despair. We will meet him again, and soon.

Mitango's departure threw Ching Yeng into a state of confusion and depression. He lost his appetite, slept less, and his eyes showed signs of fatigue. In the office, his colleagues were concerned about it. He acknowledged that he was going through a period of mental stress but, in the end, he would survive. He said "I have not lost the desire to fight for the truth."

Later, the chief editor confided in one of the reporters, "He is getting too deeply involved with the poverty issue and the orphans. He is a Communist model. With him here, our country will have only success."

In November 2005, in the city of Xian, China, a dozen Catholic nuns resisted the expropriation of their land. The government planned to sell it to real estate developers. A bunch of young people armed with sticks assaulted the nuns and severely hurt some of them. One lost an eye and another suffered a broken arm. The rest of them received minor injuries.

Ching wasted no time in criticizing his government's intentions. The Chinese authorities called him immediately back to Beijing. Ching packed his suitcase again and boarded a plane. The police were waiting for him with an order to apprehend him and throw him in jail. The passengers deboarded one by one, but Ching was not among them. It took about half an hour of phone calls to Africa to realize that he had taken a flight with destination Ottawa, Canada. He left a note to his supervisor, who was ill at the time, that he was going to attend a symposium on "Journalism and Truth."

The lightning action took the other reporters by surprise, as well. For China, the sudden defection of one of its brightest and world-renowned journalists constituted a blow to its international image. China's News Agency, the government mouthpiece, labeled Ching a traitor, a transformer, a radical extremist and a megalomaniac. The whole front page was dedicated to his purported cowardly behavior. Realizing that his life was in danger, Ching changed his name to Chau Mau, but we continue referring to him by the original name to avoid confusion. He also underwent facial plastic surgery.

In Ottawa, he established his temporary residence. After a while, he decided to settle in Montreal, where the Canadian Secret Service advised him to play it safe by not exposing himself to the point he would alert the Chinese spies. He dismissed that fear and, after a month living in the heart of the city, he took residence on Rue de l'Eglise, near Ile de Soeurs, which is on Le Fleuve de Saint-Laurent. The apartment, on the second floor of a building, was small and modest, but it met his needs. He found a job as a reporter at the Mont-Royal Star, which printed his articles in Chinese, due to the large Chinese community living in the city. Because of the long hours of work and for his desire to keep a low profile, he hardly associated with anyone.

Ching's first big article cast light on a baby-smuggling ring in China. The American and Canadian families, which had adopted many children from the orphanages of Zhuzhou, were perplexed and enraged when the Chinese government claimed the adoptions were illegal. The scam caused an outrage in the capital and stopped any adoption that didn't follow legal routes. Those who had already paid were in a state of limbo. The Chinese government arrested some ring leaders, who sold the children to orphanages for a couple hundred dollars each and these, in turn, put them on sale to other orphanages or directly to foreign buyers for a sum greater than four thousand dollars. The ring organizers usually kept a vigil on the families living in the most squalid misery and contacted them proposing a cheap deal before they placed them on sidewalks and left to die. In many cases, they abducted the babies without paying anything. The Chinese authorities downplayed these shameful and outrageous incidents, stating that it was not a widespread practice, but a single, isolated case. They claimed that those countries that fueled the fire of propaganda lacked credibility and were demagogues and counterrevolutionaries. To assuage foreign criticism, they announced an intensive hunt for baby speculators and condemned certain renegade journalists who continued to highlight the deplorable sale of orphans in their acrimonious articles. In Canada, they sent to their ambassador the following fax: "Search and destroy operation." It gave them carte blanche to silence any criminal engaging in those lurid activities.

Life for Ching was proceeding smoothly. He was well known and esteemed by his colleagues. Two years went by and he began to contemplate the idea of devoting some of his energies toward exposing, in a book, child abuses across the globe and abuses of the elderly in health care institutions. At that time, it was already rumored in media circles that the Canadian government was secretly planning a project for the same purpose.

Prior to his official departure, Ching's department threw a party in his honor. Only a few special guests were at hand. The editor made this toast, "To Ching, a man whose humanity has no bound." Another reporter and friend, having sipped a few drinks already, added, "Drink and be merry, for tomorrow is another day." The participants cheered.

At a corner table, a secretary was chatting with an elegant, handsome young man.

They ate, drank and talked. Suddenly, she said she'd like to introduce the new acquaintance to Ching. They got up and went to his table. The secretary approached Ching and said, "May I introduce you to this distinguished journalist."

"Of course."

"He lives on the other side of the city. We invited him to stop by and wish you well."

"That was a great idea. Very happy!"

"My pleasure, Massimo Camp."

"So, you are a …"

He didn't finish the sentence that Massimo responded, "I'm a neophyte."

"Don't be so modest! Welcome on board."

"Thank you. I'm trying to navigate through the complexities of this profession."

"I take the license of giving you a suggestion. Don't overdo it. Each day has its aches and pains. I, for instance, am embarking on a new career, closely related to journalism. If I succeed, I may win the Pulitzer Prize," and started to laugh.

"Don't laugh! A well known reporter like you has every right to believe in a glorious future."

"Easy, easy! Let's not mention glory. It's a word unheard of around here."

"Don't be facetious! The royalties will be coming like a steady stream and you won't know how to spend them."

"Massimo! Did I pronounce it correctly?"

"Yes, perfect!"

"Don't you think that you are putting the cart before the horse?"

"I smell success in you."

Ching got serious. He took Massimo by the arm and led him in the hall where there was more privacy. In fact, he looked around to ascertain that no one would hear him and voiced his doubt even about publishing the book, "Do you realize how hard it is to find a good agent?"

"That goes without saying. No publishing company wants to talk to you or to me, even though we belong to this business."

"You are absolutely right. No editor promises anything. Only one word rings loudly in the ears, business."

"Let me relate to you a couple of details that indicate how hard the publishing process is for anyone outside of the writing business. Now, everybody wants to write. They haven't the slightest idea that writing is an art. They write to show off. Let us not mention the audience. A very few understand a good book. Not even many English teachers do. Listen! You write a novel. It could be the worst ever written, but if you go on a popular television show, you make a mint. Readers from all walks of life will acclaim you. But we, who have the writing ability in our DNA, will continue our profession because this is our bread and butter."

"I agree with you on every point. My suggestion is to take a leave of absence. If it doesn't work, then ..."

"Thank you for the advice."

"Remember, the agent! A relative of mine thought of publishing his book in Italian, so he called an international publishing company based in Milan. Guess what the editor told him?"

Ching got curious, "What?"

"Your agent can call us," and dismissed him without allowing him to ask any further questions.

"That's bizarre!"

"The truth is that there is no Terrestrial Paradise here."

"You are absolutely right! " He looked at Massimo from above the shoulders and attempted a smile. "Really, I don't do it so much for pecuniary reasons. I have a debt with the human race."

"What do you mean?" asked Massimo with mixed emotions. "We work for money; we live for money; we ..."

"No, no, no!" interrupted Ching. "Life has to have a reason for living otherwise we might close the book."

"I don't believe anymore in a divine presence here or above, therefore ..."

"It's that and other ... We can't look at humanity's frailties and close our eyes. There is no compromise to make. Either we stand on the side of reason or on the side of evil."

"People have to be prepared for disappointments. The bare truth is that everything rotates around the almighty dollar. Business is business, but you are a lucky man."

"How do you figure that?"

"Because I'm going to show you a short cut."

Ching rolled his head from right to left and reversed from left to right in order to relax his neck muscles. The exercise over, he placed his ear close to Massimo's mouth. Massimo smiled and said, "Call my cousin in Toronto. She is the head editor of the major newspaper in the city. If you would rather have me make the phone call then, at the completion of the project, give me a ring and I'll make the connection. Here, I'll give you my card. Wait, I have her card too." Ching looked at it for a long while, as if he were trying to remember something, and placed it in his wallet.

Massimo said, "You didn't tell me how you are going to spend your money."

Ching laughed, "Again with the money? My mind isn't on it; however, if I strike a gold mine, I plan to build an orphanage in Africa."

"Noble idea! Do you have any country in mind?"

"None in particular."

"And the flame, this desire to help abandoned children, how did it start with you?"

Ching frowned. His face changed color, but he managed to overcome his emotions. He shook Massimo's hand, "You are a sincere and great friend. I'm honored to have met you." Massimo patted him on the shoulder and said nothing. Ching went back to the main room and joined the rest of the guests. Massimo stayed outside thinking for a while. He finished his glass of champagne and rejoined his friend, the secretary.

On May 19, 2005, Ching's life took a new twist. A government representative got wind of his plans and decided to contact him. Shortly after, even Fania, the Toronto editor, had a phone conversation with him. In the following days, he made sure to sign a contract with the parties involved. The investigation place would be San Lazarus.

San Lazarus was not completely new to Ching. He had heard of it and seen some pictures on the computer. To get a better idea, he visited a friend's parents. It was before Christmas and the brief visit left a scar in his soul, as he revealed later. It was a terrifying experience. With a couple of questions he asked, he realized that the cost of health care was astronomically high. He found out that the monthly fee for each resident was seven thousand dollars. If the patient couldn't afford the payment, Medicare would pick up the fee, but the patient had to turn over the pension and any asset he or she had. In the event that one of the spouses was living at home, the government allowed either one of them to keep in the bank up to eighty-five thousand dollars and to live in the house. With that scenario, rich people shunned Medicare and purchased a personal medical insurance, most likely "The Joy of Life."

The headquarters was on a big estate across from the hospice main entrance. The company's activities spanned from all types of insurances to caskets, and who knows what else.

The building had the shape of a hexagon. The facade was of Greco-Roman style with Corinthian columns and arcades of different sizes. A monstrous fountain, about twenty-five feet away, had the statue of Pluto holding a fork in his hands. The fork sprinkled water continuously in a large cement pool with the statue of Diana at the center. The water sprinkled as far as the entrance, so that the visitors or customers had to wipe their feet on the rug before entering. At night, the lights cast a light bluish color on the water offering a spectacle that enchanted visitors and patients alike.

In the atrium, a Venetian chandelier of gigantic proportions dominated the hall. People marveled at the glass art and wondered how the glassmakers were able to produce such a piece. "That must have cost a mint," said a man in his fifties. "How they are able to make them with all those intricacies, I have no idea."

A woman next to him, who could have been his spouse, replied, " A million dollars, I bet. When it comes to art, you name it, the Italians have no equals."

A lady in her seventies heard the conversation and interjected, "If I may … look at this leather jacket, the shoes, the silk scarf, I purchased them in Florence."

The man looked at the old lady with apparent surprise and asked her if she had any relatives in Italy.

The lady smiled and made a gesture of denial with her head. "I know what you are trying to get at, but no. It's their nature. They have art in their DNA. Whereas in another country you hear about a good movie director, in Italy you can count twenty, thirty. I don't know. Certain things can't be explained."

The man remained silent. He was still waiting for the woman to provide additional information. He was fascinated by the chandelier. His wife pulled his arm and pointed at the external walls made of Carrara marble, white and yellowish with red veins moving from one end to another. The back part was swallowed up by the hill behind it. Nobody knows up to now if it stretches its tentacles beneath or ends there. Except for the secretaries, who were all American, the rest of the personnel were Chinese. Around the perimeter, ten guards worked day and night in plain clothes. Ching Jeng didn't have in mind to investigate a specific insurance company. The work ahead of him was complex.

The abysmal deficit caused by the exorbitant costs of health care alarmed the government, who decided to keep the Medicare Department under close scrutiny. The President's critiques argued that from the services transpired three endemic problems. First, the old folks were inadequately assisted. Second, the workers were underpaid and, thirdly, the insurances companies were uncooperative and secretive. Criticism was mounting rapidly on the social and political spectrum. A parliamentary inquiry was initiated by the Lower House. To be better prepared to answer to both political parties adequately, the Health minister contacted Ching to launch an investigation to unmask corruption on a large scale in order to cause public outcry. At first, the journalist was reluctant to embark on a secret mission dealing with old and sick people. He had in mind to pursue a project in a literary and personal context. The idea that external forces charged him with political responsibilities and dangers didn't please him. As mentioned earlier, before giving his consent, he had a long phone conversation with Fania. She assuaged his fears by assuring him that working at St. Lazarus would be an enjoyable experience, rather than a burdensome assignment, because reliable sources indicated the presence of a patient who spoke Chinese. That news alone spurred his imagination and curiosity. By the time the conversation was over, he had made up his mind. He felt more convinced than ever that the mission, although fraught with risks due to the government's involvement, it was worth the gamble.

That night, Ching didn't sleep well. He tossed in bed from left to right. Strange visions appeared in his mind. He got up a couple of times and drank hot milk at first, and chamomile later, trying to sedate his nerves. It was all useless.

He welcomed the daylight with a blessing. At nine o'clock, he went to the Medicare office and announced to the supervisor his availability for the project; however, he asked, as a condition, the freedom of publishing, at the end, his collected material without restriction and under no obligation from anyone. The supervisor didn't object, but reserved the right to preview the manuscript and to erase any material he considered classified. There was a brief tug of war between them. When both sides reached an agreement, they negotiated the salary and signed the related documents.

The Canadian Health Ministry had launched a program three decades earlier that became the modus operandi of some European countries. It was an experiment on a small scale with the purpose of decentralizing the state run health institutions. The elderly were returned to their immediate families or relatives who received a financial incentive. The Conservatives in the Parliament hailed it as a New Beginning for the elderly. Their contention was that eventually health would have improved and longevity increased by employing only certified aids with a dual objective: visit the patients on a daily basis and keep their spirits high.

In theory it seemed a terrific approach to an old problem, but in reality the project had its shortcomings which prompted the authorities to change the course of action over a long and bitter debate. The opposition argued that the New Beginning had many presuppositions of a failure and charged that the data furnished were inaccurate, unreliable and tainted with political flavor. The initial success was an artificial fire, which got extinguished rather quickly. "We want to go on record," the leader shouted, "that we ought to give a harder look at the hospices (who runs them and how they manage the budget), but also at the families' performances when they take care of their loved ones. There is hard evidence of psychological trauma shifting from the patient to the family."

In a subsequent stormy debate in the capital, the Health Minister acknowledged that there were occasional glitches in the patient-family program, but that everything was under control. At that point, the leader of the opposition took the floor, looked around and smiled sarcastically. He asked permission to read some unclassified excerpts he had extracted from the Health Department Record Book. A storm of protests drowned his voice, but, when order was restored, he raised some papers in his hands and yelled:

"Lend me your ears, my colleagues, politicians! Lend me your ears, my countrymen! I know that no one here is willing to listen to these stories, but I'm going to pass around copies for you to read. Then, we are going to discuss the skyrocketing costs of health institutions." These two statements appeased the Chambers for the time being.

What the papers related were some incidents that cast doubts on the benefits of the program. The first project was spearheaded a few blocks away from Notre Dame Cathedral. A war veteran was struggling with his wife's loss. When it became evident that he couldn't cope anymore with it, he fell into a deep depression. His three sons, then, opted to transfer him to the Veterans' Hospital. The situation worsened and the man became on the verge of mental collapse. After many discussions, the older son decided to take his father back home with the acknowledgement that his father would take care of himself during the day. In addition to the well known ailments, the old man suffered from arthritis in the left knee. The pains resulted from lack of lubrication in the kneecap.

The man, who was nearly ninety and lived on the second floor of an apartment house, dealt as best as he could with the solitude. At times, some neighbors joined him in card games. One morning, he fell down the stairs and injured his back. His daughter-in-law took a short leave of absence to attend to his immediate needs, hoping that the situation would ameliorate in due time. Her hopes were shattered when she realized that his condition was stagnant after a couple of months. In various circumstances she couldn't control herself and began to give voice to her rage, "Because of you I'm living this type of life. I'm jeopardizing my job, do you understand?"

The old man was able to say in a feeble voice, "I'm sorry!"

"If it were up to me, you would not be here, not a single day! Your place is St. Lazarus! They have all the comforts there and the nurses can attend you 24 hours a day. Once in a while, we would visit you, and that's it!"

Her father-in-law couldn't hear well, but the tone of her voice was sufficient to sadden him. He lowered his head and sank into a subdued state. She raised her voice even more, "You are a burden here to both of us!" When she noticed that the old man was unable to perceive her words, she dropped the pillow on the floor and ran out to smoke.

The days passed by slowly. The old man's daughter-in-law decided to reduce the food rations, but he refused to eat. "Do you think for a moment you irritate me with your stubborn attitude? That will be the day!" The sick man made a strenuous effort to get up and sit on the chair. She stared at him with curiosity, not knowing what he was up to. She looked at the many barbiturates on the desk. She opened some of bottles and let a few pills drop in her palm. The old man, in the meantime, made a desperate attempt to rise from the chair and gain access to the door. His head began to spin in an eternal crescendo, like a tornado that carries destruction and death. He was unable to see anymore. Suddenly, a thunderous noise shook the entire apartment as he banged his head against the wall, fell backward on the floor, and tumbled down the stairs his body gushing blood."

The daughter-in-law said, "Finally! It's over! I don't have to deal with him anymore. It was too much for us. We just couldn't take care of him." She lowered her head in a state of momentary discomfort and muttered, "I have to call my husband. And what about the police? Who am I supposed to call first?"

Another episode shook the entire community of Ottawa and most of the people still remember. Half a mile from this building, a nurse was assigned to assist a sick old woman at her home. The nurse loved to play cards with her friends nearby. Each time she came back to relax, she found the bed wet or pictures and cookie packages scattered on the floor. One afternoon, she said to her friends, "How much do you want to bet on the next card?"

"Ten dollars," responded a tall blond lady.

"Very well!"

"Wait a moment! Don't you have to take care of your patient? She has been alone for quite a while."

"She can wait. Cards are more important to me. Should I say that they have top priority in my life?"

"Is that so?" replied the woman as if she were offended.

"Honey, I don't tell her to get nervous. Why should I?"

"Aren't you being paid for your job? Listen, I can't continue playing. I may contribute to your wrongdoing." The nurse looked at her with dismay, dropped the cards on the table, gave a stern look to the others and left.

The patient's house was across the street from where the nurse usually played cards. When the nurse opened the door, she placed her right hand on her heart and fell down.

Half an hour later, one of her friends decided to find out if the nurse was ready to play again. The spectacle in front of her shocked her. She emitted a loud cry and the rest of the company ran over. Behind the door, the nurse lay motionless and across the room dangled the body of the old woman.

The final straw came on a hot summer day. A sick lady of about eighty was living alone in a small house in Newfoundland, 20 kilometers from Musgrave Harbor.

One nurse provided her assistance during the day; another was on hand at night.

On a Monday, toward lunchtime, smoke billowed from the woman's house. A neighbor promptly called the police. Five minutes later two police cars arrived on the scene followed by a fire truck. The firemen first knocked at the door and then yelled for a response. The smoke was forming thick clouds and flames were gushing out of an open window. At that point two firemen, brandishing hatchets, broke their way through the kitchen and the stairs scattering any piece of furniture they found on their way.

Some members of Parliament got restless and began to pound the floor with their feet "We are tired of these banalities," one of them yelled in anger.

"The gentleman may have to display a bit more patience because I'm about to wrap up." The boisterous members of both Chambers laughed with disdain.

The speaker pressed on. "The second floor presented a gruesome spectacle. The body of the old woman was enveloped in flames. The firemen directed the water hoses there to extinguish the flames. More police and firemen reinforcement arrived on the scene and ordered the crowd to stay back. The firefighters' truck raised a ladder and their colleagues were able to bring down the woman. By the time they touched the ground, the woman was deceased.

"Several bystanders told the police that they had just stopped a car. The driver dropped both hands and her head on the steering wheel and stayed in that position for a while. The air was sultry. She made an effort to raise her head and start the car, but she was blocked. The police put on the blinking lights and the siren screamed. Her body shivered. She looked at her immaculate white uniform. One of the policeman handcuffed her and said, "You are charged with murder." She became pale and was unable to utter a single word. A medical examiner arrived at the scene and pronounced the old lady dead. He covered her body with a blanket and turned toward the mortician and ordered him to take the body away."

A week later, with both Chambers attending, the President somberly reported the dismal state in which the health system agonized, "The family, traditionally the bastion of our society, is fragmented due to the loose bond between parents and relatives and the lack of professional responsibilities. There is no doubt about the profound crisis our healthcare system faces." The orator stopped and looked around for approval. Those of his Party gave him a standing ovation; The others stood silent and were visibly embarrassed. Both Chambers agreed on one issue: There was a need for a large scale investigation.

The wide media coverage of the Canadian tragic episodes caused a global uproar and inspired many governments to pass laws for the protection of old and sick people in institutions protected by state and federal laws. Japan was the first country to enact such a law in 2004."

It was a terrible blow for Canada and for the experimental program. The next concern was the Health deficit, which ballooned on a monthly basis. It had surpassed its budgetary limitations for the fifth straight year, and Medicare was the scapegoat. They Health Minister reassured continued medical support to the elderly, but it could do it only by bringing the cost under control. It was in this heated climate that he secretly commissioned Ching to carry on the investigation .

In a relatively short period of time, Ching Jen collected a voluminous amount of documentation that occupied ninety per cent of his manuscript. He needed only the last chapter to complete it. To accomplish this goal, he needed to examine the records at Saint Lazarus's vault in the unit called "Elixir" where the hard core cases were located. He was aware of the hurdles that he would encounter. To overcome them, he had only one approach available: work as a volunteer and, later, force his way through or gather the information in another way.

First of all, he had to be accepted, and that was not easy for anyone. The applicant had to go through a rigorous personal scrutiny. If he passed the preliminary screening, the candidate had to sign a document of secrecy. No one was supposed to talk about residents to the outside world, not even to their families. Most of the volunteers were forbidden to talk to the residents, unless they had special permission. The janitors and cooks could only exchange information related to working activities. This latter rule rendered the atmosphere gloomy. Being a journalist, Ching was an easy target for rejection. He pondered over it for a while; then, he went to the police station for another identification.

As expected, the preliminary interview was very rigorous. He tried to ingratiate himself with the head nurse, a beautiful young woman by the name of Venefungus Moors (hereinafter called "Venus" for the sake of simplicity, even though there were rumors that her original name was different; we would not be able to inform you about this detail were it not for the assistance of a "deep throat," even though the revelation occurred much later). Venus was certainly influential in "hiring" Ching as a volunteer, even though we are not in a position to determine what prompted her to give the final approval.

Venus was conceived in Yemen and born in Nairobi. She was tall with long, dark brown hair that cascaded onto her shoulders. On the job, she wore her hair in a French twist, against which the white cap rested solidly. When she smiled, she showed a perfect white set of teeth, and the lips were tiny, curved in a V shape. Her voice was soft, almost inaudible, at times. The nose was small, a bit on the flat side, and her eyes light blue. The bust was prominent, and the rest of her body was curvaceous. Her hands were long and thin. At the time this book was being written, she was thirty-five years old. People described her as polite and introverted. Occasionally, she entertained female friends, but rarely showed up to their parties.

Not much was known about her. As a matter of fact, nobody knew anything at all! If someone inquired about her parents, she would courteously decline by saying, "This is a private matter." Her co-workers respected and admired her, even though some of them would not admit it in private. She lived near San Lazarus in a one-family brick house. The window curtains were always closed and the lights rarely on in the evening. The furniture was arranged with decorum. On the living room walls, she had portraits by Cezanne, Dali and the Mona Lisa of Duchamps. In the hallway that led to the main bathroom, she hung paintings by Apollinaire and Matisse. In her bedroom, she had Botticelli's Primavera. The fireplace was across from the kitchen, but she lit the fire only once. She liked to use natural wood; however, the smoke darkened the ceiling. In order not to have to paint often, she opted to keep the chimney for exterior beauty and made the fire in the cellar fireplace.

The cellar was huge. It could accommodate about two hundred people. The ceiling sparkled and one sidewall was covered with white stucco. She had three huge mirrors where the guests could admire their physical beauty, the rare times they were invited.

Around the chimney, she arranged her books, organized according to subject. Someone suggested that she not keep them close to the chimney, but she scoffed at the idea that one needed to be careful. In fact, she protected the books with ceramic tiles and concrete stones whenever she lit the fire. In a corner, she built a bathroom and, close to it, a kitchen. The laundry room was attached to the kitchen. She kept her house very neat, to the point of obsession. She couldn't stand dirty dishes and washed them immediately after eating. She loved her house and didn't miss the opportunity to brag when she spoke on the subject with some close friends.

She owned a Maserati, but used it only for out-of-town trips. For local errands, she drove an Alfa Romeo. In the spring and summer, she walked to work.

At St. Lazarus, her office was sober. On the main desk, she kept a computer and her mother's picture. The printer lay in a corner on her right side. Five television monitors hung on the wall in front of her and, with those, she controlled the whole building. The only odd feature was a red divider with a sign "No plus ultra." It stood just before a vault covered by a painting, close to the window. She had the ribbon there even during her office hours. The janitor could cross the line to clean, but only in her presence. A couple of corpulent men, with Chinese somatic features, walked back and forth in the halls.

Ching Jen began his volunteer work in the Olympus building, which was divided into units. People undergoing therapy after a knee or hip operation usually ended up at the Olympus unit. Normally, they would stay for two to four weeks, depending on the individual recuperation ability and the nature of the surgery. At times, a patient stayed up to two months. In Units B and C, there were old residents with various ailments, who couldn't take care of themselves at home or the family would not or couldn't assist them adequately. It was here that Ching collected the material that comprised most of the manuscript. To complete it, as I mentioned earlier, he moved to an adjacent building, the Elixir, where the conditions of the patients were more desperate. In fact, many of them were considered terminally ill. The atmosphere at the health center was somber and there was no room for errors.

After completing an application and using some communication skills, Ching's request finally got approved and he started working at Elixir, where Venus was the supervisor. Not to jeopardize his security, the police assisted him with providing him a new identity card.

The first day, Venus assigned him to drive the residents to the cafeteria during lunch time. He wore dark glasses and threw occasional glances left and right. As the time went by, he came across Venus's office. Everything inside was as it has been described. He didn't see anyone inside. A tag on the door said, "Head Nurse." There was no name, nothing.

His job was tedious, but he put a smile on his face. At times, he noticed Venus watching him from underneath her eyeglasses at a distance. The days, weeks and months went by without any notable progress. He realized that to put his hands on the information he was seeking he needed access to the rooms and talk to the residents. That was the only way he could finish the last chapter of the manuscript and get out of that asphyxiating place.

One morning, someone caught his attention. While he was transporting a patient to the cafeteria, he saw a door half open, and heard the raspy sound of a coughing. He looked inside, amid the presence of two bodyguards on each side of the entrance, and saw an old man. He wanted to stop and go in, but repressed his impulse. The guards would have stopped him. Instead, he drove the patient to the cafeteria.

On the way back, he couldn't resist the temptation. The guards were inexplicably absent. He grabbed a broom and pretended to sweep the hall. He looked inside the room at the man again. The two stared at each other for a while without saying a word. It appeared some interior chemistry was going on between them because the young man wanted to ask about something, but didn't dare to follow it up. Moved by curiosity, the old man reciprocated with his staring. It appeared that both were doing mental research. Ching shifted his attention to a desk, where lay a biretta and the picture of a child. The old man placed his head between his hands and fell in meditation. Ching moved automatically forward. The man placed his right hand on his heart. It was vibrating and the blood rushing furiously to the brain. Ching got scared, and started to tremble. He heard voices and ran out just in time. He rushed to the dressing room, hung up his uniform and headed for the parking lot. He stood in silence for a while, alone in a sea of automobiles. He looked up to heaven searching for an answer that never came. A couple of minutes passed by. It seemed an eternity. He walked on the grass, stumbled, and fell. He remained in a prone position with his eyes open. The birds were chirping; the ants began crawling on his ears; and a squirrel, from a tree branch, dropped a nut that fell on his head. He was immune to the sounds and feelings of mother nature. When he finally woke up from daydreaming, he took a handkerchief and wiped his eyes. The air was cool. He made no effort to get up and regain his poise.

In Elixir, Venus had been alerted to the presence of a sweeper outside room 85 and moved expeditiously in that direction. The presence of two husky men reassured her. She waved at them and proceeded to another unit.

Ching couldn't sleep that night. He couldn't believe that he had run across an "old friend" from his African reporter's experience, yet he was not at liberty to speak to him. He contemplated trying to meet him again, but couldn't think of a safe strategy. Bit by bit, he was beginning to place the pieces together in a dangerous game. A sense of discouragement prevailed in him. He felt worthless. He felt incapacitated, incapable of accomplishing his goal. The severely restrictive rules were hindering him to accomplish his work.

On Monday morning, the sky was overcast when he went to San Lazarus at 11:30 a.m. He wanted to stay home and work on a newspaper article about an Indian enfant prodige on his computer while he was stationed in India. In hisn'tebook, he had written, "boy, nine years old made personal internet site and had an emotional meeting with Gates. The child told him that he knew the alphabet by the age of two and that he wants to be a web designer when he gets older. He also had the honor of meeting India's Prime Minister."

Ching looked at hisn'tes over and over again. The life of that little genius fascinated him. He thought of returning to India and make a film of him. It was only a dream. He knew he was barred from that nation and was also cognizant of the danger he ran if he ever took such a trip. He was also aware that the Chinese Intelligence Agents were scattered all over the world and waited for a small false move on his part. He placed the notes in the last drawer of his desk and stood up. He walked back and forth a few times. His mind was clogged with thoughts. Finally, he decided to leave. He got into the car and drove to the hospice. The air was humid and the wind cold. The clouds ran one after the other and overshadowed the sun, which appeared, occasionally, only to disappear immediately after. When he arrived, he greeted a couple of volunteers and went to the dressing room to put on the red uniform.

On the way back, he passed by Venus's office. No one was inside. In the hall, hardly anyone went by. There was an unusual calm in the area. Most of the residents were still in the cafeteria listening to a concert. Ching was overwhelmed by an uncontrollable temptation. He took out of his pocket a master key and inserted in the door. He turned the knob. The door squeaked a bit and opened.

He entered and lowered the curtains. Then he hastily checked through the papers on the desk. He slipped on the floor and hit his head against a wall. Botticelli's painting began to swing back and forth. To his surprise, he saw a vault encased in the wall. His desire to check was greater than his self-control. Venus had forgotten to close it. He grabbed a bunch of papers and began to read. He rushed to the door and saw nobody. He couldn't believe what he read. This material was sufficient to complete his manuscript, and he didn't have to struggle anymore. As a matter of fact, he could have quit volunteering altogether from that point on. He took the micro camera and frantically began to snap pictures of the papers. His heart rate increased to the point that he had to stop and take deep breaths. He realized that he was walking on a minefield, so he had to try to get out of there as fast as he could. He didn't have the time to think of the consequences.

He got clumsy a couple of times. His fingers nervously slid off the camera. He began to sweat and his tongue got dry. He heard Venus's voice on the speaker and got scared. He wanted to abandon the operation, but he was close to the end. A nurse stopped and knocked on the door. She called Venus, but heard no answer and left. Ching squatted quickly behind the desk. His hands were wet with sweat. A knot was developing in his throat. He was alone with his fear. He heard voices from the end of the hall. He couldn't close the vault because he didn't know the combination and hung back the painting. The voices got closer. He raised the curtains and opened the door, but could go out. The voices were too close. Instead, he ran to the window and jumped out. He fell on the grass, but the impact was hard and he felt pain in both legs. He dragged his right leg up and skirted the building until he reached the old man's window. It was open. He threw the camera inside and tried to get to the street next to the parking lot.

Mitango heard the object falling on the desk and rushed to the window. He saw Ching with tears in his eyes and with a grimace on his face. Mitango's face changed color. He became suddenly pale. Without caring about the clothes he had on, he dashed out of his room and ran through the halls to get outside as fast as he could. He bypassed residents and nurses. The cellulars were clicking. The two guards got nervous and followed the action.

Ching stretched his hand trying to reach a tree. He couldn't. His hand wasn't strong enough, and he slipped and fell down. He made a final effort. Maybe he should rest briefly, recollect his thoughts and energy and drag himself to the car.

Venus, in the meantime, returned to her office. Two men were following her at a close distance. She noticed the painting swinging lightly and ran over to it. She moved it and saw the vault open. She remembered she left it like that. Her mind was combating many doubts. Her eyes stared at the open window. She instantly alerted her guards and whispered something in their ears. They disappeared. Venus grabbed something from her desk drawer and ran our right behind them. The guards were young and fast. They passed Mitango and ran directly to the tree where Ching had sought temporary refuge. As soon as the guards arrived, they frantically searched through Ching's pants and shirt pocket. Having completed that task, they stuffed his mouth with a small rag. One of them grabbed his neck with both arms and twisted it at first and banged it against the tree after.

The jerk was quick and the concussion fatal. Ching turned his head to one side and his tongue came out from between his teeth. The men had no time to waste. They gave a quick glance at the main entrance to ascertain that no one was watching them and ran away in the direction of the The Joy of Life building.

Venus, who had passed Mitango too, arrived on the scene. Ching was about to give up his spirit. Venus took off the scarf from around her neck, but when she noticed something in his mouth, she pulled it out. She looked at it and threw it in the grass far from her. She lay Ching on the ground and attempted the resuscitation technique by pressing her hands on Ching's chest, but they slipped further and further toward his throat.

Mitango arrived. With a swift movement, he freed Ching from her hands and laid him on the grass. Venus fell and rolled all the way down to the street. He pressed his hands on the dying man's chest in a frantic race against death. When his efforts to revive him failed, he held him in his arms straight up against the tree. This position appeared to bring life back to Ching. It was a relief of a short duration. Ching almost lost consciousness and reclined his head on Mitango's right arm now. Mitango caressed him as does a father with a dying son. He whispered something into his ears. Ching attempted to spell out a word, "fat ... h ... This was meant to be my las ... t chap ... ter, my l ... ch ..." His eyes rolled back. His throat gurgled until it rested. Mitango was holding back tears. He tried to revive him in vain. He knew it was a hopeless fight against time. He laid him on the ground again and placed a handkerchief under his head. The sandals had fallen off Ching's feet. An idea flashed through Mitango's mind. He took off the sock of the right foot and saw something that horrified him. He cried out, "Son ..." The shout shook his chest and his voice became feeble. The sweat soon covered the entire forehead. His vision became blurry. He turned around for help. He saw nobody. He raised both hands to heaven and murmured a prayer in Latin "Lord, don't take him. Don't ..." He bent over Ching and said, "Son, I wanted to be so much with you ... Be brave, like your father. You will make it. I promise you...." And gave him the Last Rites. Big tears fell down his cheeks and disappeared in the dry ground. The dead man seemed to stare Mitango in the eyes, then his eyes rolled backward and he expired. Mitango emitted a loud cry. Big tears fell down his cheeks. He dropped on his knees. His arms were stretched on both sides. Shortly after, he composed himself, pulled a crucifix from his shirt and placed it gently on the dead man's forehead. The sound of the wailing sirens grew nearer. The sirens finally stopped screaming and the ambulance pulled briskly on the side scratching the asphalt, raising a powerful asphalt odor, and stopped. He sat upright position and realized his cheeks were wet. He wiped them with piece of cloth he pulled from his back pocket. He closed his eyes and joined both hands in prayer. He stood there a couple minutes in deep meditation until a paramedic touched him on his shoulders and invited him to step aside.

Mitango couldn't hear. Close by, Venus got up, dusted off her clothes and watched the scene intensely for a minute. A lightening bolt of terror and hatred crossed her eyes. A man with a stretcher approached her to ask some questions. She turned around and, without glancing at anyone, gained access to the hall that led to her office.

Soon, the residents came out and formed a crowd. The medical examiner arrived also. He exchanged a few words with the paramedics and pronounced Ching dead at 3:00 o'clock under the tree where he had sought refuge. He attributed Ching's death to an overdose of barbiturates that plugged the carotid vein causing a brain damage. Most of the residents rolled their eyeballs and twisted their faces. Someone didn't hesitate to show his disagreement and shouted some incomprehensible words, but he was quickly silenced by two muscular young men.

# FANIA AND MASSIMO

Fania Lesaca, chief editor of the Toronto Globe, was tall and slender with blue eyes and light brown hair. She loved acting, and also played the violin. Whenever she had to strike a deal with someone, she would first resort to a violin performance. She would entertain the guest for a half hour and then talk business. In her thirties, she was a skillful communicator, who knew how to turn to her advantage any negotiation. She had read Ching's incomplete manuscript and was convinced that it had all the characteristics of a best seller, which could have produced millions of dollars in the editor's coffers. There was only one annoying detail. The last chapter was missing. She picked up the telephone and dialed a number. A masculine voice answered on the other end.

"Hello?"

"Hi, handsome!."

"Who is this?"

"Don't you recognize your sweetheart?"

"Oh, Fania, quit joking."

"Listen, I apologize for interrupting abruptly our last conversation."

"I suspected that something drastic happened."

"You got it! Here I am as I promised, to reiterate my offer."

"Let's hear."

"Ah, ah, ah! You know better than that. I don't discuss gold mines on the phone anymore."

"Quit playing games."

"I'm dead serious! I keep my word."

"If that's the case, let's talk ..."

"Tomorrow, be at my Toronto office on College Street at six o'clock. By that time, everybody will have left. Do you remember how to get here?"

"Yes. You got it."

Fania dropped the receiver on the cradle, causing an awkward sound. She closed her eyes and reclined on the chair.

Massimo Campbell, by the age of 28, had already achieved a notable journalistic stature by uncovering a case of corruption that involved one of the Prime Minister's cabinet members. Tall and blond with light blue eyes, he had a captivating smile. As a child, he looked fragile and gaunt. Once, when he was two years old, his grandpa held him up by one hand. His daughter cautioned him to handle the child with more care. Any sudden jerk could have snapped the bone out of the socket. As he grew up, Massimo took karate lessons and became a black belt. By the time he graduated from high school, he was a robust young man, handsome and respected. The girls chased him, but he kept everybody in line.

When he smiled, he showed a perfect line of teeth. His mother made sure that he had the best dental care. She used to say ad absurdum that there is nothing worse for a young man or woman than to have crooked teeth. As a student, he had been on the honor roll from the first grade. Because the teachers unanimously stated that he was ahead of his class, his grandfather suggested that he skip a grade. In college, first he studied law, then he turned his attention to journalism. In his senior year, he studied at the Sorbonne in Paris. He took a doctorate in communication and went on to work for the Red Quebecois, the most famous local French newspaper.

The call from Toronto couldn't come at a better time. Massimo was punctual. He parked his Ferrari at the back of the building in the space reserved for visitors, and walked upstairs to the second floor. He disliked elevators. He thought that only lazy people use them. He rang the bell and the door opened. "How lucky I am to see the future number one reporter in North America. But now, we will try something a bit different." She hugged and laid a kiss on his cheek. She laughed. The lipstick had left its mark. She grabbed a tissue and wiped it off. "Don't worry! Your girlfriends won't see it. Massimo, some people are born with silver spoons in their mouths. Everything runs smoothly for them. Others, no matter how hard they try, don't seem to do anything well. You belong in the first category."

"That remains to be seen."

She poured two cups of coffee and invited him to sit down on the couch. "I can help you to make a bundle."

"How much?"

"One million American dollars."

"You are kidding!"

"No, I'm not."

"Doing what?"

"Easy money! You have to write the last chapter of an incomplete manuscript."

"May I see the manuscript?"

"It won't do you any good."

"Why is that?"

"You need your personal experience to write it."

"What kind?"

"You have to collect information about senile and terminally sick people at San Lazarus."

"Wait a minute! This is unfinished business!"

"You are quite right!"

"Now, I begin to untangle the bundle …"

"Which is?"

"No, nothing! I mean, it's not a big deal, except …"

"Never mind! Remember that the area where you ought to operate is under tight control."

"By whom?"

"That's up to you to find it out. I think the Health Department is interested in you."

"I have a big problem."

"What's that?" replied Fania anxiously.

"I don't like to be around old and sick people. I get too sick."

Fania didn't expect that answer. She challenged him, "Are you made of straw?"

"Don't be silly! I'm talking about emotions."

"And I'm talking about a million dollars. Do you understand? Hard money, man!"

"I need time to think."

"Are you insane? Anybody would jump at the opportunity. Listen, you could start at Olympus, which is the first building, where there are healthy people too with some sort of physical or even light emotional problems, but nothing so severe as to compare it to the residents of the Elixir building."

"Let me think about it. I'll give you an answer in three days."

"Cool! Oh, before I forget it. Change your hair color; grow a mustache and beard and, above all, make sure to change your identity. Whatever you need to disguise yourself...."

"Got it!" The two exchanged news on relatives and Massimo closed the conversation.

At this point, dear reader, my task is temporarily over. I leave you under Massimo's tutelage. He will continue this monumental task of writing the Last Chapter.

# Massimo

I was born in Milan. My father was a Canadian diplomat, so I was automatically a Canadian citizen. At the completion of his mandate, which came immediately after the operation, we moved back to Quebec City. I finished my university studies and became a journalist.

At a young age, we rarely think of the years when we will most likely be confined to a wheelchair. We have everything: youth, strength, time, work and money. Well, in 1996, I was in my fifties, still young, strong, with a teaching position and financially stable. I always shunned hospitals. The presence of a sick man or woman made me nervous. When I was a young boy my father underwent an operation for throat cancer at San Raphael of Milan, headed by a world famous oncologist, Doctor Veronesi. My father was a heavy smoker and, even though he was tall and muscular, he couldn't prevent the inevitable.

The surgeon cut a hole in my father's throat without anesthesia. Or if he did give him a shot, it didn't take effect. The vision of blood had always horrified me. I didn't visit my father before or after the operation. I closed myself in my impenetrable shell of fear and refused to see him in his hospital bed. My eldest brother didn't push the issue. Perhaps he realized my emotional weakness and dropped the topic. I have been grateful to him ever since. He would never impose his own ideas on anyone. If it was just repulsion to blood or a grudge against my father that impeded me from showing up and giving him consolation in his time of agony, I'll never know. Looking back, it could have been a combination of the two. The crudity of the operation, as my brother recounted it, remained embossed in my memory to the point that I have shied from funerals and hospitals ever since.

I have no intention of hiding behind any plausible excuse anymore. I was self-centered, eccentric, and insensitive to the needs of others. I felt like an outsider to society. Age hadn't molded my character yet. I resembled an unripe cherry. The sun was not there yet, nor was it sufficient enough for me to ripen. I was too introverted and obtuse. I didn't have the respect, the compassion and the courage to pay my father a visit. It's true. I was empathic and obsessively emotional, but I was also a coward. I could barely repress a sense of culpability. It took God's patience to let me get rid of my guilty conscience. I loved medicine. Nonetheless, I came quickly to the realization that it was not for me. My other brothers reproached me harshly for my cold character, insensitivity and unchristian values. I reflected upon them quite often, until I concluded that I needed a humility bath. Later, I tried to limit the damage by visiting Lourdes, but without conviction I dipped in the coldwater pool asking a miracle of the Blessed Mother. The response in my subconscious came rather quickly. "You must emerge from the polar waters of your arrogance, jealousy, envy, asocial behavior and egotism. You have to learn to walk like a baby on the path of humility if you really want to transform your inner being. You have other problems, but right now, these are of the utmost urgency."

San Lazarus, aside from the professional consideration, seemed to be the perfect place for my moral rehabilitation.

Fania Lesaca's offer to write the Last Chapter of an incomplete manuscript came, therefore, as a surprise. I was young and single and I spent the money lavishly with girls and games. As a junior reporter, my salary was decent, but I was always broke. The three-day expiration term was approaching and I was supposed to give Fania an answer. The problem didn't consist of accepting or refusing a once-in-a-lifetime opportunity, but in completing a project with all my well-known emotional limitations. The time was flying and I was still deadlocked. Finally, I realized that to overcome the employment hurdles I had only one path to pursue. I would seek a volunteer position. In that way, It would be easier to step in the building and do my work. At the same time, the job would help me to strengthen my emotions. So I made up my mind that I would start first at the Olympus building at St. Lazarus, and later attempt to gain access to the infamous Elixir.

I must confess I was not prepared for the challenge. If it were not for some motivational factors that played a significant role in the initial stage, I would have been doomed to failure. Certainly, I was influenced by Manzoni's, I Promessi

Sposi (The Promised Sweethearts), where the great writer gives a vivid and touching account of the tragic events of the Milanese epidemic of the 1600s, during the Spanish occupation. But it was Cardinal Borromeo's unselfish and indefatigable efforts to allay the pains and save the lives of the dying people that softened my hard stance. Equally important to my decision was the memory of Father Damian, who gave his life working among the lepers on the island of Malachi, in Honolulu. All in all, I believe it was an invisible hand that drove me to a world of pain and suffering, although I resist the temptation of admitting it publicly. I was about to learn firsthand lessons in humility and charity, and that alone was sufficient. I also felt the impulse to close the emotional distance that existed between me and my father. Whether there was one factor that played a major role in the decision making, or a synthesis of many, I felt impelled by the desire to pursue a noble cause, though I had financial responsibilities.

# SAN LAZARUS

San Lazarus looks like a dormant giant, raising its head on a hill close by Saint Agathe des Montes, a sanatorium, where people affected by tuberculosis sought asylum. It's close to Mont-Tremblant, where route 15 merges in with 117. Located on the west flank of Montreal, it's distant about one hour of car by the metropolitan city.

San Lazarus consists of a vast array of flat buildings. The highest is four-stories high. It's subdivided into units, excluding the immense belly of a subterranean intricate quarter with its own subdivisions. The hospice is surrounded, for the most part, by a wide semicircular parking lot. One section is reserved for visitors, another for the volunteers, and the rest for the disabled. Behind it, there are woods with dense vegetation, whose only inhabitants are squirrels and deer that graze freely in summer and rarely show up in winter. Across the entrance, there is a circle reserved for the ambulance and wagons used for patients' transportation. It's an area easily accessible to the residents, located about a quarter of mile from the main road, thus avoiding intense traffic, and offering a relatively tranquil surrounding. The only building facing the hospice is "Living Joy Company," about three hundred feet away, whose facilities stretch deep into the hills.

Inside, San Lazarus is well organized. Two large cafeterias can simultaneously accommodate three quarters of the residents. The rest go to eat at a different time.

One building is exclusively set aside for therapy. Specialized nurses provide their assistance and experience on a daily basis to patients who have had hip or knee surgeries and have to undergo a period of rehabilitation. The exercises last from two to eight weeks, after which some of the patients return home, although they continue to observe a long term individual exercise plan. Most always, a nurse will follow through by visiting the patients and by continuing the educational process until he or she feels certain the healing process has reached a satisfactory level. Those who are fortunate enough to return home are reminded to have a rail installed on the steps of the entrance, use caution while walking and apply a bag of ice on the knee in the event it swells up.

Adjacent to the main building, there is a south wing, added at a later stage, where minor surgeries are performed. It typifies the extension of an urban hospital, yet it operates exclusively for San Lazarus's patients. The extra wing has dark glass windows all the way around. Guards, with the aid of metal detectors at the entrance and exit, utilize the strictest methods of search. A sense of mystery surrounds this section because, although it's visible to everyone, no news ever filters through it.

At San Lazarus, another aspect worth mentioning is recreation. The daily agenda, even on weekends, is full of activities. There is bingo, language classes, concerts, painting and decorative arts lessons, just to mention a few. In summer, in particular, the residents are taken to watch football games or they have picnics in the parking lot. In the cafeteria, a priest celebrates mass on Sunday or on special holidays, but it's not unusual to find an inter-religious service officiated by ministers of different denominations. Eucharistic ministers are available on a daily basis to give communion to those who request it. A gift shop is open seven days a week to allow anyone to buy all sorts of articles. Recently, a coffee stand was brought in on the ground floor where one can find sandwiches and cookies before noon. There is no such convenience on the higher floors.

The only plausible criticism that visitors lodge against the institution is the elevators' sluggishness. Like Cyclops, they are excellent for heavy loads, but in terms of speed, they have a long way to go. Somehow, they missed the train to modernity. There are times when visitors laugh at hearing the elevators' groaning in ascending and descending from one floor to another. Even their number is insufficient to meet the demands of the traffic, especially as they are also designed to carry laundry carts, food trays and four wheelchairs at a time. To avoid lengthy periods of waiting, some nurses or patients' relatives opt for the stairs, but there is the omnipresent danger of inadvertently touching an emergency metal detector placed on the side of the door, thus causing the alarm system to sound and sick people to worry about possible fire. The concerns quickly abate as the head nurse scrambles to find the key to shut off the alarm. During that time, the personnel assures that no one leaves the floor or the elevator.

During hot, humid summer days, residents prefer to relax in the interior gardens and watch the birds and the flowers from underneath the lilac trees. The smokers prefer to spend their free time outside of the compound or in the smokers' room. I saw more women smokers than men. If someone smokes a cigar, a volunteer has to stay outside for one hour in his/her company because it takes that long for the cigar to finish.

Next to the main entrance, there is always heavy traffic. Ambulances come and go, along with vans that take patients to stores, video arcades or restaurants. The incessant emission of exhaust from the vehicles makes it difficult for most residents to breathe. Many times they choose to move to an area populated by tall trees and dense vegetation, behind the huge parking lot. They enjoy the coolness and the greenness of nature. If deer roam by, they take pictures. On certain days, the management arranges antique auto shows on a section of the parking lot. The rest is blocked off to allow visitors and residents to move about freely.

It's curious to note that St. Lazarus is like a floating city. A beauty shop is open eight hours a day to accommodate ladies' hair requests. Actually, it's a unisex parlor. The two hairdressers are busy all the time. To pay their bills, the residents go to the small local bank and withdraw the money from their accounts.

The kitchen department employs about 100 workers, including cooks, helpers and waiters. The administration department is made up of 125 people, including the top executive, ten supervisors, and various bosses and secretaries. The smallest department is the cleaning staff. Ten men and women clean the floors and wash clothes. The health department is by far the largest. 150 of them work on the 7:00 a.m. to 3:00 p.m. shift; 100 work from 3:00 p.m. to 11:00 p.m.; and the night shift employs only 50 nurses and runs from 11:00 p.m. to 7:00 a.m.

'The Order of San Lazarus'

Before I began my volunteer work, I inquired about the hospice's history. Its first name was San Lazarus. Later, they changed it to St. Agathe des Montes, and back again to its original name because there was already a St. Agathe des Montes. The funny part about it was that no one could explain the reason for such a name. It took me hours of research before I found out the real story.

The Order of San Lazarus was established, without doubt, during the First Crusade.

The members built a hospital in Jerusalem where they treated people affected by leprosy, both local and pilgrims alike. Some historians dispute the accuracy of the claim and purport that San Basil founded the Order in the seventh century. We are confronted here with centuries of inaccuracies and, therefore, even this claim lacks credibility because it has no historical background. We do know, however, that King Luis VII of France in 1154 changed the Order's goals. In fact, during those years, it lost the character of a religious institution and acquired a military personality. At the beginning, until the thirteen century, people made no distinction between them. Regardless of the role the Order played, it didn't bring much luck to the brothers who ran it. In fact, most of them contracted leprosy and eventually died. From this perspective, the hospital didn't have to fear an enemy attack. An enemy wouldn't dare occupy it. So the military connotation attached to the hospital had no practical significance.

In 1265, some diplomatic maneuvers began. The king allowed the pope to annex the Order of San Lazarus and unite it to all other leprosy hospitals under the papal jurisdiction. But it was destiny that the Order would not enjoy stability. The name and the fate of the Order underwent some changes within the Church itself. No one knew what was going to happen to the Order anymore. It looked like, as Dante would have defined it, a boat in stormy weather. An obvious example were the Papal bills which appeared in contradiction of each other. One issued in 1489 (which carried the title "Cum Solerti") reversed the previous one and practically wiped out the existence of the Order by subordinating it to St. John, the Order of the knights of Malta. In the sixteen century, another policy, under the authority of the Prior of Capua, returned to the Order of San Lazarus its original identity.

In the aftermath of Waterloo, King Victor Emmanuel I wiped out once again the independence of the Order and made it coalesce with that of San Maurice. Despite the fact that the name fell into oblivion in the succeeding centuries, it was finally resuscitated by hospitals, hospices and health centers in the Western world.

# ARIAN

Arian was 24 years old, of medium stature. Her hair was black, black like charcoal, but coarse and dense. Her eyes were black, too. Her skin was light brown and shone under the light. Everything she had was tiny: lips, nose, ears, and hands. She had a very gentle demeanor, a soft and captivating voice. She came from a rich family. Her father owned a microchip company, perhaps the largest in Canada. After graduating from high school, he sent her to study medicine at the University of Lugano, in Switzerland. However, the family fortune crumbled and the company filed for bankruptcy. Her father argued that unfair competition drove the prices down and he could no longer stay in business. The government's position was different. It held that he was involved in ballooning the cost of shares, which caused false expectations in the public. The stock market fell and his company was reduced to ashes. There ensued parliamentary inquiries that attempted to establish the relationship between her father and some high-ranking politicians, but the only one who paid the consequences was her father. He ended up in a federal prison near Ottawa for five years. Through good behavior and the mediation of some members of the Parliament, his term was reduced to two years. As a result of the financial disaster, Arian interrupted her medical studies in Switzerland and returned to Canada. She continued her education at the University of Ottawa where she graduated Maxima Cum Laude in biochemistry.

My first day was quite exciting. When the guards' routine inspection was completed, I asked the telephone operator about the volunteer department office. The well-groomed lady there, with a gentle voice referred me to another guard, who had me sign a visitors' book. Then, he pointed at a chair, made a phone call and asked me to sit until someone could assist me. I closed my eyes and, for a while, heard nothing. My mind was elsewhere.

In Lugano, a young lady on her last night of vacation had just finished eating at a fashionable Italian restaurant—"Il Sogno"—alone. It was apparent that her mind was in turmoil by the way she was shaking her head. A young man approached her and asked permission to join her. She made a disconsolate gesture of acceptance. After the young man ordered food, he introduced himself as Massimo Campbell and asked if she cared to eat something. She declined and gave her name as Arian Dedalus. He asked if there was something bothering her and if he could do anything to assist her, but she looked him straight in the eyes and shook her head in a sign of refusal. When he told her that he too was from Canada, she regained her composure and took courage. They talked and talked. They drank too. At one point, he left the table briefly and when he came back, he invited her to dance. He was not a good dancer. Conversely, she had music in her blood. She took her shoes off. In the middle of the dance, he extracted a red rose from underneath his shirt and put it in the girl's mouth. She smiled. From that moment on, she appeared to be much more relaxed. He already gave signs of exhaustion after three or four dances and was sweating profusely. Any dance master can attest to the demands that dancing imposes on the heart. Even athletes feel a bit tired after dancing a few minutes. The two young people needed a rest, so they sat. He paid the bill, and led her outside. The moon made her hair look lustrous. Her eyes were shiny. He unhooked the necklace from his neck. On the bottom, there was the image of the Blessed Mother and two capital letters: M&C. He placed it around her neck. She felt happy and threw her arms around him. "I'll never forget this dream," she whispered in his ear.

"We will keep this dream alive forever."

"We will never extinguish the fire that lit in our hearts tonight."

"The moon is our witness."

"So be it!" As soon as she was loose from his tight embrace, she unhooked a golden heart with a cross from her sweater and pinned it on his shirt." He tried to help her, but his hands were trembling. She noticed that the last two fingers of the left hand were unusual. They were not separated completely at the base. In fact, a re-growth kept them joined for about half inch. She thought it was a birthmark and didn't inquire. He murmured, "From now on, your heart is joined to mine." She laughed. He caressed her hair and kissed it. "I will never forget this night," he added. He put a card in her pocket and accompanied her home.

The following morning he wanted to take her to the airport, but he overslept. She was deeply disappointed. She tore apart the card and threw it out of the window. The wind did the rest. She was pulling out her necklace with the intention to destroy it, when the taxi honked the horn and she ran down the stairs.

My dear reader, that young man was me.

The First Day at San Lazarus

At San Lazarus, I waited for ten long minutes before a nurse arrived at the waiting room. She saw me in a sleepy mood and said, "Is someone in dreamland?" I didn't hear her the first time. When she touched my hand, I woke up. I realized that I was sweating and took a handkerchief to wipe my forehead. She smiled and asked me to follow her to her office, where she was going to review the rules and regulations.

Once in her office, she invited me to sit and started with a long list of don'ts. She emphasized not to sell or buy anything from the residents, not to offer any food or accept any from them, not to converse unnecessarily with anyone, except to answer to their most immediate needs, not to be personal or talk about my family, not to mention anyone's name or anything related to the outside world, and not to engage in sexual activity with any resident. I responded that I had no problems with any of that. She took note and informed me that I needed to take a TB test and a physical examination at my expense. This I disliked, but I agreed. I didn't raise any question or objection because, if I wanted to be hired, I had to make a good impression on her. There were moments of silence that made me think the worst. I was waiting for her to give me additional instructions. Instead, she pulled a tape measure from a drawer and measured my shoulders. She handed me a red jacket, and all my fears disappeared. For a moment, I felt proud. I had taken the first step. She realized that I was in a state of joy and invited me to take her for a ride in a wheelchair. She handed me a pair of plastic gloves and warned me that rubber gloves were sine qua non whether I served at Olympus or Elixir.

At the end of the trip, she commented favorably on my driving skills: I had passed another test. She then changed her tone of voice, became more polite, and invited me to follow her. When we arrived in front of the head nurse's office, she said, "Mr. Campbell is here." The head nurse was reading a document and without lifting up her eyes or turning her head, she motioned me to go in. It was then that she got up and introduced herself, "Arian, a pleasure." I can't hide that I felt an incredible sense of emotional turmoil. I tried to control myself and said, "Massimo Campbell." She stared at me, and I could tell she was instantly nervous. The attending nurse returned to her duties and I was alone with Arian. "I was waiting for you, sir; my compliments for choosing San Lazarus as the site of your volunteer work." While she was talking, she didn't raise her head. When she did, I could tell she was startled. She stared at me again until I felt uneasy. I had a beard and long hair. I returned the staring. She had blond hair and long eyelashed. I was not sure if she used contact lenses. If they were, the blue color was very deep. We were studying each other. She remained pensive for a short time. The reader may remember that I changed my name for obvious reasons. I keep the same name here to avoid confusion. She inquired about my profession. I answered, "I'm a collector."

"And may I ask of what?" She asked a bit annoyed.

"A collector of thoughts...."

"So, you live on thoughts. That sounds good."

"I mean, a philosopher, you know...."

She didn't seem to be pleased with my answer, but pretended to be unaffected by it. "Why do you want to volunteer here at Olympus?"

I explained to her that I felt an urge to help old people. She interrupted me and, changing the tone of her voice, said, "Mr. Camp, oh, I'm sorry, Mr. Campbell."

"No, it's fine." I quickly assured her. "But, if you don't mind it," I added, "I would prefer Massimo."

"As you wish.... I was about to inform you that we don't provide service just to old folks, even though they are predominant, but people from age forty on."

"I was not aware of that," I responded courteously.

"In this department, we offer services to sick people and to outsiders, who in the aftermath of surgery, seek our therapeutic expertise. On the other hand, in the Elixir building, you find terminally ill people with all sorts of diseases. Are you ready to accept the challenge?"

"I'm going to try. With your help, I can do anything." I could tell she liked that answer by her smile. A pause followed. Neither of us spoke. She covered her face with both hands. She appeared to be in a state of confusion. She broke the ice and said, "Follow me."

She led me outside into the garden where people like to relax during the summer. On the way back, she muttered, "I'm not so sure about you and the reasons for coming here. I have my doubts."

"I'll help you to get rid of them."

"I'm sure you will. May I give you some friendly advice?"

"Of course."

"Walk straight. Keep your chin up. Everything is under surveillance here. Any act of imprudence may cost you dearly." I nodded.

"Another word of caution," she added. "What I told you is internos.

I nodded, and we exchanged a last glance that pierced my heart.

That night I didn't sleep a wink. Her voice, her demeanor, everything about her were so familiar and yet unfamiliar to me. I felt deeply troubled.

My dear reader, that meeting shook me up from the bottom of my feet. Despite the pecuniary advantage that would eventually come from writing the last chapter of the manuscript, I don't know why I got involved in this assignment. Yes—the books, the emotions, moral values ... but I have been reflecting on it and I'm not sure if what I'm doing is right. I repeat. I'm a journalist by profession, but I never reported on sick people for a simple reason: I'm overly emotional. Suffering and pain just overwhelm me.

The next day, I took a deep breath and reminded myself that I had to honor a commitment. I was well aware that I couldn't complete the job unless I personally observed the patients, but how? Who would give me permission to conduct interviews? The idea of being stuck for a long period of time in a nursing home setting didn't fit my plans. I was not going to quit my present job, but I was not going to perish in the hospice either. I was troubled to the point that I spent many sleepless nights. Finally, I called Fania back and explained to her that in order to have access to certain sources of information, I needed to work longer and harder than what I had envisioned initially and I asked her to relieve me from my duty even if the monetary loss was enormous for me.

She calmed me down and offered me words of hope. She said that everything would work out for the best.

I took a sabbatical from my job and went back to San Lazarus. The nurse who took me around the previous day informed me that we had to complete the tour. She encouraged me to ask any questions I might have. As we passed by unit A, in the Olympus section, I heard a continuous lamentation, "Help, help, help. Nurse, help me!" I looked around and I saw one who was attending another patient. Further down the corridor, I heard a cry, "Oh, my stomach, my stomach! It hurts! It hurts!" Another patient nearby got tired of listening and shouted, "Shut up!" We passed to Unit B, and I saw a woman who must have weighed four hundred pounds. Her legs were as big as tree trunks. She looked serene, but as soon as she saw me, a look of pain crossed her face. I asked my guide, "What have they done to deserve this punishment?"

"Many brought these conditions on themselves." I was going to ask another question, but she gestured to move on.

Finally, we arrived at Unit D. Here, cries and high screams filled the air to the point that I began to cry. I wiped my cheeks and asked my guide who these people were. She replied that it was not proper to ask such a question, but because I insisted, she replied, "In other places, you will see worse scenes, so get ready." I covered my face with both hands and I started to sweat. She noticed my discomfort and handed me the set of rules I had to abide by strictly. When we reached the end of the hall, she stopped me abruptly and assigned me to the transportation group of volunteers. She looked at me and wished me well. If I needed any further assistance, I could rely on her.

I remained speechless.

The third day was like the first two. This time, however, I was on my own. I stood motionless in the hall for a while, pensive, with my eyes closed. A visitor stopped and stared at me. I made a reassuring hand gesture, and he left. I sat on a chair in the corner and I debated with myself for some time whether I should continue or drop the whole idea. When I got up, I had made up my mind. I realized that money alone was an insufficient stimulus to continue the job. I needed something stronger than that. I needed to psyche myself, to despoil myself of the armor of arrogance and insensitivity. The project lost the monetary motivation somewhat and assumed a new dimension. Suddenly, I felt the urge to assist these unfortunate people. A compelling force, stronger than writing, prompted me to look elsewhere to fulfill my life's expectations and dreams. Writing no longer occupied the top priority in the new environment, or so I thought. I struggled to find a rationale for the sudden change in my attitude. I felt emotionally involved in these people's lives. While I was thinking, someone tapped me on the shoulder. I turned around and saw Arian. She forced a smile and asked me how I was doing. I felt suddenly regenerated and I tried to remember her face from years ago. I was resolute to solve the problem and I asked her for a date. She said in an almost imperceptible voice that my request was imprudent and inappropriate.

The message was quite clear. San Lazarus was not a place for romance. I explained to her that something else prompted me to extend that invitation. She cautioned me again to refrain from making such advances and not to push my luck too far. A cold feeling, like an icy ball, ran up my spinal chord. I felt myself pale and I trembled for a minute or so as if that ball were lodged in my body. Arian left immediately. Her nurse attendant came and brought a cup of coffee, which I drank. My body reacted favorably and I gradually regained my composure and began my routine. The nurse returned to Arian's office, where I could see the two of them talking.

Before I move on to the next chapter, I want to make sure that the reader knows there's no place like home, and that those unfortunate brothers and sisters suffer every day away from the social mainstream.

Mitango Africanus

After Ching's death, Mitango became a hermit for a while. His visibility was at a minimum. He severed his ties with the Living Joy Company. As a result, he lost the conspicuous monthly subsidy that the insurance company delivered to him, even if his prestige had declined. He refused the honorary guards and warned them that any attempt to curtail his freedom would be considered a hostile act against the Church. Under such circumstances, his legal adviser, the brilliant Anna Lisa Casale, from Ottawa, would withdraw his memoirs from the Vatican's vault and read it to the world. From then on, there was a tacit reciprocal understanding not to step on each other's feet.

I stumbled on Mitango Africanus by mere chance. Because of a hip surgery, every day he came to the Olympus building to undergo therapy. He was of medium stature and stocky. He wore reading glasses and a hearing aid. His curly, scarce, hair was black and gray. His lips protruded, and two of the canine teeth were covered with gold. His nose was quite flat and his ears big. He smiled and laughed most of the time making his black eyes even more lucid. After he dismissed the bodyguards after Ching's death, they still kept a somewhat close vigilance in front of his door even though they made an effort not to be very visible. Their presence gave me the impression that he was either an African politician or a tycoon. I met him briefly in the main hall while he was trying to pick up a letter from the floor. I bent immediately and handed it to him. One of his guards, from afar, ran to prevent me from doing that act of courtesy, but Mitango looked straight in his eyes and the guard left. From that moment on, he remained a mystery to me. In getting up, I felt a pain in my back and I cried out "Porco Diavolo!" He turned to me and asked, "So, you speak Italian."

"Certainly! I was born in Milan of a Canadian diplomat. When he retired, we moved to Canada. Do you speak Italian, too?"

"Well, I try."

"What do you mean by that?

"I get by. I visit Italy sometimes...."

"Where did you learn it?"

"Well, well, well." He didn't answer.

"You sound like my uncle, the priest." When he heard that, he looked surprised. He grinned and invited me to a nearby table.

Mitango was born in the outskirts of Mlolongo, near the major traffic artery that runs from the port of Monbasa toward Nairobi and stretches out all the way up to the border with Uganda. There, the truck drivers take a pause before crossing the border, eat, drink and look for night company. They don't waste any time because girls swarm the area dressed in bikinis and high heeled Italian shoes, and keep their breasts quite exposed.

Mombasa Street is flanked by motels of different qualities. After all, in a desert, truck drivers don't expect a five star hotel. During the weekend, starting at dusk, the area swarms with people, resembling a market place. Men strike deals with women, who compare themselves to any other factory-worker. Prostitution is illegal in the country, but at Mlolongo, life continues unperturbed without police who are scarce and underpaid. A Kiswahili word 'hanya-hanya' best characterizes the prostitutes activity. In the year of the Jubilee, the local authorities tried to tax the ladies who sold their company to truck drivers, but the reaction was extraordinary. The prostitutes showed up at a meeting at the municipal building and offered a bag of condoms to the mayor and trustees, then put red roses in their mouths. The police intervened to protect the politicians and to restore order. The women argued that the government had no right to levy taxes on them because they didn't sell or buy anything. One of them owned a massage parlor, right in the main square. When the police got the word that something fishy was going on, they threatened to close her down. She claimed that she was a psychologist and her professional objective was to make men relax. By frequenting her establishment, men discharged their frustrations and anxieties and actually got along better with their wives. In a span of ten years, she had accumulated a fortune and got into a business partnership with a local engineer. They made plans to build a twenty floor skyscraper, "Freedom Sky," but to make their plan work, they needed financial support from bankers. Their goal was to imitate other investments abroad, but on a much lower scale. They looked into an American consortium which was going to invest 500 million in Moscow to build an 85-story tower, the highest in Europe. They also studied the Taipei Tower of Taiwan with its 101 stories, completed in 2003. On their desk was the picture of the Jim Mao Tower, with 88 floors, completed in 1998 in Shanghai, China. For a while, they had in mind a grandiose project equal to the Kuala Lumpur Tower in Malaysia, with the same height of the Jim Mao Tower, inaugurated in the same year. That skyscraper appealed more to them because of its two towers, but they couldn't carry out their plans for lack of capital. As a last resort, they contacted the prince of Dubai to start a joint venture, but he had a project of his own. He was also embarking on the construction of a tower, unrivaled not only in the Middle East and Africa, but the world. It was designed to be 160 stories high, at a cost of 900 million dollars. He had already hired the Italian stylist Armani to decorate the first 37 floors of the hotel and the 235 rooms of the other apartments. In the adjacent area, he planned to build an artificial lake with hotels, golf courses and restaurants. The woman and her partner hadn't given up their dream, even though they were not prince and princess yet. They even made contacts with some drug lords from the village of Malana, India. By the following year, hotel construction, 20 stories high, began and their prestige rose immeasurably. It didn't matter if the rest of the town was squalid.

Mombasa Street, in Mlolongo, is infamous for another reason. It has become the epicenter of AIDS in Africa and holds the record for the highest death rate in the world. The churches in Africa are very vocal on this issue, but the struggle is long and hard. The rumor is that the only real winners are the manufacturers of condoms, but they have nothing to laugh about. Condoms don't assure complete safety and the financial gains are offset by the sad perpetuation of an epidemic of vast proportions.

Lately, a new positive energy seems to be seeping through the streets of Mlolongo. There is hope that change will occur. A few people are beginning to make a difference in the fight against prostitution. The President of Uganda and his wife are Born-again Christians. They have launched a campaign of abstention and prayer to replace condoms. Pope Benedict XVI has once again reiterated that the best weapon to fight AIDS is chastity. In the meantime, the uncontrolled epidemic has added another sinister statistic to the record: 15 million children are without a mother or a father and six million are dying every day.

The hygiene in Mlolongo is at an all-time low. Most of the motels are infested with lice and other bugs. In the past, the plague reached biblical proportions. To avert the intervention of the national health department and the shut-down of their operations, the motel owners took some action. They hired additional workers from neighboring countries at low wages to contain the epidemic. The irony is that bedbugs operate at night by sucking the blood of the victims, who bear signs on their skin. The tiny animals may live in a perfectly clean environment, but it's the use of special disinfectants that kills them.

Mitango's parents were around seventy years old and still worked because they didn't receive a pension. His mother worked as a janitor in one of the motels; his father was a clerk. Every day, they rose at sunrise and walked three miles to reach their workplace. Mitango used to help his parents when he was young. He saw the girls with miniskirts, and their breasts mostly exposed, walking with truck drivers up and down the aisles, drunk, smelling of beer, vomiting sometimes in front of the rooms, and falling heavily on their beds. Some of them wore shorts and t-shirts. Their sandals were covered with sand and their hair stank of gasoline. Some men were so disheveled that half-unbuttoned shirts couldn't cover their prominent bellies. Whoever wore a beard had them discolored by dust and the scorching sun. There were times when young Mitango asked about an unusual noise or the low, broken voices coming from the bedrooms, but his mother was quick to shut him up. "Mind your business and respect the privacy and profession of the ladies. Without them we couldn't hold our job," she used to say, somewhat irritated. The boy would not reply. In the evening, when no one was around, he stopped in the hall and placed an ear close to a door. His mother caught him once and reprimanded him, "If one of the ladies sees you, the owner can fire you."

One day, an Italian missionary arrived in the small plaza. He drove a motorcycle that left behind a cloud of sand. The motorcycle coughed a few times, shook, and finally fell silent. He carried a guitar on his shoulders, a Panama hat to protect himself from the scorching sun and a Bible, hanging at his chest. His whole body was covered with dust. Soon children gathered around him and he began to play and sing religious hymns. He brought along a parrot, which rested on his head and, occasionally, repeated a word or two. The children were fascinated by the scene. The missionary stopped singing and wiped the sweat and dust from his brow with a long, rough handkerchief, which looked more like a short hand towel. The children tried to place their fingers on the chords of the guitar and the musical notes that came out of them sounded more like shouts. A little boy climbed on the motorcycle and put a finger on the parrot's beak. The missionary told the parrot to say "ciao." The bird repeated the word. The boy laughed loudly, his mouth wide open. As soon as he stopped laughing, he pointed out to his friends that the parrot spoke to him in a foreign language. The boys and girls performed a local dance with circular movements and sudden back steps. The missionary applauded and passed around a few candies he had left in his pocket. The older folks gathered around too.

The missionary, noticing that the crowd was increasing, took the guitar and played some local songs. Everyone cheered. Still holding the guitar in his hands, he stood on a chair, and with a soft musical back up, he began to preach both against female slavery and the exaltation of sex. A giant of a truck driver, half drunk, snatched the guitar from him and broke it on the man's head. The parrot escaped, shrieking, but came back as soon as he saw his owner getting up from the dusty ground. He touched his head. Fortunately, there was no wound and no blood. The children cast stones at the truck driver who threw some punches in the empty air and left, mumbling words that can't be repeated here. A little girl approached the missionary and tried to dust off his clothes. He caressed the girl and gave her a chocolate bar. She hugged him and, in a soft voice, asked him, "Why did he break the guitar? Now, how are you going to sing to us? That man is mean." The missionary placed his dirty hand on the girl's shoulder and said, "Someday, I'll come back with a new one and you will sing for us." The girl agreed and looked at him with her big black eyes.

A week later, a Buddhist monk appeared on the main square and sat on the ground in a traditional meditating posture. His head was shaved and his face serious. He walked barefoot and dressed in typical Buddhist garments. The sandals were covered with dust. He was corpulent, weighing over two hundred and fifty pounds. He was almost motionless for an hour. The people looked at him with intense curiosity waiting patiently to see what he was going to do. When he finally opened his eyes, he began gently stretching hand and arm motions. No one proffered a word or made any unnecessary noise. The monk invited the curious bystanders to sit in a circle and he started to explain that meditation is the vehicle that propels man to Buddha. The crowd started to laugh, not knowing what he was talking about. One of them asked him, "What happens to the woman? Does she get lost in space?" The crowd got slightly unruly and was ready to toss sand at him, if it were not for an older man who intervened by saying, "Let the man speak! Don't you have any respect for foreigners?" The people's faces slowly got serious and the monk was able to continue. "Through meditation one can acquire peace in one's heart."

"When can anyone become Buddha?" asked a boy.

"Actually, there is no age limit," replied the monk. When he realized that nobody believed him, he said, "A young boy in the district of Bara in Nepal has sequestered himself in a tree cavity for the past six months without touching bread or water."

Once again, his last words were accompanied by laughter and disbelief. He remained composed and continued, "Even scientists are visiting the area in the Himalayan kingdom, about one hundred and fifty kilometers from Katmandu, near the district of Lumbini, where Goutama Siddhartha was born. According to popular oral tradition, he became the Buddha (which means "The Illuminated") through long periods of meditation." At that point the crowd became restless. One of them shouted, "It's a lie!"

The monk replied, "The Lumbini Development Trust is carrying on an investigation, but at the end, it will prove that the boy is a true follower of Buddha. He is in the cavity of papal."

"At that age he is already a pope?" a boy asked.

"No, that's the name of a fig tree where Buddha stood for six months without touching food."

A man in his forties, from the last row, stepped foreword and said, "How is it possible for a human being, even though he is a young man, to stay in a sitting position with his eyes closed in a cavity of a tree without food for six months? Do you think Africans are dummies?"

"He simply becomes invisible at night. This is another proof of his sanctity."

"You are absolutely right! "exclaimed one old man with a bird. "What you didn't tell these ignorant people is that his followers lower a curtain in front of him."

"That is not true."

"If it's so, how come he is in good health and doesn't lose weight?"

"The fact that he is weak proves that he isn't tasting any food or drinking any water. The doctors themselves disputed it initially. Now, even they are admitting that there is nothing fraudulent in the case."

"You mean the doctors have actually checked his health?"

"I don't think so."

"If the Buddhist authorities forbid the doctors to visit the boy, something is fishy."

"The boy is a saint. Anyone can see that he uses a scarf just like the Buddha did."

"What do we care about the scarf?

"I can understand your rejection," replied the monk in his calm posture. "His own mother had doubts. She didn't believe that her son was going to be a Buddha. That has changed and she speaks wonders about him."

"What else does she say?

"He is following in the Buddha's footsteps. Allow me to provide a brief background of the Buddha. He was born in Lumbini about two thousand five hundred years ago and became what he is in Bodh Gaya in Bihar."

Some of the prostitutes incited discontent among the crowd. One of them yelled at the monk, "Who cares about this nonsense! If you want to talk to us, get rid of the tricks and let the doctors and scientists visit him, otherwise everything is fake. You can fool the Indian, the Nepalese and all other people in East Asia, but not us."

The monk didn't have the chance to reply. The young people got rowdy; they grabbed his belongings and destroyed them. Before they could put their hands on him, he got up and hurried out of the town, mumbling imperceptible words.

Mitango didn't show up for a while on the job. His family searched for him to no avail. They suspected that the Buddhist monk had brainwashed him and left the town with him. The police had no clue of his whereabouts. One day, a shepherd came to Mlolongo and told the family that he had found Mitango in the desert under a palm tree in a state of meditation. He had lost a lot of weight and his health was precarious. Mitango's parents couldn't find words of appreciation for the shepherd who had saved his life. Since then, the townspeople didn't allow any more Buddhist monks to stop among them, not even for a short time.

A couple of months passed after the desert experience. The missionary returned with a new guitar, as he had promised the girl. He gathered the children in the center of town and began to teach them how to sing religious songs. The children accompanied the music by stamping their feet on the ground. The little girl finally had her chance to sing and proved to have a fine voice. The missionary glanced often in all directions to see if there were any unwanted guests. He didn't have any intention of having his guitar broken again, nor his head.

One morning, Mitango jumped on the back of the missionary's motorcycle and they rode off.

In the capital city of Nairobi, he marveled at the many buildings, police officers, traffic and people from every continent engaged in all sorts of activities. He thought he was on another planet. His eyes couldn't avoid the opulence in some districts and the poverty in others. At night, he watched the girls in miniskirts walking up and down the streets and wondered if they had anything in common with those of Mlolongo.

The missionary thought the boy spent too much time looking at girls and asked him, "Can you guess what they're up to?"

"Not really, but I can imagine."

Suddenly, the missionary departed from diplomacy and asked him, "Do you like girls?"

"Not that type."

"If someone wanted to marry you, not now, how would you feel about it?"

The boy smirked, "That isn't going to happen so soon."

"Ok. I have a proposition for you. How would you like to study in this Catholic seminary. You will get your education and eventually become a priest, if you wish."

"What does it mean?"

The missionary patiently explained the life in the Seminary that led to priesthood. The boy liked the idea of forming a bright future for himself. The missionary read his thoughts, "Mitango, my boy, you don't seek personal glory, but the Lord's."

The boy looked in the street at the girls again. His young mind was clogged with a myriad of thoughts. The missionary insisted, "You have to train yourself to give them up if you wish to pursue a holy life."

"That's not easy! All my older friends have girlfriends."

"They live in a secular world. You are already part of the ecclesia. You have to honor your commitment with the Church. She will be your spouse and you have to honor her."

The boy didn't respond. The missionary kept staring him. The time was flying.

Finally, the missionary asked him, "Do you want to go to school?"

"What's that?"

"You will learn how to read and write … and be able to add and subtract numbers."

"That isn't a bad idea."

"You can also learn about other people and Jesus."

"Who is he?"

"He is our Savior."

"Where did you learn that?"

"Well, attending a seminary, you will learn that and much more."

The boy didn't answer. He was thoughtful. The missionary looked at him with a mixture of curiosity and suspicion. "You can always withdraw from school if you don't like it. You will regret it if you do, no doubt about it, but …"

"Why not give it a try?"

"Fantastic!"

"Wait a moment! Is there enough food?"

"Of course! But, think more about the other food."

The boy thought that he was alluding to extra food and nodded.

"Next week, we start. In the morning, we have educational sessions and in the afternoon we will train you in prayer and fasting. These are two great defensive instruments against temptation."

The boy protested, "Just a minute! You told me that there is enough food and now you tell me that I have to fast."

"Don't worry! These are exercises."

"I hope that they are just exercises and not real stomach sufferings because I'm not going to deny my body certain things."

"Frivolities!" replied the missionary. "You will conquer these weaknesses in a brief period of time."

The boy stared at him as if he wanted to grasp the meaning of the words, but the missionary invited him to the cafeteria for a snack. The boy jumped out of the chair and followed him.

That same evening, it was hot, but the missionary wasted no time in introducing Mitango to the other students of the Catholic seminary in Nairobi. Mitango needed a special intensive course on reading and writing. Being a brilliant, enthusiastic and aggressive young man, he learned rather fast. Later he joined the more advanced classes that led him to attend regular classes.

The meals were not according to Mitango's expectations and he soon made it known to his classmates. The cook told him that he had plenty of time to satisfy his juvenile hunger. The evening meal, appeared especially meager to the boy. It consisted of a slice of bread with nuts and some fruits. One advanced student remarked, "In medieval times, one could have considered it fasting or, at least, hunger control, but not at the end of the 20th century or at the beginning of the new millennium." One teacher explained that the frequent appeals that the mission made to foreign countries fell on deaf ears. And so they had to learn how to survive on their own terms or with the generosity of some good-hearted souls.

The Seminary was not just a place of seclusion with long and arduous hours of studies. As soon as supper was over, the seminarians had various tasks to accomplish. Mitango was assigned to clean and mop the kitchen floor. Very quickly, he realized that he had to face many temptations in that place. The smell of various spices and cheeses tempted his palate and nostrils every single day.

The credenza was the food guardian, so to speak. There, the missionary kept the perishable foods. Mitango sat for a long time in front of it, staring at it, perusing it, trying to come up with credible answers. Sometimes, he stuck out his tongue on the glass window pretending to lick the food or squashed his nose on it to smell the aroma. He was ready to give up playing that game when an idea flashed through his mind. He attempted to move the credenza, but to no avail. It was too heavy for one young man. He checked all over the kitchen for some tools, but there were none.

The first week, Mitango was unlucky. Fortune didn't smile at him. As the days went by, he resorted to a stratagem that only a locksmith would be able to devise.

The missionary was not a scrutinizer, or an oppressive priest. He never deprived any seminarians of anything within his means. All of this, however, changed. One evening, he noticed that a piece of Parmesan cheese was missing from the closet. His religious brothers made a mockery out of him. "You drank one too many," one of them said.

"Brother, I didn't drink anything last night. I had a migraine headache."

The new day arrived and he noticed a half-empty bottle of wine in the credenza. The tension increased in the missionary's mind and suspicion began to take root. He inquired among the students, but he obtained no clue that could lead to the explanation of the disappearance of the wine.

The brothers didn't wish the incident to be blown out of proportion and suggested to the missionary that he was having illusionary visions. He felt humiliated, and after that, he avoided any reference to the food issue. After all, he didn't want it to become an obsession. At the end of the supper, he placed a bowl with ten olives in the credenza and locked it. Two days later, they were missing. This time he raised the issue with the seminarians, but no one was in a position to provide a clue that could lead him to the identification of the culprit.

The whole situation was becoming unbearable for the missionary, who took the bold initiative of approaching Mitango, privately, "Have you seen at any time, for any reason, anyone, even a seminarian, opening the credenza?"

"I never saw anyone. I swear!"

"It's a sin to swear, but an honor to be honest."

"Don't you have the key?"

"Right here, in my pocket!"

"In that case, the only one who could do the job would be you."

The missionary smirked, but didn't answer.

"Well, then, it has to be a mouse," added Mitango.

"A mouse in the kitchen! Why didn't I think of it before?" admitted the missionary.

"Why do you sound so surprised?"

"In reality, I shouldn't be. You are absolutely right. After all, the whole area is infested with rodents. Every month we need the assistance of a pest control man."

The missionary suddenly became pensive. He placed the index finger on his nose as if in a meditative mood. Mitango was waiting for the conversation to continue, but to his disappointment, the missionary got up and started checking every piece of furniture in the kitchen. He removed every item far enough from the wall, except for the credenza, which, being heavy, remained a few inches away. When he exhausted his search, he exclaimed, "Not a single hole!"

"I'm still convinced that we have a mouse around here."

Again, the missionary looked at Mitango with a mixture of incredulity and suspicion. It was the first challenge in a long time that he failed to meet. On the door, he had a sign, "Never give up!" He stared it for a while and then he stood silent waiting for a response from Mitango. The young man must have been tired because he turned around and walked toward the door. The missionary caught him in time, "What if someone has another key."

"How could that be? You are the only one who has it."

"Exactly! Somebody could have stolen the key from me, gone to a locksmith and made a duplicate. Later, he could have slipped it back in my pocket. It makes sense, doesn't it?"

The missionary shook his head and pointed out that such possibility was very remote because he had always slept with the key in his pocket. He was apprehensive and, without waiting for a reply, he said in a soft voice, "It would be a risky operation."

"It's easy to find it out. You could check with the locksmith," said Mitango.

"Be serious! There may be hundreds of locksmiths around ..."

"Start asking!" challenged the young man.

"Oh, don't be silly!"

"Don't like facts? Then use your imagination. You have a good one!"

The missionary thought it over and said, "Imagination, my ... eye!"

"Then, someone has a second key. Still, I don't believe that someone would steal your key. I'm dead sure!"

"Don't bet on it!"

"Why would they take the key?"

"To open the credenza and steal the food from it."

"The food? I insist that's a mouse's job."

"It's an educated guess, but I discard it. I don't see crumbs of any sort on the shelf."

"You won't. The mouse eats them."

The missionary turned to Mitango, half irritated. He had heard enough of word games and justifications from a young man who was not in a position to teach him any lessons in logic. The allusion to a mouse being the culprit of the missing food didn't fit in his puzzle. He dismissed Mitango and continued his work.

In the following days, there was a repetition of the previous mishap. The missionary complained this time that a whole chunk of cheese and half loaf of bread disappeared. A closer investigation revealed that even the sausages and the two bananas were gone. Now, he excluded altogether any mouse theory and was determined, instead, to allow the events to run their course. "In one way or another, the train has to reach its destination," he murmured. He brought an old armchair into the kitchen and decided to sleep there during the night from then on. For this tight vigilance in the kitchen, he neglected his other duties. He kept that schedule for approximately a month, but not even a clue turned up in his favor. Tired of his own suspicions, he resumed his usual working routine, allowing that everything was back to normal. At least, he felt half assured that if nothing abnormal happened during that month, it was due to a severe dosage of discipline and honesty he had imparted on the seminarians.

The days were passing by monotonously at the Seminar, until another incident shook the compound. A banana cake was missing from the credenza. The news brought new concern in the mind of the missionary, who almost lost his customary patience. He displayed an unusual series of authoritarian actions that caused discomfort among the young students. In an impromptu general meeting, he warned the youth that he would no longer tolerate such mischievous conduct and would severely punish the guilty. "He will feel the full price of my indignation," he shouted, pounding his fist on the table. He reminded the audience that the mouse traps he put in and around the credenza had failed to catch any rodent, but he did it to please someone's curiosity. From then on, he would resort to different traps. The brief meeting ended with comments of innocence on the part of the seminarians. One boy said, "What evidence does he have to accuse any of us? It may be the work of his fellow brothers, or other assistants."

A friend replied, "He is basing his accusations on assumptions."

The missionary stumbled into Mitango on the way out. The two exchanged a brief greeting, and that seemed to be all. However, the missionary stopped shortly after, and turning to the young man he said, "I have the gut feeling that this is a job of an expert, a very precocious young man." Some passing boys repressed their laughter and ran away to avoid any confrontation with the missionary, who again lost his customary serenity and exclaimed, "I don't tolerate privacy invasion!"

Mitango stood there and said, "Maybe it's an act of a mouse or a colony of them." The missionary took it as a statement aimed more at irritating him than helping him. He tightened his jaw muscles, but refrained from making any further comment.

Mitango had no intention of upsetting his mentor and invited him to the kitchen once again to check every single piece of furniture. Frustrated, but willing to show cooperation, the missionary agreed. He checked everything scrupulously and finally he arrived at the credenza. He placed his hand at the bottom of it and his middle finger got stuck in a hole. As soon as he disengaged it, he turned suddenly pale. Whatever Mitango had been telling him all along shaped up into a logical and plausible possibility. His voice faltered, "How ... can ... this ... happen?"

"Very simple! They want to survive."

The missionary's face was a discolored ball of emotions. He insisted that he had taken all the precautions, but that the mouse still had its way. He looked like a defeated man. Then, he rushed to get a hammer and nails and taped the hole with a piece of cardboard.

Two days went by and a whole salami was gone. The enraged missionary stared at Mitango, waiting for an explanation. The young man, by no means disconcerted, put his right hand in his pocket and pulled out a mouse. The missionary stepped backward. Mitango laughed, "You are afraid of a little animal like this," and began to pet him.

The missionary grimaced. "Get rid of that immediately! That's an order!" Mitango obeyed and the missionary resumed a false calm. Mitango said, "Let us go to the kitchen and I'll show you how this animal gets his way through."

"You're not coming with that ... are you?" Mitango tossed the mouse into the street. "He is harmless."

"Never mind it!"

In the kitchen, the missionary was nervous. Mitango showed him another hole. The missionary was appalled at the sight of it, "I'll tape it immediately."

"Why waste your time? It's senseless. Another mouse will replace the first and make more holes."

"What are you suggesting? That I give up and let everything be at the mercy of thieves?"

Mitango didn't like the word "thief," but made no fuss about it, "It's not a question of stealing; it's a matter of life and death, of survival. Do you understand?"

The missionary stared at him so intensely that the young man got up and walked out.

That night, the missionary was unable to close his eyes. He tossed left and right until he couldn't bear it any longer and got up. He got a drill and bored a hole in the attic floor, above the kitchen. From the attic, he hoped to control the action.

One evening, while he was on guard, he heard some steps in the kitchen. He placed his right eye over the hole and waited impatiently to catch the thief. The pupil of his eye dilated when he watched a young man taking in a hurry the hinges off the credenza. He cast a few glances around, grabbed a jar of marmalade and a slice of bread and laid it on the table. Then he proceeded to replace the hinges and bolt, and he left on tiptoes.

The missionary remained speechless and spent the whole night in the attic.

At dawn, he got up and descended cautiously from his improvised bedroom. He didn't bother checking anything else, but hurried to the locksmith to order a chain with a special lock on it.

Later, he visited the seminarians and joked with some of them. When he located Mitango, he rushed to him and exclaimed jubilantly, "I caught the mouse!"

Mitango played it cool. The missionary was standing there, in front of him. His eyes were inflamed, "I finally caught the mouse in the act!"

Mitango didn't respond. The blood began to rush to his face which felt like a ball of fire. A friend heard the missionary and shouted, "It was just a game!"

The missionary didn't appreciate the statement and sent him for detention. He walked back and forth in the room for a couple of minutes, then he added, "Honesty has been finally restored in this religious community. It took my energy, patience and perseverance, but in the end, I can declare that the mission has been accomplished."

"If you caught the mouse, where is it?"

"I let him free for now. He won't come back anymore. He is so scared that he won't dare to fall into the trap again. If he does, he is going to stay there."

Mitango smiled. The missionary walked backward to the door never letting his eyes off Mitango.

# MRS. DUBLIN

I didn't see Mitango any more at Olympus. The rumor was that the administration applied restrictions on him by changing the time of his therapy sessions. His seclusion, whether planned or desired, prevented me from pursuing my main objective. His background was shrouded in secrecy. I checked on the internet and sought help from other professional sources. The result was unanimous. His name appeared nowhere. I thought about Fania and the reason for assigning me this task. I repented for having accepted the offer. It was too late. I scoffed at the temptation of abandoning the whole project and started to plan on the next step to take. After all, for the scanty notion I had of Mitango, as a person, he appeared to be quite interesting. So, I decided to move on and transfer to his building.

Not everything was that simple. Prior to making any inquiry on the procedural methodology, I got the news from a private source that I needed special permission to have access to Elixir, where Mitango resided. I took a deep breath and my plans remained in an embryonic stage, at least for the time being.

To make matters worse, during this trial period, Arian's private secretary approached me informally and whispered in my ear, "Starting Monday, you will work only the east side at Olympus. You will feel more comfortable, less stressed. The scenes there are not as unpleasant as elsewhere."

I looked at her with surprise. My mind was in turmoil. Suddenly, I felt as if my head were spinning and I was unable to stop it. I looked around me. It was dark, darker than midnight. I tried to walk, but I stumbled. The nurse helped me to stand up. I made a clumsy attempt to find out the motive for the restriction. She reminded me in a soft voice, "You are a volunteer here and, therefore, you must submit to the rules without questioning them." She twisted her lips, attempted a smile, turned her back to me and left. I followed her steps speechless until she turned at the end of the hall and was no longer within my vision.

The atmosphere was somber. I stared at the floor. No one paid attention to me. Volunteers passed in a hurry in all directions, pushing wheelchairs. It began to form in me, the feeling of being worthless. The new orders spoiled my plans. I was well aware that *The Last Chapter* could only be completed by working at Elixir. Despite the temporary setback, I armed myself with prudence and patience and I slowly began to push residents to their destinations.

One morning, I ran into Mrs. Dublin. She was the oldest woman in Syracuse and probably one of the oldest in the world. A very affable and softly spoken lady, she had a good sense of humor. She always wore her hair straight and it was very shiny. I don't think she applied any products to it; it looked naturally healthy. Well, I should add that the nurses were always at hand to fuss over her and on a couple of occasions I caught them fixing her hair. Yes, there was a beauty shop in Section C, but she never went for any work, not even for a hair cut, a nail clipping or hair coloring. Her skin was healthy, typical of the old matrons. She experienced hearing difficulties and the hearing aids could help only to a certain extent. She wore reading glasses, and her children, to ascertain that she could read their phone numbers, wrote them in big characters on a piece of cardboard she kept within reach. She was very well mannered. Her demeanor reflected the gracious education she received within the domestic walls. In her youth, she must have been a beautiful woman. She had a perfect nose and sparkling blue eyes. She wore different clothes every day, sometimes colorful, sometimes plain, indicating her good taste. When she was younger, she would shop in the most fashionable shops of New York. On the nightstand, she proudly displayed a picture of her with the President, but never bragged about it. She spent her days in a wheelchair, but never complained. Being an ultra centenarian, she was the center of attention. At times, newcomers or visitors peeped in to get a glimpse of her or inquire about her secrets of longevity. In answer, she claimed she'd done nothing special. "I controlled myself and led a normal life." She was very religious and recited the Rosary every day. When I found that out, I asked permission to pray with her whenever I came to Olympus. The first reaction was negative. The lady in charge of the religious program didn't show any enthusiasm at my request. She informed me that it was not necessary since the residents gathered in the chapel each Monday to pray. I said to her, "Look, not everybody can attend the prayer group. Some patients are too sick to move from their beds. I don't think there is anything wrong in going to their rooms to say the Rosary. I'm willing to come even on weekends."

She looked at me somewhat annoyed and said, "What for? I already told you that we have it once a week in the chapel." I closed my eyes, thanked her and left.

The religious program leader disappointed me enormously. The good news was that I felt unshaken in my project. In front of my eyes, I saw, as in a movie, history repeating itself. I remembered when I was fifty-eight years old and I tried to embark on a religious mission, but the bureaucracy became an obstacle. I bent my head and whispered, "Rules and regulations are meant at times to obstruct, not to facilitate or fortify faith. Let us not mention communication and the desire to reach people. Fortunately, those of us who feel we have a mission in life don't give up, and continue undaunted, undeterred in their quest to serve people, thus enjoying personal and spiritual satisfaction." That personal failure with the person in charge of the religious program reminded me of the boy who encased himself in the cavity of the tree in Nepal. In my case, not once did anyone attempt to discuss the matter with me to a greater extent. I was never invited to a meeting; never asked for input; never recognized for my religious work; and never did they try to communicate. I felt isolated, but not doomed; beaten, but not defeated, ignored, but not silenced.

Mrs. Dublin was very fond of me. She smiled as soon as I appeared on the threshold of her door. Often she broke the ice with interesting remarks, "Are you a priest?"

"Not at all! I'm a sinner in search of redemption. Prayer helps me to achieve salvation."

"Listen to him! What should I say?" she replied.

"Mrs. Dublin, I don't want to sound like a preacher, but it's very common for us to judge from appearances. 'A habit doesn't make a monk or a nun,' they say in Italy." She shook her head in disbelief, stared at me and laughed.

On another occasion, she told her daughter that I was a holy man, and all her relatives held me in high esteem after that. They spoke to me almost with reverence. That scared me, and I tried to stay away from her whenever I heard she was enjoying their company. If I inadvertently stumbled into them, she made sure I was recognized. Her son told me once that she looked foreword to saying the Rosary with me. She was happy in my presence. When she saw me arrive breathless, she would say, "I hope you don't do this because you feel obligated." When I told her that it gave me great pleasure to pray with her, she would smile. Many times, we got interrupted by the telephone during the Rosary. She picked up the receiver and, regardless of who was on the other side, she would say, "Call me later." The caller guessed that I was around and quickly hung up, but not before sending me greetings. If her family came and heard us praying, they would wait outside. As they got to know me, they entered and joined us in prayer. It was inevitable that Mrs. Dublin would misplace her Rosary. In fact, she lost it most of the time. To prevent the unnecessary search and waste of time, her daughter suggested that she wrap it up in a napkin, hang it on her neck or place it on her wrist. Nothing worked. There were times when she kept it in a jewelry box, or locked it in the nightstand drawer. I had to search all over to find it.

At times, Mrs. Dublin experienced a loss of memory. Once she asked, "Do you know what today is?"

"Absolutely!"

"What is it?"

"It's Tuesday."

"I thought it was Sunday." Then, she added, "Don't get offended, but I think you have an accent." I started to laugh and she did the same. When I regained my composure, I looked on the nightstand and asked, "How did you get the picture with the President?"

"Well, she stopped here. I didn't know her."

"You are very popular," I insisted.

"Oh, stop it! Don't be silly!"

During the summer in particular, the floor was the scene of unwanted "visitors." Mrs. Dublin munched crackers during the day. The crumbs fell on the floor and attracted ants, which multiplied in a matter of minutes, if not seconds. I had to move my feet not to become a visiting-place for them. I kept quiet for a while, but then I got tired of it and told the janitor. No matter how many times she came to sweep and mop, the insects would reappear. Mrs. Dublin appeared oblivious of their presence or if she was cognizant, she didn't make any fuss about it. Evidently, she didn't see anything wrong, and I never alerted the janitor again.

Mrs. Dublin had a sweet tooth. Her children brought her chocolates galore. I wonder if the ants ever got into the closet.

Between Mrs. Dublin and her hearing problems, and her roommate, who was blind and deaf, communication between them was practically nonexistent. It broke my heart when their children called. "Ma, ma, ma, can you hear me?" and got no response. Occasionally, I would take the phone and tried to convey some information to them.

Mrs. Dublin had a calm temperament, even when the fellow across the hall cried out, "My foot, my foot!" intermittently all day long. Occasionally, she'd ask, "What is he complaining about?"

Her children took turns visiting her. The oldest son showed an uncommon tenderness toward her, speaking softly and with kindness. His eyes glowed with love for her. He was the picture of tenderness and love. He visited her three or four times a week and treated her with the same love she must have showered him with when he was a baby.

Mrs. Dublin's son was a very devoted man, and so was the whole family. Sometimes, he arrived at San Lazarus to visit his mother while she was reciting the rosary. He stepped in silently, sat on the bed and joined us in prayer. His faith was like a light in the middle of a dark night.

His daughter had been involved in a Vatican inquiry. She was diagnosed with a malignant tumor in her early twenties and her health was declining steadily. The doctors didn't give any hope to her parents. According to the newspaper articles, she was the object of a miracle by Mother Cope, a Franciscan Sister from Syracuse, in Upstate New York, who had devoted her life to sick people on the island of Molokai, in Hawaii. She was later beatified by the Vatican.

A volunteer lady found out that I was saying the Rosary with Mrs. Dublin and came to see me. Afterward, she looked at me with awe and promised to join us the next time. I reminded her, "Do you know that when you say the Rosary with someone else, there is a higher indulgence?"

"I didn't know that."

"Oh, yes, it's true."

"I don't dispute it, but the indulgence isn't the driving force in this string of prayers."

"You are absolutely right, but we can't discount the benefits."

"Oh, yes, it's true and I would like to join you." This pleased me immensely, but to my chagrin, she never showed up.

Yesterday afternoon, I visited Mrs. Dublin again. She was not in her wheelchair, but was lying in bed. I thought she didn't feel well. She had a serious look and, on her nose and forehead, I noticed a few scars. I didn't ask her if she fell or not. I went on to other subjects. I didn't want to hurt her feelings or intrude on her privacy. Suddenly, she had a flash of memory and asked me how my sister was doing. "I'll pray for her," she said. She had remembered from a previous conversation that she was not doing too well.

Spring came and the flowers were blooming. The birds were chirping. Mrs. Dublin said to me, "Now, be a good boy and I'll pray for you." She reclined her head on one side and fell asleep. All her children, grandchildren and great, grandchildren were in tears, around the bed.

When I returned the following day for the Rosary, she had fallen into a deep sleep from which there is no return.

Never again did I meet a woman of her stature inside or outside San Lazarus.

The news of her death reached the White House and The President took time to attend the funeral. The crowd was crying at such a gesture of humility and friendship. The Canadian people were honored and showed their appreciation by waving white handkerchiefs. The mass media reported the event at length. It was a tribute to honesty, fidelity, and faith, but also to one of the oldest people in the history of Canada.

According to the foreign press, Mrs. Dublin was four years younger than Virginia Dighero, the oldest woman of Europe. She was born in Genova on Christmas eve of 1891 and worked on a farm all her life. She is believed to be the seventh oldest woman in the world, at this date. Yesterday, she received the well wishes of the Italian President Ciampi.

Mrs. Dublin's death threw me into depression. I had spent almost every day with her, praying the Rosary. She represented to me an anchor of salvation. I didn't have to push a wheelchair or look for friendship with other residents. I had a place to go and I enjoyed being with her. In this context, Olympus was very rewarding. I felt at home in Mrs. Dublin's company and had the chance to meet very interesting people, who came to visit to her. I didn't realize that everything received the approval of Arian, who acted like my occult guide, even though I rarely saw her.

On the other end, I became restless. The time was flying and I hadn't made any headway. On a door, I saw a sign, "La paciencia lo alcanza todo." Patience allows you to accomplish anything. St. Teresa's words had a beneficial effect on me. They restored my spirit of perseverance and optimism. A lady by the name of Sonia helped me regain my sense of humor.

She was quite fat, and when she talked, she showed a mouth without teeth. She kept her dentures in a nightstand drawer. She had a fantastic outlook on life. She exuded joviality from every pore. Her clothing, although worn out, was flowery and bright. She wore no socks. She looked like a multi-decorated soldier with all sorts of medals pinned on her chest. I asked her, "Where did you earn all these medals."

"I earn them."

"You look like a general, but without an army."

"Well, put it this way. I like them. If you have one, bring it to me."

"I don't have any medals, but I do have some foreign money." I should not have said that. From then on, she pursued her goal, to get as much as she could from me. To get her out of my hair, one day I brought her some Italian coins. I suggested she get holes punched in them and pin them to her sweater. She was overjoyed. In the subsequent weeks, I gave her some additional meaningless objects that she kept as a prize. Whenever she saw me, she yelled to catch my attention. If I pretended not to hear, she shouted again in the hall, "Did you bring me anything?" I began to feel embarrassed, and responded negatively. Sometimes, instead of calling me, she would beckon to me with her index finger. I responded that I was searching for something to give her. Then, she would feel satisfied, but she made sure to remind me not to forget my promise. Later, I found out that she was an artist and she proudly showed me her drawings. I congratulated her and expressed my admiration for her work. She opened her wide mouth and joyfully thanked me.

She sat on the same spot every day and made sure to control the traffic all day long. On one occasion, I showed her the book, *A Fistful of Happiness*. She looked at it and said, "What a nice color! Can I take it?"

"I'm sorry! You can buy it."

"Oh, I don't read books anyhow. Don't forget to bring me something the next time." I nodded.

Once a year, I did spring cleaning. Whatever I didn't need, I threw in a bag and brought to her. Each time I brought a bag, I made sure she would not be in her room so she wouldn't see the contents. She might have rejected it and I would have to make another trip. I got away with giving her a lot of junk. She seemed to be pleased to no end with whatever I threw in the bag and she acknowledged it, publicly, even though I would have preferred a certain degree of secrecy because volunteers were not allowed to give anything to the residents, neither to accept anything from them.

Once, when I went to visit her, she had passed away. On the wall, there was a crucifix—the only companion of her solitude.

# THE BASKETBALL
# TEACHER—ROOM TWO

The man in Room Two was 95 years old and almost seven feet tall. He had been a basketball player and teacher and though at his age he couldn't walk, his body still showed his former vocation. The doctors operated twice on his back, but the problem persisted. He had dentures and still read books with the aid of eye-glasses. His wife had passed away ten years earlier and they had no children. He delegated his finances to a nephew in Chicago. In his younger days, he ran for county office on the Democratic ticket. He was especially proud of a picture taken with Robert Kennedy, who came by to help him get elected. He used to say, "God has been good to me." When I asked what he wished the most, he replied, "To live with my family. If my nephew were here, I would stay with him, but he is a doctor in another city." He spent his days watching T.V. and reading books. He didn't mind living like that because everything was done for him. Sometimes, I saw him throwing his hand in the air, then closing it into a fist. I wondered, "Is he trying to catch nonexistent flies?" I didn't pursue the matter. He was a happy and quiet man if it were not for the family. I asked him what thoughts crossed his mind most of the time and he said, "Death, but I'm not afraid of dying."

I didn't return to Room Two for a couple of months. When I finally did, he was no longer there. I refrained from asking his roommate. I knew where he had gone. The hospice contacted the nephew in Chicago. He came, arranged a quick funeral and left in a hurry.

# MEIN KAMPF—ROOM 50

Mickey was 89 years old with a head full of white hair. He was skinny as a string bean. He moved to Canada from California after his discharge from the army. He married a nurse, Mademoiselle Francoise, whom he met at the hospital where he recovered from a wound. Even at 89, his blue eyes still sparkled above his aquiline nose. His voice was naturally inquisitive. Whatever the nature of a comment that I made, he would sound surprised. I was not sure if it was due to a lack of general knowledge of or current events. I never saw a visitor in his room, but he didn't seem to be bothered. He told me his wife had passed away and that he had a girlfriend five years younger. She was also suffering from some ailments that forced her to call him rather than to visit. The rare times she visited, they spent the time playing cards. He had intended to marry her, but she would not hear of it. She didn't seem to be fond of children and houses. Not that she looked like a movie star: she walked slowly and hardly spoke a word in my presence. Her skin was visibly old. Extra fat was dangled under her throat when she moved.

Mickey didn't say much about his wife, "She lived here for nine years, but everything was useless. I came three times a day to help her, but she disliked the food and the cafeteria."

Whenever I asked him about his health, his reply was a sort of fatalistic resignation. He was reluctant to talk about doctors either. "A doctor found polyps in my colon and he took care of them. Later, he told me that there was a regrowth. This is monkey business! What kind of talk is this? How can they grow back? What are they, mushrooms? First, they took them out and then they gave me more bad news? I don't know how that can be possible. In the army, it was totally different. A man's word was his word, if you know what I mean."

"Exactly! So you were in the army?"

"Yes sir! I was a marine. Even my grandson is one of them. He came back from Virginia just to visit me."

"Did you serve during the war?"

"Of course! In 1941, I was in the Texas National Guard, 36th Division. I fought in France and Germany. I was in Lensburg, a town in East Germany, where Hitler wrote *Mein Kampf*."

"Did you visit any concentration camps?"

"Oh, sure! I was stationed for a short while near Dachau. There were a lot of Polish prisoners. The stench was awful! I couldn't understand it! I saw the gas chambers, the ovens ..."

"Who was your commander?"

"Patton. When he died, I General Clark replaced him. My unit reached Berlin. I didn't know how to swim. We had to use rubber boats, but we got shot anyway. I was sent to Eastern France to convalesce, and there I met my future wife. I received the Bronze Star. At Eganot, France, I saved a lot of friends who got hit with small bombs. They were even more deadly because of the sharp steel. I carried some of my wounded friends on my shoulders through a river where the water level reached my waste. So the army awarded me the Bronze Medal. Later, I got other medals in the Mediterranean. I landed at Anzio, in Italy. You should see the beautiful girls!"

I laughed, "You still like to reminisce about them...."

"How can I forget them?"

It was time for me to leave. He exclaimed, "Aren't you interested in knowing how I got here? You asked me all sorts of questions related to war, but not this?"

I apologized and assured him that I was very attentive.

"I suffered a stroke. My children took turns helping me, but when I had a second one, they decided to put me here for my own safety. They felt that I was going to be better off in a health care institution." At that point I was tempted to ask what made him get involved romantically with a woman who would not share the rest of his life with him, but I didn't pursue the matter. I didn't wish to appear too intrusive. I also feared that my inquiry could have been interpreted as offensive. His youthful outlook on life was contagious and I didn't want to spoil it. A couple months later, he passed away. I didn't see his girlfriend or any of his relatives. Only his medals kept him company in his final rest.

# Room 25

I knew the woman in 25 from her younger days. Her husband was a carpenter and a motor operator in a large company. He visited the gym every day, summer and winter, and stayed half an hour in the steam room. When he passed away, his wife went to live with her son. I don't know why she didn't live with any of her daughters. After all, they were respectful to her. She was short, but quite attractive even in her seventies. Then, senility crept in and neither the son nor the daughters could take care of her. The next step was San Lazarus.

During my visiting time, I spotted a patient in the corner of a living room, which served also for recreation and dining. She lay in a sleeping position. The following days I returned to get acquainted with her. I witnessed the same scene until I got curious and inquired of the nurse the identity and the condition of the lady. When I heard her name, I placed my right hand on my mouth in a state of astonishment. How could such a pretty lady be reduced to this condition, receiving no meals and no liquids? I looked up at the crucifix and shook my head. I went back home and talked to my cousin and she confirmed my information. She was Mrs. Francis! I expressed my deep concern. She replied, "Why should you worry about it? She has children."

"But I don't see them," I protested.

"Well, she isn't responding anymore to external stimuli."

"Is that a reason to abandon your parents?"

"No, it's not, but what can you do. They grabbed the house and the money. Now they figure they can't help her."

"Grabbed who? What …?"

"You know …"

"Never mind the financial aspect! She is a mother and a human being!"

"What do you want me to tell you?"

"She is a vegetable. If you were to see her …"

"They are waiting for her to die. The doctors keep her alive with medicine."

"Is that what her children told you?"

She didn't reply.

A few months later, death came almost without notice. The family didn't make any display of the casket. They had a small funeral that most of her friends didn't attend due to freezing temperatures.

# THE FLOWERS

Arian was eluding me. She didn't come by anymore. At least I was able to see her occasionally from wherever I was strolling, like a ray of sun piercing through the clouds in the midst of winter. A riddle of hypotheses was taking place in my already turbulent mind. I was searching for clarity among them, for a definitive answer that would serve me as a guideline, but every effort careened in a bay of dead responses. Her invisibility became a torture for me and I couldn't explain it fully. It was in my subconscious and I was unable to repress it. Also vain were my efforts to locate or contact her. Her initial predisposition to conversation and advice suddenly evaporated. Whenever she was in the office, she locked the door and pulled down the curtains. The sign "Unavailable" became omnipresent behind the glassy door. If before I expressed gratitude for her tacit support of my wandering around, now I felt baffled by her persistent disappearance. How dreary it was without her presence! I became a skeptic in a skeptical surrounding. No one can conceive or imagine all the beauty, unseen and unseeable in a woman! No one can imagine her gracious power to alleviate the pains of love. Nobody is in a position to explain the gentle power of joy she can promote in a male companion. These are secrets of nature, secrets of the divine sparkle in the human species, incomprehensive gifts to the feminine domain.

A few days passed by and I devised a new strategy. I was well aware of the risks involved, but I needed to put an end to my obsession. It was an inevitable course of action if I wanted to keep my sanity. I pleaded to the Lord but I didn't get an answer.

A week later, a UPS carrier knocked at Arian's office door. The secretary raised the curtains and opened the door half way. He handed her a package and a paper to sign and left. She read the name and passed it to Arian. She opened the package and found a red rose with a long stem. She motioned with her head to the secretary, who moved temporarily into another office. Arian looked at the rose again. The temptation to smell it became irresistible. She placed the rose close to her nose. The fragrance that emanated from the rose invaded her lungs and she felt inebriated. She reclined on the chair and closed her eyes. For a while, she was unable to think. When she finally returned to an upright position, she pulled the card from the white envelope. The scent of violets in it inebriated her and once again she fell backward on the chair. She sighed deeply. For a few moments she forgot of being the severe head nurse at Olympus. She felt transported into another reality. Slowly, she read the card, "Spring will return and it will never depart from us." She dropped like a dead body on the armchair, both arms dangling. Her head reclined on her left shoulder as if she'd fallen asleep. The rose and the card represented to her, as she admitted later, a mixture of thrilling, complex and troubling reality. Still, she was not absolutely sure of what was going on. The events were taking a new twist in her life in complete contrast with the severity of her profession. She earned close to $200,000 a year, but she had to abide by the rules of secrecy and celibacy.

These two worlds came suddenly into conflict one morning in September. She remembered how Massimo failed to show up the morning of her departure and how she had destroyed his telephone number. The only memory was the necklace. She touched it. Deep emotions began to well up in her heart.

She put the necklace back on and covered it under her uniform. Years of separation had dug deep furrow between the two people. In her new position, she felt security, protection and satisfaction. For the time being, she was not going to give it up only on account of a rose. She was not ready to jeopardize what she had built with patience, hard work and determination. She had her father in a dream. The prospect of shattering her mosaic was terrifying. She turned her head to one side as if someone were talking to her and said, "What if this is a trap?" She remained in her office most of the day.

# ROOM ONE, "THE SWEETHEART"

I visited Room One for the first time on a Sunday morning. Jimmy was a sweetheart. He was in his seventies with a lot of straight hair. He came to Canada for a job opportunity after the war. He met a girl from Quebec by the name of Segonelle and married her in two months. He was thin and of medium height. His eyes were small and brown. He was very reticent, but extraordinarily courteous. On the wall hung a purple and a silver medal he had won for heroism in the Philippines during World War II, but he never bragged about them. He was very reserved, but as I began to visit him every day, he felt more relaxed, and even extroverted as the time went by, to the point that if I missed seeing him one day he would inquire about it. He felt the urge to open his heart only with me. To this date, I don't know what caused him to feel that way when I was in his company.

This man's background was evident from his facial expression: a veil of sadness. I never saw him smiling. I asked him what bothered him and if I could help in any way. He had apparently been waiting for that question to relieve the pressure of his life. He said, "I worked at Carrier for 40 years. I get two pensions, one from the company and one from the government, besides Social Security."

"Why do you get two pensions?"

"I was a prisoner of war. The Japanese captured my platoon at Mindanao Island during a patrol mission. We couldn't see them. Their bodies were covered with foliage. After our capture, they put us in a cage for seventeen months. Some of my friends died of malaria. I barely escaped the disease. I guess I'm immune to it or the mosquitoes don't like me."

"I suppose you suffered very much."

"Let's not talk about it! At least that passed. There are other things that linger with you for the rest of your life. And, let me tell you, they are terrible."

"I'm sure you have the support of your family to alleviate some of those pains." He raised his head and looked at me with surprise as if I had proffered a blasphemy. He lowered his head and replied in a soft voice, "My wife gets all the money. At the end of the month, she signs the checks and cashes them."

"You can't blame her. She has to live. Do you have children?"

"One daughter! She is fat and lazy."

"I'm sure you want their wellbeing."

He appeared slightly irritated by my comment and said, "What about mine?"

"What do you mean?"

He continued in an almost imperceptible voice, "My wife visits me once or twice a year."

"Does she live far away?

"No, she lives here in the city."

"I can't believe it!"

"You better believe it! She sends me a postcard once in a while, as a reminder that she is alive."

"Does she drive?"

"Of course she does. She doesn't like to come here."

"Is it the precarious conditions of the old people …?"

"She claims that she vomits each time she comes."

"And your daughter?"

"She never comes to see me. I already told you how she is."

"I'm at loss of words, my friend."

"Yeah, they have been sucking my blood all along, but don't have time for me."

I remained silent, as did he. I couldn't take it, so I got up and left without saying a word. His eyes were fixed on the floor.

I didn't feel well the whole week. Emotions overpowered my state of mind. I was insensitive to noise. I returned one Sunday afternoon to Jimmy's room. I saw another name on the door. No, my dear reader, he didn't change rooms, neither did his wife change her attitude. I think of him and his family relationship I feel nauseated.

The news of my friendship with Jimmy somehow reached the main office, and Venus confined me in an uncomfortable area where they commissioned me to the onerous task of dumping the trash and transporting the residents to and from the cafeteria. Occasionally, I took them to the therapy section of the building, or to other menial activities. Soon, I realized that these activities, although honorable, were not part of my repertoire. I had another predisposition. Besides the writing aspect, I needed to motivate myself by talking to people, to console them, encourage them and reinforce their faith, if possible. I had grown sensitive to the patients' plights. I sent a written request to grant me permission to the visiting program only.

The reply came shortly after. The supervisor ascribed my ill feelings to external situations incompatible with my volunteer work. Nonetheless, she realized that I could give a greater contribution in a field in which I had more ability and left the door open for reconsideration.

Two weeks went by. I was on the verge of an emotional collapse. I didn't go to church anymore and hardly talked with anyone. One morning, Arian's assistant handed me an approval note. I jumped with joy. I had the freedom to move and to talk to anyone in my building without restriction. I was free at last, but not quite! There were vigilantes in every corner of the building. I had to use discretion and common sense. When I talked to the residents, I limited my questions to general topics unless they volunteered to reveal their privacy.

# ROOM THREE

Pedro, nearly 100 years old, and a lawyer by profession, was so influential in the Democratic Party of Montreal that no candidate could win an election without his support. He was also an obsessive gambler. We don't know whether the last time he came out of the casino he was broke or filthy rich. We can only report that when he ended up in San Lazarus, he claimed that he was already impoverished by medical expenses.

His character was arrogant and defiant, and his tongue resembled a sharp blade, ready to slash anyone he disliked. His own relatives refused to visit him because they were ashamed to hear indecent language. He treated the nurses with disrespect and humiliated them regardless of their rank, and pushed them to the point of tears. He made no exception with his family. His wife passed away ten years earlier and he had no children. If his relatives visited him it was mostly out of familial duty, not because they cared much for him. He had a daytime nurse on his payroll, but despite her presence his pants were always soiled and spotted with food. His shirttails hung out. He hated being at San Lazarus and firmly believed that, eventually, he would go back home. His house was grandiose. It faced a mountain in an extensive garden of trees and flowers. I could understand why he missed it.

To achieve his objective, Pedro needed a nurse who would take care of him during the night. He asked me more than once if I could help him in that matter. I promised him that I would investigate. In a week, I gave him the name of a girl and her phone number. He lost the card. A second time, he misplaced it. A third time, I called his nephew's secretary and gave the information to her. I don't know what he did with it.

He was a heavyset man, which complicated his daily walking exercises even more. The therapist gave up at the end of the third session. According to him, he lacked strength in the upper part of his legs. Pedro's dream of walking again, with or without a cane, was shattered forever. Related or unrelated to it was the fact that Pedro couldn't bend. Many times, I had to tie his shoelaces. He could barely eat on his own. Not that he disliked only the food. He hated everything and everyone at San Lazarus.

The summer was particularly challenging because I had more time available and my visits were more frequent. I used to take him for lunch or supper and, when we arrived at his table, he insisted that I wait for him and even eat his food, which I refused in a very courteous but firm manner. He could hardly hear and I had to help him to dial a number, write notes on a paper or speak myself on his behalf. What made me uncomfortable was his request to accompany him outside to smoke a cigar, which took him an hour. He complained that the nurse would not allow him to go alone because she was afraid that he would burn himself. I didn't want to spend the whole hour being inactive and from then on I tried to avoid him, which made me feel more than uncomfortable. For the first time, I started to experience a sense of guilt—not for the most powerful politician of Montreal—but for a human being. After all, I liked to be in his company. We had interesting conversations on legal issues, but I couldn't bear the smell of smoke.

In other circumstances, he revealed private information, which I can't disclose for professional reasons. We became somewhat close friends. When I told him that I had to call a lawyer for the deed on my house, he emphatically assured me that his nephew would do it for me for free. I thought it was unethical for a volunteer to use a sick man's friendship to attain financial benefits, and I never mentioned it again.

There were malicious rumors flying around that his sisters-in-law were interested solely in his property because he was a widower. I'm not in a position to substantiate those claims. We should give the benefit of doubt.

The day before the observance of the French Revolution by the French-speaking people in Canada, I stopped in the hall across from Pedro's room. I noticed a slip of paper falling off his pants. It looked like the one I gave him. A nurse picked it up and went straight to her office.

Two days later, I paid him a visit. He was sleeping. His shirt was out of his pants and his shoes were old and had holes. His head was inclined to one side.

Some barbiturates were strewn on the floor. I didn't make anything of it at the moment. I looked at him. He stirred in me compassion and irritation for his lack of care. I felt embarrassed for him. He, the most famous attorney of Montréal, was alone and forgotten. He had commanded the political scene for decades, and now was alone with no one watching him to leave the stage of this world. I murmured a prayer. I did the sign of the cross and got up to leave. A nurse was watching from the hall.

# ROOM TEN

Joanne came from a large French family. She was in her sixties, but her skin gave her a younger look. She wore a wig year-round, but I never asked her why. I thought it was for a special, personal reason and I considered it improper and imprudent to delve into her private matters. None of her relatives disclosed the nature of her sickness, but I inferred that it had to be something serious. She hardly spoke, but stared at her visitors for long periods of time, to the point that one felt uncomfortable. Not even the nurses or volunteers escaped that intense scrutiny. Her speech pattern was uncoordinated, often blurred by amnesia. Her husband, a saintly man, got up in the morning, prepared a package for his needs and went to the hospice to keep her company. He departed at five o'clock in the afternoon when a brother or sister-in-law would relieve him from his duty. His had the patience of Job. He never complained. Before leaving, he kissed his wife on the forehead, yet some of the relatives privately chastised him for being insensitive. In all frankness, I was unable to explain this position. He told me that he took her for a walk in the morning, but due to her bad coordination, she was able to make only a few tenuous steps at a time. One day, he decided it was not worth the effort.

They didn't have children, but the love of the relatives kept them warm.

Joanne had Parkinson's disease, which affects each patient differently, but the basic treatment is daily walks and exercise, just as a singer has to train his voice daily; otherwise he may lose it altogether. Others may have memory lapses. Besides that they function relatively well, until the conditions get out of control, so it was explained to me.

Joanne's symptoms were unique. She alternated between long periods of silence and repetition of one word or phrase. Her memory suffered a long, slow process of deterioration. Most of the time, she didn't realize what she was saying. Her language even became offensive until her family intervened.

I admired the love her relatives poured onto her. Particularly worth mentioning was that of her brother Cole. His turn to attend his sister at five o'clock in the afternoon came about three times a week. Upon entering, he stared at his sister and said, "Joanne, look at me. Do you know who I am? Are you happy now? Are you happy now?" As soon as she nodded, he would start feeding her and accompany each spoon with a word of consolation and hope. Many times, he cooked for her and the genuine, compassionate and intense care he lavished onto her will always stay with me as a moving force toward the sick. She was still living at the time of this writing.

# ROOM 20

This man was almost immobile in the wheelchair when I met him. He complained that his shoulder was causing him unbearable pains. Slowly, I gained the perception that all patients had a propensity toward complaining. He must have read my thoughts and said, "Look at my upper arm. It's out of the socket. I have been at the Veterans Hospital and instead of fixing it they made it worse."

"They have good doctors. How did it happen?"

"You tell me. I was better off before. My back is killing me, so …"

"Are you able to walk?"

"How? My legs have no strength."

"Do you go for therapy?"

"Don't mention it."

"Why don't you change doctors?"

"I can't. I was in World War II. I have to go to the army hospital. If I want to see an outside doctor, I have to do it at my own expense."

"Did you enlist or did they draft you?"

"Well, my story is long. I left Canada and joined the American marines. Their government is paying my expenses."

I didn't wish to be intrusive so I quit asking him questions. Being noontime, I offered to take him to the cafeteria. He declined the offer, claiming that the nurse brought lunch to his room. I was ready to leave when he started a tirade against the food, which he hardly ate most of the time. Then, without further comment on my part he said, "In the army, we ate good. We didn't have fresh fruits and vegetables, except when we reached a village or city, but it was good." He gasped for a few seconds and I wondered if he smoked. On his own, he admitted that during the war the soldiers couldn't smoke, and so he never did. I exclaimed, "That was good!"

"No it wasn't!"

I asked for an explanation and he said, "The captain gave breaks to the smokers. I had to be on guard because I didn't smoke. I wish I did." His daughter and grandson were listening and asked questions occasionally. I was surprised that they participated in the conversation because he had informed me during other visits that his family relations were strained. Suddenly, to my astonishment, he started to talk about women. "The Japanese government sent women on the front line, but we didn't have any."

"Those were most likely Chinese women."

"Who cared? It was war time."

"And the American nurses?"

"No, they were way back attending injured or sick people."

"Did you miss a woman next to you?"

"Of course!" His daughter blushed, while her son laughed. I caught the mood and asked him, "Were you all vaccinated against diseases?"

"For some, yes, but for others, the doctors had nothing. We made beds by tying a canvas between trees."

"No mosquitoes?"

"Are you kidding me? We used a net with a zipper around us. They gave us some medication against malaria, a pill before meals, but that was it. Those mosquitoes ate the net and many soldiers contracted malaria. Some of my friends would get red skin and, shortly after, die. The mosquitoes poisoned the blood whose temperature rose very high and then you'd sweat a lot. Unlike some other diseases, malaria doesn't leave any scar on the face, but it's deadly. There was no water to take a bath and we couldn't make a fire because we didn't want the enemy to detect our position, which would have endangered our lives. But we didn't have time either. We were too busy defending our positions. Unfortunately, what I didn't catch then I'm getting now. Look at me!" He pulled up his shirt. "I already had a triple by-pass and I can hardly breathe or move."

"What is that medal for?"

He didn't turn around. Ha paused a moment and said, "At Guadalcanal, I received the Purple Heart. On a hill, the Japanese command had built a train passage in the hills. From there, first they opened fire and quickly closed the doors. I got hit and ended up in an emergency hospital made of coconut trees, where I stayed for a month. I was twenty-one years old and I lost many friends."

"Didn't you have good doctors?"

"Oh, the Australians were excellent."

"How was the food?"

"They provided us with lamb all the time. That was their favorite meal, but I didn't like it." His face was getting hot.

"Let's come back to the States. How did you meet your wife?"

"We knew each other from high school and we exchanged mail while I was at the front. When I returned, I went to work in a hospital, where she was a nurse." He stopped talking. A tear found its way down his right cheek. I took a tissue from the box and handed it to him. He wiped his eyes and I bid him goodbye.

The following week, I found him in the same position, all alone. He invited me to sit and said, "Now, we may continue our conversation." I didn't wish to disappoint him and nodded.

"My wife had a boyfriend and I didn't find it out until I came back. She was no virgin."

"But you married her …"

"That was my greatest mistake. She told me her grandmother was an Indian chief's daughter. What good did it do me? I should have married someone else."

"Why?"

"She went to her sister's house all the time. They were very close. I warned her to stop that monkey business, but she didn't pay heed to me."

"Children …?"

"Five! After a while, I couldn't take it anymore."

"What happened?"

"She took the children and moved out."

"Just like that?"

"Exactly!"

"Divorced?"

"No! I don't believe in it. When I married my woman, I married forever, not like these movie actors that change one in each corner."

"You are a role model."

He made an effort to straighten his position and added, "And do you know what? I have not touched a woman for the past twenty-eight years."

"I can't believe it! You are a hero."

"I never betrayed my marriage vows. If it were not for these maladies, I would be OK. It all started last year when I got a stroke. I had no previous symptoms, mind you. I fell in the bathtub. The next thing, I ended up in the hospital, where I got a second stroke. I couldn't move or talk for a long time. They warned me not to move unless somebody was with me. What a case! Hardly anyone visited me."

"Then, you recovered."

"Temporarily! The doctors took five months before they diagnosed me with arthritis. Later I broke my leg and the ambulance took me back to the hospital. This time I cautioned the doctors that unless they found out what was really wrong with me I would not have gone back home. The verdict came rather quickly. I had a tumor on my spinal chord and needed a surgery. They kept me on the operating table five hours. They cut off a tumor as large as a golf ball, but dislodged my arm out of its socket."

"Are you fighting the case?"

"Yes, but only my grandchildren will see the results." He rested, trying to catch his breath.

I said to him, "With the time and with your family's support you will be able to overcome all these obstacles."

He looked at me with dismay, took a deep breath and replied, "Are you joking? I never see my wife, and my children rarely visit me."

I felt embarrassed. I had made an inappropriate comment.

He turned to me and added, "The only time I see her is when there is a party in the family. Last year, my grandson graduated from high school. They picked me up and brought me to the party. That was the only time I saw her!"

"That's unfortunate."

"Well, I don't think about it; otherwise I go crazy. But I know one thing. She has a boyfriend. After our separation, I went to see her one day. She told me to wait in the kitchen, while she went to the bedroom. After that, I heard a noises for a few minutes."

"Did it cross your mind to leave?"

"No, I stayed like a fool."

"How could she do that to you? She bore your five children."

He turned off the radio and stared at me and in a surprised mood he exclaimed, "That's what I mean!" As soon as he finished the last word, his face became suddenly serious. He turned toward me and said, "Actually, I don't think so."

"Wait a second! Didn't you tell me that you got married …"

"I did, but it doesn't mean that all of them were mine."

"How can you make such an assertion?"

"Very simple! My first son is black."

He saw me pensive and said in a low voice, "That's reality …"

His eyes got watery and I decided it was time for me to leave.

In the following days, I saw him moving around the halls with his battery powered wheelchair. I told him that he looked regenerated. He replied, "They gave me a machine, but how good is it if my health has deteriorated?" He pointed at his shoulders and said, "Look! I have to go to the VA for an operation. I have to go to an American hospital.

He turned the radio on and began to chew a stick of gum. He offered me one, but I courteously refused. He threw back the blankets and uncovered his body from the sheets. His legs were as thin as a stick. I wondered how longer he could stand the ravages of the infirmities and age. My mind went blank. When I finally found my composure, I reviewed as in a film myself being in his place, the whole humanity since Adam and Eve in his place. I closed my eyes and I don't remember when I opened them again.

In the successive meetings he reiterated his firm belief in the sacredness of matrimony, "For better or worse, for rich or poor." Those words reverberated in the hall and I couldn't stop admiring him for withstanding almost thirty years of chastity without his wife's company or comfort. He spent all that time without his children.

He is still alive at the time of this writing.

# ELIXIR

After my tenure at the Olympus building, I manifested my intentions to Arian that I would like to move on to Elixir. I had to discover new frontiers if I wanted to carry out my plan. I had gained enough experience and I had met so many people, but it didn't give me a passport to the next building. The system was so rigid that, in order to volunteer there, one had to work first at Olympus, and then needed a special authorization. Ching's death had stiffened the rules and it had become even more problematic to enter the premises without a special permission and a passage through the metal detector.

She called me to her office, clicked a couple of buttons and the monitor went blank. She extended her hand, as to invite me to sit, and explicitly indicated that she was not keen on the idea of my moving to Elixir. "I caution you not to be so eager. First of all, that place may be extremely risky for your safety. This angel can't be there to save your skin. I recommend that you reconsider your position. Secondly, don't think that they are waiting for you with open arms. You have to apply for it and fill out many questionnaires. Only after a meticulous scrutiny of your papers and a follow up investigation, they may accept your application and call you for an interview."

I ignored the word "angel" and I replied, "Why would they refuse me?"

"It's not a piece of cake. Only recommended people enter those premises.

"Well, you can recommend me."

"No, I won't."

"I thought ..."

"You thought what? That I would put my reputation and job in jeopardy, and your life too?"

"I don't understand."

"That place is for terminally ill people. Don't let me say anything anymore."

My head dropped, and I sank into a state of sudden depression. She looked at me with interest and suggested that I go home and relax.

As expected, my transfer request to Elixir was denied. The days went on drudgingly and I languished to almost a point of no return. During a fire drill, I noticed that a piece of paper fell from Arian's pocket. I picked it up, kept tight in my hands and rushed to the bathroom to read it. It was a copy of a memo she had sent to Venus. To my astonishment, I realized what I never wanted to read. I didn't return the paper to her although she searched all over for it. Even if she looked suspiciously at me, she never dared to question me. The revelation didn't deter me from redoubling my efforts to leave Olympus.

Venus was the 'deus ex machina' that controlled the whole internal apparatus. I wanted to soften her stand by sending her my request along with a box of the famous Perugina chocolates available in the Montreal stores, but I discarded the idea. It appeared too simple, too naive. I invented a more sophisticated plan, but this didn't satisfy me either. Finally, I decided for a third alternative. I would send her a second application with Arian's approval.

Three days went by and the florist delivered a box of red, white and yellow roses to Arian. She hesitated a while before opening the box. She cut the plastic ribbon around the box and opened it. A fresh and sweet fragrance inundated her nostrils. She breathed in the perfume, not once, but twice and sat on the reclining chair. She pulled out the card and read it:

Mademoiselle Arian, May you accept this humble token of friendship from me. I venture to take this opportunity to invite you to dine with me at the Cheval Blanc in Montreal, away from everybody. I have an urgent matter to discuss. I renew my admiration for your beauty.

I kiss your hand.

Respectfully Yours,
M.C.

The last two letters made Arian quiver. The card slipped off her fingers and fell on the desk. She sat gently, like an automated machine, and began to touch her forehead with both hands. She was sweating. Her lips changed color. She felt dizzy and fell backward on the armchair. The telephone rang many times, producing the same monotonous sounds. It took a good ten minutes before she fully regained her contact with reality.

During the weekend, she tried to write a response, but after a few lines, she ripped it up and threw it in the wastebasket.

Monday came. She sent her secretary for me. As soon as we were alone in her office, she detached a plug and the monitor was shut down. She proceeded to unplug another cord until a machine in front of her became inactive. I was awfully nervous and I expected a tempest to fall on me at any moment. Contrary to my suspicions, she thanked me for the invitation and reiterated her concern over my determination to be transferred to Elixir. The worse part of it was that I failed to garner any support from her, "I can't help you in this matter. I wish you well."

She stopped talking. I did too. During the long pause that followed, she glanced at my hands which I protected with plastic gloves. I pretended not to notice it and I explained to her that I admired her intelligence in the matter, but I felt a professional urge to move on. She raised her eyes from my hands for the first time and they met with mine in very intense scrutiny, which to me lasted an eternity. We both blushed. As soon as we regained our serious demeanor, I apologized for having been a bit indiscrete in my message and I made an attempt to rephrase it. She interrupted me, "I know perfectly what you would like to say, but please, stop lying to yourself. You are afraid to reveal your cards, but I know what is underneath them." I opened my mouth, ready to confess. She stopped me and continued, "First of all, I don't accept any invitations from anyone."

"But, I'm only a volunteer."

She raised her voice, "And stay here, then!" She realized that the tone was unusually out of line and apologized. Her face got red, and she lowered her head and said nothing for a while. I was in a similar mood. Slowly, she raised her head and looking straight in my eyes, muttered, "It's too dangerous for you there."

I shook my head and protested with firmness, but gently, "It's not a criminal institution."

"She opened the door and said, "I don't trust you." I looked into her eyes. They were lucid and penetrating. Neither one of us was making a move. I realized that it was a lost cause to try to persuade her. Her eyes spoke the language of determination. I didn't wish to push the issue and jeopardize my volunteer work. I turned my head away. I felt hurt, deeply hurt. I got up and walked toward the hall. I felt the urge to shout. I gave a glance around and noticed people everywhere. I considered it unwise to get engaged into an altercation that would have destroyed the castle in a few seconds. I opted to observe silence and returned to my duty. An hour went by and I began to think about the whole matter. I concluded that, for once in my life, I had reacted responsibly.

Two weeks more of hell dragged on slowly. I saw my dream shattered. I was only physically present at Olympus and I hardly talked to anybody. I looked in the mirror and I saw a beaten man, devoid of energy. I became apathetic. I lost weight, and all my ambition.

On the following Monday, I smiled at people by the force of inertia. Lunchtime came. A guard handed me a letter and left without explanations. It came from Venus's office. She had received my second application and, after much consultation with her staff, had agreed to concede me an interview. My mood changed instantly. I was jubilant, and determined to carry out my plan. I hurried home and called Fania.

Dear reader, at this stage, take a deep breath and relax. After talking to Arian, I'm not at all sure if I can trust Massimo to continue on in his role as a first person commentator; consequently, I decided to relieve him from his position. It's common knowledge that a writer who addresses the audience in the first person for too long, may lose part of his credibility because he perceives reality more from a subjective standpoint. I assure you that I took this action with a broken heart and was compelled only to ensure credibility. I wanted to clarify this point, so that your reading may proceed in a linear and pleasant fashion. Let us follow, now, Massimo as he continues to move in this new and risky enterprise laden with incognitos.

On the date and time specified, Massimo arrived at Elixir. A guard invited him to pass through a metal detector and another searched him from head to toe. With this check finished, a nurse accompanied him to Venus's office.

Venus has been described in an earlier chapter, as the reader may remember. I missed only a couple of details, which may assist you in better understanding future events.

She had olive skin and a birthmark right below her earlobe known only by her parents. Her mother lived a very reserved life in Montreal. No one ever met or saw her father. There was an aura of secrecy around him. She never mentioned him in her conversations even with the most intimate friends. By thirty-five, she had reached a prominent position. The executive committee appointed her as supervisor of the whole Elixir building, which she ruled with an iron fist. A close acquaintance, who wishes to remain anonymous for fear of retribution, said, "Intellectually, she is bright, but in terms of social behavior, she is cold and lacks charisma.

Massimo arrived ten minutes early to the interview and waited in the hall, until Venus's secretary spotted him and invited him in. He said "Glad to meet you."

Venus didn't respond. Instead she stretched her right hand. He kissed it. She tried to smile and sat. "I was expecting you. Please, sit down," she said without inflection. "Do you care for a coffee?

Massimo made a denial gesture with his head and added, "I'm not a coffee drinker."

"Would you prefer a glass of soda?"

"No, thanks, I would rather drink water, but at this moment, I'm not thirsty."

She called a secretary and ordered a glass of water with ice. Massimo didn't object.

As soon as the water arrived, Massimo took a sip and wiped his lips with a colored handkerchief.

Venus realized that her guest was more relaxed than before and began, "I have a good report on you from your ex-supervisor. After much pondering, I've decided that you may make some valuable contributions in this institution. I expect you to live by the tenets of the glorious tradition of San Lazarus. I demand punctuality and a 'clean nose.'"

Massimo responded, "I believe that you have the same rules that govern the rest of San Lazarus."

She raised her voice and Massimo got somewhat intimidated, "Here it's different! I don't tolerate any infraction of my written expectations. Do you see that poster? It says, 'silence and work'. That's the motto. Of course, I'll enforce against any violation."

"I fully understand my responsibilities."

She liked the answer and exclaimed, "Good!" She was about to close the file when she turned to him again and asked, "By the way, monsieur, why have you sought this position with such great determination and obstinacy?"

"I really want to help these people."

"I like your answer. The attending nurse will complete the interview. Good luck!"

"Thank you, mademoiselle Venus. I'll do my best."

"I'm sure you will," and went straight to the door.

The attending nurse, upon a gesture from her boss, went over with Massimo a list of prescriptions and proscriptions about the privacy of the residents and briefed him on the main health rules. Before discharging him, she cautioned him to refrain from giving liquid to residents who had a yellow band around their wrists even if they requested it. She showed him how the alarm system worked and dismissed him, "We wish you the best," and she closed the door in a hurry.

Massimo looked back to her, surprised by the quick manner he was treated. Luckily, he remembered Arian's warning and headed for the volunteers' office. In the vestibule, he stopped to read a sign in Latin. He didn't get the whole meaning, even though he had studied for a few semesters in high school. From the little he could gather from it, it was an admonition to abide by the rigorous system of norms and be extremely discreet in talking to the patients. "Why is this ominous sign hung up there?" he muttered. "Does this serve as a deterrent to imprudent volunteers? Maybe it refers to the residents? Whoever is the governing body is utterly insensitive to the plight of these miserable souls. This is an abominable inscription and it should not be displayed. It's reminiscent of the inscription that Dante saw on the door of Hell."

A nurse was watching him from nearby. She pulled a cellular phone from her pocket and listened. Then, she closed it and approached Massimo. "Is there something bothering you?" She queried.

"No, not really, I was trying to understand the meaning," and he pointed at the sign. "I studied Latin a long time ago."

The nurse tried to downplay the significance of the sign. She smiled and said, "That's a warning for me, so that I may live a better life." Before he could even respond, she made a gesture that meant "follow me." She led him to a dark corridor, where she said, "I have instructions to show the premises to neophytes and to instruct them on the more stringent responsibilities. You may interrupt me at any time if you have questions."

They passed through units A and B, where he overheard various patients complaining. As they passed through Unit B, the nurse asked "Do you have any questions?"

"Not at this point. Maybe later."

"Don't hesitate to ask anything you wish."

"If that's the case, may I ask you if you are single?"

"I think it's time to move on.

They walked to Unit D, where cries and screams filled the air to the point that he couldn't hold back some tears, just like his first visit to the other wards in San

Lazarus. The nurse smiled again and handed him her handkerchief. He pulled his own from his pocket and wiped his cheeks. "I have it. Thank you."

"Apparently, you are very sensitive to other people."

The nurse sat on a wheelchair and ordered him to take her for a ride. When it was over, the nurse gave him a few suggestions and led him to the volunteers' office. In handing him the red jacket of Elixir, she said, "You are being assigned to the transportation department. "Honor this coat and be proud of it. Not many people have this glorious opportunity. You must sign the sheet and write the time of entrance and exit."

Massimo remained with the jacket in his hands while the nurse closed the door behind her.

The first working day wasn't that thrilling, but it offered a glimpse of curiosity and suspense. Five residents defied the restrictions imposed on them and protested within view of Venus's office. In the cafeteria, they carried signs printed with slogans like "Cat food;" "We are tired of being treated like beasts;" and "If you don't change the food, change the leaders."

The place became crowded in a matter of minutes. The nurses surrounded the protesters while management rushed over to cool the malcontent. Venus arrived at the scene a little later, short of breath. She'd been attending a meeting when the incident occurred. She invited the protesters to her office for an exchange of ideas. At the end of the meeting, she accepted their grievances and vowed from that day on they would receive meals with special nutritional values. To corroborate her promise that evening, she supervised the meals that were being served to the group. The fresh and high quality food restored confidence in the building. To demonstrate her good will, Venus added Italian pastries to the menu and the reactions were extraordinarily enthusiastic.

Three days passed by and, within the rebellious group, there emerged signs of abdominal spasms, followed by vomiting and diarrhea. Massimo remained speechless before that inexplicable event. He was waiting for the doctor to show up. No one came. The attending nurse invited everyone to be calm; however that seemed unattainable because of the fear that the condition was contagious. For precautionary reasons, the area was quarantined.

Massimo and other volunteers were forbidden access to the compound and were temporarily asked to operate in another unit. During one of his routine jobs pushing a resident to the therapy room, someone caught his attention. He stopped and stared at the patient, who was entering and leaving some rooms. From the last room, he heard Latin, but understood only "*Requiescat in pace.*" This gave rise to a deep suspicion in Massimo's mind. When the two finally crossed paths, Massimo stared him, but the other appeared to be in a hurry and kept on going. Being inquisitive by nature, Massimo paused at the door of each room. He glanced inside and saw that a nurse was standing beside an immobile body. Before such a macabre scene, Massimo was petrified. He tried to push the wheelchair, but it was unusually difficult. He almost panicked. He wanted to shout for help, to cry out, when he saw two nurses and some men with a stretcher approaching from the opposite side. The main doors in the middle of the halls were closed. Two of them grabbed Massimo by the arm and pushed him out of the big door ordering him not to come back until further notice. He ran to the bathroom and puked. The presence of dead people made him sick. He had only the strength to pick up a mop and clean the floor. No one saw him.

The few residents who lived nearby were the only ones who were able to take a peek at their unfortunate friends. As soon as the guards arrived, they pushed them back in their rooms. The following day, during their morning talk, they claimed that their departed neighbors were natural and beautiful.

Venus arrived late. She looked serene ands among a dozen nurses. At first, she ordered the guards to leave the rooms and, then, she secured a carton of milk from a dresser and placed it in a large plastic bag. Outside, she handed it over to one of the guards for quick disposal. Massimo secured the box from the dumpster and took it to an outside analyst who ascertained that in the milk there were traces of isopropilthioxanthone or Itx, which is a compound used for the process of labels. The local health institution wasn't informed and the medical examiner's report determined the deaths to be from natural causes.

# ROOM TWELVE

The man in Room 12, Mr. Iceland, was in his seventies, bald and handsome, with blue eyes and a tiny nose. He made sure to remind his visitors that his vision had been greatly impaired by his condition. His torso was reminiscent of a stout physique long gone. He had one leg, which was unusually skinny and darkened. The other had been amputated. He worked as an engineer for 28 years in Spy Mission, and had to take an early retirement due to a severe case of diabetes. It was then that his downfall began. His wife passed way five years before he entered San Lazarus. Painting was his main hobby and the walls of his room had the aspect of a museum. His preferred themes were nature and historical bridges, like those of Venice. Soon, he became a respectable painter and exhibited his art in the hall twice a year. Art lovers were willing to pay good prices for his work, but he didn't succumb to the temptation. He hung a sign on the door which said, "Painting is a source of my life satisfaction. My work is priceless." He wrote in his testament that at his death the family could do as it pleased.

Mr. Iceland had four sons and one daughter. His sons seldom visited. He said that one of them lived in another state and the others had their families to take care of. His daughter made up for her brothers' absence. She visited him almost daily and during rare moments of family memories, he showed no emotions. I never heard him complain, except for food. He was a realist and, perhaps that accounted for his detached attitude about life in general. He moved around the building in a self-powered wheelchair, but preferred to go out in the open air to smoke his favorite cigar.

During one of his frequent visits, Massimo asked him about his condition and he said, "Sugar did the job on me. It caused what they call a "purple toe syndrome."" He paused for a moment to remember the facts and shook his head. "The doctor couldn't believe it when he first checked me. Two weeks later I was diagnosed with gangrene." Massimo opened his eyes wide in disbelief and asked him about the symptoms of that disease. He said "The skin peels deep enough to make a half-inch hole. The biggest problem is that gangrene moved from one foot to another, so doctors amputated my left leg and now my right leg is so skinny and black that I'm going to lose it, too." Massimo exercised extreme caution in getting too close to him. His concern increased when the nurse came in to change the bandages. She put on plastic gloves and wore a mask. After the nurse left, Massimo asked him why he didn't use a protasys. He explained that he lacked the necessary strength of the upper body to sustain him.

Massimo wasn't allowed to stay in any room for very long. From the main office, they kept an eye on his movements. At times, he saw Venus watch him from behind the curtains of the upper glassy door. When their eyes met, she immediately withdrew. She realized that Massimo was aware of her spying activities and she pretended to ignore him for a while, which provided him an opportunity to stop and talk with some residents.

The following afternoon was sultry. The air conditioner was doing extra work to keep up with the unbearable heat. Massimo knocked at the door to Room 12. As soon as the old man recognized his voice, he begged Massimo to sit down, which he did. Mr. Iceland then pointed to his left leg and said, "The stroke causes the skin to fall." Massimo made a gesture of repulision and fell backward. His discomfort didn't go unnoticed. Mr. Iceland assured him it wasn't contagious and, then, he went on, "The blood coagulates in the brain. From that time on, you have two hours to unplug the veins."

"What did you eat to cause these problems?"

"All sorts of fat food …"

"You are not obese."

"Oh, yes, I am. I weighed 250 pounds when I came here."

"Obesity is a national problem and no one takes the initiative to change."

"You know why? You like what you eat. Take potato chips. They are tasty, but full of sodium. Mothers are the real culprit. Either they are not acquainted with nutrition facts or are fat themselves and are unwilling to bring about necessary changes. Children should have the right to sue them!"

"Well, let's not go that far."

"But it's true!"

"We would be more politically correct if we placed more blame on the government. They don't do anything in Ottawa to stop this problem. They let the food companies get away with murder. Do you know that they put in canned food, to give you an example, additives that drug you up, in the sense that you feel the urge to go back and buy the same product?"

"It sounds like we should take business people and politicians to court."

"You left out the mothers."

"Oh, yes, I did."

Massimo didn't wish to dwell on the same subject anymore. Instead, he asked Mr. Iceland if he missed his house. He replied, "I loved it. I spent $30,000 just to install an elevator to facilitate my movement in and out of the house." Massimo noticed a box of Cuban cigars on the nightstand and inquired about his smoking habit to find out if there was any direct correlation with the stroke. To his surprise, Mr. Iceland didn't show any sign of uneasiness. Indeed, he was very candid in admitting the danger that smoke represented to the lungs. "I used to smoke in bed. Just last week, I made a hole through the mattress. My daughter got upset. Now, I go to smoke in the backyard or outside." I asked him if he knew the Medicare rules. He went into a tedious listing of acknowledgements that any candidate must report before even being considered as a resident of San Lazarus. "You must surrender all your personal records. Then, you need a good lawyer.'

"Whom did you hire"?

"A bozo! I lost $30,000. Then, I learned my lesson and called Anna Lisa Casale, a brilliant lawyer from Italy, who had opened an office in Montreal. She saved my house because she suggested that I put it in trust of my children. Despite that, I couldn't live in it. I needed three nurses to work every 24-hour period. I couldn't keep up with their pay and the house maintenance. I also understood that if you have life use of the house and the children sell it, fifty-three per cent goes to the patient, who in turn, has to give it up to Medicare and forty-seven per cent to the children. I asked the attorney what to do. She replied, "Omit 'life use.' Don't write it in the will."

"Did your new attorney understand English?"

"Sure she did! She even speaks French."

"So what happened with the savings?"

"In Canada, there is a social system, but for the Americans, Medicare will pay. Now, they are saying they are running out of money. The result is simple. You go to the bank and drain your piggy bank. Currently, I draw $3,000 a month between Social Security and the company's pension. I don't even see a penny. San Lazarus grabs it all."

"There's no way out?"

"No, each time you draw $8,000 to make San Lazarus's monthly payment, you can give $6,000 to a family member. The main thing, however, is to get rid of your possessions five years prior to the recovery. If you are still single and young, you don't have to be concerned about it."

Suddenly, he felt a sharp pain in his left leg.. He looked at it and added, "When I visited my mother-in-law in the hospital, I walked from the parking lot to her room, but I got out of breath. The doctors prescribed me medicine that, in high dosage, they use to kill rats."

Mr. Iceland had gone through two leg operations and, unfortunately, the upper parts became too weak to sustain his body weight. As a result of his inability to move, they'd accorded him a battery-operated wheelchair. However, his painful story doesn't end here. In addition to the gangrene and stroke, he suffered from glaucoma and a heart condition. In a six-hour operation, the surgeons changed a valve and three veins. Some patients die during this procedure, but he survived.

Massimo was curious to know Mr. Iceland's reaction to his past and present conditions. He tried to smile and said, "In life, one should be realistic. I had a wonderful profession and a lot of money. I loved my house and garden." He paused for a moment without showing any emotion and continued, "Now, I'm what I am. I can't change the wheels of fortune. The doctors did a job on me and here I am paying the consequences." Each time he stopped talking, Massimo would inevitably look at his leg and feel a mixture of fright and compassion, not so much about the man, but about human destiny. The last time the nurse changed Mr. Iceland's bandages, Massimo witnessed something repulsive. As she touched the area above the ankle, her index finger went right through the flesh. She withdrew it immediately and a mixture of pus and blood surfaced. Massimo ran out in search of a bathroom. Once he got there, he locked the door behind him and began to vomit. That day, he went home sick and didn't touch any food or liquid.

# Room Seven, the Kind Man

Earlier in his life, Massimo ran a radio program. He interviewed people from every walk of life, and taped the programs in the diocese's studio. The director was a pleasant young man by the name of Timmy. He divided his time between the radio station and St. Ignatius College, where he thought sociology. Timmy looked good and moved swiftly. He had a split lip, but it was natural. With passing years, when he reached his thirties, Timmy began to experience something strange with his hands. His fingers started to curve inward. It was hard for him to stretch them all the way even if he wanted to. Slowly, his legs began to give in. He came to a point when he had to quit both jobs. He lived alone in his own house. He was single and had no relatives around him.

After a year, Massimo met the man in Room Seven at San Lazarus, in the Elixir building, first floor. He was stunned to see it was Timmy, and inquired about the reason for his being there. He didn't say much. He assured him that his stay was only temporary and soon he would be returning to teach at the college and regain his job as a T.V. director. Massimo didn't respond, but in his heart, he felt his vision was simply utopian.

A couple months later, Massimo ran into Timmy again. He had moved from the first floor to the second, Room 99. Timmy invited him in and started to tell him his story. Unfortunately, Massimo had lost his notebook and decided to postpone the interview.

During the summer, it's breezy at San Lazarus. The residents prefer to stay outside until dusk. One evening, Massimo put some blank papers in his back pocket and went to Timmy's room with the precise objective of obtaining some information from him. He didn't find him. He went out and met Timmy next to a bench doing hand exercises, pulling light weights up and down by their attached strings. To Massimo, it seemed strange to engage in exercises on a warm evening, even though it was breezy. Usually, residents are requested to go to the gym. In that location, there was no one. So, Massimo pulled the papers and the pen from his pockets and said, "Now, it's the perfect time to tell me your story." Timmy was surprised to hear that. He stopped doing his exercises, wiped his forehead and took a long breath. "Where were we?" he said smiling. After he collected his thoughts, he became loquacious, probably thinking that he was going to be in a newspaper article. "I tell you, Massimo, I'm plagued with debts and if I don't pay them, I'll lose my house."

"Doesn't the church help you?"

He lowered his head at the word "church" and said, "Nobody knows anything, but it did assist me immensely with insurance and with a lawyer."

"I suppose that isn't enough, because you want to pursue your dream."

"Exactly! I plan to live in my house as soon as I get better. Despite the fact I live alone, I can take care of myself."

Massimo shook his head, but Timmy insisted that he could. Massimo shook his head a second time, but Timmy was quick to reiterate his conviction that everything was going to be fine.

The following week, the scene was the same. Timmy disclosed what Massimo had feared. He had to sell the house to pay all of his debts. He was practically a pauper. He looked at his friend and said, "I had no other solution. If I didn't pay, they would have taken over my house. So, no matter what you do, you can't fight City Hall."

"I'm terribly sorry about it."

"Well, let us put it this way. If I didn't have MS I would not have lost the house."

"Is there any chance for you to get out of it?"

"How? MS stands for multiple sclerosis. It's a disease." I got alarmed and asked him if it were contagious. He responded, "No it's not. It's a strange disease."

"How so?"

"It strikes at any time, mainly in adulthood after the late teens. Most people get it in their late twenties, and it's common in European countries, such as Scotland and Ireland, but there are also black people who get it. Yet, people near the Equator tend not to get it."

"That's strange."

"It is. There is no known cause and no cure, only treatment. It's not genetically inherited either."

"It gives me the image of a bee that moves in all directions. You can't pin it down."

"Exactly! You mentioned the bee and you know what? There are people who claim that they have benefited from the sting of a bee. I got stung, but I didn't get any benefit."

"What are the symptoms?"

"Every individual is affected differently. MS attacks the coating around the nerves in the brain and this causes a miscommunication or lack of coordination between the central 'bank' and its 'clients.' The brain nerves don't 'talk' anymore with the nerves of the other organs of the body. This isn't to say that there is no feeling in the various parts of the body, although it's uncommon. The neurologist was surprised to find that my leg responded when he hit it with a small hammer."

"What organs does it affect in your case?"

"My fingers and toes mainly and the loss of coordination. It's like a line interruption while you are talking with someone on the phone."

"What about your ability to think logically?"

"Fine! MS rarely affects memory. I can't stretch my feet or hands."

"Can you walk?"

"No!"

"Have you tried to use braces?"

"You don't seem to understand. My feet refuse to coordinate with the rest of my legs; otherwise, I would be able to walk. The therapists can't figure out how to use the braces because the strength in my back is practically nonexistent. To complete the description, I must add that there are people without any symptoms at all. It's a very strange disease." He looked at me with powerless eyes and leaned forward.

"Is there anything you can't tolerate?"

"The heat! The air conditioner is indispensable in summer."

"It seems that we are paranoid with the hot weather in this country. How do they survive in Africa?"

He laughed as if I made a ludicrous remark. He straightened his back and said, "They suffer a lot. In my room, during summer, if the air conditioner isn't on, I open all the windows. I tell you ... I need air, cool air."

Massimo smiled faintly. His adversity to air conditioners was proverbial. Whenever he entered an office, he put on a jacket and a hat. People thought he was an alien, but he didn't pay attention to them. He turned to Timmy and said, "What kind of medicine do you take?"

"I take Bacolafem, twenty-five milligrams, six times a day. Some patients take it with interferon, which is used for muscles and cancer treatment."

"What does it do to the muscles?"

"The legs get stiff, but the blood circulation remains unaffected. The nerves are shot. There is no sensitivity. The medicine relaxes the muscles, but it doesn't go to the root of the problem."

Massimo stayed seated, motionless for a minute or so. He was dumbfounded. Two minutes passed by, then he muttered, "I have no explanation for human suffering, except within the faith context. We are made of flesh and bones and subject to all sorts of diseases. This is what it is to be human!"

Three weeks passed by. Massimo didn't return to Timmy's room. When he did, his friend had already packed up some cases. "Timmy, what are you up to now?"

"I told you I was going to leave."

"When?"

"I have to be out of here by the 31st of the month."

"Where are you going?"

"Downtown." He was determined and happy.

Massimo scratched his head. Timmy watched him with a bit of apprehension, not knowing what he was going to say. "Why in the world would you want to abandon this comfortable room, all for yourself, and venture into Nowhere Land?"

Timmy made a gesture of reassurance and said, "It will be a different ball game. I must go! I can't stay here any longer. I need to go on with my life."

"All alone? Without assistance? In your predicament?"

"Well, as I told you before, I'm going to work."

"Where? How?"

"With the computer. After all, I can move around without difficulties. A nurse will be with me a couple of hours a day."

"Well, good luck!"

"Wait a minute! I need something."

"What?"

"A couch with sheets."

"A couch, I can. The sheets … I'll see what I can do."

The nights were getting longer. Massimo returned in the evening to inform Timmy that the sheets and the couch were available. He thanked him and told him that a friend would shortly stop at his house to pick them up.

One morning a young man of about twenty-five and a short, fat lady stopped in Massimo's driveway. They had come to pick up Timmy's couch. Massimo looked at the woman and twisted his nose. "Is there something wrong?" the man asked. Massimo invited them in the cellar and showed them the couch. The two tried to raise it, but dropped their arms. "This is too heavy. How can we carry it?" said the man.

"I must confess that when I saw your wife, I didn't think you would make it. No offense to anyone."

"We didn't know it was this big. It's made of iron. You need a crane to pull it outside." His wife confirmed her husband's comment with a nod of her head.

"We have to call more friends," the woman finally said, "otherwise, this monster ain't goin' to move." Her husband assented and they went back to their car.

It was very humid when at noon of the following day a wagon stopped in front of Massimo's house. Four stout men looked outside first to make sure they were in the right place. The doors squeaked as they opened. The men talked a while among themselves before picking up the couch and then, with their big arms, surrounded the piece of furniture and dragged it out. One of them looked at his friends and said, "Who is going to pay us? It should be double time with this weather."

The tallest of the crew replied, "This Timmy pay to no one. He no have money."

Massimo went to visit Timmy for the last time at San Lazarus, but the room was empty. Everyone he spoke to predicted that Timmy would be back shortly. To this date, he is still out.

# THE CANADIAN COUPLE

Massimo had a hard time reconciling his profession with the volunteer work. Each time he thought he had gained a full understanding of the complexity of the hospice, another event occurred that made him change his mind. In the morning, he used to cater to residents who went for coffee and cookies in a special small cafeteria. There, he met a couple from Ottawa, both in their nineties, short and cute. They were the types that didn't bother anyone. Both spoke French. She displayed an elegant demeanor, while her husband had more rustic manners. He hardly spoke and communicated mostly with his head or hand gestures. He couldn't hear too well and she had to repeat questions twice. He looked at her lips and was able to decipher what was being said. They formed a lovely couple living in the same room. Actually, there were rumors that she had been a nun, who renounced her vows after she met him in the garden.

Both came from a middle class family. Their infirmities had dissipated all their savings. Like the other residents, they paid the Joy of Living Company in advance for the expenses of the casket and funeral, thus avoiding any future price increases. The cost of living, however, rose dramatically in Canada in the first decade of their residency at San Lazarus. In fact, it almost doubled. The couple didn't have any children, and the relatives were not willing to bear the financial burden. It happened that the husband fell seriously ill and died. For two days, his wife was unaware of her husband's loss and told the nurse that he didn't want to eat. The nurse, seeing him in bed in a sleeping position, didn't bother to wake him up. The residents became uneasy when a foul smell started coming from their room. They suspected that some spoiled food was underneath a bed and urged the janitor to check the room. What she found alarmed her and she alerted the office. Whether the old woman was motivated by insanity or by fear of solitude, we don't know. The fact is that she put a mannequin in her husband's bed and his body in a wheeled suitcase. Then, she proceeded to the gate and passed through the checking point. How she was able to do that is still a matter of heated discussion. According to a person who spoke under an assumed name for fear of being fired, the area was deserted at that moment. A couple of police near the traffic light, alerted by Venus, hurried to stop the lady. The unspeakable stench almost drew them back. When they asked her where she was headed, she replied, "To the post office. I have to mail this package." The officers got suspicious and opened the suitcase. The macabre scene was reminiscent of a Hitchcock movie. The traffic jammed and reporters arrived. They sensationalized the event by associating it to an analogous episode that occurred in Kingston a week earlier. A drug addict, searching for food in a rubbish can, noticed the arm and leg of a deceased person. The lady was in a state of confusion and couldn't provide clear information.

The episode at San Lazarus took place in a public street. The city police launched an investigation. The results were never publicized.

Venus and the Joy of Living staff were furious. They harshly reprimanded the guards and suspended them for a month without pay. The lady was taken into custody by San Lazarus and transferred to the third floor in a room with a balcony. The residents soon forgot about the dead man in a suitcase until another deadly incident occurred. The body of a lady lay immobile on the garden floor with her arms widespread and a fractured cranium. Fear overtook the whole unit and the doors were locked. Venus arrived on the scene with ample delay in company of a doctor. She looked calm, passive, indifferent. The doctor placed the stethoscope on the woman's heart and pronounced her dead. She had joined her husband.

# ROOM FOUR

The latest events had noticeably shaken Massimo, but he was determined to finish the chapter. One evening, on the ground floor, he saw the door open in room 23. He stopped in the hall and saw a tall blonde woman in her fifties, dressed in an elegant silky nightgown. He greeted her and she invited him in, introducing herself as Madame Jolie. After the ritual preliminaries with questions and answers on both sides, she looked at her leg and said, "Look at it! I'm disgusted."

"How long ago did you have the surgery?" inquired Massimo.

"Three weeks ago. I was in the hospital three days and then they transferred me here for therapy."

"Well, that's the normal course of the healing process."

"I hope so. My roommate went home after two weeks. I'm still here."

"Convalescence depends on many factors, chief among them the nature of the knee condition. It's different for each patient."

"The nurse told me it takes a bit longer for me because I'm heavy."

"I don't think so."

"I'm so glad that you disagree with her."

"No, anyone can see that you are in the normal weight range."

"She was trying to find an alibi for my long treatment process. Maybe my case is more severe than others...." She uncovered her leg and showed him the stitches. He tightened his teeth, but made no comment. He helped her move from the bed to sit on a wheelchair. He emphasized the need for rest and left. She offered an apology, but begged him to come back the following day.

Massimo returned to inquire about the healing process and she was happy to see him. She had sprinkled violet perfume on her hair and was resting on the bed. Madame Jolie told him that she was a widow and, as soon as she could walk fairly well, she had planned to go to Toronto for business. She raised her head and looked him straight in his eyes, "Would you like to be my chauffeur?"

"Unfortunately, I have a commitment with my volunteer work."

There was no quick reply. Madame Jolie was thinking. She made a proposal that startled him, "Voulez-vous coucher avec moi?"

"Mais, oui madame. C'est mon plaisir."

"Tomorrow, at seven." Massimo stood there speechless. No woman had so blatantly invited him for a "joy ride." He couldn't believe what had just happened. He turned around and threw a kiss. She did likewise.

In the corridor, Massimo felt dazed. He was living between two states of mind. In one, he felt elated; in the other, guilty. He was walking sluggishly. He didn't realize the direction he was taking. Accidentally, he passed by Venus's office. Inadvertently, she had left the door slightly open and was playing the tape recorder. He recognized his own voice in the conversation he just had with Madame Quatre. A cloud obscured his memory. He hurried to a meeting room and sat. He placed his head in between both hands and began to breathe heavily . If Venus sent that tape to a newspaper or to a police station, his reputation would have been damaged for the rest of his life. No one could have saved him from the charge of sexual misconduct with a patient. Nobody was in a position to protect him from a long jail term. Massimo started to sweat profusely. He ran to the bathroom. It was empty. He looked in the mirror and felt ashamed of himself. He threw a punch at himself in the mirror and broke it. The blood was gushing out of his knuckles. He rinsed his hand and rapped it with a bandage he had in his red coat. He stood against the wall with his arms wide open gasping for breath. He opened the window and felt a breeze rushing on his face. He sat on the toilet seat and locked the door. He panicked and banged his head in all four directions. He heard voices outside and stopped. He cleaned the broken pieces of mirror from the floor and placed them in a garbage bag, along with the frame. When the voices subsided, he opened the door. The hall was clear. He hurried in the courtyard and threw the bag in the dumpster. On the way back, he signed out and ran home.

All alone, in his room, Massimo couldn't believe that the whole place was being wiretapped. He remembered Arian, her warning and her opposition to transferring him to Elixir, but his professional duty prevailed over her opinion. He started to cry, but quickly wiped his face for fear of exposing his emotional fragility to himself. He was restless, and decided to find out if the wiretapping had its source in the National Security Agency, which was engaged in fighting terrorism, or if it were a practice typical of San Lazarus. The word "terrorism" was unheard, but the Interior Ministry was on the alert.

He turned on the American channel and got even more nervous when he heard that in the U.S. there was an analogous system in operation. Through the satellite and the telephone companies' cooperation, the government intercepted and screened all the conversations dealing with national security. The Pentagon had no recriminations when it came to monitor Islamic activities in major times of tension. Initially, the government began to control the international communication. Later, it extended its activity to the interior of the country with the code name "Daytona," which was already operating to control corporate frauds.

Waves of protests have clouded the latest political events in the U.S. The citizens feel cheated, defrauded by the federal authorities. What seems to catch most attention is the posture of prominent national lawyers, who are defending terrorists at Guantanamo with the accusation of denying the right to privacy to the detainees. They also challenge the legality of wiretapping on the ground that the information gained could be used against the terrorists in court. At the present time, no one is sure whether or not wiretapping has been influential in criminal cases at all or to what extent. Some legal experts claim that the Bush administration didn't have the legal power to order the eavesdropping. The government claims that the President is warranted by the Constitution to promote wiretapping for national security. This has split the population into two segments: one prefers security to freedom, while the other claims that no one has the right to listen to private conversations, especially if they relate to business, domestic affairs or love. The growing controversy may jeopardize faith in the surveillance system, no matter who emerges as the victor. Only the future will be the judge of this political battle.

Massimo looked outside of the window and said, "From now on, everyone should be careful what they say on the telephone or what they do in any place, at any time. There is no question in my mind that the Big Ear is listening."

He returned to the couch and sank into it. His cellular rang. He hesitated in picking it up. Finally, he did. "Massimo, it's me, your buddy. I called you to inform you that a Canadian was caught in Siberia trying to snap pictures of military installations."

"Spying activities take place globally and the clamor is proportionate to the extent democracy is exercised."

"But Canada has always been clean."

"Don't kid yourself. Nobody is clean. We are all dirty." His friend looked at his cellular and hung up.

Massimo wasn't interested in his friend's call and was glad he had hung up. He had his hands full and couldn't find a remedy. He pronounced a name, "Arian" and remembered when she warned him to "keep his nose clean." He didn't pay heed and, now, he was in deep water. He didn't know what to do. The events were running out of his control and he was worried about the grave repercussions. He drank a big cup of chamomile tea, but still was unable to sleep the whole night.

Dawn came to his rescue and he got up in a hurry. He went to Olimpia to look for Arian. He spotted her while she was heading for her office. She was surprised to see him at that hour. He told her that he needed to speak to her urgently. She wasn't one who would give in to the first request, but he troubled her to no end and she, for once, was willing to accede promptly to his request, despite the anomalous time and place. She invited him into her office and pulled a couple of plugs from the outlet. The monitor fell immediately dead. He followed the action with his eyes, but said nothing. Venus asked him, "What can I do for you, sir?"

"The main reason for being here is …"

Arian followed him with her eyes and waited until he added, "I have bad news to report. I have failed you in many ways."

"Could you be more explicit?"

"Yesterday, I was talking to Madame Jolie and she invited me …"

"I surmise that you acceded to her request."

"Only verbally …"

"What do you mean by that?" She replied in an irritated tone.

"You have every right to be upset at me. You warned me to be careful, but to the extent that my conversation was being wiretapped, no."

"How could you be so naïve? You put yourself in a big mess!"

"I know. This is the reason why I'm here. Maybe, you can help me for the last time."

"Do you realize that you are jeopardizing my job, my profession and my livelihood?"

"I do now and I'm deeply sorry. I'll make up for it. I promise. If I ever get out of it."

"I don't believe it! How am I going to help you if you endanger my position? Who is going to help me in case I need help?"

"I do. Don't worry about that."

"You do, eh"? And, gave him a questioning look.

Massimo placed his hand on her shoulder to reassure her. She looked at his hand and he withdrew it. "I have to do something. I feel Damocles' sword dangling on my neck. I never thought I could be so weak."

She looked at him and said, "What did you do with her?"

"Nothing, absolutely nothing. We have a date for this evening."

"You do, eh!"

"I'm not going. I promise you."

"I guided you like a child and you failed me."

"And I failed myself too."

"That goes without saying. Look at yourself! You are the opposite of what you were when you first came here."

"I didn't sleep the whole night."

She looked at him with compassion, then, she grabbed some biscuits and filled a cup with coffee. She placed them in front of him and said, "Take them. You need to perk yourself up. I bet you didn't eat anything."

He shook his head in a gesture of denial. "Here, take it." Her voice became sweet. He sipped the coffee and munched on a biscuit.

She waited until he finished and said, "How did you find out that you were being wiretapped?"

"I passed by her office. The door was a bit open. She was playing the tape and I recognized my voice."

"Just pray that she doesn't call the police. In that case, nobody will save you from a stiff jail sentence." She looked at his hand, "What's going on here?"

"That's another story …"

"What story?"

He recounted what he did in the aftermath of the tape. She opened the drawer and pulled out the gauze, alcohol and bandages. "Give me your hand, but don't get any ideas."

He smiled and placed his hand in hers. "I give you my hand and my …"

"This is no time for jokes."

"It wasn't. OK. Should I go back there?"

"Sure! Pretend that nothing happened. And don't be such an imbecile as to see Madame Jolie again." Massimo didn't reply. He got up and fixed his hair. She kept on staring at him. She wasn't absolutely sure of her thoughts. She got close to him and whispered, "Remember that the walls talk. Will you remember?"

He nodded. Before he closed the door, he questioned her, "What if she threatens me."

"Don't respond. Let the events run their course."

Massimo resumed his work the next day. He needed a good night's sleep. He was exhausted emotionally and physically. When he woke up, it was six o'clock. At seven o'clock sharp, he was heading to Madame Jolie's room. He planned to clarify his position in regard to the statement of the previous night. He wanted to explain to her that it was a joke. He knew that he was going to be taped. He planned to tell her that he was joking when he agreed to her request.

Madame Jolie was offended and irritated by Massimo's failure to show up at the date. She had prepared to meet him in an elegant black night gown. She sprinkled a couple of drops of Nina Ricci's perfume and rested on the bed. Massimo never arrived.

Massimo stopped a moment to help a resident whose wheelchair got stuck. Suddenly, he heard a scream, then he smelled smoke. He looked at the end of the hall and saw firemen dashing from every corner. Madame Jolie's room was on fire. In a matter of minutes, the flames devoured everything in the room. By the time the firemen extinguished the fire, there remained only her skeleton. Massimo ran to rescue her. It was too late. A game of love had turned into a tragedy. He felt deeply troubled.

Massimo went back to Arian to report the event. As soon as he entered the office, he fell on the chair. His face was dark, dark from the smoke. His left hand was slightly burned. He was a mask of sadness. Arian locked the door and closed the curtains. She got close to him and washed his face and hands. She took his hands into hers and leaned her head against his. No one talked. Ten minutes went by. She whispered to him to go home and rest. The death of Madam Jolie had robbed him of his peace.

The smoke rose very high in the sky and called the attention of the local police, who intervened immediately. Venus indicated that it was the work of arsonists and that her staff would collaborate with them to investigate the case and bring the culprits to justice. In Canada the control and the prevention of fire was and is under the care of the police and firemen. Mrs. Jolie died without any relatives. After four months of fruitless investigation, San Lazarus and the police agreed to close the case, dropping the charges against a couple of alleged arsonists, who were completely uninvolved with the tragic event. The final report stated that a cigarette butt from Madame Jolie's room had started the fire.

# Violette, the Nurse

Violette was a tall, blonde nurse. Many young men had been having her in their dreams. Maybe they perceived her plans of self-glorification. She wanted to become an actress and took every opportunity to show it. She had a sinuous shape and pronounced lips. Her smile was captivating and male residents often made no attempt to hide their desires. They ignored one of the nurses' main requirements, if not qualities: her smile. A smiling nurse and a few sweet words can raise patients' morale. Hospitals and health institutions share the same idea. Some men, however, consider that approach a passport to inappropriate language and rude gestures. Yes, even old and sick people do it! The eyes and the mind play dirty tricks, and the repercussions are always unpredictable.

A man in the thirties came to visit a friend in room 34 on the second floor. He wore tennis sneakers with his pants folded upward. His shirt covered his pants about five inches below the waist. His black bangs fell on dark sunglasses, which made the color of his eyes indistinguishable. On his fingers, he had rings of all shapes and sizes and from his ears two long gold earrings dangled like a pendulum. A pack of cigarettes stuck out of his shirt pocket, along with the top of a blue pen.

He entered the room and, instead of finding his friend, saw Violette sitting on the bed with her legs crossed. The nurse remained unperturbed by the sudden appearance of a young man. Instead of repositioning her legs, she started to clean her nails. The visitor was puzzled. He didn't know how to initiate a conversation. The nurse perceived his moment of hesitation and decided to remind him that, according to the hospice rules, a visitor is to knock before entering a room. He didn't reply, but stepped back a few feet and knocked on the door, then closed and locked it. Violette realized that she was in dangerous predicament. She tried to push the alarm button, but it was too late. The young pulled from his back pocket a knife and warned her that any wrong move could be fatal. He motioned for her to take off her clothes. His eyes were constantly on her. He took off his shirt and t-shirt. She unbuttoned her uniform and began to take off her stockings. He took off his sneakers and socks. She got up and started to unhook her bra. With one hand she loosened her bra; with the other she pressed the alarm button, unbeknownst to the young man. His face was a furnace of fire as he loosened his belt and watched her at the same time. She touched her panties and started to pull them down. At that moment, the door broke open. Two large guards jumped in and with a karate chop threw the intruder on the floor. Before they laid their hands on him, he managed to pull his knife from his pocket and brandished it at them them. One of the guards kicked him on the ankle and the man screamed in pain. The knife fell on the rug. The other guard stepped on his throat and arms; kicked him on all sides; grabbed one of his arms and pulled him up and, with a lightening jerk, hurled him out of the window.

Violette was shaking. The two bodyguards left and she was able to dress in a state of agitation.

Five minutes later, Venus was waiting for her in the office for questioning. By the time the police came, she was ready to give a report. She filed a lawsuit against the assailant charging him with sexual molestation. When the sergeant asked her how he ended up outside, she explained that as a result of her screaming, the man jumped out of the window, probably thinking to fall on a soft spot of the lawn. The police looked at her intensely, as if to read her mind and said, "Mademoiselle, there is no need to file any charge."

"Why can't I?" she replied with indignation.

"I repeat: there is no need. The man is dead."

"Oh, I wasn't aware of that," she said with indifference.

Massimo was in the hall when the police passed by. One of them suggested that the other file an accident report. His colleague frowned, but made a gesture of deference at Venus, who was talking with her aids.

# THE DEADLY SALAD

One week passed and another grave incident occurred. A lot has been said about nurses and much more will be added in the future. Some people argue that nurses are provocative, and patients, regardless of their ages, succumb to temptation resorting to all sorts of subterfuges. Many male residents wrongly believe that one of nurses' tasks is to provide sexual stimuli. Massimo himself tried to express that thought in one instance and the nurse rewarded him with a big smack on his face. He was lucky that she didn't report it to Venus.

Sexual harassment is often in newspaper headlines. Violette's incident didn't serve any purpose because the news died inside the supervisor's office. Venus was a very sly manager. She had lights installed in every corner of all corridors and TV cameras wherever she deemed it necessary. However, the problem of inappropriate behavior continued, at least for a while. Younger patients attempted to entice charming nurses to indulge in intimate behavior either when they were being assisted in bed or in the bathroom, when they were semi-nude. Several nurses complained that men patted them on the buttocks or touched their breasts. On the other hand, there were a few nurses who considered those behaviors innocuous. Hustling with many job demands, they got used to it. Venus, instead, made it clear that she would not tolerate such actions. With the passage of an anti-discriminatory law, sexual harassment subsided in health care centers and hospitals in Canada, but it didn't extinguish itself completely.

The day passed by very quickly at San Lazarus. The daily activities were written on calendars posted everywhere. By evening, everyone was tired. On the second shift for supper, Massimo was serving food to about ten residents in a moderately large room used as a dining room and relaxation area. While they were eating, he went downstairs for a brief volunteer meeting. Juliette, a charming brunette nurse, was the only one on duty to assist them. She made sure that everything was under control by checking all the tables one by one. As she arrived at the end, a man touched her fanny, while another made sexual advances. The sexual rejection caused laughter in most of them. As she moved around them, someone pinched her, touched her legs and made other attempts to reach private areas. Young people, who were visiting their relatives, were having their feast day. The nurse became red as a beet and told them that their behavior had gone too far. They threatened her with retaliation if she divulged the news.

Juliette smiled faintly and promised to come back shortly with a salad that would excite their senses. They approved and waited excitedly. But, first, she took the ladies to their rooms.

Ten minutes later, Juliette returned with two trays holding many plastic dishes. She told them that it was typical salad with radicchio, romaine lettuce, carrots, spinaches and sunflower seeds that would spur their imagination to the limits of the universe. The young visitors shouted for joy and one locked the door and stood on guard in front of it. The nurse passed the salad around that the residents and their relatives devoured. The female patients were spared the pleasure. Five minutes later, all sorts of sounds filled the air. They complained and groaned. Juliette assured them that the type of radicchio she used in the salad would give out its benefic effect at any moment. She tried to calm them down by explaining to them that that unique radicchio is wild and grows above 1,500 m. of altitude on days following the spring thaw. However, the pain increased and then, suddenly subsided, until everybody fell asleep. The adulterated oil present in the salad intoxicated them all.

Juliette walked out on her tiptoes, gained the hall and reached Venus's office. When Massimo returned to ascertain that everything was in order, he found everybody dead.

# Room Number Eight

There was a thirty-five year old brunette patient with dimples in her cheeks and a captivating smile that could launch a thousand ships. Even Massimo was tempted to glance at her more than once. She noticed him and blushed. She had a hip replacement and was undergoing therapy. On a Saturday afternoon, around four o' clock, Massimo intended to stop and talk to her. An old man was struggling with his wheelchair and asked him for a push. Massimo agreed. At his destination, the two continued their conversation that lasted for about half an hour.

A health care provider came twice a week to give her treatment sessions. During the last meeting, the worker got too affectionate with her and she accused him of sexual molestation. Venus, Massimo and other volunteers from Elixir attended the court case. A grand jury indicted the health care worker on a felony count of a first degree sexual act attempt and a misdemeanor of a third degree based on sexual abuse. The charges were quite serious. He was released on his own cognizance and suspended with pay, pending the arraignment results.

At trial time, the defense attorney and the prosecutor did their interrogations of the witnesses. The judge dismissed the rape accusation and reduced the charges to abusive language and misconduct of a negligible degree. A commotion erupted among the spectators and the judge threatened to evict anyone who disrupted the case. The police restored order and the case continued.

Finally, the grand jury was called to proclaim their verdict. The pronounced a verdict of "not guilty" based on the consensual act. The victim was furious and shouted revenge.

Outside, before the press, the indicted man explained that there was nothing unusual in his behavior. It was a matter of interpretation.

The prosecutor had a completely different view. He challenged the verdict by stating that only a DNA test would do justice.

The molester rejected the proposal and called his work, "Medicine of the body." He said, "Women suffer from psychological syndromes, therefore, my therapy has a healing power on them and dispels all sorts of pressures from them."

Venus was enraged. She spoke of injustice and warned the man not to set foot again at San Lazarus.

Massimo remained perplexed by the verdict. For once, he sided with Venus, but made no public display of his feelings. He realized that at San Lazarus they dealt with all the cases within their jurisdiction, but this one fell outside of their jurisdiction because the molester wasn't employed by Venus. The verdict definitely convinced Venus that the time was ripe to tighten even more the control over anyone entering or leaving the compound.

Massimo, for his part, realized that the death frequency and other related incidents were on the rise. He decided to discuss the matter with Arian or Mitango, if he had the chance to meet him again.

# THE EMPTY CASKET

Unit R, at Elixir, was reserved for the wealthy. A guard screened anyone who entered that section of the building. Venus had jurisdiction over them, but consented to the creation of a self-governing body, as long as they didn't impinge on the constitution of the hospice. A high metallic fence surrounded the vast edifice. Armed guards protected it 24 hours a day and visitors and employees, without exception, had to pass through the main gate. It was rumored that in emergency cases, the fence was equipped with high voltage devices. At times, cats, woodchucks, raccoons, dogs and even deer were found lying dead on the ground, or clinging electrocuted to the fence.

They served food three times at day and the evening meal was the most luxurious. Massimo stopped there casually once and only briefly. He had to carry a personal message to a resident from a relative in Olympus. He noticed the tables in the cafeteria were covered with all sorts of fresh fruits and vegetables. The predominant ethnic group appeared to be Arab. The leaders had their heads covered with white turbans; the women dressed in silky clothes with their faces covered. The only strange thing that called Massimo's attention was the smell of tobacco, different from the regular cigarettes. He got particularly concerned when he began to feel inebriated. Before leaving the premises, he saw a nurse unpacking some small envelops containing white powder. He murmured without being heard by anyone, "How did they bring that in? That's cocaine. Where does it come from? India? Colombia? Afghanistan? They chastised Ching for unveiling the problem. They should have hailed him as a hero instead." He recognized an old man coming from the same unit where he worked and struck up a conversation with him. At first, the man was reluctant to talk. The red uniform and the charm of the young volunteer reassured him about exchanging a few words. "It must be nice to have friends around here," said Massimo.

"Absolutely! If you don't have them, you are bound to create friendship."

"Even if you don't like a person …"

"That's right. But, here, everybody needs each other. We are all in the same boat. You have two candies, you share them. You have a bottle of Coca—Cola, you offer a glass to the other person. We have a great sense of comradeship."

"I agree. By the way, why don't they allow patients to smoke marijuana. They should, at least for medical reasons."

"Of course! Take the leaves of Coca! The business people use them to make drinks, but the government penalizes us if we use it for pain."

"There is no question about it that those drugs are not the product of the culture of South America. If the Aymara, the Quechua or the Parani' produce it in great quantity it's because exterior factors have imposed it on them."

"Well, that isn't an accurate portrayal of the case. The Indian population cultivates it because for them it represents a means of survival."

"In Canada, we don't have a drug problem on a large scale. The U.S. is inundated with it. But that's not all. With the pretext of destroying the drug cartel, Washington dictates its policy on the Andine's region or tries to build military bases there. A few million dollars, and the deal is done."

"The people resent such interferences."

"No doubt …" At that point, the old man was showing signs of discomfort. Massimo placed his hand on the wheelchair and said, "There is no way the governments can stop the cultivation of those leaves and shrubs that produce drugs. They need a concerted effort."

"Why stop it? In the hospitals, it's a good thing to have it around. When medicine is unable to create a joyful feeling in the midst of so much depression and when it can't control effectively the horrible and unbearable pain of a disease or the aftermath of a surgery, why not use it?"

"Yeah, but how do you pass it through these gates?"

"Oh, you could never have it here. Drug dealers have tried in the past, but they were arrested at the entrance of the building and ended up in the cage."

"I didn't know that."

"This is a clean place, my dear young man."

"If you say it, it must be so. I'm new in this place."

"Take some advice from me, pal. Don't even discuss this topic again with any-one here. They can throw you and me out, right away, if they hear us talking about cocaine."

Massimo remained pensive and the old man sped away in his battery-powered wheelchair. A loud voice shook Massimo from his thoughts. Behind him, a bearded man was pushing a casket and was cautioning the residents to move aside. Massimo was surprised to see a casket inside Elixir. They always carried the deceased persons to the Joy of Living, where they would embalm and place them in the casket. Curiosity forced Massimo to say something to the man, "Excuse me, are you sure you are in the right place?"

"I have been doing this for a long time."

"Forgive my ignorance. Who is in this casket?"

"No one at the moment …"

"You mean somebody died? It's not possible. I have just come from there and I didn't see any dead person."

"You are right. Nobody died."

"Are you bringing back a dead person, then?"

"Why would I do that for? This isn't a cemetery!" To reassure Massimo, he opened the casket. It was empty. The man took the handkerchief out of his pocket to wipe the sweat from the brows. Some dollar bills fell on the floor. The back door to the garden suddenly opened, and the wind blew the money throughout the hall. The man ran after it. Massimo looked at the pillow. The fabric was of leopard skin. On the side, there was a small zipper. His temptation became irresistible. What he saw inside knocked him off his feet. He touched small bags and felt white powder in it. He hurried to close the zipper. The bearded man caught up with his money and was back. He closed the casket in a hurry and cursed. Massimo tried to hold him back, but the man dismissed him with his hand and proceeded toward the exclusive section of the building. Massimo remained semi-paralyzed. People passed by him and launched inquisi-tive glances. Others made sarcastic remarks. He couldn't see or hear. His mind was elsewhere. When his mind cleared, he looked at his fingers and went to a nearby fountain to rinse them off.

A week passed and the same bearded man came back, this time with a bag in his hand. Massimo recognized him and asked him if he had buried the man. "Mission completed," he replied.

"How many people die on a monthly basis?"

"I have no statistics at hand. I don't discuss this matter with anyone. It's not my concern."

"What is your concern?"

"To keep people happy …"

"Is that why you bring the caskets here?"

"That's normal routine. People in that unit like to see the casket before they depart."

"Only in that unit they like to see it?"

"Well, let's put it in this way. They are more sophisticated."

"You are absolutely right."

"Well, my friend, have a good day."

"Wait a minute! What are you up to now?"

"I have embalming fluid to show to some of my clients." The word "client" stimulated a new interest and suspicion in Massimo. The man was set to go, but Massimo leaned on him and asked him, "Why would people want to look at the fluid? Isn't that crude?"

"It's like oil. You like extra-virgin olive oil, another prefers pomace olive oil and others, corn or vegetable oil."

"With oil, one tastes the difference. With embalming fluid, the dead person can't taste or smell."

"People are funny, my friend. They live in fantasyland. They believe that the other world is a replica of this one. Woe, if you oppose their belief."

"You would be incinerated."

"Exactly! People are vain. What can you do? Well, my friend, don't think too hard. You may blast your brains. It's human nature to touch or smell before buying."

"Not always!"

"Take care of yourself!"

"Take good care of your oils. They cost a lot of money."

"Everything costs nowadays."

"It depends on the quality. There is the more expensive and less …"

"You are not far from the truth."

"Have a good one!"

The man smirked and disappeared at the end of the hall.

Massimo felt utterly confused. He wanted to know more about it. Arian was the only one who could provide him with verifiable information. "If I could see her even for a couple of minutes, it would be sufficient," he muttered. During lunch time, he paid a quick visit at Olympus with the uniform and gloves on. His old friends were happy to see him. After a few hugs and kisses, he headed toward Arian's office. She was on the threshold of the door ready to check on a patient.

He excused himself for the inopportune time and without warning, and asked to exchange a few words. She reacted with surprise, "What in the world are you doing here dropping by without making an appointment?" Her face changed color. She felt sorry for having made that comment and invited him in. She reached her chair and unplugged some wires. Massimo said, "You look splendid!" She thanked him and showed him his chair. Massimo didn't take his eyes away from her. She noticed it and asked, "What's on your mind?"

"Are you still mad at me?"

"The battle isn't over. There is a lot that I want to know from you, but not now."

"I hope you don't hold any grudge against me."

"What brought you here?"

"I would like to know something about the embalming fluid."

"Where did you get it?"

"I don't have it."

"Did you commission someone else to purchase it for you?" It took Massimo a good five minutes before she was assured that the question had no personal significance. It was only then that she explained, "Embalming fluid is being used for many purposes. It racks the brains. It drives the neurons on rampage."

"Why would someone in the right state of mind cause havoc to his brain until his behavior becomes uncontrollable? Do they apply the fluid on the head?"

She laughed, "You know, you are so naïve. A person dips his cigarette or marijuana into it."

"Is this phenomenon widespread?"

"No, it's uncommon. When you smoke it, it has a psychedelic effect. You feel euphoric or the opposite. The phencyclidine is similar to the embalming fluid. Sometimes, you may mix them. But, watch out!"

"I didn't know that."

"In the U.S., on November 2, the police department in a city was confronted with a case where a man on top of the roof was doing crazy things …"

"Don't divert my attention elsewhere."

"Aren't you interested in knowing additional information?"

"You said enough. I thank you immensely for your knowledge and kindness."

He got up and started to walk toward the door. She accompanied him. He turned off the light and kissed her on the cheek. She was stunned and touched her face with the palm of her hand. She turned the light on and looked for him. He had disappeared.

# THE FROZEN DEAD

Massimo was accumulating a considerable amount of knowledge, and getting increasingly uneasy about San Lazarus. Arian had warned him, but he scoffed at the idea of being in a risky place. Much time had elapsed since then, but now, he feared that one of these days he could end up in a casket himself. His blood pressure rose some days to 162/98 and his hands shook more than normal. He boiled ten clover of garlic and drank part of it every day for four days. He saw the pressure dropping down to normal and gained more self-assurance. His mother had taught him from an early age, "Drink garlic water whenever your blood pressure rises!"

Summer was hot, but at San Lazarus the temperature was cool. One morning, Massimo showed up half-drowsy. He hadn't slept well that night. He had wild dreams. Dragons were bullying him. One of them threw him in the air and, when he fell on the ground, he became a cat. He woke up and couldn't close his eyes for the rest of the night until, at dawn, he dreamed about Arian. The kiss had changed his attitude toward her. Yet, his project kept him away. He went to the bathroom and looked at himself in the mirror. He didn't like his face, his nose, his ears. He threw some cold water on his face and wiped it with a towel. In the halls, there was the usual movement of wheelchairs, nurses, volunteers and management.

At ten o' clock on the dot, Venus called all the volunteers to her office to lead them to a short visit to the mortuary of Joy of Living. The purpose was to explain the physical symptoms of a moribund ready for the transition to the world of eternity and how such passage could be temporarily averted by repeated head and chest massage techniques.

The group traveled in a minibus through a narrow subterranean passage for about two minutes. They got off and climbed a winding staircase. They entered a cold room at the right side of the platform and saw a 95-year-old man laying on the table. He had died the previous month and was kept in the freezer. The person in charge lined the visitors up around the casket. Tension rose. He took a club and hit the deceased on the hand and on the legs to show that he was, by all means, dead. To increase the belief in the man's absolute state of inertia, he placed a mirror on the mouth and nose to demonstrate the absence of breathing. To complete the list of steps that proved death without doubt, he listened to the heart and there was no beating; he touched the pulse points, one by one, and there was no pulsation. The man wasn't yet embalmed. His relatives from Portugal were en route to San Lazarus to take him back to his native country. As soon as they arrived, the medical examiner was at hand with the personnel to discuss the legal procedures for the transfer. The morticians picked up a plastic bottle and sprayed a lacquer on the dead body to prevent stench.

The volunteers didn't know what to make of it. They were absorbed in their thoughts and waited for the dismissal signal, when the unthinkable became reality. The dead man coughed, opened his eyes and tried to get up. The nurses and secretaries began to scream. The volunteers drew back in a corner. The lady sweeper shouted, "Miracle! Miracle! Lord, help us! The dead resuscitated!" The men in the managerial staff, were apprehensive, and searched for space. Some ran back to Elixir. Others frantically sought refuge in the labyrinth. The guards arrived with the rifles drawn. In the midst of the panic, they were disoriented and didn't know what to do. Massimo was skeptical about the miracle and suspected that it had been arranged by the supervisor. He shoved anyone in his way and returned on foot to Elixir, where the news had already spread like lightening. Everybody was curious to know the truth. He told them that the old man had never died. He had gone into hibernation. One lady, more than anyone else, insisted in asking him to prove his doubts. He shrugged his shoulders and declined to explain the causes of heart and pulse stoppage.

In the following days, the Lisbon newspaper, *O Jornal de Noticias*, gave ample footage of the extraordinary event. It reported that the man was already in his country, in good health and was going to celebrate his resurrection with his family and friends. In the meantime, San Lazarus gained the reputation of being the place where the dead come back to life.

# THE TWO PRIESTS

The news of the man declared clinically dead and resuscitated after spending a month in Hades, as the ancient Greeks believed, did the "*tour du monde*." From China to Canada, in the markets and in the theaters, in the stadiums and in the streets, there many interpretations. In Sumatra, they claimed it was the result of magic. In India, the fakiri, people who walk on hot charcoal, maintained that the power of the mind is infinite. In Tibet, The Dalai Lama refused to comment. Nonetheless, a Buddhist monk explained that meditation can let one die and bring him back to life. In Japan, the leader of the new religious sect, Body Power, insisted that he was an old samurai, who returned to earth after half a millennium. In South Africa, the Zulu representative called it "a return from a vacation." In Mongolia, a nomadic tribe of horse riders, closely associated to the Siberian church of "Boiling Ice," refused to accept the "transmigration." According to them, the man had fallen asleep so deeply that doctors couldn't detect the heartbeat. When he woke up, the whole body returned to its normal function. In Teheran, the Ayatollah described the event as bizarre and controversial. In Iraq, Ayatollah Sistani remained neutral. The Catholic Church, following its traditional stand, made no comment.

In San Lazarus, the focus of the conversations was "the man who beat death." Massimo did his best to abstain from the topic, but it wasn't always possible because he was one of the volunteers who witnessed the "resurrection." He was walking in the hall when he accidentally ran into Mitango. Massimo tried to strike up a conversation with him, but the other made a 360-degree turn on his wheelchair and went back to his room. Massimo followed him, but two guards, with large crosses on their chests, stopped him. He explained to them that his aim was to hear Mr. Africanus' reaction to the event of the previous day. They were insensitive to his plea. All of a sudden, an acoustic signal from inside communicated with the guards. They stepped aside and let him in. Massimo noticed a big cross on the wall and a red biretta on the nightstand. He was terrified by the idea that the man in his presence was a man of God. Mitango made the sign of the cross. Massimo tried to imitate him, but was too clumsy. Mitango scrutinized him deep into his heart. "So, you were Chingo's friend," he said, and launched a profound look that pierced through to Massimo's spinal chord. Massimo remained silent. Mitango paused a moment and added, "To respond to your question in the hall, the Church doesn't make any pronouncement on these matters. We leave it up to science to solve physical and scientific matters. The Church's mission is to save souls. Remember that only Christ resuscitated from death after three days, according to the Scriptures. All the rest is fiction, fruit of popular imagination, utopia and ignorance. Now, you may go newsman. Wait, not yet. Fall on your knees, confess your sins and say the act of contrition."

He said, haltingly, "I, I don't know it. I, I'm not a believer anymore."

Mitango looked at him with surprise. "Aren't you a Catholic?"

"I was ..." Massimo struggled to say.

"You recited the Rosary in Olympus ..."

"It's true, but I did it without conviction, to help others to believe, because we need faith to go on living. What is life without faith?"

Mitango didn't respond for a minute or so. He just kept his eyes on Massimo, who was completely lost in a sea of recalcitrant thoughts. Massimo lowered his head and said, again, "I used to believe ..."

"What made you withdraw from Christ?"

"I lost faith on account of a girl."

"A girl ..." Mitango stopped as if he was overwhelmed with thoughts that rumbled through his head like a herd on a stampede. The silence seemed to be eternal. Finally, he continued, "You may come back some other time." He did the sign of the cross again. Massimo fell backward in the attempt of standing on his feet. He got up, gave a glance once again at Mitango, withdrew backward to the door and left disgruntled and confused.

Massimo felt very uncomfortable to go back to Mitango. His lost faith, the relationship, if any, between Mitango and Ching, the presence of a powerful churchman prevented him from being at ease. On the other hand, he realized he needed help in order to complete his mission, a lot of help. Each time he moved around, he found insurmountable obstacles. He started to believe that someone was obstructing his plan. Restrictions on top of restrictions were making his life miserable. Undaunted, he kept on pressing, took a deep breath and furtively went to visit Mitango. Evidently, the guards had already been briefed because they didn't even question him. He knocked at the door. A feeble voice ordered him to enter, "Come in."

"How are you today?"

"Not perfectly well. The humidity makes my arthritis flare up. Old age is creeping in."

"I wouldn't say that. You are still young. Pretty soon you'll finish your therapy and you'll be hopping again like a rabbit."

Mitango tried to smile. "So you are back ..."

"Well, Ching's work is in my mind and unless you act as a guide ... the clock is ticking."

"Swear on this Bible that you will never reveal my secrets."

"But I don't believe anymore."

"Swear anyhow! Someday, you will."

Massimo agreed and went through the ritual that Mitango read from a book.

The oath didn't last too long and Mitango asked Massimo to help him to straighten up his position on the chair and to open the door. The hall was empty. Outside, two men were feeding the birds in the garden. Mitango leaned over to Massimo and whispered, "As long as Ching delegated to you the task of this completion ..." He turned his head toward the window and said, "Do you see that man?"

"Which one?"

"The one with the black shirt and a Panama hat. He is throwing seeds to the birds."

"Yes, I do. Is he important?"

"He's a priest."

"Really?"

"The other sitting next to him is also a priest. The community has lodged different accusations against them."

"Unbelievable!"

"Why do you question my word?"

"No, I wasn't dubious. I wanted to make sure I understood." He took a deep breath and added, "The way they dress nowadays, it makes you wonder. It seems that they are ashamed of their black vestments."

"If it were for the vestiary aspect ..."

Massimo felt embarrassed to have spoken so bluntly about the liberal wind sweeping the Church in certain respects. He apologized, "I should have not been prejudicial, but without rules to abide by, without referring points, without examples, people will soon lose their faith." He realized he had stepped into another issue and stated, "He looks healthy and young to me."

"Remember, never judge by the clothes."

"It may be a stupid question, but if he isn't sick, what's he doing here?"

"Your doubt is well taken. No healthy person wants to live here."

"Did the church exile him for inappropriate behavior with another man?"

"You have a very narrow mind." He stopped as if he wanted to change the subject of conversation. He looked at Massimo, but his silence was stronger than the desire to quit that topic. He gestured here and there using some Latin phrases. Massimo had studied the language for a while, but could only understand a few words. He wanted to ask for a translation, but he didn't. The air conditioner kicked off and produced an irritating noise. When it stopped, Mitango rubbed his face and looked outside. The sky was rumbling and the clouds gathered darker and ominous over San Lazarus. Thunder soon shook the air and lightning followed. Soon, drops of water fell on the ground, and a storm broke loose. Mitango coughed repeatedly. Massimo asked him if he needed the nurse. His chest rattled a few more times, but he refused any help. He stretched his chest foreword and became serious. Massimo stood waiting until Mitango said, "I don't know where we are going."

"You keep on being evasive."

Mitango motioned with his head to the man dressed in black and said, "He hired a private detective."

"For what?"

"Good question! The priest who preceded him in his parish was a homosexual."

"Is this the revelation of the century? I don't wish to be their defense lawyer, but young seminarians are not selected to be priests on the basis of their sexual orientation."

Mitango took time to respond. He sipped cold coffee from a cup offered to him by one of the guards, who had entered for that purpose, and continued, "Theoretically, your reasoning makes sense. The Church has her hands full of homosexual priests, but the problem goes beyond that. The priest spent too many long hours in the rectory with a man. As you may expect, rumors flew around like leaves in the wind. They went on vacation on exotic Caribbean islands and the priest bought many gifts to his companion, always according to the rumors."

"But rumors can be false too!"

"Absolutely!"

"If the accusations have some truth, where in the world did the priest get the money?"

Mitango made some wide gestures from which Massimo attempted to extrapolate something, then, he said, "He defrauded the Church for hundreds of thousands of dollars."

Massimo couldn't control his astonishment, which culminated in laughter. When he reestablished his normal poise, he replied, "But if the churches are broke.... Look, youngsters don't attend Sunday Mass and the retirees can't afford higher donations. In many instances, people drop a dollar in the basket."

"Not quite so at St. Jeremiah! Each parishioner donates nine thousand dollars on a weekly basis."

"Do you expect me or any reasonable man to believe that?"

"Listen, St. Thomas, I'm talking about the richest church in Montreal. If my words sound unrealistic, math is available for anyone who disputes it. The other priest has been accused of diverting the funds ..."

"It's unheard of! And supposing that the parishioners have turned into a flock of King Midas's, what does that have to do with the priest outside?"

"The investigation! The Bishop considered it an abuse of power and declassed him, in the sense that he can't celebrate the Mass for the time being, nor he can hear confessions."

"The controversy doesn't center solely on the alleged sexual relations or embezzlement. The role model of a priest comes into question ... Nonetheless, we have to be judicious and wait because charges, at times, may be reduced to pure fiction by the defense."

"It's no longer fiction when the parishioners rebel against the Bishop who exonerated the priest."

"Why?"

"People consider the priest's demotion as immoral and unjust and unless he is going to be reinstated the cash flow will eventually stop."

"I can understand that priest's demotion, but to relegate this other one in a "prison" for his quest of honesty and morality calls for a reassessment of the whole judicial system of the Church. The sentence killed the man in his conscience."

"*Sic transit Gloria mundi.*"

"I understand that, but this priest can't languish for pursuing the truth."

Mitango agreed, and for a while the conversation came to a halt. Neither one of them could find a plausible justification for the Church's action. Mitango took the floor again, "Time is still. The whole process of dialog is stagnant. The Church needs renewal. Everyone knows it, but few dare to challenge the status quo."

Massimo rested a short while and remarked, "The priest feeding the birds shows signs of depression, although he is young and healthy."

"How can you tell?"

"From here, I can spot deep lines on his forehead."

"Did you study Depression Aesthetics?"

"No, but it's common knowledge nowadays that the more you open and close the wrinkles the higher the state of depression. I'm fully convinced that there is constant communication taking place between the facial expressions and the brain. There has to be. The body communicates constantly in all its activities on various fronts. It's the most perfect machine ever devised. This has been evidenced even by a recent medical study. The brain causes the skin to assume a certain color or expression based on the "e-mail" it receives. Therefore, it's the mirror of the soul."

"Very interesting! Medicine has made gigantic leaps in recent decades."

Massimo appreciated the compliment and felt encouraged to go on with the previous topic. He took a long respite, then said, "Are you in a position to explain to me why these problematic situations arise only within the Catholic Church?"

"Could you be more specific?"

"Like the one we were discussing …"

Mitango ran his fingers through his hair and took his time to answer. It was hot. He asked for a glass of cold water and gulped it. The hall had become unusually deserted. He pointed to a man in a wheelchair in the hall and said, "Do you see him? The one dressed in a robe?"

"Yes."

"Another priest."

"More?"

"He is here to convalesce for a nervous breakdown."

"Too much stress?"

"Exactly! The government expropriated a building to a man of questionable morals and donated it to a church, which turned it into a playground for youth."

"I can only surmise the reaction."

"In fact, this priest's car was blotted with blood and hundreds of bullets were left in a sack next to the church. He also received a death threat. You can imagine his reaction. His mind was so shattered that the Bishop had to send him here for a while."

"Repulsive!"

Both took time off and drank a cold coffee. They looked in the hall and saw a volunteer transporting a resident to the therapy room. Massimo looked inquisitively to his guide to find out if he had anything to say about him too. After a couple of minutes, he felt disappointed and got up. Mitango patted him on the shoulder and invited him to sit back down. "That man is another court case."

"Another?"

"You told me to guide you toward knowledge because you are to complete your mission …"

"Oh, yes, please, do so."

"Did you see that man with the olive skin? He is alive by the doctors' courage."

"We would expect it from a medical doctor."

"But courage acquires a higher connotation when it works against current. It converts into heroism."

"I fully agree with you. What is atypical about him?"

"He is a Jehovah's Witness."

"I've heard about them. I don't intend to criticize them, but some of their beliefs don't make sense to me. Of course, for their faith everything is justifiable . To us their behavior is funny, strange, bizarre."

"Easy on that! They don't believe in blood transfusion."

"That's common knowledge!"

"But what you ignore is that his family is taking to court the doctors who saved him."

"How is that?"

Mitango scratched his head. He didn't want to enter into a distant feud with another religious denomination. At the end, he gave in, "Last month, they transported this man to the emergency room at San Joseph Hospital. His relatives warned the doctors not to attempt any blood transfusion otherwise they would be liable for lawsuit. The doctors followed their professional motto "Save human lives at all costs!"

"That's the most admirable expression of human love!"

"Not for the Jehovah's Witnesses! For them the doctors impinged on the man's freedom of choice."

"Freedom of choice my …! Don't they make sense?"

"According to us…. Now, the doctors are confronted with a court case."

"Where did this happen, in Montreal or in Quebec City?"

"It doesn't matter the location. The Jehovah's Witnesses are spread all over. It's not a location issue, but one of Bible interpretation."

"It's unthinkable that God would allow his creatures to bleed to death when care is available. That is such a distortion of the word of God ... such confusion ... and most of the time for pride, individuality, independence, hegemony, materialism. And when I look a these people suffering, I can't avoid asking myself why God leaves us alone. That's why I'm not a believer anymore. I lost it all. God's silence overwhelms me.

Mitango looked even more serious. His face showed the signs of Father Time. His silence too was beginning to bother Massimo. Finally, he murmured, "What about me? Why do I deserve this?

"Yes, why do you deserve this when you still possess youthful energies. You are in the prime of your life."

"I think we have to postpone this issue until a later date. Right now, I'm able to see something of your future. You will come back to God someday."

Massimo didn't share the same conviction and made no secret of it. Mitango didn't think it was the opportune time for engaging in a hot theological debate and changed the subject. He noticed a little gold cross with a heart on the lapel of Massimo's jacket, but didn't make any comment or question. Massimo realized that the cross was being scrutinized and said, "It was a gift, not a proof of my Christian belief. I keep it here as a remembrance."

Mitango smirked. Massimo was reluctant to get engaged in a discussion related to his past life and commented, "She was a true gem!"

"I can imagine. Such a handsome young man deserves a pearl."

"She was!"

"Don't you see her anymore?"

"No, ... well ... Some unfortunate events occurred and I lost hold of her. Nonetheless, I have reasons to believe that some day, some how, I'll be able to meet her again. It's going to take time before this murky water clears up. Only then will I begin to live my real life."

"Time is on your side."

"If you feel so confident, I'll let your wisdom guide me."

Mitango smiled. His mind appeared to be fraught with preoccupations. The wrinkles on his forehead were more pronounced. He scratched his head, but didn't reply.

Massimo was lost in his own contemplation. Suddenly, he shouted, "I see the light! You will lead me to good pasture."

Mitango seemed to wake up from a dormant state. He looked with compassion at the young man and said, "Control your voice! Remember that only God can lead you there. I'm but his tool."

Massimo felt disappointed by the answer. He shifted his attention on a painting of the Chinese Great Wall and other colorful artifacts. He observed them one by one with an expert eye. Mitango didn't wait for any questions, informing him they were not for sale. Massimo didn't hear him. He stooped before a large vase with serpents and dragons decorations. Mitango grabbed some pictures and other small items and pushed them in the desk drawer. He didn't feel comfortable with his objects being scrutinized. "Interesting aren't they?"

"Absolutely! Where did you buy these fine treasures?"

"They're not for sale. They come from China."

"Did you visit recently?"

Mitango coughed and laughed simultaneously. "I wish I did! No, I lived there many moons ago. Huge country with an immense population!"

"And still mysterious, isn't?"

"I suppose so, until yesterday. Lately, the authorities have embraced an open door policy and the country is booming with business. The only barrier that exists is the opposition to the Catholic Church to expand and prosper."

"They've made some progress . ."

"Not like the old times when Valigiano, a priest of profound culture and patience, did his apostolate in those lands."

"Who was he? I never heard of him."

"An Italian missionary who understood the importance of the local culture in the evangelization process. He gained enough experience to teach him how to dress, eat, speak like them before engaging them in a religious conversation. In fact, by the year of his death, 1606, the North American missionaries had learned the lesson when they tried to convert the natives."

"You spoke of his fabulous patience. He must have been another Job."

"Perhaps, even better! Initially, it wasn't so in his native Venice. He exhibited a notably irritable character that led him to a scuffle with a woman whom he knifed. Accused of physical violence, he ended up in jail and he would have remained behind the Venetian bars for the rest of his life if it weren't for the direct and incessant intercession of Cardinal Borromeo."

"What a lucky guy he was! And you mean the unexpected freedom caused such a profound change in his personality?"

"No doubt!"

"Did he compensate the Cardinal?"

"Of course, by pouring all his energies and love into the evangelical mission. He sojourned in Rome where he studied theology. When he found out there was an opening for the mission in the Far East, he accepted the challenge wholeheartedly. He possessed a genuine and original vocation in dealing with the indigenous population, so that he became the point of reference for future missionaries, as I mentioned earlier. He even mastered the Japanese language, which made his conversion efforts much easier.

"Anyone would have called him a dreamer when he outlined his plans, but in time, he made Nagasaki the main Catholic religious center in the whole country."

"What about the obstacles?"

"That's another issue. Inner struggles between the Franciscans and the Dominicans. Each order tried to assert its own character, so to speak."

"The Pope couldn't control them?"

"It's not that easy. The distance and the Flemish Protestant Reformation helped significantly to spark the flames of division."

"That tells you the role that envy plays in all aspects of our lives."

Mitango commented sadly, "Let's not make a rule out of an exception."

Massimo frowned. He had had enough for the time being. He excused himself to return to his work, promising to return.

Three days passed by and Massimo didn't visit Mitango. On the fourth day, he finally showed up. The guards recognized him and let him pass.

"Good afternoon, my guide, I hear a massive jubilation taking place in the Unit B. What could it be?"

"All the confusion you hear is the result of a miracle."

"What miracle? Another figment of your imagination …?"

"Are you predisposed to accept only pessimistic news?"

"No, but miracles are no longer part of my writing repertoire."

"Read the newspaper this evening or listen to the TV news."

"What's the scoop?"

"I'll tell you in a nutshell. The noise that you hear relates to a lady, on the threshold of ninety who has been in coma for the past two years. She was a fan of a television program dedicated to the Blessed Mother. Every day they recite the Rosary or have guest speakers, and so on."

"Was she terminally ill?"

"I'm not so sure about that. I only know that she was a 'vegetable' and her family couldn't take it anymore. They were exhausted. There were rumors that one of them favored the cessation of life support."

"I can't believe it!"

Massimo departed abruptly and visited the scene of the purported miracle. He inquired with one of her relatives, who summarized the miraculous event with these words, "I turned off the TV and dozed off a bit, along with my brother and nephew. Suddenly, she started to call us one by one by name. We woke up instantly and thought we were dreaming, to hear her voice again. We rubbed our eyes and ears and we realized that she was staring at us. I swear her lips were moving. Imagine our reaction! We couldn't hold back our tears because the doctors had informed us that she was clinically dead."

"I'm convinced that music is a loyal ally of physiotherapy, but not to this extent."

"Oh, yes! Music is the voice of our soul. She used to recite the Rosary every day."

"Are you positive that something else in the nervous system didn't trigger the valve that brought her back to consciousness? This is fantasy and science mixed together."

The lady felt offended. She withdrew with other relatives and joined other patients in the festivity.

Massimo returned to Mitango completely stunned. He dismissed the event as a genuine miracle, but he was visibly disturbed. He tried to hide his feelings as long as he could. Mitango exclaimed, "I have seen many faith transformations in my life, particularly that of a young man like you. After many tribulations, his beliefs took a parabolic descent. He never claimed to have witnessed something supernatural. It was an inner metamorphosis. I'm absolutely certain that in this building an event of purported divine origin isn't shaking up only your conscience from its foundation, but also of those who share your convictions."

Massimo looked back at Mitango with resentment. He wanted to run away, denounce the hypocritical behavior of the elite, the credulous nature of the populace, but he opted to cool off. He stared at the ceiling for the next five minutes. Neither one of them was willing to restart the dialogue. Each one was engaged in reading the thoughts of the other. Not a word came from either man. The noise of the silence was overpowering both. Massimo finally made a gesture with his hand and departed. Mitango took a cloth and started to polish the cross that lay on the table.

# THE DOCTOR'S LONG HAND

It was sunset when Massimo received permission to enter into Mitango's room.

All day long an oppressing humidity kept the air conditioners busy to the utmost of their capacities. Hardly anyone roamed around San Lazarus's perimeter, not even under the tall trees whose shade was visible from a distance. No wheelchair was on the sidewalk. Occasionally, the trucks that came to unload the food made shrieking noises, leaving on the asphalt a black streak and behind a cloud of smoke, which resisted dispersion in the air.

Mitango disliked any artificial cooling system and opened the window. He stuck his head out and, from the south wing section of the hospital, a group of people caught his attention. He tried, but couldn't identify anyone. He took off his eyeglasses, cleaned them, and took a second look. This time, he recognized a doctor walking handcuffed, head down, among guards. In proximity of a security car, the leader approached the doctor and seemed to whispered what appeared to be monosyllabic words or coded messages.

Massimo, too, was watching the scene with a mixture of tenderness and curiosity. "Master," he said, "What is it going to become of that man?"

"Son, he is a doctor who violated the law of conduct."

"Is that all?"

"He molested a patient. Do you see his hands? They're longer than ordinary ones.

"How old is the lady?"

"Only 39! She went to his office for a back pain."

"My understanding was that only patients from San Lazarus can avail themselves of medical service here."

"Exactly! She had a hip operation and was sent here for a three-week course of therapy. During this period, she experienced a back problem. The doctor abused her. She would cry, but was too ashamed to report it. As soon as he went to the lavatory to wash up, she got up slowly and made it to the hall without making any demonstration against the doctor. Limping, she got to the street, but she stumbled on a clod of dirt and fell. It was then that a police car from nearby came over to assist her. Under interrogation, she revealed her personal and sad experience."

"How well informed you are! When did this happen?"

"Yesterday …"

"It took all this while to arrest him?"

"Legal matters, you know … or something else intervened in the meanwhile."

"You mean, they didn't give the opportunity to the doctor to put up his defense?"

"By all means! He claimed that he was victim of a rapture. It's on today's paper."

"You have to realize that in most instances legal cases are carried out here quickly."

"I thought so."

"How did the police build their case?"

"Aside from the witness's allegations, the police found a picture of the victim, naked, in his pants pocket.

"What was his justification?"

"He claimed that he needed it to make some analyses."

"It was a credible defense, no?"

"By no means! He had other female clients, but he did it only with this one."

"Where does he stand now?"

"Being a local matter, he may get away with a reprimand, a dismissal or even a punitive action. San Lazarus's image is at stake here. The girl may seek psychiatric help and later hire a reputable lawyer. In that case, the insurance company of the Health Center will have to pay a lot of pennies. The Canadian police don't tolerate physical violence against women, especially when they are patients."

"This place scares me more every day."

"You will get used to it."

"But, the doctor, where is he going now?"

"At a detention place in San Lazarus. Later, they will decide."

The days dragged on nervously at San Lazarus. No one was in a position to anticipate the young lady's next step. It was a Monday afternoon when she called the press to hand over her memo. Venus immediately sent an emissary to her house. He called her to one side and handed her a big envelope. She opened it and counted what was in it. She felt somewhat relieved. When the reporters arrived, she dismissed them, raising all sorts of suspicions.

# DEATH BY NURSES

As we have seen, Venus was extremely sensitive about San Lazarus's public image. A negative portrayal of the hospice could have had catastrophic repercussions. She made an attempt to restructure the managerial level and lend more emphasis to the rigorous application of the rules. She sent a memo to her subordinates that outside patients coming for short periods of therapy should have constant supervision, especially young women. Terminally ill residents who never received visits, on the other hand, would no longer live in Olympus or Elixir. Having fixed the basement of the hospital wing, she arranged for their permanent transfer there. Those who didn't respond to conventional medicine, but still received visits, were to stay in the main building.

Venus called the new unit "Oblivion." To keep expenses to a minimum, she hired unemployed foreign workers. The following is an interview she had with one group of them.

"What is your name?"

"Rashim."

"Where do you come from?"

"Ramallah, Palestine."

"They are having a tough time, aren't they?"

"Well, Jews take all land."

"Do you speak English well?"

"Perfect!"

"Jobs are scarce nowadays."

"What you mean?"

"The job market is low. Not too many jobs are available."

"That's why I come here."

"Good! Are these ladies with you?"

"Yes, one is from Russia and the rest come from Pakistan."

"Let me see if I can help you." She opened up a book and read something. She raised her head and asked one of them with blond hair and blue eyes, "Are you Canadian citizens?"

"No, nobody knows we are here."

"You mean you are aliens with no legal status?"

The ladies looked extremely concerned. Only when Venus assured them that she would not report them to the government, did they gave a sigh of relief. They were poorly dressed and their faces showed signs of a rough life even though they were in their thirties. Venus explained to them that she could only pay them minimum wage, but if they wished to earn a lot of money, they had to work overtime. None of them objected. The most important thing for them was job assurance and no police interference.

In Oblivion, no one ever supervised the new "nurses" from the other side of the world, so they started to create their own rules. One of them, who was a bit aggressive said, "Svetlana, let us take the food home whenever we can give our patients the left over."

"No problem, Natasha. It sounds good. We need something extra here to make ends meet. Pass this news to Rashima and Malika."

"These "dry sticks" can't smell or taste. What's the use to give them all the good things. Life must be good in this country. Look how many there are here!"

"If a few of them die, what's the difference?"

"Somebody gets the insurance."

"I wonder who...."

"We talk about it some other time."

Winter came and the "nurses" were busy downtown, visiting shops, buying clothes and looking for fun. "Rashima, you don't have to worry. Those old people can't hear or see well. They don't have the will to eat. So why bother?"

"Malika, but we have to run our own mini food market away from here."

"Excellent idea! Let's work on it."

"What if someone spills the beans?"

"Who can do that? The residents have no idea where they are. Every month someone dies. And so ...?"

"Wait a moment! If they die, we have no job. Take it easy!"

"Don't be too conscientious."

"Yes, but a lot of them are dying ahead of time. If they keep on dying like flies, we won't have a job. Stop this unnecessary carnage."

"Not a chance! People get old every day. They have to die somehow."

"Last month, an old man complained and Svetlana cracked a pot on his head. Last week, Natasha threw the dish in the garbage because a lady complained about the food."

"Let's not go too far because if we break all the dishes and pots, how are we going to explain it to the supervisor, unless we buy them."

"Korosho!"

Three months went by. The nurses had started a mini market and had full control of the compound at San Lazarus. The police officers who usually made their routine check never had a complaint against them, except that one evening they smelled a foul odor and wanted to get to the root of it. Initially, they suspected that a dead animal lay in the vicinity, but when they inspected the cellar, they remained speechless. What they saw was beyond their belief. Some old men were tied to the beds. The odor of urine was so pungent that the guards had to place handkerchiefs over their noses. They also discovered a couple of corpses on the bed which emanated an unbearable stench. The food on the table was spoiled and covered with flies. A pile of clothes on the floor prevented anyone from crossing to the next room unless it was removed. Some of the sick people were yelling for help, The medicine was scattered all over the night stands. The police checked the dates and found out that it was expired. There was hardly any light in a dark rectangular hall.

The purported "nurses" returned late that night. They were tired. At the door, they found the police, who handcuffed them and took them to jail. They were charged with homicide, derelict behavior, abuse of power and of false profession. Thirty people died during their service time. San Lazarus's executive board sent a documentation of false statements on the part of the foreign nurses to their many political friends. The Canadian government, instead of convicting them for homicide, decided to expatriate them and asked their countries to prosecute them.

The hospital wing cellar was closed. Venus was tried and convicted for poor supervision and neglect in the death of thirty patients. The judge condemned her to thirty years prison and withdrew her nursing license. Her defense lawyers appealed, and presented to the judge documents that exonerated Venus from any guilt because she had rented the basement and the supervision to the foreign nurses. Once again, San Lazarus's executive board come to Venus's rescue by providing the judge false documents and forged signatures. Once again, Venus walked out freely, but she gambled her life away.

The Canadian police kept a special file on San Lazarus. Once a week, one officer would walk through the door of the main office and demand they turn over the books for a regular inspection. After an hour, he left without lodging any complaint or making questions about the computer material. Everything appeared normal to him and he left in good humor.

Despite the government's vigilance, patients continued to die at the hospital wing on a daily basis. Venus reported to the board of directors that the deaths were the result of old age or heart attacks. In one month, thirty people had passed away. This long series of deaths didn't go undetected and alerted other agencies. The Health Center was collecting Medicare. The Joy of Living headquarters at San Lazarus controlled the whole financial system from insurance to pensions to Medicare. They even bought life insurance for the residents in a web of controversial and sometimes obscure deals.

# EUTHANASIA

It was close to noon. Massimo knocked at Room 99. The lady looked feeble. She had been waiting for some time to go to the cafeteria. At the left side of the same room lay a woman who was over 100 years old. She leaned on one side of the bed. Her left arm was dangling. The air was filled with an unbearable odor of urine. Massimo took the handkerchief from his pocket and held it over his nose. Her respiration was erratic, clumsy and disturbing.

He greeted her, but there was no response. He turned to the other lady and asked, "Isn't she feeling well? She has to eat lunch."

"Don't worry! She isn't going to eat."

"Why is that?"

"I don't know. She has been like that since I came here."

"Which is …?"

"The past two years."

"You mean … She never eats?"

"Exactly!"

The echo of Massimo's astonishment reverberated throughout the room and hall. He disregarded the foul smell and exclaimed, "How is it possible to survive without food?"

"There are other means, young man."

Five minutes later, Massimo passed by the guards at Mitango's room. Massimo rarely felt introverted; he was always open to conversation. This time, however, he had a gloomy face. Mitango asked some questions, but he didn't receive any answer. Finally, he told him, "Have you lost your tongue?" Massimo shook his head in a sign of denial and continued to be engulfed in his contemplative mood. Mitango thought that something serious had happened to him, but didn't pursue the matter.

The pensive attitude lasted about ten minutes. Slowly, as the ice began to melt under the sun's rays, so Massimo began to speak under the anxious scrutiny of his guide, "I have just visited a woman over a hundred. She is unresponsive to any physical or mental activity. Moreover, she has lost her vision, the speech ability and her hearing power is limited. She lives in a vegetative state. They have to feed her intravenously to keep her alive."

"Don't talk any further. I know perfectly well your aim."

"Then, why does your Church condemn euthanasia. Do you like to perpetuate human suffering?"

Father Mitango drew back in his armchair. He was visibly irritated, "How do you dare to proffer such a blasphemy!"

"I see it with my own eyes! A human being can't even die in dignity. When technology keeps people "alive," it carries violence to the dignity and free will of an individual, not to mention to nature itself."

"You have to realize that a doctor's main responsibility is to keep a patient alive. The ancient philosophers considered the breath the very spirit of a human being; consequently, pulling the plug would do violence to the spirit."

"I'm referring to only one organ that keeps pulsating. The rest of the body is oblivious to life activities."

"I believe, instead, that the right to die is in juxtaposition to the right to vote, to free speech, to work ..."

"Don't mix them, please. The rights that you mentioned originate in man, in a society. The right to die or to live originates in God. He is the only one who can exercise that right."

Massimo exhibited symptoms of restlessness. The prelate perceived his distraught mood and waited. Massimo smiled, "OK, OK. Let's look it from a family perspective."

"For instance?" answered the Bishop with an ostensible apprehension.

"A patient doesn't eat for two years?"

"She may be in a state of irreversible condition, a coma."

"How can the relatives witness this slow process of self-destruction?"

"The Church has to deal with these cases too in a very cautious way."

"I don't appreciate this apologetic, sibylline posture."

"It's not sibylline. It's factual," insisted the Bishop.

"I surmise that you take in consideration the individual's right for self-determination."

"Of course we do!"

"Why, then, doesn't the Church allow to be written a clause in a testament or delegate the right for a final decision to the immediate family survivors?"

"The Church can't accept that position even when the bodily and mental functions are apparently irreversible."

"Hogwash!"

"Listen! We appoint a special medical commission to ascertain the irreversibility of the illness and then, we must also consider the international guidelines."

"Again, if the cessation of mental health has been established, why does the Church hold with obstinacy to such a rigid position?"

The prelate closed his eyes to let them rest a few seconds, then he wiped his glasses.

"My friend," said he very calmly, "This issue, too, is utterly sensitive to human life. We have no control over it. God alone has power over it. It's not an issue that belongs to the realm of science. You must understand that we are human beings, not robots."

Massimo shook his head in disagreement. "I respectfully dissent from you. We are equipped with a rational process."

"I'm with you."

Massimo looked through the window at the statue of Zeus in the garden of Joy of Life and continued, "Man is god on some occasions."

"Don't be so naïve."

"Look! Many of these patients could relieve their families' anxieties by living at home the last days …"

"Not everyone can. You need facilities: the ramp, bathroom conveniences, a special bed … And a wheelchair alone costs $4,000."

"You don't need all of that with a person in a coma. He or she is going to die soon anyhow."

"Don't be so sure! There have been cases where the person came back to life after eight years. This is why the Church is so ardently opposed to any violence to life. Don't be polemical! Admit it, for once, that the Church is right."

Massimo didn't respond. He was looking outside.

The conversation was assuming the character of a heated debate. Massimo had no intention of keeping it at that level so he quit talking, and moved closer to the window. Father Mitango was curious to see what he was up to and turned around. Massimo was looking in the direction of the statue of Zeus. Without addressing his companion, he said, "Only despots weigh the fate of their subjects on a scale."

"This is compassion, human sensitivity, respect for the wish of others."

Neither one of them would submit his convictions to the other. The priest showed signs of fatigue. He made a last attempt, "The respect for life is the respect of a free will, and when someone pulls the plug it's homicide."

At that point, Massimo couldn't hold back his impatience, "It's a matter of culture! No one would have accused a Roman woman when she committed suicide to protect her honor. Father, we are talking about a person who is oblivious of the real world, and without that cognition can't be considered responsible if so wished or if another family member made the decision based on the length of suffering and irreversibility of the case. If she wishes to die, her right should be respected. If her husband would pull the plug, it would be a sign of real love toward her because she doesn't want to suffer anymore. He would exercise the right of extreme fidelity and love."

"Look! It's like abortion. When a woman aborts she commits homicide."

"You are opening another scenario, a scenario of life and not of death."

"I told you before and I repeat it. There is no respect for life unless there is respect for free will."

"And I told you that life belongs to God."

"Your dialectic is convenient in an ecclesiastic environment, not in a secular one. I, for instance, don't believe in God anymore. How could it affect me?

"Not believing in God doesn't justify your action before a responsible conscience."

Both of them were tired. Massimo smiled and told him that he would be happy to reopen the debate at a later date. He bowed his head and went to take on his activity.

# THE COST OF MEDICINE

In Canada, the government provides free medicine. The cost has skyrocketed. The pharmaceutical companies mushroomed. The Health Department called for a volunteer lowering of prices. Unfortunately, it didn't happen. Some intercepted conversations between the Joy of Living headquarters and the manufacturers revealed that San Lazarus had a ten per cent share investment. They also lobbied for governmental non-interference in the private sector. Very simply, it pressed the politicians to leave Medicare prices floating, while they could bargain for cheaper prices on generic medicine. The estimated cost of the drugs for the following decade was going to be around $750 billion. With a diluted bargaining power, that estimation will eventually rise. The Medicare system suffered from internal bleeding and the taxpayers were bearing the financial burden. Zoo, a cholesterol drug, for instance, was being sold to a private hospital at $167. To Medicare, it cost $1,155.

Massimo checked the drug prices on the hospital wall and made a comparison with those in the drugstore. The discrepancy was humongous. One day, Mitango dispatched him to Room 88. The patient was reticent in talking to him. The diffidence disappeared when Massimo told him that he worked as a volunteer and he was referred to him by Mitango. It was a visit of courtesy.

The patient was actually a doctor, who had been diagnosed with a rare lymphatic disease. His candle was dwindling and he felt he didn't have anything to lose anymore.

He asked Massimo to give him his word of honor not to reveal the content of his conversation with anyone in the building. Having agreed, Massimo sat on the chair and listened to him, "What they do here is uncivilized, inhuman, unjust. If you don't play their games, one strike and you are out, if you know what I mean."

Massimo nodded and gave a glance outside of the door to ascertain that no one was spying on him. The doctor noticed his apprehension and said, "Keep cool! I'm about to leave this earthly house."

"I wanted to make sure that we are in a safe place," Massimo reassured him.

"Nothing is safe here."

Massimo sat back in the chair. The doctor said, "Don't be naïve! Last week they killed an old man with boiling water."

"No way!"

"Listen! They did it!"

"Why?"

"He doesn't have any relatives. The man was being critical of the drugs' high price."

"Was that all?"

"Well, they gave him other pills. This time he complained that they made him sleepy."

"There was nothing wrong in reporting the collateral effect of the drugs."

"Not to the office. They placed him under a shower head and dumped boiling water on him. Prior to that, they tortured him."

"This is cruel, unthinkable!"

"But true!"

Massimo got up and said, "I can't take it anymore! For today, it's more than enough. Thank you for sharing your thoughts."

"Are you leaving so soon?"

"I need a week of rest now." He dashed out of the door and returned to Elixir to report to Mitango.

# OTHER IMMIGRANT NURSES

In the last decade of the 20<sup>th</sup> century, a wave of immigrant nurses, all legal, from the ex-Soviet Bloc, moved to Canada. For them, reaching the Canadian shores was an oasis of peace and opportunity, a place of security, a dream come true. Those fluent in English found jobs quicker by taking an integrating course and a final test.

The nurses with a language barriers worked as attendants in hospices. Two of them, through some intermediaries, were employed at San Lazarus without scrupulous scrutiny. As they became proficient in English, they took the necessary steps to obtain their licenses. Two of them, unfortunately, got involved in a tragic episode that rocked the health system from its foundations for many years to come. We protect their anonymity by calling them by false names, Jolie and Juliette.

On a Friday afternoon, the two girls punched their timecards and walked back to their apartments. The streets had been paved during the day and the steam was still rising in the air giving an acrid, unbearable odor. They took the narrow sidewalk flanked by all sorts of shrubs. They never accepted a ride from drivers, regardless of their age. They loved to exercise, smell the fresh air and enjoy nature. Often they exchanged greetings with people they met on the sidewalk, but there were times when the greetings stretched into conversations, which they cut short by saying, "We have to go! We have to go cook." Someone dared them occasionally, "Can we taste your food?"

"Oh, no!" was the answer. We don't have room in the kitchen."

"We can eat outside."

"Oh, no! It's too hot!" or "It's too cold!"

That day, a man they didn't know approached the girls quickly. Within a close distance, he spoke to them briefly, then showed them a roll of 100 Canadian bills. The girls listened with interest, asked a few questions and, at the end, grabbed the money, each securing part of it in their bosom. The man wrote a few notes on his pocket calendar and disappeared with the same speed with which he had arrived.

At San Lazarus, at four o'clock in the afternoon the following day, Jolie and Juliette were joking with two elderly women. The patients complained about the rashes on their legs and stomach caused by an unusual heat wave. Jolie and Juliette promised them that with an injection of lemonade, every ailment would go away. They took two syringes, spilled a few drops and stuck the women in their arms.

During the night, the two ladies experienced the worst nightmares of their lives. The next morning, they felt unusually weak and noticed various bluish spots all over their bodies. Soon, their conditions worsened. Their sons called in their own doctors and the prognosis was terrifying. They had contracted the HIV virus. Jolie and Juliette didn't show up at San Lazarus anymore. "Someday, I'll get them," said Venus.

Not a month went by that both nurses were seen handcuffed at the local police station.

It was cold toward the end of October. The President of Joy of Life appeared at the penitentiary where the new detainees had been transferred. The attending guards stood on attention and allowed him to enter without searching him or passing through the metal detector. A third guard led the visitor to the room where he would met the prisoners.

The girls were waiting. They stood up immediately when they saw the President. He closed the door behind him, sat and said, "I came to see how you are doing."

"Jolie replied, "What do you think Mr. President? We have been locked up in this Garden of Eden. Adam and Eve cried before they were evicted. We cried when we entered and the bars closed behind us."

Juliette asked anxiously, "Is there any chance of getting out of here soon?"

"I'm afraid that we have to defer that question to another visit."

"Could you, at least, help us to get extradited? In our country, we could get a far less harsh punishment with one of our judges."

"That's your country! Listen carefully! My lawyers are in contact with the ambassador. I can't make any further mentioning of him. Our conversations may be wiretapped. I'm not certain that this place isn't equipped with a listening device."

Jolie got up and started to walk up and down the room until she stopped and looked at the man in front of her. "Mr. President, we could very easily incriminate you and the deliverer. We don't wish to do it, but it doesn't mean we won't unless you find a way to free us."

The President became suddenly pale. His glasses fell down his nose and he started to perspire profusely. He took a handkerchief and wiped his face. He cleaned the glasses, put them back on his eyes and said, "You do that and you shut the door to any reentry to your country."

Juliet was trembling. Jolie put a handkerchief over her mouth and drew back a couple of steps. In a shaky voice, she implored the President, "Sir, we are at your mercy, but you do owe us a favor."

"Yes, yes," responded the man annoyed ad nauseam. "For my favors, I pay a high price."

He looked at his daybook and said, "I have to go! I have an appointment with my lawyers."

He got up and kissed the prisoners goodbye, and whispered something in their ears. Their faces glowed from joy. Jolie exclaimed, "That sounds wonderful!" Jolie scratched her head and said in a thin voice, "I never thought of it."

The jail was located in the middle of nowhere. It was two hours from Montreal. It accommodated 2,000 prisoners of both sexes. The high walls were equipped with sonar devices, barbed wire and cameras. It had the reputation of being the only prison from which no detainees ever escaped.

The changing of guards occurred three times a day, at seven in the morning, at three in the afternoon and at eleven at night. In front of the main door, there were two guards. The two relieved guards slipped in their cars and left behind a cloud of dust. The other two rushed to the cell where the two girls were sleeping and handed them two police uniforms. The prisoners took no time in dressing. The guards opened up the cell door and walked them out of the compound from a secondary gate. A car was waiting for them. The guards from the tower top and on the roof watched the scene, which appeared a normal routine to them.

One hour later, the girls were a plane that took them to their homeland. When the alarm was set in jail, it was too late.

# MITANGO'S MISSION

My dear reader, I'm detecting signs of impatience in you. You want to delve into Mitango's life to find out how he got in this "self-imposed exile." At least, this is the impression that emerges from the material available. But, to think that you are the only one to be interested in his past, it would be a distortion of the truth. In fact, there is another important person who wishes to get his hands on it.

It's with great pleasure, therefore, that we open the curtains, and look at the background, focusing on the seminary mouse events. Up to that period, Mitango's private and religious life was in the public domain. With the passing days, the sun became increasingly pale in his sky and fragments of dark clouds followed him in his daily activities. The Church considered them murky. He defended them as crystal clear. The fact is that his whole figure became impenetrable.

The heat was oppressive in August, but Venus installed a new generation of air conditioner at St. Camillus, so that the temperature was constant and comfortable 24 hours a day. The garden was closed to prevent the residents from getting a heat stroke or shortness of breath. Mitango disregarded the sign and went to rest under a vine's arch. He started to sweat and puff. His heart gave symptoms of palpitation. He touched his chest and felt a vibration. He pressed a button to alert the guards. They accompanied him to his room, where he rested until he felt at ease again. He got up and drank a lemonade. He was experiencing abdominal pains and ran to the bathroom, where he started to cough.

It was at that point that Massimo arrived. He had heard that Mitango didn't feel well and took the time to see him. The room was empty and he decided to sit and wait.

Massimo wasn't one who gave up easily before an obstacle. He possessed an investigative impulse that led him most of the time to the target. Despite this natural ability, he was only able to build sketchy and inconclusive results. His visits were always characterized by the utmost caution. He didn't wish to lose the trust of his guide. A misstep would have cost him a valuable friendship. Whatever he touched or looked at, he did so with extreme discretion. The intermittent coughing coming from the bathroom disturbed his thoughts. He noticed in a corner a black briefcase equipped with a digital clock and a digital lock. It was secured to the desk. Mitango never made reference to it, and Massimo was discreet enough not to make any inquiry. In the meantime, the blood in Massimo's veins was boiling and rushed to his temples, causing a terrible tension. The temptation was mounting. He walked on his tiptoes. He leaned over the case and read on a videotape, "Top Secret." His brain was beaming incessant impulses of curiosity. He grabbed the video, hid it underneath his shirt and walked out. On the opposite hall, he stopped. His heart was pumping furiously. He lost control of his rational process and stood motionless against the wall. His temples were pouding at high speed. He had taken a road of no return. He was unsure if he had taken the right road. He had no time to waste. Every second was precious.

Five minutes later, he was at Arian's office. He knocked at the door, but nobody answered. He needed her urgently even at the cost of submitting himself to her. He stood there immobile. He remembered the time when Arian told him to keep an eye on Mitango's briefcase, but it had escaped his memory. A nurse passed by him in a hurry and the timid greeting got lost in the space. A second nurse went by. He asked her about Arian, but she was very vague. The same nurse came back shortly after and handed him a note, "Sir, please, wait in my office. I'll be back soon." While he was reading, she opened the door and invited him in. She looked at him with curiosity, smiled and disappeared from his sight.

Massimo locked the door and searched all way around with his eyes. Against the wall, there was a dubbing machine. He pulled the tape out of his shirt, grabbed a new one and inserted them both in the proper openings.

The dubbing process lasted about twenty minutes. He turned off the machine and wrote on a note, "Dear Arian, I couldn't wait any longer. Thank you immensely. M." Arian just missed him. She ripped the note and threw it in the basket. She let herself fall onto the armchair and bit her fingernails.

Mitango had just flushed the toilet and pulled up his pants when Massimo arrived. He proceeded directly to the briefcase and dropped the tape in its original place. Avoiding any unnecessary noise, he sat and waited, pretending a false calm.

Mitango was surprised to see Massimo. Instead, of greeting him, he dropped on the chair and began to breath heavily. Massimo saw him in distress and was about to call for assistance. He gestured not to bother and blamed the heat for being the cause of his diarrhea.

Massimo protested, "A virus causes the runs, not the heat."

Mitango wiped the sweat from his face with a towel and said, "My dear, the heat can do a lot of damage." He looked back at him and added, "But, I don't discard that possibility or a combination of the two." Massimo smiled.

The visit didn't last long. Before departing, Massimo suggested he call a doctor or nurse to get a restrictive bowel medicine. He had one at home, but refused to give the name for fear it might interfere with other medicines Mitango was taking. Mitango insisted that he stay, but Massimo reassured him that he would come back later. In the meantime, Mitango needed rest and the doctor's advice. He patted his shoulder and bid him goodbye.

Massimo had been gone ten minutes when Mitango's eyes rested on the open briefcase. He raised his eyebrows and rushed over to ascertain that everything was in place. Then, he closed and locked it.

Massimo didn't even eat that afternoon. He went straight home, put the tape in the VCR and watched it.

Mitango was a bright student, as we have seen him earlier in his career. He excelled in philosophy and theology. Eventually, he was ordained priest in 1958, at the age of 28, and his first destination was Shanghai.

In China, the Church was living underground and in duress. He did his best to organize it. His first act was to hire a pretty, 28-year-old secretary, who helped him beyond her call of duty. She didn't believe in God, but it didn't bother Mitango, who in a short while converted her to Catholicism. They traveled together in the far provinces of the country to determine the number of Catholics and proselytize, acting always with discretion, due to the Communist regime's vigilance. The money that Mitango received from the churches in Australia was insufficient to meet his needs, but Uncle Sam, through the CIA, provided additional financial assistance. Mitango was very liberal in his spending and kept on requesting money. He dreamed of building an orphanage and, subsequently, a church in Shanghai with the government's approval. He had charisma and used it in all its potential in a country where there was no religious freedom. Although the Communist authorities made him feel their presence everywhere, he didn't drop his plan. He mingled with all sorts of people at the markets, plazas and universities. With the help of a local engineer, he developed the blueprint for an orphanage and, with the support of various foreign embassies, was able to accomplish the project in less than a year. It wasn't a big church. It was rather sober, built with cement blocks. It had a wooden Crucifix on the altar and no statues. The pews could accommodate 100 parishioners. The orphanage was attached to the sacristy and had four big rooms, a kitchen and a bathroom. It wasn't a colossal architectural feat, but it fit the immediate needs of the few Catholics scattered around the city. The construction took place with the tacit consent of the rigid Communist hierarchy and that represented an enormous success, per se.

Mitango added a small apartment for himself. His secretary moved in and assisted him in all menial and religious activities. Their concerted efforts to establish a solid basis for Catholicism gave also rise to rumors. Old folks whispered that they saw them embracing more than once, and a neighbor insisted he saw only one light on in the evening.

It was nine o'clock in the morning and the secretary hadn't gotten up yet. The priest celebrated the Mass and headed straight to her bedroom. He knocked at the door, but no one answered. He opened it and noticed that she had her eyes open. "What's the matter, dear?"

"I feel … so … tired."

"Maybe, you're over-stressed. You are working very hard."

"No, it's not that."

"What else could it be?"

"I'm pregnant."

"Wha …?" The last letter got lost in his throat. He fell on his knees and his head leaned on the bed.

A long silence followed. Neither one of them had the will or the strength to talk. When he finally got up, he said, "Oh, my dear, I don't know what do."

"You could ask the Vatican for an exemption."

"I can't. I made a chastity vow."

"File a petition to be married. Explain to them that in view of the risks that the Church experiences here in China, it would be much better if you could acquire a marital status. In that way, you are not going to be a target of the authorities' incessant stalking."

"If I send that request, I'll cause concern among the Curia members."

"What do you propose to do?"

"First of all, you have to be certain."

"I know I am. All the symptoms are there."

He looked on the Crucifix hanging down at his chest for a long time. He said, "This is the greatest challenge of my life. I'm going to lose now, but I promise that in the future I devote all my energies to make a change."

She sat up and replied, "Let's not talk about the future. We are dealing with the present, our present."

He looked straight in her eyes and said, "I can't leave the Church. I'm a priest. A man who marries a woman becomes one with her. I'm already one with the Church."

She grabbed him by the arm and said, "Do you realize what they will do to me?"

"I do. Therefore, we will wait until the birth of the child and then we will put him in an orphanage."

She lowered her head and cried.

Nine months later, Mitango's mission in China came to an end. Orders had arrived from the Vatican for his work to continue elsewhere. She wanted to follow him, but the Chinese government denied her the visa.

As far as we know, he always provided for both her and the child in the means and manners he could afford.

# BACK TO MLOLONGO

Our story picks back up when Father Mitango is eventually assigned in the mid-80s to his hometown of Mlolongo, Africa. Mlolongo reserved a hero's welcome to her illustrious citizen. There were no protests, only festivities in his honor. He delayed his appearance in public for days. He was still weak and tired. The colorful shops resembled gardens of flowers. The windows displayed the national flag, and the street in front of the church was covered with rugs and palm tree branches. The façade of the church was decorated with colorful bows of silk, flowers and yellow flags. A wave of euphoria and optimism swept the town. The prostitutes disappeared from the sidewalks and people became polite and friendly as never before. When Father Mitango finally decided to make an appearance, he was met with an unprecedented wave of enthusiasm.

The Vatican had transferred Father Mitango to his hometown with the specific task of taking charge of the AIDS plague. He wasn't too thrilled about the new assignment; in fact, he accepted it with a mixture of fear and awe. He wasn't enthusiastic about returning to a place where AIDS was rampant, but he obeyed. It was the toughest task he would undertake since his ordination. He confided to his family that the project was far beyond his capacities and ability, but at the end, he had no choice and began with his usual fervor and dedication. Initially, he had absolutely no idea what to do and how to start. He had nothing to work with and no church to rely on. He was all alone in a desert of people without guidance and without self-control. His friends hardly recognized him. He had gained weight and wore reading glasses. The white collar put the prostitutes on the defensive right away after the initial euphoric stage. His first act was to buy a huge tent and build a table under it to use as an altar, and placed some candles on it. He had the chalice, the priestly garments and some other accessories pertaining to the Mass. His compatriots thought he was setting up a circus, but the absence of animals made them wonder even more.

The first Sunday, he stood in front of the tent and invited the people in, who, motivated more by curiosity than any religious idea, glanced inside. The absence of interesting objects or food made them quickly disperse.

Father Mitango wasn't a man who got discouraged easily. He used a loud-speaker to call them back. As soon as the crowd took shape, he announced, "My fellow citizens! I come here in all humility to talk to your heart. First, let me tell you something about the Spanish Fever. My grandfather was a victim of it." The congregation ignored completely the disease, but hearing that his relative had died, they sat on ground to listen.

As they got comfortable, he addressed them in this way: "The Spanish Fever didn't originate in Spain as it was erroneously believed. In May of 1918, a Spanish newspaper reported an outbreak of the fever that, in actuality, an American soldier had spread in America. In four months, the disease attacked 100 million people throughout the world and killed 50 million of them. One million died in the U.S. and thousands in Canada, particularly in Toronto and Montreal."

The crowd made some loud reactions of disbelief and urged him to continue. He understood that the message was touching their minds and hearts and said, "The Spanish Fever came in waves, three in total, and a year later had already abated and eventually finished its course. All public places were closed. People got so hysterical they ran away whenever they spotted a sign of the epidemic. In New York, the police fined anyone who sneezed $50. In Stockholm, the theaters were shut down, and Paris and London looked like ghost towns. The Spanish Fever killed more people in one year than the Black Plague of 1453, which lasted four years. Only the island of Morajo, near the Amazon River, in Brazil, was spared. World renowned doctors have tried to give a plausible explanation, but often their theories contrast with each other."

The people got restless. They began to be suspicious about the authenticity of the information. They began to shout that it was false news and doubted that such immense tragedy if true could happen again. Father Mitango waited until the noise subsided and added, "The Spanish Fever claimed millions of lives at the beginning of the century. Now, there is another epidemic without control. It's a silent killer and it's in our midst."

The spectators looked at each other for an answer. It didn't come. They turned to Father Mitango to hear more about it. "You know what I'm driving at.

The new Spanish Fever has another name and a different source. We call it AIDS. It's a disease that has already wiped out 20 million lives in Africa alone. You and I must defeat this enemy together, hand in hand."

Women and men stretched their arms and held hands. He raised his voice, "Yes, it's good what you are doing, but I don't mean this. There are three waves by which the enemy attacks."

The old people looked around, but didn't see anyone coming. "The first attack comes under the form of infidelity. Remember! The best defense is chastity."

"The second attack comes with drugs. And, do you know who is reaping the profits? The businessmen! Don't think that only the poor and unemployed are the victims, but many, among rich people, resort to them for the purpose of getting high.

"The third attack comes in the form of personal and collective risk. This disease is contagious. Our society has been paying a high price. We must educate the ladies in the streets here that they are contributing to …"

He was unable to finish. A woman threw her shoe at him and hit him right on the nose. The loudspeaker fell on the dusty ground causing a thunderous noise. A driver started his pickup truck and ran at full speed through the tent, smashing everything in its way. At that point, a pandemonium broke loose. People were running in all directions yelling and crying. The police questioned some of them. They accused the demons for wrecking the tent. Obviously, they were not content with the preacher's sermon. Suddenly, they heard a loud noise. The rest of the roof fell flat on the ground. From the street, two truck drivers and two fat ladies approached the site where Father Mitango was. They reproached him sternly and warned him not to get involved again in 'family affairs.' Not content with that, they lifted him up with their greasy hands and threw him in a big barrel and let it roll until it hit the post of a gasoline station. Somehow, the drum ignited and Father Mitango barely escaped from being burned alive.

The gasoline manager pulled him out just in time. The diagnosis was minor burns that would require a month of rest to heal.

On a Monday morning in July, the area where the priest had raised the tent came to life again. People watched Father Mitango and an engineer busy measuring a piece of land on the main square across from the site where all the prostitutes convened to attract their clients. The truck drivers, motel owners, and their cohorts conspired to get rid of him, but they hadn't counted on one thing. About 20 men arrived with picks and shovels to dig the perimeter of the new construction.

Many women were alerted and arrived shortly after, but with a different design in their minds. They were ex-prostitutes, who had prayed to St. Catherine to give them back their dignity. They were married to wealthy men and came to assist a longtime friend to carry out his financial project. Father Mitango planned to build a replica of the church of St. Catherine in Pigalle, Paris, in the red light district across from the Moulin Rouge. With the generosity of the ladies of Mlolongo, Father Mitango was able to accomplish it in the record time of three months. The church had the essentials. It was unpretentious and sober. When it was finished, he called it "San Catherine of Mlolongo." Once it opened, people jammed the church during Mass. Among them, one could see some prostitutes who knelt before the saint, lit candles before the saint's statue or prayed. Occasionally, someone cried.

On the feast of St.Catherine, for the inauguration ceremony, Father Mitango spoke to an attentive congregation. Not a single seat was empty. The pews could accommodate up to 500 people. Most of them felt the beating heat, but they didn't let it bother them. He took the floor, saying "My dear friends, I come to you as a fellow citizen, as a priest, who has been blessed to carry the name of Christ to you and to the rest of our great nation. The king of Zimbabwe has purchased for his wives cars with the value of eighteen million dollars, yet his people are dying like flies in the grip of AIDS. In Malawi, half of the population of twelve million people is on the brink of starvation. These are two of the most dramatic examples of an Africa which is dying slowly and the world watches without sending doctors or medicine to prevent another tragedy like that of 1918."

An old man ventured to raise his bony and weak hand just above his head. He looked frail, but well dressed and determined. Tradition doesn't allow anyone to interrupt a priest during a sermon. Father Mitango smiled and let him speak. "Father, don't the governments realize the role that poverty plays in the spread of HIV? Why does nobody talk about it?."

"I'm talking about it! It's not just this government, but others as well, that are slashing programs that combat AIDS on a global scale. It's common knowledge that mortality rises where there are inadequate health care delivery systems. The existing community resources are not available to the public. Politicians don't seem to care. Where people live below the poverty level, infection soars and spreads quickly."

"Does population have anything to do with the spread of the disease?"

"Of course, it does! Geography also has a great impact on the spread of AIDS. In rural areas, like those in China and India, whatever propaganda they disseminate, people are not getting the necessary medical care. They need to be educated;

otherwise, they are going to lose the war. I'm talking from an experiential perspective and not from literature."

"Is the disease the only problem?" insisted the man. The prelate didn't expect to be engaged in a dialog during a sermon. He said that he would be happy to have a discussion in a public forum, but the church has a different format. However, not to be discourteous, he would take one last question. "These are exceptions that take place only in Africa," he said with a smile. The congregation erupted in a sonorous laughter.

He concluded, "The orphans represent another thorny issue. Zimbabwe accounts for a half million of them, at the present time. But adults are not the only ones to be infected, my brothers and sisters. Children account for 15% of the AIDS cases. You are blessed that some governments are living up to their responsibilities by opening counseling centers. By now, it's no longer taboo to talk about these problems. The capital, Harare, is making strides in that direction. We commend them. Now, the rest of Africa should follow their example and get rid of foolish traditions that are in contrast with medicine."

A politician, with a crooked nose and a ponytail, who displayed more a fact-finding look than devotion, said, "What can people do? It's not their fault. That's the way life is. We realize business people are there to make a buck, but the government has been helping."

The priest was irritated by that interruption. He hesitated a moment, then, he replied, "Give enough incentives to research hospitals and you see the results."

The same man answered, "The government has pumped millions of dollars into research and the hospitals have shown absolutely nothing up to now. It provides funds even to the pharmaceutical companies, but they have discovered no vaccine up to now. Everybody cries poverty."

"We realize that human nature is weak, but we need to invest more if we want to save millions of people affected by this terrible disease."

The politician got annoyed and took a harder position, "Don't you think that priests and ministers of other denominations would do a great service to humanity if they dedicated their activities to the spiritual wellbeing of the people? Leave the health issue to the doctors and to the pharmaceutical industry."

This new challenge bothered Father Mitango. He became red in the face and almost lost his patience. For a few moments, he remained silent, then he replied, "Hear this about the pharmaceutical companies! Many of them are dropping out despite the billions of dollars that have already been invested because of the astronomical research costs. World authorities are hopeless about halting or reversing the spread of a pandemic in the next decade unless we provide additional financial assistance."

"Let the private sector conduct its own researches," responded the same politician.

"Splendid! Nonetheless, non-profit organizations also can't sustain the enormous burden."

"I don't believe it!"

"It's your prerogative."

"Let the Church finance the research. It's rich."

"You are very right! The Church is rich in spirit. Indeed, I have made my own researches, and I have come up with a vaccine valid for all generations."

The man was stunned to hear that news, as were the parishioners. "I know you are longing to find out what it is."

"Yes, we want to know it," they replied, almost in unison.

"My friends, my vaccine is simple and costs nothing."

They looked at each other and laughed loudly. When the ushers restored silence, the priest continued, "My vaccine's name is 'abstinence.'"

Everybody smirked and looked once again at each other with a heavy dose of skepticism.

Father Mitango, unperturbed as usual, continued, "My appeal to the world is: abstain, abstain, abstain. Chastity is the best preservative, the most effective method of curbing and, eventually, eliminating the disease. Even, if they find a cure in the medical field, there is no substitute for a clean life in the pre-and post-marital time."

There was silence. The congregation wasn't sure whether or not he had finished. When they realized that the sermon was over, they began to scream and dance. All the prostitutes, who were present, fell on their knees and cried profusely. It's said that most of them left their vocation the same day. Father Mitango helped them to find an honest job in the community. They proclaimed that it was the brightest day in the history of Mlolongo, Father Mitango's crusade against prostitution and AIDS split the city in half. One side lauded him; another supported the idea of forming a club with the main objective of fighting back at the priest.

Of one thing we are sure. Since that day, many prostitutes attended the morning Mass, lit candles before St. Catherine's statue and even contributed generously to the collection.

Father Mitango launched another project. Whoever wanted to abandon her sinful life, he would help her to find a job and to provide food. His popularity climbed. During the festivals, he joined the crowd eating, drinking and dancing. He loved to bring with him a python on his shoulders. Children ran away at first, then, kept themselves at a distance. Finally, they got used to it, but not entirely. When he wanted to scare them, he grabbed the snake by the neck and put it close to them. They drew back immediately, shouting words of fear.

A lady, who planned to build a skyscraper, was the first to organize hotel owners, truck drivers and cleaning ladies to create an anti-Mitango front. The local economy was sluggish. It began to show signs of recession. The trucks no longer stopped in town, but outside it. The business lady was also losing her shirt on the account of a reduced clientele at her hotel. Undaunted by the criticism coming from the priest, she prepared a feast and arranged a band to play loud music in front of St. Catherine's Church to disrupt the Sunday Mass. She made an effort to bring back in the corral her sheep that had run astray, but it was useless. They had made the choice of a new life and enjoyed new jobs and opportunities. Despite their immoral pasts, a few got engaged within the Christian community; someone found husbands.

The lady masseuse, who claimed that she healed her "patients" from all their psychological problems was in deep water. She suggested to the audience to come up with a plan to revitalize the town and the economy. Some supporters declared to be in favor of the prelate's physical elimination. According to them, he was the cause of all their problems. By taking out the bad apple, peace and prosperity would once again be restored. However, two old men advised against it. The priest could count on many relatives and friends. If the aggressive ladies' party prevailed, bloodshed could possibly ensue, and everyone would flee the town. After endless argumentations, a new force emerged. They called it "the hit and run" party. They reasoned that, by harassing the priest, they would, eventually, force him to abandon the church and sell it.

They hired a dozen young ladies who, prior to the Sunday Mass, were willing to walk up and down the church exposing their breasts. At eight o' clock, the ladies began their promenade. One of the parishioners reacted in an unusual way. He grabbed the hose and sprayed cold water on them. A melee followed and many got hurt. To avert a major confrontation, Father Mitango declared a truce. The ladies stopped appearing in provocative apparel and the hot-tempered parishioners promised not to resort to inappropriate actions. A temporary calm settled in, but it was the calm before the tempest.

The truck drivers were furious. They joined the prostitutes, the business people and drug traffickers in a newly created club called "Lifesavers," where they examined strategies to drive the church out of the town. At the end of a meeting, they reached a consensus to set up ice cream and game stands near St. Catherine. Children could eat and play at ten o'clock on Sunday morning, at Mass time. Somehow, the strategy was initially successful. Children, against their parental intimidation or approval, put their hands on whatever they could get free. Needless to say, the priest was infuriated. He changed the Mass hour, but so did his opponents. This time, it was Father Mitango to change strategy. In fact, he decided to attack them on their terms. He announced that he would offer the same amenities, but only after the celebration of the Mass. This tactic seemed to pay off.

The club responded with some innovations. It organized a series of festivities with music, dance and food twice a week. The church responded with a similar plan. When the Lifesavers realized that the priest was a hard man to deal with, they decided to pass to more drastic actions. A truck driver proposed to destroy the church by driving his vehicle through it. The priest got wind of it, and built massive cylinders of concrete around the church's perimeter and connected them by steel chains.

Young ladies used to spend evenings with Father Mitango when they had finished their chores at home. It wasn't unusual for some of them to depart from the rectory at late hours. To this day, nobody knows what they said or did, but, the local newspapers wasted no time in providing spicy innuendos. Interestingly enough, the satire against him turned out in his favor among the prostitutes. They too expressed the wish to spend a evening in his company.

The Lifesavers, dissatisfied by the turn of the events, conceived of tightening the noose around the priest's neck. With the assistance of their intermediaries, the bank doubled the interest rate on the church's mortgage. Anything flowing in and out of the church compound passed through a rigorous fraudulent control system to financially suffocate it. In the stores, in the markets, anywhere the church bought something, the price was purposely jacked up.

The priest wasn't the type to give up easily. He gave orders to his aids to purchase the supplies and do other types of business in the neighboring town. He applied and obtained the same loan from another bank and paid off the debt by the end of the year. The bank's president couldn't believe how he was able to get that much money in a relatively short period of time.

The club realized that it was being outsmarted, got furious and planned a revenge, but its plan was foiled. After another impasse of a relative calm, the club decided to hire a Muslim martyr. He was a bum and drunkard. They promised him ten thousand dollars to his family if he would explode himself in the church. As for his personal reward, he would find seventy virgins once he entered into the kingdom of heaven. Both parties agreed, but at the time of the operation, the self-proclaimed hero got nervous and missed the correct trigger on his belt of explosives. A couple of young men saw him and subdued him immediately. He got a five year jail term and, when they released him, the priest offered him a custodian job. It's said that the man gradually saw the light.

The government, alerted by a parishioner, sent a crew of federal police to disband the club and to warn them of severe punishment if they pursued their objective of disruption and destruction. The club continued to operate secretly and to discredit the priest. Indeed, much could be said about the schemes they devised to shoot down the church, but it would be too long to report here.

Father Mitango was a visionary. He didn't sit idle. With his charisma, broad smile, and a predisposition to mingle with the simple people, especially in social events, won a great victory in his native land.

# THE CABARET

The cabaret Mau-Mau was the main attraction in Mlolongo. Every evening, starting at 11:00 p.m., showgirls would exhibit their artistic talents, disregarding the dress code. At the end of each performance, they would mix with the audience and share some drinks. The auditorium was packed seven days a week and there were times when truck drivers were denied entrance for lack of seats. Most of the time, they left in disgust and gave the manager a piece of their mind. In some cases, they became violent and threw beer bottles against the doors or windows. The police, which was stationed around the block, had to intervene occasionally, even lock them up for the night.

In August, the cabaret looked particularly glamorous. Colorful neon lights illuminated the whole area and the sidewalks were swarming with the "ladies." The cabaret sponsored fireworks that gave different bright and vivid colors to the sky for the first two weeks of the month from midnight to one o'clock in the morning. Hardly anyone slept in those days, such were people's expectations.

One of those nights, the cabaret announced a special attraction. A famous singer was going to perform. The soft breeze mitigated the day's sweltering temperature. From time to time, a disheveled truck driver would show up on the sidewalk, grab a "lady" and drag her away. Usually, there was no resistance on the part of the female companion. That evening, across from the cabaret, a yellow Maserati stopped. A distinguished gentleman, white gloves on his hands, opened the door and an elegant woman in her fifties stepped out, placing her hand on an assistant's arm.

The lady was tall and slim. Her long black hair flowed gently on her bony shoulders. Her smile was captivating, as was her Portuguese accent. She had spent a short period of time in jail, where she decided to study. Eventually, she graduated from college and upon her release, she decided to "retire" from the sidewalk and engage in a business activity that made her both rich and famous. Her name was Pretty Angel.

Her bodyguards jumped out of the car and flanked her, glancing rapidly in all directions. Such a visitor couldn't leave the cabaret personnel indifferent. They kept on staring at every movement she made. The bodyguards had their work cut out to keep curious onlookers of all ages from crowding around the luxurious car. The temptation of plucking out a "souvenir" from the car was too enticing. The lady's visit lasted five minutes. She was satisfied with what she had seen and left the bystanders guessing.

The following day, Pretty Angel was already at work. She brought a lawyer along to negotiate the purchase of the building across from the cabaret. Both teams sat down and reached a tentative agreement. The transaction was finalized in a matter of days.

Pretty Angel first renovated the ground floor, giving it a classical look. At the entrance, she added four columns and a double Roman arch, a palm tree at each side. The display window was spacious and well decorated with exotic flower paintings and women dressed in silky clothes that left nothing to the imagination.

The second floor was turned into a large oval conference room with a huge table and wooden chairs. The floor was covered by Turkish tapestry. The main chair at the head of the table was arranged like a throne. A crown lay on the table, to be used only during special conferences.

One month went by and Pretty Angel opened up a clothes boutique she called "Tramputique." What mostly attracted the attention of the clientele were the gowns which opened on the front and on the back with a zipper, and lovely cotton shirts with a deep V shape on the chest. Another center of attraction were the high heeled shoes in various styles. A wide selection of intimate clothes could be seen in a separate window. All the merchandise had the brand name of the most famous Italian designers.

At the grand opening, Pretty Angel provided food and drinks galore. Musicians played all sorts of African music and some visitors improvised local dances. The main visitors were showgirls or who were interested in the new fashions. The rest consisted of smelly truck drivers, unshaven and dirty looking, who were present with the idea of browsing around in search of a gift to give to their favored "lady." No doubt, others, young and old, flocked the boutique with the sole intent of satisfying their appetite for food.

Pretty Angel had many projects up her sleeves. She invited all prostitutes, active and inactive, to attend a meeting at the oval office on a Saturday afternoon at sunset. She opened up the meeting by saying, "Wonderful, indispensable and proud beauties of Mlolongo, today my dream came true. This is a new avenue to reap additional revenue for those who have an extra luster on their faces. I mean business is coming to town. I give you my business."

The windows were open and the voice was carried to the streets. A truck driver, standing on the sidewalk, shouted, "Monkey business!" Pretty Angel disregarded the uncalled-for comment and continued, "I have already hired fifteen saleswomen and I plan to add ten more, who are willing to work as models." The hall resounded with exclamations of joy and most of the guests raised their hands. The speaker acknowledged their ovation and said, "There are plenty of opportunities here to increase your wages. To legitimate our enterprise, we are going to invite the mayor and the local priest to bless our premises. This is an offer that neither one of them can refuse." At that moment, the audience in the oval office burst into laughter. When it subsided, an old lady, who attended the meeting more from curiosity than the desire to find a job, raised her hand and said, "Father Mitango will never accept this type of invitation."

"Perhaps, he will, for me...." She whispered the last words looking straight in her face. The rest of the women were listening attentively. The chairman's comment had a beneficial impact on them and they instantly responded with a frantic display of approval. The main speaker waited for the noise to abate and concluded, "Ladies, money talks!"

As with a single heart and mind, they responded in unison, "That's for sure!"

The orator appeared satisfied at that point; therefore, she thought of wrapping up the meeting. A bodyguard handed a note to her. Upon reading it, she quieted down the crowd and said, "Before you leave, I'm going to 'fire a shot that will be heard around the world.' Everyone quieted down and waited for the chair to draw a gun. Reading their minds she said, "No, no, no! What I meant is that here and now I'm going to create a "Free Women Union. Whoever is an honest worker can join it." Everybody raised her hand. Pretty Angel motioned them to exercise self control and said, "This Union will protect your rights; will work for a better wage and it will establish a pension for you all." She didn't even finish when a pandemonium broke out. Screams of exhilaration filled the oval room and they almost mobbed the chairwoman so high was their enthusiasm. The meeting was adjourned and the bodyguards quickly escorted her to another room.

The news of what went on at the boutique reached Father Mitango's ears. He made a brief statement to his congregation, "It's all we need now, the Union of the Lost Souls! Who knows what tomorrow will bring us ... Maybe a Union of AIDS Victims, a Union of Thieves and Criminals ... What this place needs is a revolution of faith."

The days dragged on lazily, but not for Father Mitango, who was constantly active teaching the catechism, visiting the sick, inviting the poor to his church, fighting against immorality and organizing a Catholic Lady Club. He sat on the veranda on a Friday evening, looking tired. His aids suggested that he go to bed early and have a good night of rest. Before he withdrew, he asked the custodian to lock the door.

In the sky, a slice of melon illuminated the earth. The desert sand saturated the air, and rendered breathing difficult. Even the dogs sneezed in the streets and the townfolks covered their faces with cloths. Occasionally, the distant roaring of a lion reached the ears of those living in the suburbs. The trucks coming from inland screamed, coughed and stopped altogether for a pause. In front of the cabaret a truck driver was having an animated discussion with a woman. Suddenly, he grabbed her by the arm and pulled her away from the sidewalk. She disentangled from the grip and said, "I told you that I made up my mind. I am disgusted with you, with the cabaret and with this life."

"Since when?" the truck driver responded indignantly.

"I have been pondering it for quite a while. Now, I want to join the ranks of Father Mitango."

"What?" exclaimed surprised the man.

"You heard me."

"You mean you are joining the club of that greasy ball, lady-man, clown preacher?"

"He is a decent priest."

"And I guess he is going to provide you with bread and butter, right?"

"It's no longer a question of money, but of values, of conscience, of our future."

"Listen to her!" said the man in a derisive tone. "Did he convert you too?"

"What is wrong with being converted to a new life?"

The young lady's talk was beyond the man's comprehension. He started to laugh loudly and made an attempt to kiss her. She pulled away, "I'm out of this vicious circle, out of the Cabaret, out of the modeling business. My whole mind is polluted. I need some oxygen."

The truck driver became serious, "Hear me! You walk out of my circle and you lose protection. The oxygen is right here in my pocket."

"I don't need it anymore."

"Listen to this newborn Christian. You are all drugged up with this religion. I'm the doctor. Come to me and I'll heal you," and he tried to touch her.

"Keep your hands off me!' She turned around and fled.

"I suggest you think it over. Come to me or you'll be sorry," shouted the driver.

"Don't talk to me like that or I'll call the police."

"You will, eh?"

A couple of rough men were watching the scene from across street, in front of the boutique. The girl walked away at a fast pace. The truck driver pulled a cellular from his pocket and dialed a number. The girl increased the speed. There was no doubt in her mind that she was being followed. In front of the church's main gait, she looked back to ascertain that she was secure. A nightly silence reigned around the area. Suddenly, a scream lacerated the air. The lights of the rectory were lit. The priest dashed out of the kitchen in shorts. He didn't have pajamas. He reached the front door of the church and found the girl's hand still holding the handle. He talked to her, but she didn't respond. He touched her pulse. It was still. He shook it, trying to revive her. He quickly gave her the Extreme Unction, "*In Nomine Patris et Filii et Spiritus Sancti, Amen.*" His assistants sent for a doctor. One of them said, "She was such a nice soul!" The priest didn't move his eyes from the dead body. At the sound of the police car, he stood up and said, "*Requiescat in pace.*"

The police called for a pick up truck to take the body to the mortician. The examiner arrived and pronounced her dead. The police tried to find witnesses. Nobody stepped forward. The leading officer asked Father Mitango if he had a statement to make. Without turning around, he said, "Yes, I have." He faced the officer and said, "I will fight these criminals to the end of my days." The officer was shocked to hear that comment. He stood at attention and gave the order to his police subordinates to remove the dead body immediately.

# BRIGITTE

The news of the girl's death plunged the town into a fearful mood and shook up the prostitutes, who feared for their lives. Father Mitango continued undeterred his rhetoric against immorality. He ignited the conscience of people against evil wherever he went. As a result of his relentless evangelical work, that part of Africa infested with AIDS began to show signs of progress and his name spread all over Africa and beyond with an incredible rapidity. China kept a close eye on him and so did Rome.

In the evening, Father Mitango rested on the veranda. He loved to watch the last part of the sun setting on the horizon. A Norwegian reporter, by the name of Brigitte V., heard about him and came to interview him. She worked for Oslo's main newspaper, *Melting Ice*. Her beauty and her smile were stunning. She was tall and blonde with blue eyes. Her manners were elegant. The prelate agreed to speak to her only on condition that she would describe the plight of the sick people and the terrible price that Africa was paying in terms of human lives.

The two met at eight o' clock in the evening. A relatively cool breeze brushed the patio, where they were sitting, and made the conversation more enjoyable. An aid to the priest prepared tea for her, while the priest opted for a cold beer.

"So, you have come all the way from Oslo," began the priest.

"I go to any spot of the globe where the game is."

"The game is unhealthy here."

"Unfortunately, it's not confined here. My country too accounts for thousands of HIV-positive cases."

"Why did you come to me?"

"Your success has reached our shores and we would like to learn from your experience."

"I'm not endowed with a medical panacea. My prescription is abstention from sexual activities until marriage. I have no magic potions to mix."

"Forgive me for my boldness, but aren't you being a bit unrealistic? Do you, actually, believe that prostitution is the cause of all human misfortunes?.."

"Certainly! To answer your question more accurately, I would say that it's people who create the problem. In some Eastern European countries (Bulgaria, Rumania, Russia) and in South East Asia (Viet Nam, Cambodia, Thailand), unscrupulous pimps create sex trade centers. They recruit young girls for local houses or lure them in foreign countries as prospective secretaries. It's an economic boom for those areas, but the price they pay and we pay is inconceivable. Children have become the focus of this as yet unforeseeable catastrophe."

"Children.... You seem to be obsessed by children."

"I ought to be! I'm a priest, a missionary, a representative of Christ."

"Don't you think it's a lost battle? We are dealing with humans, not objects."

"From a human perspective, I agree with you. It's hard for a young man to restrain his sexual appetite. But man isn't a beast. He is a rational being capable of controlling himself. If he doesn't exercise restraints, then there is no difference between him and the animals." He looked up to heaven and continued, "The Creator made a distinction between the animal and human kingdom. Let us not mix them up. The real problem consists in our deliberate search for short cuts, all the time, in whatever we do. The long road is tortuous and only a few are willing to take it. Liberalism is going to kill all of us if we don't control our behavior."

"How can you persuade your people to change their lifestyle?"

"It's more than that. We must shake up our consciences."

"Do you think it's within our potential?"

"We can do almost everything if we really want to. We are dealing here with suffering, life and death."

"AIDS spreads like wildfire more in impoverished areas."

"Of course! Poor people are mostly uneducated. They don't realize the seriousness of the danger that looms in the corner until it strikes them. This doesn't mean that some rich people don't succumb to the temptation."

"And you, are you tempted?"

"No comment."

Father Mitango didn't elaborate. The journalist was still writing notes, when they heard a big bang. The back door sprang wide open and five masked men surrounded them and ordered them to follow them. The journalist was terrified by the presence of the armed men. The priest was surprised, but not scared. The men had en emblem of the moon on their turbans and spoke Arabic. They pointed Kalashnikovs, Russian machine guns, at their heads and said not to make any noise or any attempt to escape. They would have not hesitated to shoot. They allowed the lady to carry the hand bag she had with her, while they suggested to the priest, to pack up some intimate clothes.

The captors left the rectory through the back door, avoiding the people standing on guard at the front entrance. They boarded a black Sedan and drove away at high speed. The sun was getting pale.

Two hours passed, and the masked men stopped at an airstrip in the desert flanked by long lines of palm trees. Only a barracks stood on one side of the runway. Two men came out of it and exchanged a few words with the pilot of a small private plane waiting for them and pointed to an old pick up truck resting behind the shed. The lady understood the danger and, without looking at her companion prisoner, began to shed copious tears. The captors too were aware of their own lives being on the line.

In the distance, the jungle was about to come alive. They heard the lion's roaring and other animals' cries. The rest was a picture of solitude and silence. The sky was clear, except for a few clouds overhead, and a few more clustered at the horizon as if they were gathering for a meeting. This time the sky rumbled. The crew attended to their immediate needs and boarded the truck. They didn't want to be caught in the rain. They tried to avoid cities. They stopped at gasoline stations, bought some food and beverages and continued their trip. Three of them were twelve or thirteen years old, who had started their perverted lifestyle in Mlolongo. A gang leader gradually cajoled them into his ranks by offering them money, at first, then hashish, cocaine and heroine for free. After a while, he trained them to steal and forced them to sell drugs. If they refused, he threatened to burn their parents' houses. In this new environment, they were completely at the mercy of the leader and of the drugs. Their eyes were glazed and they appeared to be lost somewhere in space. Occasionally, they injected in their arms some kind of drug. They held Kalashnikovs in their arms and could be brutal if circumstances demanded it. They smoked often and the aroma made the priest and the reporter a bit dizzy.

The following is the account of the odyssey that the journalist wrote daily during their ordeal. She kept the diary secret for years before publishing it in a women's magazine. We pass it over to the reader because the authenticity and the accuracy are uncontestable:

"We traveled through deserts and mountains for 35 days, by plane, by truck or on foot. When the truck broke down, someone arrived with a car. The captors talked constantly on the phone. We lost many nights of sleep because we moved in darkness. My sneakers wore through after a week and my feet began to bleed. Fortunately, they got me another pair of shoes, stronger, but not comfortable. At night, it was cold. They provided us a blanket with the help of some shepherds we met on our way. We never knew our geographical location. They hardly talked to us. The priest was stoic. He was exhausted like me, but never showed it. He cracked jokes to keep me away from depression. He was always hopeful that the Vatican had alerted every African country of our disappearance. I think they also asked for help from the KGB and CIA. All the people we met must have been accomplices. They spoke in low voices and covered their mouths with their hands. The only time they left us alone was when we went to the bathroom. What bathroom? We went behind a dune in the desert, rock or brush in the mountain. Fortunately, I had brought two rolls of bathroom tissues. In a few occasions, we stopped at waterfalls. Those were the only instances in which we were able to take a bath and scrape off the dust that had stuck on our bodies like hard crusts of bread. The cold water had such a chilling effect on me that I forgot about the hunger.

After a month of peregrinations, we arrived in Yemen. We saw the sign. The cellular phones rang much more frequently. They fed us with whatever food the shepherds passed to them. We arrived in the region of Marib, the site of the legendary reign of the queen of Sheba. We didn't know the reason of the abduction. We presumed that they wanted to kill the priest or even make a deal with the Vatican. Their aim was to get rid of the priest from Mlolongo and destroy the church. If the Church's hierarchy would have accepted the deal, they would have freed us. This seemed the most credible conjecture and which turned out to be the most veritable. They took me along because they thought I was going to write favorably about the priest and the spiritual progress he had initiated. They considered me a western spy. After 35 days, I lost thirty pounds. The priest grew a long beard. He looked emaciated, but didn't lose his sense of humor.

In the last five days of our captivity, they put us in a hut in a mountain stronghold and left us alone most of the night. We understood that some sorts of negotiations were brewing between the crew and the tribe, which offered us hospitality. One morning, a government official showed up to talk to them. Evidently, they had been tracking us down. He was calm and made them understand the futility of running. The young men were about to pull the trigger of their gun, but the oldest members held them back. In Yemen, there is a death penalty for the abductors. The Minister of Tourism announced on the radio that kidnapping is bringing the country on the edge of collapse due to the fact that it thrives on tourism. He went on saying that it also damages the image of the country around the world and the reputation of his people.

To show their muscles, the government forces surrounded the area and were ready more than once to attack, particularly when the captors broke off the negotiations and stated without equivocation that they were going to kill us. The Norwegian authorities and the Vatican asked the government of Sana'a to use caution and diplomacy. Within the stronghold, we moved to another location with the headlights turned off. We found hospitality in another house. They offered us tea and some fruit. We felt relaxed and encouraged when we saw the boys moving to eat in another room. They placed their Kalashnikovs on the floor and started to devour whatever they could put their hands on.

The only one who didn't place the Kalashnikov on the floor, but held it on his knees during the frugal meal, was the leader. He was about 60 and had a cyst as big as a golf ball on his forehead.. He wore a beret a la Che Guevara and dressed the jalabia. He had lost most of his teeth in a fall during a jail escape two years earlier. In the last week, he moved us constantly at night. We walked without a lantern. The only light came from the moon or from the cigarettes they smoked. At times, we slept on the bare earth, covered only with the blanket they brought along. We heard shots in the distance. The echo got closer. We were afraid that the government forces would engage the captors and they would kill us. I told them that I was a Muslim, but being white, they didn't believe me. They hid us in a cavern and warned us not to make any noise.

The Yemenite security forces were tightening their grip around the area. The captors got irritated and warned them that they would kill us if they didn't stop their strangling tactic. Unconfirmed reports from the tribe and from the legal authorities caused such a havoc that the situation might have exploded at any time.

The new day arrived. The captors led us out of the cavern. We couldn't stand the daylight. We had to cover our eyes. Gradually, we got used to it, but we were exhausted. We had hardly slept. We saw an airplane flying overhead. The boys pointed the machine guns at us and ordered us to lie down. We were afraid that the pilot would drop a bomb and wipe us all out. A tribesman, who appeared to have some sort of authority, maybe due to his old age, arrived with a box in his hands. The crew bowed and showed signs of respect. He brought cheese, milk and bread. We ate it with great appetite. The leader's cellular rang. I could understand that he was talking about a ransom. He didn't trust us, and distanced himself from us. He returned shortly after to inform us that we had to follow him.

Against a palm tree, a young woman of about 25 was wailing. Her boyfriend tried to persuade her to stop, but she kept up even more her mourning. A small crowd of shepherds slowly gathered. From what I could understand from their gestures and, later, from our captors, the young man refused to marry his girlfriend. She was pregnant and he wanted to abort. She would not hear of it. She picked up the gallon at her feet and spread the liquid on her body. Everyone was staring at her. The air was saturated with fear. She drew from her pocket a lighter and ignited her body. Her boyfriend fled.

We marched to another hamlet. I kept on looking backward to the flames that were consuming the young body. The smoke rose in different dark figures. The stench was horrible. The leader stopped us 100 yards from the first hut. A great deal of commotion was going on around it. A father had contracted a marriage for his daughter with an older man from the city. He was missing a canine tooth on the row, was bald and obese. He was a distant relative of the royal family. The girl was supposed to meet with his parents and relatives. At the beginning, we thought it was a dispute over the livestock. As the bickering continued, the man slapped his daughter several times. She ran inside and came right back drenched with a smelly liquid. In her hand, she carried a torch. Suddenly, the noise subsided. The jaws of the bystanders were visibly tight, their eyes fixed on the girl. Her father's face became like red coal. He had already previewed the drama. He went inside to get his shotgun. When he returned, he found a ball of fire. I started to shake. The priest did his best to calm me down.

We had no time to waste. We walked quickly for about twenty minutes until the leader stopped the caravan. He pushed us in a small cavern where we spent the last two nights. They covered the entrance with a huge rock and found refuge in the vicinity of it.

The first night, we tried to sleep, but explosions and shots didn't allow us to close our eyes. It was cold inside. We huddled in our blankets and talked almost the whole night. In the darkness, we couldn't see, but only touch each other. We had no matches, no flashlights, nothing. We were prepared to die. As a Muslim, I didn't accept what the priest was telling me about his religion. We do believe in Christ, but only as secondary Prophet, not as the Son of God. Allah is One and Mohammed is His Prophet. He shook his head in a sign of discouragement and said, "My religion came from Christ 2,000 years ago. All other religions are either a copy of it or false." I must admit I didn't know what to answer.

We discussed our irreconcilable differences for a long time. Neither one of us was going to give in, so we shifted topic and talked about human life. "Why don't you get married?" I asked him.

"The Catholic religion forbids us."

"What do you think?" He touched his back pocket. He had forgotten something. He had a small candle and two matches. He lit it. We could see each other. The echo of our words reverberated throughout the rocky prison. The flame sent our shadows on the walls. They looked dark and ugly. After forty days of captivity in the desert, we had developed a frank and solid friendship. He looked at me and said, "I have been blasting my brains since my early days in the seminar."

"Don't you think that it's ridiculous to expect a man to live without a woman?"

"It's a long tradition. You can't break it."

"Does it make it right?"

"Married life entails, per se, many sacrifices. The family is the top priority for a married man or woman. I have no such worries. I go as I please to hospitals, church, rectory. I don't have to report to my wife or children. I'm married to the church. You Muslims don't understand the beauty of celibacy. We priests give our whole life to the Church. It's our faith. We have to live up to rigorous standards. That makes us what I call beautifully different." He seemed to fight within himself what every man fights for. He weighed each word before he spoke it.

"Don't you wish to have a woman that waits for you; cleans the house; prepares the meals; advises you; cares for you in times of sickness and gives you children? Isn't this the beauty of the union? Doesn't God want this?" I waited for him to answer, but he remained silent.

He shook his head and said, "In theory, the rationale is valid, but ..." The flame trembled. One of us, I don't remember, touched the stone on which we laid. We took turns in warming our hands against it. I said, "I guess you are not interested in this topic."

"It's not that I don't want to discuss it. We have no choice."

"I realize that, but who made the rules?"

"The Church has the power. Christ delegated it to us."

"He told you not to get married?"

"Didn't your Church establish certain rules that govern the faithful?"

"Yes, but they are human. Everybody can submit to them without problem."

"Why, ours are inhuman?" His smile didn't convince me. I scratched my head. He looked at me and broke out in a loud laughter. The eco resounded against and above the rocky walls and came back to him. I got up and went next to the entrance. I placed my ear on the circular flat rock that covered the entrance. I didn't hear anything. I sat next to the candle again. His face shone. His eyes were semi-closed as if they were about to sleep.

"Look! Why do you want to deny that this rigorous religious tenet on celibacy isn't for every man. Don't you agree that's discrimination? Not allowing a person to follow his own nature?"

"Nobody forces you to join the army of single people."

"You still insist on the logic of purity."

"I have been trying to explain to you in the past hour that these are the values of the Church. Take them or leave them."

"You are not following me. We are discussing a concept. Man wasn't created to be alone."

"Will you concede that everybody is the same?"

"I do. Then, those who are predisposed to celibacy should go for priesthood."

"And those who have a vocation and can't respect celibacy?"

I couldn't reply.

The daylight came and woke us up. We had to move again. Our captors led us up to a hill with rare vegetation and a small pond infested with snakes. I was frightened to death seeing those animals swarming on each other. The priest didn't show any emotion. He touched my right arm and with his head told me to go on. They ordered us to find refuge under a line of palm trees. The sun was hammering and the heat was baking the stones. I was visibly uncomfortable and tired.

A group of unknown people showed up and engaged in discussions with the leader who didn't show any interest in me. He was concerned about the negotiations going on. The group left abruptly and disappeared behind the dunes. Finally, the leader decided to take us among the rocks, which provided more security.

A shepherd brought us some food and water. I grabbed the goat skin container with the water and drank it all. The priest remained with his hands upward waiting for me to pass him the precious liquid. He didn't complain. His lips were dry. A white line was developing on them. I felt so ashamed that I gave him my food ration. His body demanded it more than mine. The shepherd pushed us to a mud house where we were supposed to stay the night. A man inside acted as our host. He had gentle manners. He welcomed us and invited us to sit. The walls were covered with graffiti. We could only decipher a few words. In one place, it said, "Allah, help me." On the other side, we read, "The one who cures you, will kill you." I shivered and got closer to the priest. I didn't understand what they meant. Only later, I captured the significance of the cryptic words. We were expecting bread and water. The man, instead of satisfying our needs, talked about things that not even our captors could make heads or tails of. They made gestures among themselves indicating that the man had lost his reason. In fact, the host motioned us to follow him to another room, where he pulled a cord tied on the floor and lifted up five planks held together by nails. I almost fainted. There was the body of his mother who had died long ago. He used to visit the tomb every day, and bring flowers to her. He uttered fragments of a mystical delirium, "I chased out the enemy of the human race, and "I'm the deliverer of mankind." On the floor, where his mother's tomb was, he left a written testament, "I was still attached to her womb. I didn't want to be independent, free. That scared me. I couldn't walk alone." We found out later that the man for years had forged his mother's signature on pension checks. We were nauseated and lost any desire to eat for the time being. We perceived the captors' malcontent and one of them was ready to pull the trigger on the shepherd if it were not for the leader, who had other plans in his mind, and cautioned him not to let his emotions prevail. At that point, we got the sensation that our kidnappers were acting on the orders of druglords, who had some sinister designs for the priest. As for myself, I couldn't come up with any rational explanation of my role in the whole story. I was only a journalist.

With the daylight, a man who spoke fluent English joined us and informed us that he would fly us to South Arabia and then back. I asked him, "Why?"

"We are going to Hajj', Mecca, or maybe to the last stage of it, called "Mina."

The priest tried to find out the reason for it, "I have no intention of watching pilgrims launching three stones against the three posts that represent the devil."

"How do you know that? You are a Catholic priest."

"I'll also tell you that this rite commemorates an episode that occurred on Mount Moria. The devil didn't want Abraham to sacrifice his son Isaac. The Patriarch grabbed some stones and threw them at him."

"It was Ishmael."

"Muslims don't agree on this."

"You have an encyclopedic mind. Tell me, if someone is old or sick and can't take the trip to the holy city of Mecca, then, what?"

"It's common sense that if they can't, somebody else will do it for them."

"Everyone has to go to Mecca?"

"According to your religion, yes ... It's called the fifth column or pillar. If you have the economic means and are in good health, it's a commandment."

"And what is the purpose of the pilgrimage?"

"As Catholics went to Rome during the Jubilee Year for the indulgence, so the Muslims take on the trip to purify their souls from sins."

"How many stages are there?"

"Seven."

"Why is that?"

"As Catholics during the Holy Week do the Stations of the Cross, so the Muslims commemorate the seven stages that the Prophet Mohammed undertook."

"I can see that you are very prepared on the Koran."

"How come you are not familiar with it?"

"I was trying to test you."

"That wasn't nice."

"Let me say this. It appears that you know more than I do even in my religion. Now I realize why priests are celibate. They need time to master knowledge."

Upon hearing the word "celibate," Father Mitango stopped talking and his face got serious. I smirked.

The plane arrived. We were ready to board it when the phone in the cockpit rang. The call lasted about three minutes. The pilot turned to us and said, "The trip has been canceled."

"Why? I'm Muslim. I would like to go."

The pilot turned toward me surprised that a European was Muslim. He waited to recollect his thoughts and said, "There has been a tragedy at Mina, outside of Mecca."

"What kind of tragedy?"

"On the Jamarat Bridge, clumsy pilgrims caused a stampede. Everyone wanted to get closer to the pillar and hit it. According to South Arabian news report there are 354 dead and more than 300 wounded."

"How is it possible to die just trying to hit a pillar? I suppose that's what makes people believe. Was this a single incident in the history of the pilgrimage to the Mecca?"

He shook his head and frowned, "About twenty years ago, 400 Iranian pilgrims died. In 1990, more than 1,000 people died, suffocated in a gallery, but still others went. Is this faith or stupidity? I don't know. In the last fifteen years, there have been four tragedies. Just in 2004, 250 pilgrims died for the same stupid reason. How much longer shall we go on making the same mistakes?"

The priest was listening. The pilot, not hearing any objection added, "This time, what made it worse, was the determination (or stubbornness) of the pilgrims to pursue their objective even in the face of the tragedy. I honestly begin to have my doubts about my religion. It's not the pillar that saves us, but our deeds; how we behave with others; what we harbor in our hearts. The rest is lack of practicality, of realism. When religion reaches this level, it becomes a drug."

We were stunned. My faith began to dwindle like a flame in the wind. I was going to ask him something else, but our captors arrived and took us back. The pilot stopped at the foot of the plane's short ladder and looked toward us. I only had the chance to wave goodbye to him.

In the evening, they brought us back to the same cave, They gave us two candles and a box of matches and left. I stood with my ear next to the big, circular stone that covered the entrance. I could hear a lot of commotion going on. We had to wait and see. Fortunately, this time they gave us also some wood.

We made a fire and warmed ourselvese. To keep our minds busy, we kept on talking. I started, "If you were not a priest, neither one of us would be a hostage."

He hesitated a few instants and said, "We must pray, my friend, pray." I looked at him. At least, he sounded optimistic.

"I think this is our last night. Either they free us tomorrow, or we will meet in heaven."

"Easy, lady! The Vatican isn't being idle," the priest tried to reassure me.

"My family has no leverage in this matter."

"Be patient and, when you return to your country, you can write many articles about our detention. You will go on vacation and resume your activity as a journalist."

"And you will continue with your life of a faked celibate."

"Wait a minute!"

"Let me tell you something, Father Mitango. I'm a journalist by profession and I know more about you than you think."

The priest looked at her perplexed. She continued, "Why all of you, who can't reconcile your carnal passion with celibacy, don't get married? In that way, you find peace in yourself, and people will respect you more. Take off your mask."

"What mask are your referring to?"

"You know very well the type of mask I'm referring to. I tell you, I have more respect for that priest who left the church and got married."

"Which one?"

"That priest whose temptation for a woman was greater than the passion for Christ. It happened in Sicily, in a poor neighborhood, where the police chase the drug-traffickers. And the children, well trained by their parents, stoned the officers. The bishop tried to justify this event to the lack of experience and too much socialization. No one disputes the rationalization behind it, but it's utopian to expect in our modern society that a young priest lives separated from the flock."

"It's possible that he entered the seminary too young. It can happen. It could be an isolated case."

"Nonsense! It was premeditated. He said goodbye to the parish and never returned."

"His marriage is invalid without the Church's dispensation, not to count the automatic excommunication. Only the civil matrimony counts for him."

"Don Mitango, you call that an isolated case? According to the Vatican, 36,000 priests have abandoned their mission in the last 36 years. Foundations which deal with the problem go even further back. They claim that there may be more than 100,000. In the years, 1976–1977 alone, between 2,000 and 3,000 priests asked for dispensation."

"The Pope is the only one who can concede it, and the time involved is long. I'm not aware of anyone receiving it up to now."

"What makes the case even worse is that priesthood stops at marriage. In other words, the celibate and priesthood form an indissoluble knot. Are we kidding? This isn't freedom."

"Freedom from what and to what?" asked the priest a bit irritated. Then he added, "If the priest can prove that he was forced to study for priesthood, or that any other form of coercive force was applied, his investiture would be declared invalid. It's not easy to prove it." He took the time to think and continued, "You don't have these problems in your Church because the Iman can have up to four wives. What a nice way of circumventing marital obligations!"

"I don't believe in that either. I want a man only for myself."

"You like a marriage of convenience, half way between Catholicism and Islam?"

"No, I'm simply arguing that God gave the most beautiful gift to humanity: freedom. It doesn't justify the authoritative action of a pontiff to change it arbitrarily."

Father Mitango, shook his head. He was losing patience. He said, "The Magisterium of the Church has determined that celibacy is a fundamental part of priesthood and some priests may not make the road to chastity."

"Then, they should stay out of it!"

He looked at me as if I said something bizarre. He muttered a few unperceivable words. He rephrased himself, this time clearly, "If the candidate is stirred by real vocation, he should be able to stand up to the temptation of getting married and, if he can't take the life of celibacy, he should not enter in the seminary in the first place."

"You are denying to yourself that we are human beings and, therefore, subject to change. A young man may have all the good intentions in the world when he enters the seminary. He may still be chaste by the time he becomes priest, then, a beautiful girl comes by. If he has deep convictions, he can continue his life undisturbed. However, if the subject realizes that he is weak, he should quit for the Church's sake and for his own. His initial good intentions have not withstood the challenge. What is wrong with this? Why do you want to deny this basic principle of nature? Is my logic preposterous? Am I speaking an alien's language? Why do mortals want to impose rules which don't spring from divine source?"

The priest listened without interrupting. He was exhausted. I was in the same shoes, but we had to kill time to survive. We spent most of the night talking and we didn't know what to expect at dawn. Finally, he said, "How beautiful it is to be true to oneself and to God! How great it is to live in purity!" He spelled out the last two sentences in a monosyllabic fashion, lay his head down and closed his eyes. Mine did too. The candle was about to die out. I raised the blanket and lay next to him.

The daylight was celebrated with gunfire that lasted for almost an hour. We woke up, but couldn't see each other. We didn't have any more candles. The sun was opening its way through some holes at the entrance of the cave and I could see some sparse clouds floating in the air. Our dungeon was a surreal picture of fear and unpredictability. We murmured words that I promised not to ever report. As the gunfire abated, we heard dogs barking and human voices. This time, they were not those of our captors. The flat stone screeched. It moved slightly, then, it rolled. The police introduced us to a Vatican emissary, who was on the scene to assist us.

They took us directly to the hospital for a checkup. The doctors kept us for three days under observation and released us. We had been hostages for forty days. The ordeal was over. Another cloud was appearing on the horizon of our lives, much more serious than the captivity. The radio announced a statement from the Ministry of the Interior. He stated that anyone involved in the foreign hostages plan and execution would face the death penalty.

The Yemenite authorities offered unconditional health care and two months of paid vacation to Father Mitango. He stayed only four more days to regain his strength. A Vatican envoy assisted him during the brief convalescence to ascertain his safety.

I decided to leave on the same day of my freedom despite the fact that I needed additional time to re-establish my physical and emotional conditions. Before departure, I hugged Father Mitango and whispered something in his ear. He was startled. His face became like the color of wax. He attempted to spell out a word or two. He couldn't. He fell on the chair and closed his eyes. I looked at him with a sense of compassion and human understanding. I had the feeling that I would never see him again. A few tears made their way down my cheeks. I sobbed. He touched my hands and held them tight until the Vatican emissary motioned to me that it was time to leave.

# THE CHASTITY VOW

My dear reader, the diary of the Norwegian journalist ends here. Upon her return to Oslo she resumed her normal life. Two days later, she didn't feel well. She experienced stomach problems. She thought that dehydration and malnutrition during the desert captivity were the cause of it. The condition persisted and her female colleagues advised her to see a doctor.

The doctor made a scrupulous check up. At the end, he emerged with a smile and exclaimed, "Congratulations!"

"For what? What are you talking about?"

"Miss, you are expecting a baby."

The newspaper reporter was stunned. If on one hand, she was relieved that the stomach ailment wasn't symptomatic of a hidden disease, on the other, the whole world seemed to fall on her. She couldn't believe that it had happened with all the precautions she took. She didn't know what course of action to take. By no means, she wanted to disrupt Father Mitango's religious life and mission, but she wasn't going to abort either. After days of indecisions, she decided to call him, "Hello, Father!"

"Hi, how are you doing? I'm so pleased to hear from you."

"I'm not so sure that you will be after you hear the news."

"What? Something terrible happened?"

"No, it's wonderful, indeed, at least for me. I don't know about you."

"What do you mean? Could you be more explicit?"

"Of course, I can! Do you remember when I gave you that unconfirmed news before my departure? Now, it's official. I'm expecting a child."

"How? When? How did it happen? Who?"

"Don't pretend to be a dummy. You know very well who and when."

There was no response on the other end. Finally, Brigitte said, "Don't worry! I won't ruin your career, profession or mission. Call it whatever you want. Goodbye!"

Father Mitango remained pensive, with the receiver in his hand for quite a while, then he broke into tears.

A curious event took place thereafter that caught the attention of the whole continent and of the world. A group of fifty young girls convened at the main entrance of St. Catherine Church in Mlolongo. They wore white veils on their heads and held a lily in each of their hands. They formed a circle, held hands, recited a local prayer, then broke the circle, forming a line. A lady of about 40 approached them with a water bassinette and a towel. Each one washed and wiped her hands. A man, also dressed in white, came toward them with a Bible. He stopped at a close distance. The girls stretched their hands toward the Holy Scripture and pronounced in unison, "We solemnly swear to offer our virginity as a gift to our future husbands. We are poor. Our dowry is chastity. To this end, we will spend all our energies. St. Catherine is our witness."

The ceremony was in response to Father Mitango's bracelet campaign. He asked boys and girls to wear it. On it was written, "Chastity 'til Marriage." A group of adolescent boys arrived on the scene and flanked the girls. At the signal of the man dressed in white, they all raised their arms to the heavens and pronounced the following words with absolute glee, "Lord, give us purity or give us death."

Bystanders gathered from the plaza. At the conclusion of the event, they applauded, ignoring the real significance of it. Someone approached them and explained the nature of the event. It was then that they broke into a prolonged ovation. They were still applauding when a band of drummers showed up from a street corner. The musicians placed some old rags on the ground and placed their instruments on them. They sat on improvised chairs and began to play local songs. Two ladies walked around with trays full of food and drinks. The crowd welcomed the unexpected party and participated by dancing.

The vow of chastity stirred the conscience of young ladies and brought them to a *mea culpa* reflection. A relevant number of prostitutes took the unprecedented step of a moral rebirth that did a tour of the world. They prepared a document in which each one of them promised not to regain her lost chastity, but to honor it from then on. They assembled in front of the church, stretched their right arms toward an older lady who held a paper in her hand and shouted, "We, the underprivileged and misunderstood ladies of this noble town, declare our determination to reinstate chastity in our lives, so that we may offer it as a gift to our future men."

The ceremony lacked the glamour and the participation of the people as before, but attracted the attention of the mass media. The Lifesavers were furious; the common people, instead, reacted with incredulity and sarcasm. "These ladies are speaking a foreign language," was the comment of a shopkeeper.

"How can anyone believe in these aliens?" commented an old man.

A well dressed gentleman said, "Let's be serious! They lost everything. No doubt, this is a bluff!"

A lady from the suburbs, upon arriving in front of her squalid hut, said to a neighbor, "I never heard such a stupid resolution. Either they are too ignorant or they come from another planet." After a while, people began to frown, then laugh.

The prostitutes' spokeswoman replied to the state of mockery in this way, "You spend your money in many different ways during a birthday or a national feast. We are going to invest some money to insure that our husbands will get their gift. What you don't know is the nature of the gift and how to obtain it."

The prostitutes action took everybody's by surprise. They contacted the best Russian imenoplastic surgeon, Dr. Fexianov and his Japanese associate, Dr. Mikuriono, who are famous all over the world and especially in areas such as Latin America, where the concept of virginity is very deeply imbued in the conscience of the women. During a recent conference, the two famous doctors explained that in other parts of the world, such as the Philippines or the Middle East, young people are not less concerned about chastity. They simply have hindrances of political and cultural background. They pointed out that in the Midwest of the United States, the evangelical churches are conducting an interesting campaign aimed at fostering self-control among youngsters, until marriage. Girls wear what they call, a "purity ring." On it, it says, "I can wait," which is a constant reminder of the value of chastity.

In Mlolongo, the local newspapers went on a rampage and reported on the front page spots of this sort, "A return to virginity!" "A return to purity!" "Miracle at Mlolongo! You can buy anything, even virginity!" The media had one immediate effect. Many prostitutes decided to invest in surgery, stay away from sidewalks and return to an honest life. In this respect, Father Mitango worked strenuously to help them to regain, not the virginity, but their dignity, finding them a job, or keeping them in the service of the church at his own expense. For better or for worse, the virginity phenomenon became fashionable among women of all social strata and ages for the psychological stigma it carried. Ever since its inception, the plastic surgery business got a boon never conceived before.

The radical or more conservative wing of the town gradually acquired a distinct and higher notion of the surgical process. They complained that it was a fraud, and by no means did it reinstate the sense of honor and dignity that one had lost. They rationalized that the method was superficial and meaningless, like the rejuvenation process invoked by old folks with the injection of a certain medicine in their neck. Nonetheless, the contentious issue wasn't settled promptly or easily. The women who thought that the plastic operation was a morale boost, didn't cease trying to achieve their goal. Unmarried women had an additional reason for pursuing their aim. They believed that, other than giving a psychological twist to their lives, the operation offered them a better chance to find a husband. The news was reported by all major newspapers in the world. The Pravda paid a special tribute to their favorite son, Dr. Fexianov, while in Japan, Dr. Mikuriono made the headlines.

Father Mitango didn't stay idle. The marriage values were taking a new twist. He purported that values can't be fixed like an object. Doctors can't operate on them. Moral values are inborn and, therefore, untouchable. He discussed at length with his aids a new project that would not replace the existing one, but strengthen it. He proposed a Virginity Certificate, an idea that found widespread echo in North Africa later on. Father Mitango explained that it was neither an old nor a new idea. He wanted the girls to assure their future husbands of their chastity.

Men, in general, and a small segment of women welcomed the idea, but those that wanted no such controls placed on their behavior caused an uproar. The protests abated quicker than expected because Dr. Fexianov explained that the new antidote to self-control could be easily sidestepped. It's true that the fee was stratospheric, especially when the girl's future rested in his hands, but according to them, the ends justified the means.

Not everything ran smoothly with the Virginity Certificate. Groups of people debated in streets and bars on who would certify the girl's virginity. They agreed that the financial benefits for the doctors were undeniable, but they disputed that they could perform a miracle. The medical code of honor prevented them from conducting any pre-marriage test. Someone suggested to assign the task to lady nurses; however, the initial euphoria soon disappeared. Girls with integrity refused to undergo the test for two essential reasons. First, they considered it a dishonor to submit themselves to the test. Secondly, they felt it was improper to pry in their privacy and declared that their word should be sufficient.

In the midst of this incredible turmoil, politicians could not ignore their importance and credibility. They attempted to mediate, but the obstinacy of the opposite factions closed the door to any compromise. They withdrew their assistance and proposed instead a referendum. At the end, everybody agreed to follow his own choice, even though the flames of the issue were not extinguished, neither quelled. The only real victor that emerged out of the whole issue was Father Mitango. On the façade of the church, he hung a big poster, "Get a Virginity Certificate. We Pay for It." Obviously, the man ended up paying the fee, which was substantially reduced to affordable means of the candidates. By and large, attestations of admiration came from all African heads of state. What they said could be summarized as follows, "Father Mitango's contribution to high morality and AIDS prevention will have repercussions throughout the continent and beyond for the present and future generations."

# BISHOP MITANGO

Father Mitango's popularity knew no bounds and the Vatican called him to Rome in July of the same year. The Pope invited him to the ceremony for the election of 21 new bishops. The Osservatore Romano published the list and Father Mitango didn't appear in it. 100,000 faithful gathered in San Peter's Square. It was sunny and the sky dressed up in the lightest blue. The Pontiff showed up at the ceremony five minutes late. Assisted by his personal secretary, he sat on the throne under the canopy, and the Cardinals, one by one, paid homage to him. The Cardinals of Camberra and Sidney exchanged some jokes with him. The others simply kissed his ring and wished him well. The chorus of St. Cecilia sang the "*Ave Maria.*" Immediately after, a clown group from Kiev performed some numbers from their repertoire. The successor of Peter seemed to enjoy them very much. Artists from various countries did their best to delight him. When it was all done, the master of ceremonies read from a list the names of the bishops. One by one, they approached the canopy and knelt before the Holy Father. He placed the red biretta on their heads and expressed congratulatory wishes. The list ended. The Pope got close to the microphone and said, 'Father Mitango, it's your turn now.' Everybody thought that the Pope wanted to compliment the priest on his good work and to express solidarity and appreciation for enduring his long and dangerous abduction. Father Mitango looked around bewildered. He was sure that it was his name. The Holy Father smiled and said, "It's you Father. Come here." Father Mitango was visibly emotional. He got up and headed unsteadily toward the throne. The pontiff placed the biretta on his head and hugged him. "Bishop Mitango," he said, "The Church expects great work from you, and not only in Africa." Father Mitango was thirty eight years old. The entire Vatican Curia was taken by surprise and so was the crowd.

The new Bishop remained disoriented for a few seconds. The Pope smiled again and helped him to stand up. An assistant pointed to the seat that belonged to him.

With the title of Bishop came a new assignment. This time, he would set his apostolic office in Nairobi.

# GHANA

The new assignment was in Nairobi at St. Peter's Church across from the Uyoma Temple, next to the Bus Terminal. Bishop Mitango's soul acquired a much needed serenity and his body welcomed once again the African sun. He was full of enthusiasm and vigor. In Ghana, at that time, lived a religious mixture of tribes attached to the shaman and to gods of nature. The Christians were a minority, divided among themselves between the Evangelists and Catholics.

In his first week, the Bishop learned a grim reality. The churches of all denominations were experiencing a deep crisis. Hardly anyone attended Sunday liturgies anymore. Most of the churches had been sold already to speculators, who had converted them into markets, restaurants or museums. This situation was reminiscent of the Stalin era, but in a democratic country, it was unheard of. The Catholic Church was hit harder because it never adopted the policy of charging ten per cent of the annual income or deducting it directly from the weekly check of the parishioners if they so wished. The Catholic problem was different. Hardly anyone was in the labor force.

Besides the economic depression, Bishop Mitango now faced a depression of faith. Only a month after his arrival, he launched a program against poverty and ignorance. He promoted culture and attracted people from every faith. In his church, the parishioners usually went into delirium in the course of the Mass. The miracles became a common occurrence. He considered himself the only exorcist in and around the city and he exorcised possessed people from all over Africa. His popularity increased tenfold. The parishioners were fascinated by his liturgy, where snakes and monkeys seemed at home. There were rumors that he acted illegally, that he used magic in his liturgy, and that he introduced local rituals. The faithful didn't want to give up their traditional gods, whom they represented with the names of the saints. A new hybrid church was born. The Vatican theologians, chief among them the Secretary of State, were not going to accept any form of "collaborationism" with other polytheistic religions.

The attacks on the Church arrived like thunders in high summer. The Protestants and other denominations grew increasingly concerned about Father Mitango's popularity and accused him of magical practices. The rumors soon became criticism, but he kept going his way undauntedly. His indifference led them to change tactic and to discredit him. They ran an anti-Catholic campaign in which they depicted the Vatican as a double standard institution using the black priests as second-class citizens..

Father Mitango's reply came quickly. In the following Sunday homily, he addressed the issue with his typical self-assurance, "Nobody told you this, but I will. After the death of Jesus, Philip baptized an Ethiopian. In the second century, a black priest, Victor I was elected Pope. During the time of Emperor Constantine, Africa gave another black man to the throne of Peter, Pope Miltiades. He reigned from 311 to 314. Later, the Church sanctified him. About twenty years later, an Ethiopian thief, who changed his life and became a priest, suffered martyrdom and Rome declared him saint. Martin de Porres, a Peruvian black friar, spent his life with the derelict and the sick. He fasted often and lived the life of a saint. Africa gave yet another saint to the world and her story is close to our days. I'm referring to Josephine Bakhita, who was born in 1869 and sold to an Italian businessman. As she set her foot in Italy, she was set free and went on to become a nun and work among the poor. She was later canonized. "Someone from the congregation dared to ask him, "Father, why don't we know these things?"

"Because nobody educated you. Other religions would not tell you that for different reasons. One of them may be that they were in darkness themselves, among the few Catholic missionaries, who made it through here.

"My dear brothers and sisters, we were too busy dealing with diseases and poverty. Now, I have come here to open your eyes. I want you to know your past because it's part of your heritage, of your identity, of your pride. You are not the only Catholics on this continent, but you are certainly among the first. Remember that there are 200 million black Catholics in the world. Be proud of it! Be proud of your ethnicity! Be proud of being Black Christians! No one becomes a saint by practicing magic."

He was wiping his brow with a small rag he had in his pocket, when a man who didn't belong to any faith shouted, "You should also tell them that the Catholic Church allowed the indigenous population of the Americas to be oppressed and allowed our ancestors to be sold in slavery!"

Father Mitango smiled and with his usual poise responded, "My friend, I'll only tell you what I know according to what I studied in the seminary. There have been some mistakes on the part of individual representatives of the Church in this respect, but were made in good faith. I surmise that you are referring to Bartolome' de las Casas, a Spanish friar, who suggested to the king of Spain to export slaves from Africa to the New World. He didn't harbor in his heart the design of oppressing them. He took their defense. They needed people for labor. As for us, it suffices to remind you that Pope Paul III, in 1537, attacked those who enslaved blacks and recommended that the owners should teach them only with the example of a holy life. Unfortunately, nothing happened and human commerce continued for centuries."

Bishop Mitango started to sweat. He wiped his face once again and said "Pope Gregory XVI lunched a harsh attack on those who conducted traffic with dark-skinned people. What does this tell you? That the Church was and is on our side. Let us be honest! Our own people were involved in that immoral business. It's not the Church's fault. And let us thank God that He has given us freedom. He gave us this freedom at birth and no one can take it away from us." He raised both arms to heaven and shouted, "Alleluia!" The congregation stood in silence for a minute, which appeared to be an eternity. Suddenly, they sang, "Alleluia! Alleluia!" and began to dance and sing religious hymns. The bishop took off his liturgical vestments and joined them.

Father Mitango's holiness, as a miracle man and exorcist, increased beyond the national boundaries. His church became a pilgrimage site for all African people who were seeking healing in body and spirit. Tourism, especially from the Americas, was still scarce at that time. The few scholars, who came here to study slavery in depth, and other foreigners, whether black or white, were called, "Obruni." The black people felt offended in being labeled by that word. They had a common ancestor. They didn't feel like foreigners at all. They came back to reestablish ties with their roots. Bishop Mitango caught the message and launched a project to the American tourists. He started to teach them the Kwanzaa, a word that takes its origin from the Swahili 'matunda ya kwanza," which stands for "the beginning harvest." In short, it means 'festival of the first fruits." This practice wasn't just common to Africa, but all the Middle East region, as well as other countries of the Indian sub-continent. Initially, it focused on the best values of the African land: to be responsible, respectful, generous, faithful, industrious, creative and loving.

Kwanzaa resembles somewhat Hanukkah, the Jewish "festival of lights," when they lit one each day for seven days. During this celebration, people share food, sing, dance and reflect on the meaning of unity.

Father Mitango worked very hard for the success of Kwanzaa. For Black Americans the idea of returning to their native country, once a year, as a symbol of cultural unity, was fascinating, but it didn't appear to stick too much at the beginning. For Bishop Mitango, it was a way of fostering tourism, boosting the local economy and reinforcing historical ties. He felt equally successful on all three fronts. In his words, he "planted the seeds of the festival in the hearts and minds of the black people of the Americas and initiated a Christian rebirth in his people."

# CONTROVERSIAL ISSUES

In Ghana's capital, Bishop Mitango had his first big headache a month after his installation. At All Saints Cathedral, next to the Ceremonial Driveway that skims Uhuru Park, a priest was accused by his secretary of embezzling $50,000 from his dioceses and using the money to vacation in a homosexual tourist center in South Africa. Besides the theft, she also accused him of sexual abuses. The bishop had emitted a controversial verdict, suspending her without pay until further investigation could be conducted to ascertain the veracity of her allegations. He also suspended the priest, temporarily, but kept him on the payroll with a monthly allowance of $1,700. The secretary was displeased with the decision and hired a lawyer, who called a press conference during which he expressed his indignation, "It's an insult that he is getting paid."

Two months went by and another, similar scandal exploded. A priest of a large community celebrated Mass and managed an elementary school. Everything ran smoothly until one day the secretary, tired of his long hands, decided to take the matter to court, this time, bypassing the bishop. She accused him of embezzling large amounts of money from the church and of sexual misconduct. In her deposition, she stated that he roamed around in a Maserati and went on vacation to Sharma el Sheik, while people were depriving themselves to give money to the church.

The truth is that a large foreign community, made up of embassy personnel, lived in the vicinity and supported the church financially, as they did with other denominations. The bishop suspended her without stipend, but promoted collections in her favor, so that she might take care of her family. The lady, dissatisfied with the settlement, complained that the amount was inferior to what she received before. Even in this case, the bishop temporarily suspended the priest, but didn't deprive him of his monthly allowance. This action infuriated some parishioners who couldn't comprehend the logic behind it. The secretary wasn't going to accept the decision. She asked for her reinstatement, money indemnity to the church, and the priest's transfer. Only in that way, her honor and justice would be served. Contrary to public expectations, the priest didn't deny the allegations, and in order to reestablish confidence between the parish and the diocese, he promised to refund the money he embezzled from the church funds. He never told anyone where or how he got the money to pay his debts. Out of those unconfirmed reports, one fact emerged clearly. The priest didn't own the Maserati any more and the bishop transferred him to a jungle mission. The Bishop's action, however, alienated a good segment of the population with his disputable decisions, but he stood by his judgment.

The first year at Hararha was rather turbulent. Bishop Mitango had to deal with two more embarrassing cases of sexual misconduct and embezzlement on the part of two priests. He demonstrated an uncommon ability to negotiate and settle issues even though his decisions remained partially controversial.

The last Sunday of February was "Slavery Day: A Day of Remembrance" and the country, especially the capital, was in exhilaration for the celebration. Thousands of tourists came from the United States, Cuba, Santo Domingo, Puerto Rico, and Brazil. The dignitaries of the various embassies attended the ceremony. Parades, enacting slavery times, began at 8:00 in the morning, before the sun began to bake the streets. There were drummers and dancers. The movie theaters were open and free. Orators took considerable time in reminding the audience about the types of transactions that occurred between White and Black human traffickers, but also hailed the progress that many Black people have achieved in Latin America and the United States. They took pride in the fact that Blacks excelled not only in sports and music, but in other fields as well, such as science and politics.

# THE ROMAN EXPERIENCE

During his stay in Rome, Bishop Mitango visited the Tivoli Fountains, a few miles from the capital. The Cardinal of Este built them at the end of the 15th century with the hard work of thousands of Turk prisoners and Northern Italians, captured in the war of the Balkans. Their rare ability to serve prompted the Cardinal to donate them to the king of Naples. The Bishop was disconcerted with the slavery issue again, but listened carefully to the guide. He became perplexed when he heard that the king of Egypt donated two dwarf slaves to Victor Emmanuel, king of Italy. Evidently, the Egyptian king forgot that slavery was out of style even in courts. His advisers also failed to remind him. The guide explained that it was very common in the past for princes and kings to exchange gifts in the form of slaves. They replaced jewels and craft work with slavery in the Occident as well as the Orient. The guide noticed that the Bishop raised his eyebrows and said politely, "It was deeply rooted in their culture. Over thousands of years, all nations, overtly or covertly, have practiced slavery as a human marketplace, which is a dishonor to every religion and civilization."

"The bishop asked, "Do they allow research in state archives?"

"Perhaps, but if they do, you will find there much human misery, Your Excellency. I mean, any scholar would be ashamed, as a human being, to see how much the human race has degraded its dignity. Take Spain, for instance. In Granada, there is still the Park of the Slaves. The name has been replaced, but the park is still there, perhaps as a reminder that women and objects had the same value on the market."

"What do you mean by "women"?

"His Excellency sounds puzzled. Men were either killed or were busy with hard and dangerous work."

"Was the Church in any way involved?"

"It's regrettable, but the Seat of Peter was silent at times and implicated at others. In 1571, after the battle of Lepanto, who do who think shared the 11,000 prisoners? The king of Spain and the Doge of Venice got the most of them. A few went to the Pontifical states, probably with or without papal consent. Civitavecchia was the Pontifical naval base. The crude reality is that the ship needed rowers." The bishop wrinkled his forehead and closed his eyes. When he opened them, he asked, "Was there any other marketplace for slavery?"

"Of course! Great slavery markets were located in Istanbul, Cairo and Ghana from where the prisoners were sent to Assyuth for castration."

The bishop shook his head, "Africa lost its youth, its present and its future. How could our countries become industrious, develop into modern states, provide progress for its people when only the sick, the old and the women were left behind? Slavery bled our continent." The guide understood that the bishop became saddened by the news and went on the technical aspect of the Fountains.

On "Slavery Day," Bishop Mitango wanted to relate to the audience his Tivoli experience, but decided to attack the problem on a wider scale.

Before various Black representations of many countries, he stood up in front of the microphone and said, "My dear brothers and sisters in Christ, today we remember our ancestors, who we sold on the marketplace like beasts. This is one of the most aberrant and despicable acts that humans have committed in the course of history. Entire generations were plucked out like petals from flowers. But, if we want to honor our people who were deported in chains, suffered, labored for survival and died in captivity, we must also honor history from a different perspective. No one is immune to criticism. This means that Blacks sold Blacks; Whites sold Blacks and Whites alike; Arabs sold Arabs. And the Church was sometimes silent, sometimes an active part of the problem. It was not until the 17th century that Muslims, Christians and Blacks met under these tents to lay some form of limitations to slavery and to end it all together. Venice, Genoa, Amalfi were maritime powers that thrived on slavery. Naples had 25,000 slaves. There were also Italian slaves in other nations." He stopped a few moments to wipe the sweat from his brow. A deep silence fell on the audience.

He continued, "Today, my brothers and sisters, we are witnessing another type of slavery: religious slavery. People are being used as human torches by unscrupulous religious and political leaders. They wage guerrilla warfare in the name of "holy war," sequester people, slash their throats, dehumanize and kill them indiscriminately. Some of them sincerely believe that they are doing a religious service. If they believe in the same God, why don't they observe the Commandment, "Thou shalt not kill"? He paused a few moments, then added, "Today, mosques are being used as battle camps and the religious leaders don't raise a word to condemn them. Their silence kills us. How can we inflict pain and death on innocent, women, unarmed people, and expect to go to heaven! The young people are being sold to infectious ideals. They are being told that they will get 70 virgins in heaven. What is heaven, a sexual camp? Don't we understand that the body remains here and the spirit flies there? Use common sense my friends! Someone has to tell you that virgins are not being given to you as slaves or as war booty. Up there, there is God Almighty, Creator of heaven and earth, not a harem! To commit suicide is a sin. To commit homicide is a sin. Where are the mothers and fathers who allow their children to become pasture for dogs! Wake up, mankind! Use your common sense! God gave a Commandment not to kill, whether it's you or someone else! Go to work and build your future!" The people exploded in a standing ovation.

A group of people from the back raised the Communist flag and shouted, "You were one of them." He took a deep breath, looked in their direction and answered, "No, I was their victim, that is, if we are speaking the same language. I suffered significantly. I'm sensitive to this issue because I was victimized."

The people were surprised to hear that and lowered the flag. The most belligerent appeared not to get along with the rest of them and tried to wrestle the flag away from his companion, but the others calmed him down. The prelate continued, "They are human beings! Whatever they did, they are still sons and daughters of God. We should treat them with compassion and care. We must teach them, not inflict torture on them. They too have dignity, whatever is their political or religious credo. We must respect them and protect their lives. Let us not try to impose our principles on them. They should make their choice in liberty."

The protesters were pleased with that talk and decided not to disrupt the sermon anymore.

The Bishop concluded, "Once, European powers, Arabic kings, Black merchants and Christian traders benefited from wars and slavery. Let us stop! They are not animals. They are human beings and we owe them respect. We must respect their dignity regardless of their crimes, political affiliation or religious identity. They too are sons of God. We should not dehumanize them. We are not superior to anyone! Let these words ring around the world. No more slavery of people, but also no slavery of ideas, of culture, of economy, of finance, of religion and of the spirit. We have one Christ! We have one God! He gave us the most wonderful gift, freedom. Let us use it for the benefit of mankind."

The crowd gave him a standing ovation, which lasted for about ten minutes. Besides the dignitaries from the various foreign embassies, there were people of different tongues from the whole African continent. They didn't feel the tiresome trip, neither the scorching sun. They were neither thirsty, nor hungry.

Suddenly, the bishop pulled out of a box a big python. The crowd drew back. The snake slithered around his body and arms. It was a long one. They brought on the stage, an old lady afflicted by rheumatoid fever. She could hardly move. Her back was like a piece of steal. She had lost all of her teeth and the hair on her head was scarce. The poor woman looked frightened by the sight of the snake. A group of young men began to beat the drums and the bishop made some foot movements as if he were dancing. Many in the crowd did the same and a sea of human beings transformed the dusty area in front of the church into a dance hall. The oppressive heat soon made some victims. A few old people suffered from heat exhaustion. The music stopped. The bishop pointed the animal toward the woman, who was about to faint, and shouted, "Evil spirit leave the fragile bones of this wretched women." He stared at her intensely and shouted, "In the name of the Holy One, get up and walk!" It took a while before the attendants could revive her. Half-dazed, she made some effort to get up, sustained by the muscular arms of the men. Finally, she made it and was able take a few steps. The crowd went wild and called it a miracle. "The bishop is a saint! He is a saint!" Bishop Mitango caressed the snake and put it back in the box. Suddenly, the sound of a trumpet crossed from one end to another of the field adjacent the church. Everybody stopped dancing and turned their attention to the stage. The bishop took the microphone in his hands and said, "And now, I invite you to eat and drink!"

The people looked around and didn't see anything. On both sides of the church, one could see only large tents. Slowly, the curtains of cloth were pulled back and large tables, covered with all sorts of food, appeared to their eyes. Like a band of dogs, people shoved each other to get first to the tables. Those who were still waiting in the rush shouted, "It was a miracle! Bishop Mitango is a saint!" When their hunger and thirst were satisfied, a band played African songs, most of them with freedom connotations. Young men and girls, dressed in their countries' traditional attire, appeared on the stage, cleared from all religious objects, and made theatrical presentations of a humorous nature. They also introduced games, to the delight of the children. Nothing was left to imagination. With the coming of darkness, the crowd became sparse. Still, one could hear, "This is the greatest day in the history of Africa. We have witnessed a miracle and we have seen a saint." The protesters looked at each other in dismay. They didn't know what to make of it. Finally, one of them threw the red flag away and joined the crowd in the festivities, shouting, "Hurrah, Bishop Mitango! You are one of us! Long live the Bishop, the savior of Africa!" They put their hands to bongos and other percussion instruments and played fast music. Some people left the food table and went over to exhibit their talent in frantic dances.

# Ester and Death on the Bridge

Ester was tall and slender. Her dark hair fell on her shoulders like the waters on the rocks. Her skin was olive. Her brown eyes were like two bright jewels. No one could escape the magnetism of her beauty. Originally, she was from Barcelona. At the age of ten, she moved to Sao Paulo, Brazil. She loved to travel, so she spent a couple of years in Patagonia. When she reached her 25th birthday, she decided to embark on a new mission and work as a UN volunteer. Two months of preparation were sufficient for her to qualify for the job. The first assignment was in Nairobi. Her initial assignment was to teach poor children to read and write. She was enthusiastic about it. The joy of doing something for others exuded from her body's pores. For six months, she walked from village to village under stressful conditions teaching children and helping old folks. The drought, the scarcity of food and water, the dust, the wild animals, always in ambush, and, especially, the lack of hygiene took a toll on her. She requested to be relieved from her position and reassigned elsewhere.

The phone rang and she ran thinking that the director had finally accepted her resignation . "Hi, Miss Ester, how are you?"

"Who is this?"

"I'm Bishop Mitango. I heard about your commitment to poor children and your distress from traveling in some desert areas. In all candor, your dedication has not passed by unobserved and we all appreciate it. We need you, here. Yesterday, I spoke to a U.N. representative and we agreed to shift your present commitment to my parish. Basically, you would combine secretarial work and children's teaching without going to dangerous and isolated areas.

"That sounds like a realistic proposal."

"How would you like to meet with me in my office on Monday, at ten o'clock."

"By all means!

"I'll see you then."

Bishop Mitango was spellbound by Ester's beauty even though he pretended not to pay much attention to it. She was overwhelming! At one point, he took off his glasses and said, "Miss …"

"Just call me Ester," she interrupted him.

"Ester, the clerical work isn't too demanding. You can do it in the morning and devote the afternoon hours for teaching or vice versa. Any way you like to work. This will be your office. It's next to mine. My secretary will show you the clerical duties. Nothing is hard, I assure you. Right now, I'm launching a financial campaign here and abroad to help the poor and the sick. I'm sure your expertise and experience will prove to be indispensable in this and other matters."

"I won't swear on it, but I pledge to do my best."

"For the rest, it's routine work. As I said, the other lady will show you what to do. Any questions?"

"Not at the moment. I suppose I'll have plenty of them as I move along."

"Make yourself at home. You may start tomorrow if you wish."

"I have no objection."

The Bishop liked to spend the evening hours on the terrace and enjoy the cool breeze blowing down from the Nairobi Hill on the south side. Ester, his private secretary, was also his preferred guest. She accepted the invitation only if she were not on a shopping spree in the boutiques of Kiniathi St. or with her friends at the Library, near the Jamai 121 Mosque. Her other distraction was the safari. Almost thirty and still single, she had no problem joining a club and leaving the city for the weekends. She bragged of being the best hunter despite the fact that she hardly made a hit.

Since she started to work at the diocese, a sense of remorse began to seep through her veins. She heard speeches by animal advocates and her participation in hunting games steadily took a dive until she stayed away altogether.

Ester joined the Bishop only at supper when she had free time. He never missed the opportunity to compliment her on her beauty. "You are the jewel of Nairobi."

"Oh, Bishop, that's too much."

"Besides your love for poor people, what led you to Africa?"

"I suppose, a sense of curiosity, a desire to discover, and hunting."

The bishop looked through the empty bottle of cognac and said, "I, too, am tempted many times to discover and to hunt."

"I assume you like to discover the universe, the infinite, the secrets of the Unknown."

"Well, I can't do that. Something else fascinates me."

Ester appeared to be in control of the situation and replied, "Be careful Father! You must dominate your passion."

"Ester, I'm bound by rules from everywhere."

Ester pulled the glass out of his hand and drank it. Her face got reddish. She blushed and covered her face with a napkin. "Your Excellency will understand. If I didn't drink it …"

He attempted a smile. She looked into his eyes. They were shiny. "I think you drank a little bit more than normal, this evening," she whispered to him. She sat in front of him and crossed her legs. The prelate looked at them and raised his eyebrows. He said in an unsteady voice, "You Spaniards. I remember one who said, "For those legs I would go to the end of the world."

She smirked and said, "Listen to the Bishop! This language should not be part of your repertoire. Where did you learn it?"

The Bishop didn't respond. He tried to pour more cognac in the glass, but spilled most of it. Her eyes were drawn to a long line of empty liquor bottles standing alongside the wall. He must have read her thoughts and said, "Even a priest has the right to drink, and thus dominate his temptations." She responded with a deep penetrating stare, but didn't say word. The Bishop made an attempt to pull her toward him, but she slipped away and said, "Monsignor Mitango, remember the vow of chastity!" He murmured something unperceivable. She went toward the door and said, "Nighty night, Your Excellency. It's time to go to bed. Tomorrow, we have a mountain of work ahead of us."

Ester went to her apartment, put on her nightgown and stopped in front of the mirror. She caressed her long dark hair and tried to curl some strands with her fingers. She made faces at the mirror, until she got serious and exclaimed, "I don't believe they should impose celibacy on a man against his will. The Catholic Church keeps captive the minds of its ministers. In my religion, a man can have up to four wives." She took a deep breath and decided to go to bed.

She didn't sleep a wink the whole night and the following morning almost stayed home. To prevent unnecessary questioning from other co-workers, she thought it was in her best interest to be in the office at the regular time.

The Bishop was unusually reserved, almost taciturn. He issued the agenda for the day and relegated himself to his office. Even at dinnertime, he was frugal with the food and parsimonious in words. At Mass, the sermons got shorter and the visits to local churches more rare. The only one who could approach him was his personal secretary, but with time limitations. Nonetheless, he would be concerned if she were not around for a while. He relied on her and not only professionally. She knew it all along and tried to maintain a professional demeanor.

The clouds hung over Nairobi one Sunday creating a surreal picture and lending a mood of uncertainty to the city. The Bishop drove to the Cathedral and locked the door behind him. He knelt in front of the main altar. Half an hour passed, and he was still in a praying position. The secretary had received an important phone call and was looking for him. The car was in the garage. Finally, she decided to go to the cathedral. The door was locked. She stepped back, then, took a key from her pocket and opened the door. She saw him, but, for the moment, didn't dare to disturb him, and sat in a pew behind a column.

"Lord, I'm in distress! I find it hard to go on like this," she heard him saying.

A voice from behind him, as in a whisper, came to him, "You must be a model to the Church."

"You want to put a burden on my shoulder that I can't bear."

"I give you the strength."

"Lord, this rule on celibacy doesn't make me any better. I need the love of a woman, like every man."

"Bear your cross."

"This is a torment. What have I done …"

"You are already married. Remember?"

"I was young, then. I don't mean that I don't want to be a priest. It's my vocation. I love it. But why can't I love? You created Adam and Eve."

"Some were born to serve as leaders, others as servants. You are a leader."

"Why don't you stop my carnal desires? I have to fight every day with these monsters. Do you think it's easy?"

"Temptations will always be your unwanted companions."

The Bishop emitted a loud cry and fell on his back.

The secretary waited for ten minutes and the Bishop still lay in the same position. When he got up, he was drenched with sweat. He tried to walk, but was gasping for breath. Ester approached him with caution. She didn't want to scare him, but couldn't leave him in that condition. He was shocked to see her in church. He leaned on her for support. Slowly, his mind cleared up and he followed her to the sacristy. He fell on the armchair and for a while he closed his eyes. He was dazed again. When he opened his eyes, he didn't know where he was or how he got there. His secretary reminded him that he needed rest and accompanied him to the rectory, where she told him to take a quick shower. She prepared the clothes for him and later the supper.

The Bishop drank a glass of wine, then another and another ... Ester said, "Bishop, I must confess something to you."

He grabbed the *stola* from behind him and answered, "For you, any time!"

She replied, "Your Excellency ought to know by now that I'm Muslim. Muslims confess only to God. So, forget about the *stola*."

"I didn't think of it instantly."

"With that word, I meant discharge of feelings ..."

"Yes, yes, you are right. My apology ..."

Ester waited until he felt comfortable and added, "You see, I always thought that priests are trained to be celibate. Did you learn anything from it?"

The Bishop frowned. He didn't like that statement. He felt it was too naïve. After a long pause, he said in a low tone, "I'm surprised that an intelligent woman like you makes a comment that only aliens without flesh and blood would."

"I don't understand your resentment. The monks, of any religion, control their carnal passions by the end of their period of trials and errors. They are exempted from temptations."

"Don't be facetious! Temptations are going to be with us for the rest of our lives."

"Listen, many married men from the day of their marriage are faithful to their wives. They may look at other women, but they don't fantasize. You are married to the Church, therefore, you should be clean of mind."

"You were correct in saying, 'many', but not 'all.' What lay people don't grasp is the individuality, the peculiarity, the uniqueness of each creature. Everyone of us has different idiosyncrasies and strengths. The policemen should be honest, but among them there those who deal with drugs. Shouldn't they be upholding the law? In their ranks we see strong and weak personalities."

"If they can't be a model of honesty, they should change jobs."

"Initially, I suppose we all have good intentions. During the trip, we encounter difficulties that we didn't experience before. The weak succumb, while the strong triumph. This is reality!"

"Do you realize the consequences of your mistakes?"

The Bishop shook his head. He didn't expect a barrage of challenges on celibacy. She reminded him of Brigitte and for a while he was silent. He wanted to drop the subject, but he made an extra effort to be polite.

"Listen, I can't even compare our temptations to those of a kleptomaniac. Our desires are legitimate. We are not violating the law. Look! Here's another example. You may wholeheartedly desire ice cream on a hot summer day, while it wouldn't even tempt me. What does that tell you?"

"I still believe that champions are special people; our champions; our heroes. They are the elite, the special force. The weak have no place in it."

The Bishop got a bit impatient, "You can't equate a fleshly need with something voluntary in nature. We are talking about two different issues."

Ester noticed that the conversation was getting heated and dropped the subject.

The Bishop asked Ester not to leave him that evening. He had gone through a turbulent time and needed company. They talked for a long time. Slowly, the eyes got tired. It was late. He went to put on his pajamas and whispered to her ear, "Don't leave me. I need you." She looked at him and smiled. He went to the bathroom. On the way back, the light in his bedroom was dim. He raised the sheet and lay down. His eyes were heavy. He turned on the right and stretched his arm to reach for Ester. She raised the blanket on her side. He started to snore. She took the pen and wrote a few lines on a paper.

Ester didn't return to work the following day. During the night she packed up her suitcase and left.

The morning came. The Bishop turned on his left side and tried to touch Ester's body, but found nothing. He thought she was in the kitchen and called her. When he received no reply, he opened his eyes and saw a piece of paper, "Dear Bishop, I'm sorry, but I had to make this decision. Neither one of us has to live a double standard of life. I made many mistakes lately, but I won't budge on my honor. I wish you well. Goodbye, Ester."

The Bishop jumped from the bed and read again the message. He couldn't believe it! "What? I can't believe it! What a world!" he shouted. He dressed quickly and made some phone calls. Ester was gone. He began to imagine having a conversation with her:

"Wait a minute! Where are you going?"

"I made up my mind. I'm going back to Barcelona.."

"If you are really determined to pursue this course of action, call me. Keep me informed. I'm not a deserter. I won't abandon you."

"No. I'm not going to ruin your mission. The best help that I can give you is to stay away from your life. It will do good for me and for you. Goodbye."

He stretched his hand as if to hold her back. Pain seeped through his chest, left arm and back and he fell backward on the armchair. The other secretary called an ambulance. Bishop Mitango had had a heart attack.

That was the last time Ester and the Bishop saw each other. She returned to Spain where she resumed her normal life. The following year she was bound for Medina. She claimed that she had to expiate her sins. As a Muslim, she felt ashamed for having been a stumbling block to the Bishop and a visit to the city of Mecca represented a consolation and a spiritual rebirth to her.

On February 1, 2004, Ester saw her dream come true. She went to Medina. On the first day of the feast of Haj, she was on the bridge of Jamarat. The trip had been long and therefore she still suffered from jet lag, but an extraordinary inner power kept her determined to go on. A tall blonde woman offered her a bottle of water. She accepted it gladly. "I'm a journalist from Oslo. My name is Brigitte."

"Glad to meet you. Ester. I'm from Spain."

"We are not too far from each other."

"Oh, yes, what brought you here?"

"Oh, I'm sorry! This is my daughter Venus."

"Nice meeting you."

"My pleasure!"

"What a beautiful girl! She doesn't resemble you."

"No, she is her father all the way from the chin up."

"He must be a handsome man ..."

"He was."

"What do you mean? Is he dead?"

"In my heart, he is."

"I understand. Men are all the same. They like to bite and go, but I didn't give him that satisfaction."

"Why is that?"

"You looked for the bb."

"I don't understand."

"He wanted to bite, but I refused to give him the bait."

Brigitte laughed.. "If he were your husband, I don't comprehend your denial."

"No, he wasn't."

"I got it. He was shopping around."

"You might say so."

"Exactly, what was he?"

"A priest."

Brigitte and her daughter looked at each other. The color of their faces darkened. Ester didn't wish to inflict any pain on them. She suspected that one of them might have had a negative experience with a clergyman. Brigitte didn't want to expose her past and asked her, "I surmise your relationship was felicitous at the end after the comprehensible religious obstacles."

Ester was unsure to return to the same subject. Finally, she replied, "Let's put it in simple terms. He was too aggressive with me. I believe that a priest has to honor his vow of chastity."

Brigitte chuckled and placed her hand on her mouth to suppress the sound. Her daughter intervened, "My mother does that when she hears a humorous statement. No offense."

Ester felt uncomfortable at that point. She didn't know how to interpret her new acquaintances' response. Brigitte was a very polite lady so, to eliminate any misconception, she encouraged Ester to continue, "It was quite interesting, I imagine."

"For him, not for me! I'm still young, don't you think so?" and made a gesture of disdain.

"Indeed, you are young and beautiful!" the reporter assured her.

"Why would I stay around an old priest?"

"And what happened?" asked Venus with urgency.

"Not to make this story long, I left him all alone in bed with his dreams and passions. I didn't want to represent a steady temptation for him. It wasn't fair. Once I realized that his desires had turned toward me, I abandoned him during the night."

"Just like that?" queried Brigitte.

"How could I have conducted myself under the circumstances? He was a Bishop and I didn't want to spoil his future."

"A Bishop?" inquired Venus full of apprehension.

"Yes, a Bishop! I didn't want to catapult him into infamy."

"You are a brave young lady. I wish I had your courage," added Brigitte.

"It's not just courage. It's steadfastness in your moral values. I learned early in life that it's far better to be faithful to our beliefs and pay the consequences, rather than be hypocritical and reap the benefits."

"You gave up a lot."

"I had a beautiful job. I enjoyed it and I loved the country and the people ..."

"Do you still remember his name?"

"Do I? You must be joking! Bishop Mitango Africanus."

Brigitte chuckled. She made an attempt to answer, but she felt like choking. She couldn't hear any voice around her, neither she felt the pilgrims' pressure. She was having a hard time breathing. Her daughter suggested that she sit down and sip a glass of cold water. She listened to her and felt better. "Heat discomfort, nothing else," she reassured them.

Ester ignored her companion's stress and added, "Incidentally, he is enormously popular in Africa. Did you ever hear of him? You are a journalist, you should."

Brigitte made an effort to camouflage her internal struggle, but had to respond, "Of course! In our profession, we travel and talk and write." Her daughter gave her a glance and got concerned. "Mom, let's drop this subject! Let's move on."

They walked and walked before arriving at the famous bridge. The crowd was immense and the spirits were getting high. Never before had they appeared so in tune with the spiritual significance of the site. The mood was exceedingly happy. Some people wore sandals, others were barefoot. The mother looked at her daughter and laughed. She didn't talk. The crowd made it impossible to perceive a word. Almost everyone was praying, singing and shouting "Allah akhbar!" Ester joined the crowd as did the other two. The sight of the columns drove many believers wild.

They began to throw stones to the pillars, to push and shove. In the excitement, an old man fell down, followed by another, and then others. Brigitte tried to hold on her daughter's arm. Her right foot deepened in the sand and she lost balance. Ester made an attempt to grab her, but both slipped even further and fell down. In the meantime, the crowd kept on pressing on. The human ocean began to create waves and each one made people fall. The waves increased in intensity and the weakest and the oldest became the first victims. It seemed that an entire army was charging a stone for the sake of washing its sins. As the dilapidation of the pillar placated, and the rush finally abated, 250 pilgrims were counted dead. Ester was lying motionless near the bridge. The scene was apocalyptic and indescribable. It looked like Dante's Inferno. Venus searched for her mother for hours. At the end she found her dead body next to Ester's. She was unable to control her emotions and collapsed next to them. It took hours before she could recover from the shock.

In a distant country full of contradictions, she will recount later, she bore the pain for her mother's loss. With the help of Saudi police, she was able to contact the Canadian Embassy, which arranged the transfer of her mother's body to Montreal for burial.

As for Ester, Venus helped the local authorities to identify her body and, with the intercession of the Spanish embassy, she was flown to her native Barcelona.

# MALAWI

The Vatican reassigned Bishop Mitango to another African destination. This time, it was Malawi. It was here where he met Ching during a conference, as the reader may remember. The Bishop took residence in the late 1980s. Upon his arrival, he realized that he had inherited a diocese in complete disarray. An old palace of the capital served as central offices for many organizations. The bishop's office was on the ground floor. Besides the picture of John Paul II overlooking an old table, the walls were unadorned and the paint was peeling. The ceilings were inundated with spiders and the windows had broken glass. The main door squeaked and couldn't be locked, for no one could find the key. Six straw chairs and an old sofa were the only pieces of furniture around. One bathroom served the whole building and was constantly occupied. It wasn't unusual to find a long line. Its interior was filthy and tissue was never available. The mirror was missing and people appeared to hurry after using it. Probably, they were afraid to catch a disease. Flies were rampant in the vicinity and from the holes in the wall, mice occasionally stuck out their heads and withdrew at the sight of people. Colonies of ants started from outside and followed their paths all over the rooms.

To buy their provisions, the diocese's employees went to Chintheche or Likoma, but many times they preferred to shop at Chizumulu, on the river Ruvuma, because food and other articles were much cheaper.

The Bishop looked at the crumbling building and disheveled personnel and made the sign of the cross. He had welcomed the new assignment as a sign of promotion, but now he was having second thoughts. He looked at his disheveled assistants and said, "This is Africa, my friends ... poverty, poverty, and more poverty." After that statement, the staff lowered their heads and dropped their arms. The Bishop had a flash of a new insight. He said, "We are going to rent the most inexpensive house nearby and begin to lay the plans for refurbishing the diocese."

One of them responded with enthusiasm, "We knew Your Excellency would inject optimism and courage in all of us. Welcome and best wishes."

Another added, "We are here to make sure that your dream comes true."

The Bishop inspected the place in detail and began his work. To give a modern and dignified outlook to the offices, he commissioned an Italian artist, whom he knew from Nairobi. Monsignor wanted to be on the vanguard even from an artistic perspective. His senior secretary objected to this plan indicating the futility of investing valuable resources into a decrepit building, "We lack the necessary funds, Your Excellency. Even if you could get something, it would not be worthwhile to carry out your project here."

"Thank you for your criticism. We have to ask for credit from the Central Bank of Nairobi"

"And how are we going to pay them back, with people starving and dying of disease all around us?" He stopped and looked at his colleagues one by one.

"Is it better to submit ourselves to the present conditions and let everything go to hell?" He raised the tone of his voice and the whole staff trembled, but they were also shocked that he had used a curse word.

"For the precise reasons that you gave me about hunger and AIDS, we can't waste our time. We must act, and now. We can't cry to heaven for help, while we lay idle," he replied staring at the secretary.

"Forgive my impertinence, Monsignor, but this is the most bizarre financial adventure that I'm about to see in Malawi."

"In my life, I have seen this and more and I'm going to prove you that everything is possible and that the impossible belongs to God."

They looked at him with incredulity, but also with respect. One older man exclaimed in a soft, but resolute voice, "If your ambitious plan to renovate this building succeeds, you will win thousands of hearts for the Christian cause. But if we fail, you will have to answer to Rome." The rest of them remained silent. They were unsure whether to sustain the Bishop's bold initiative or their colleague's courageous confrontation. Finally, they shouted in unison, "We wish you well for the sake of the Church."

"Call Lanni quickly. This is the number," he ordered the secretary.

"We have no phone, Your Excellency."

The priest showed a bit of surprise, "No one has a telephone in this building?"

"I have to ask permission to Mr. Zulu on the third floor."

"Ask a favor to anyone here. In the meantime, I'll check with the telephone company."

"By the way, who is the man I'm supposed to call?"

"Lino Lanni from Toronto. Make sure he is the one who lives on Grace Street. He is of Italian extraction. Lately, he has become a prestigious architect, building first class bridges throughout Canada."

"How is he going to come here if we can't pay him a regular wage?"

"My friends, he would not come here even for the gold of Ethiopia. But I know him well. Connections, my dear, I have connections."

The men looked at each other and shook their heads. The prelate saw them in chagrin and said, "I don't blame you for your incredulity, but from now on, when I give an order, you comply with it without hesitation. I dislike people without faith. Understood?"

They responded all together, "Yes, Your Excellency!" They learned quite soon that the Bishop was a man of few words when the circumstances required it.

The Central Bank approved the Bishop's loan and he purchased the whole building. The artist arrived the following week with his entourage.

Within three months of assiduous and hard work, they reconstructed the building façade and remodeled the interior. By the time he completed the operation, it looked like a royal palace.

The first action that the Bishop took was to establish the diocese's headquarters on the first floor and rent the other floors. That way, in five years, the Bishop would be able to pay off the debt. Then he would purchase another building with the land around it for gardens and parking space, a few blocks away. To accomplish this project, he would need an additional loan, much higher than the previous one. So as not to burrow anymore, he planned to sell the first building. With the huge profit he would make, he'd be able to carry out his plan. His staff was in awe of his plan, and followed him around meekly.

By the completion of the project, the staff numbers rose to fifteen. The piggy-bank was empty, but the diocese had no debt and owned the most modern architectural palace.

To pay a reasonable wage to its employees, the diocese rented the left wing of the building. With the steady monthly income, the Bishop implemented a free meal for needy people. "No one will go hungry while I'm here," he stated during a meeting. Yet, the diocese faced another problem of a different nature.

The Bishop's face during the Sunday Mass was grim. The church was almost empty. He summoned his staff and said, "We need to boost the attendance. We must focus on the spiritual side now."

"People are too sick to come," answered a secretary.

"I don't agree," responded another.

"This isn't a hospital, a psychiatric center or a social institution. We can only take care of the spiritual needs," intervened the bishop. "Our main goal is the salvation of souls."

"But if we don't do something for them on a material level, how can we win them over to our cause? How can we gain their trust, confidence and hearts?" said another secretary. Everybody applauded.

A younger man, in his thirties, took the floor and made this comment, "We must also provide condoms to men."

The rest of the staff didn't expect a suggestion of sexual nature to the Bishop and attempted him to quiet him down, but the Bishop brushed aside the objections and replied, "We are aware of this plague here and elsewhere. We are not doctors, do you understand? We can only make them understand the immorality of the act and the spiritual social and health consequences. The Church, as you know, is opposed to any sort of contraceptive. We will discuss this matter later on. Right now, we have to address another issue, how to increase church attendance. I want you to be aware of this: if young people don't come to Mass, I can't speak to them about the necessity to abstain from sexual activities, prior to marriage. I can't teach them."

"Your Excellency is right," said a lady who hadn't spoken up to then. "Let us work toward that goal. The question is how to attract them?"

The Monsignor took that question as the basis to lay out his second plan. "Let us distribute a free meal ticket to any needy person attending our Mass, starting this Sunday."

"That will drain our financial resources," protested his personal secretary.

"In the long run, everybody will gain," reassured him the Bishop. "You see, they don't have the faintest idea of what Christianity is, let alone what the Catholic Church stands for. Trust me on this. Once we attract them, we let them run the show without incurring in additional expenses. A volunteer committee will take charge of the organizational aspect. Each one is going to be responsible for a specific task. One will ask a contribution in meat from a butcher house, another for rice and oil from a food store, and so on."

"Your Excellency, your plan, in this embryonic stage, is worthy of merit. We are here to cooperate, assist and obey," said another assistant.

"We are in the boat together, my friends," exclaimed the custodian. "Either we sink or swim."

"Have faith, my children! Have faith! Faith is to us Catholics as gas to the car. Let us roll up our sleeves and get busy!"

"Amen, Amen!" responded the staff as if in unison.

The staff got busy. They found some volunteers and began to announce in all the streets of the diocese the Bishop's new approach. The free meal appealed to the overwhelming majority of the people and the church was crowded for the Sunday Mass.

When the liturgy was over, the spiritual minister begged the parishioners to wait a minute.

Shortly after, the Bishop dashed out of the sacristy with a python in his right hand. The new crowd cried out in fear, "Look! We've come here to die!"

One by one they started to take the exit. The Bishop thundered in a baritone voice, "No one moves!" The parishioners stopped and looked back. The prelate continued, "You have come here so that you may live. You, too, can tame evil. You, too, can take control of your lives. Let me show you what I mean."

The audience took courage and returned to their seats, uncertain what would happen next.

A man, who had been in a wheelchair for the past ten years came to the first row. His relatives pushed him closer to the altar, hoping that something good would come of it. His eyes were wide open, either from fear of the serpent or from the spasm that the pain caused. He wore a light tunic and his hair was disheveled. The Bishop didn't know what to make of it. He was sure of one thing. He couldn't let the handicapped man down. It was a time of monumental importance for the church and people's faith. He raised the animal high, so that it would be visible to everybody in the back. He closed his eyes and genuflected for a minute. When he got up, the altar boy was ready to hand him the incense. The aroma filled the air and those nearby began to sneeze. The tension was high and the clamor at a minimum. The Bishop stared in the eyes of the man, who was motionless. His relative came forward to assist him, but the priest held him back. At that point, he put the serpent on his chair and ordered him to stay put. The animal coiled on itself and remained still. The audience marveled. The Bishop called on the musicians. They were naked from the waist up. They gathered on the altar and hit the bongos with their fingers. The atmosphere was surrealistic. The Bishop stretched his right hand and yelled, "In the name of Jesus, Son of the Living God, get up! Get up! Get up!" Those from the back came forward, pushing and shoving. The moment of truth was electrifying. The Bishop took the man's hand and invited him to get up, but he didn't respond. The Bishop raised his voice in a crescendo that reverberated throughout the church, "I told you to get up and walk! I command you in the name of the Lord!" The man moved his feet, then his legs. The nerves reacted to each other's impulses. He stretched his legs, placed both hands on the arms of the chair and made an attempt to stand up. The Bishop called him towards him. The man finally stood up and, for the first time in ten years, his feet took the first step, the second, the third.... The crowd got tumultuous and cried out, "It's a miracle! It's a miracle!" The unruly parishioners pressed forward to congratulate the man. It took all the physical strength of the staff to save the man from suffocation.

The parishioners flooded the streets, like the overwhelming waters of a torrential river. They stopped the traffic for blocks around the church with cries of, "It's a miracle! The Bishop performed a miracle!" The police rushed over to bring order and also to investigate the claim. The presiding officer asked the Bishop, "Your Excellency, we have to make a report to the commissioner. Do you testify that this man was paralyzed before and now walks because of you?"

"I never made that claim. That comes from heaven. For the rest, ask him. He is old enough to respond to your questions."

"Can we take the chair to the police station?" asked the police to the man.

"You can take me, but not the chair. It will stay here as a reminder to future generations that faith can move mountains."

The police officers looked at each other, bowed their heads and left.

The clamor continued unabated in the streets. The news spread like lightening all over Malawi and beyond. In the empty church, the Bishop knelt before the altar and prayed. When he got up, he took the serpent and said, "Come on! The feast is over."

The miracle gave to the church the necessary boost for a new beginning. The Bishop kept up the tempo with other purported miracles, mixing religion and magic. His controversial style conquered the heart of the people. He didn't abide entirely with the Catholic standards. His people came from a different culture and he knew how to capture their imagination.

Every Sunday Mass was a surprise and people flocked to the church. One time, the Bishop brought a lion. The parishioners screamed and ran for their lives. He laughed at them and said, "This is a nice cat. I can't understand your behavior." Then he yelled, "People of little faith!" The lion stood on the floor lame. The Bishop looked at him and said, "Bow your head and kneel!" The lion obeyed and the parishioners returned, still somewhat afraid, to their seats. A lady asked to his neighbor, "Who is this man who orders the lion to sit and he gently obeys him?"

The other responded, "I have no idea. I only know that a maimed man walks after ten years or so, and that the animals follow the bishop like a magician. He must have magical forces in his voice that attracts and commands wild animals." Everyone marveled. The number of people being baptized grew every day, to the point that the Bishop was planning to build a huge church to accommodate them.

Early one evening, the heat was oppressive. The sky was blue. Only a tail of a cloud streaked above, but it disappeared as soon as it appeared. The Bishop was reading his Breviary, when he heard someone knocking at the door. He came down and asked the visitors, "How can I help you, my brothers?"

"Your Excellency, our friend's son is on a rampage. He has broken tables, chairs, windows. Nothing stands in his way. We can't hold him back. He has superhuman strength. Our children are terribly afraid. We locked the doors of our houses, but with his power, it's impossible to stop him."

"I understand. I'll come later."

The men protested, "If you wait half an hour, he will destroy our houses and imperil our lives. Come with us. We will take you there, so that you can see for yourself."

The Bishop didn't wish to disappoint these people and went with them.

The possessed man was wreaking havoc in his neighborhood. No one dared approach him. A couple of them did, but were hurled in the air like mannequins. The Bishop, dauntless, looked straight in his eyes and sprinkled Holy Water on him. The man covered his face and shouted, "Don't do that, holy man! It burns my face. Why did you come here?"

The Bishop murmured some prayers and said, "I'll stop sprinkling Holy Water when you leave the body of this man." The man spit in the priest's face and unleashed injurious words, too dirty to be repeated here. The Bishop called on the people to hold him down. The few who responded to his call ended up in the gutter and through the windows. When the others, who were hiding, saw that, they ran for their lives.

The Bishop took out the Crucifix and held in front of the man, whose body shook violently by that time. Two muscular assistants of the Bishop dared to intervene and tied him to a pole, but it was useless. He broke the straps and emitted shrieking sounds. The Bishop shouted, "In the name of the Living God, leave this man in peace."

"I know who sent you here," replied the voice.

"Then leave!"

"Where am I supposed to go?"

"Return to your kingdom of hell and stay there. It's your abode."

The man started to scratch his face and bleed profusely. The Bishop fearing that he would bleed to death, sprinkled Holy Water on his face again and repeated the ritual sentence, "*In Nomine Patris et Filii et Spiritus Sancti.*" The man was angry. The Bishop continued, "In the name of Jesus, I command you to leave this man in peace."

He cried out, "I don't have anything to do with him!" Then, he stuck his tongue out as long as a yard and vomited foam. This went on for about five minutes. Finally, the Bishop held the cross high in the air and said softly, "Christ is the Son of God. He commands you to leave!"

The man kicked the pole, fifteen inches thick, where he had been strapped previously, and broke it in half. Suddenly, there was no more response. His eyes returned to normal. His body stopped shaking and he assumed a normal composure. However, he continued breathing heavily for a while, as if he were trying to bring in extra oxygen to his lungs. When normal breathing resumed, he asked for some water. He was drenched with sweat and was exhausted. His family ran over, wiped him and took him inside to wash him. The crowd realized that the Bishop had exorcised a demon from the man's body, thanked God and improvised a dance. The Bishop's popularity grew without measure.

The Bishop was exhausted and sweaty. The people crowded around him to show their respect. He called one of them and said, "Hey, how about a cold, dark beer?"

"I didn't know there was any other kind!" the man replied. The crowd roared and danced to the beat of the drums.

"But your Excellency, wouldn't a glass of wine do much better?"

"Don't be silly! You lose the sense of taste in this hot weather." Then, he added, "Hey, my friend, last week on top of the ziti, I found no meatballs. How about this week?"

"They won't be there today, either, Father!" responded the woman laughing.

People cracked jokes about it. When the noise subsided, he exclaimed, "Listen to her! Since when do you deny a nice dish of homemade pasta to me?"

"Since now! If you make a miracle ..." The crowd stood silent. The air was still.

"What kind?" asked the prelate.

"I have an abscess on my funicular."

"On what?"

"You heard me! The doctor wants to cut it, but, as you know, the medical care here is still in the primitive stage."

"First of all, I don't make miracles. Secondly, if God listens to me and the miracle does occur, who is going to support the medical staff financially?"

"You! You got money! Let's take this month's collection and, 'voila'!"

"You think so? The money has to go to the diocese."

The lady didn't approve. The Bishop turned to another and said, "Are we going to dance this evening at your sister's birthday party?"

"First, you have to learn how to dance."

The Bishop's belly was almost exploding from laughter. "Are you insinuating that a Black man can't dance?"

"Not all of them know how to dance, but if you insist, I'll dance with you. Careful! not so tight!"

"Would I do that to you?"

"I wouldn't bet on it!"

As usual, a few old ladies had some unkind comments about the Bishop's word choice and their semantic echo. The overwhelming majority wasn't scandalized. They just thought he was different from the rest in his field.

Hardly a week passed by that someone didn't cry out "miracle," or witnessed an act of exorcism by the Bishop. He was bold in his actions and words and the Vatican walls trembled at times. "Satan is everywhere and I'm going to hunt him down," he shouted to a journalist.

"Where, exactly?"

"Even in San Peter!"

"On what basis do you make this assertion?"

"Don't act naively, my friend! Pope Paul VI hinted it already in 1972. You media representatives reported it. I'm not fabricating any castle of lies."

"Do you have the authority to be an exorcist?"

"My friend, the Bishop approved it when I was a priest."

Bishop Mitango had just finished the interview when he a heard the echo of a noise coming from a small plaza nearby. The vociferous pandemonium increased in intensity as it approached the church. A man of about thirty years old was blaspheming and sticking his tongue out down to the ground. His nostrils spread a black smoke full of stench that kept the crowd at a distance. Three muscular men attempted to restrain him. When they saw him breaking trees on the sidewalk with an indescribable easiness, they stopped trying. They marveled even more when the man flung three police officers in the air like puppets.

Bishop Mitango remained calm in front of the church. The man arrived proffering blasphemies in his direction. The Bishop gave him a dirty look and cursed him. The man cried out, "Priest of the Almighty, why are you standing in my way? Join instead the numerous army of Satanists present everywhere, even in your backyard."

Father Mitango sprinkled some holy water on the man, who covered his eyes and backed up. The Bishop went on pronouncing the exorcist rite, "In the name of the Father, of the Son and of the Holy Ghost, leave this man's body immediately!"

The demon yelled imperceptible phrases, then, he shouted clearly, "Damned, you, servant of the Lord!"

The possessed man suddenly appeared calm. He wiped the sweat from his brow and asked for some water.

The reporter watched the scene visibly shaken. About ten minutes passed before he was able to regain his usual composure. "How did you do that?" he asked the Bishop.

"You saw me. Why, then, do you ask that question? " After a long pause, he added, "Some superficial people think that sprinkling the holy water is sufficient to exorcise a demon. That could happen, but only in rare occasions. In other circumstances, it may take weeks, months, even years."

"Do all priests have the power to chase out Satan?" inquired the reporter with curiosity.

"It's not a question of power, but of ability, courage and determination."

"Is it true that some exorcists have died in the line of their duty?" he insisted.

"Yes. It's a very dangerous mission. Most of the practitioners are afraid. Think! In Italy, there are less than fifty exorcists. What does that tell you?"

The reporter's eyes widened in dismay.

The crowd finally dispersed, still talking about the Bishop. The exorcised young man rushed over to the Bishop to thank him and promised that he would attend Mass on a daily basis and begin to offer a contribution to the church. The Bishop laughed with passion. When he realized that the reporter was in a meditating mood, he approached and said, "What are you concerned about?"

"I'm worried about the power of your words."

"Which ones?"

"Satan smokes cigars even in the Vatican."

The Bishop placed his right hand on the reporter's shoulder and whispered, "Remember that Satan's power is great, but God's power is limitless."

Father Mitango had won another battle against evil and his popularity spread even more in the cities and countryside, as an exorcist and miracle maker. The Church grew immensely under his leadership in Africa, yet, as a good minister, he felt dissatisfied. He had another card up his sleeve to play.

During the usual overcrowded Mass, he had this to say, "My dear friends, my job is incomplete; my dream is unaccomplished. Before the Holy Sea reassigns me to a new apostolic location …"

He was unable to finish. The audience got rowdy, "We will never allow you to depart from us."

When the unruly parishioners finally took their seats, the Bishop continued, "I want to do something for your families, relatives and friends."

Again the audience responded, "Long live Bishop Mitango!"

"I want to pursue and destroy the scourge of our century, AIDS."

No one reacted to the news. A deep silence reigned in the church. When the Bishop realized that everybody was quiet, he added, "AIDS is destroying millions of lives and I'm going to destroy it!" The tone of his voice, strong and resolute, resounded under the vaults. The echo accompanied them. The parishioners voiced their surprise. The Bishop continued, "In order to win this battle, you and I must fight together, under a common ideal, and against a common foe. From now on, we are in the same boat. Round up your friends and relatives and bring them here. The more we are, sweeter will be victory." The Bishop left the pulpit, came in the middle of the balustrade and made a couple of dancing steps. That was exactly what the audience had been waiting for. Some of them put their hands on the bongos and played local music. Suddenly, they piled up the few chairs available in the corner and danced to the fast beat. The church assumed the characteristics of a dancing hall. Eventually, the music stopped.

One lady asked the Bishop, "Are you in a position to tell us about the plan?"

The diocese staff surrounded him, trying to prevent anyone from asking inappropriate questions, but the Bishop thought otherwise. He looked at the woman and said, "My plan is simple. This church will pay for the wedding of every girl who keeps her chastity vow until her wedding."

The news of "free wedding" through the chastity vow pleased the girls, who welcomed the challenge. The men, instead, were opposed and muttered that it was a heavy burden to bear.

As a result of the Bishop's offer, the girls formed a club and met for the first time to discuss the matter. At the end, they wholeheartedly embraced the Bishop's proposal. and sang religious songs. Satisfied by the response, the Bishop motioned them to wait and said, "Across the street, there is a shop where you can purchase a bracelet with the enscription, "Chastity 'til Marriage.' It doesn't cost much, but it's the passport to a healthier society. From Malawi, we launch a sanitary and moral revolution that will infect the entire continent, and, hopefully, the whole world. This is the weapon that will defeat AIDS, that's why, we need your involvement. It worked before. It can work now here."

The group of girls shouted, "We raise our hands and our hearts to heaven. With the Lord's blessing, we will bite the monster and will set a model for future generations."

The Bracelet Campaign became instantly contagious. The number of the girls accepting the challenge rose dramatically. The young men, who initially manifested reluctance and, even disdain, gradually and timidly joined the movement. Their participation was an astonishing and significant factor in the war against AIDS.

The bracelet business flourished, but so did the diocese finances because, for every bracelet sold, one dollar ended up into the diocese coffer. If the project were limited to Malawi, the end-results would have been far less impressive. The fact of the matter is that the idea spread like the fury of a wild wind throughout the continent. Regional churches jumped on the bandwagon and signed contracts with local companies interested in producing bracelets, each sharing in the profit. At times, there were signs of disorderly conduct, of chaos and apprehension, until the Vatican intervened to restore order and confidence. But the economical scenario should not obscure the tremendous moral impact that the Virginity Vow had on the young and adult population. The AIDS population remained stagnant. New cases were limited to an insignificant number among young people. The danger came also from married couples.

Two months later, Bishop Mitango proclaimed "Marriage Day." It was televised all over the world. He invited newlywed couples and the already-married. The whole thrust was on fidelity. With his action, he dared to revolutionize a nuptial tradition that had lasted for thousands of years. In a giant stadium, first he welcomed the crowd with music and dances and then he laid down the new rule. "My dear brothers and sisters in Christ, this is an historic event for married and unmarried couples. From now on, I will no longer bless your marriage ring." The spectators were perplexed. They looked at each other in search of a plausible explanation, but no one could. When the noise subsided, the Bishop continued, "From now on, you will demonstrate your fidelity to your spouse in a more meaningful way. You will do that with your own flesh and bones!" Once again, the crowd got stirred up not knowing what the prelate meant. "If you wish to preserve the sanctity of your marriage vow and preserve this generation from untimely death, I don't propose to you, but I command that you make a new fidelity ring from your own body."

"How can this be possible?" cried out the crowd.

"Brothers and sisters, we are at the last frontier of biology. The medical field has made a giant leap in stem cell research."

"This is utopia" shouted out an adult.

"Listen carefully! The doctors will extract some cells from your bones, say tooth, and a tiny bit of skin. They will multiply in vitro the cells and mix them, so that, each couple will have their combined cells that will grow into a ring with their names." The spectators grew uneasy with the new marriage ring. idea. The Bishop felt that the doubt persisted in their minds and added, "The money you would pay for the gold ring, will pay for the clinical process." The crowd didn't feel comfortable and began to display its displeasure by making noise. The Bishop took the microphone and shouted, "Do you want to reduce and eliminate AIDS from our society, yes or no?"

Everybody replied, "Yes!"

"Then, listen to me. The new ring is made safe by the biotechnology and will prevent the loss of millions of premature deaths." A deep silence fell upon the crowd. The bishop said, "If you love your family and yourself, then step forward toward my podium and give your names to my assistants. They will insure that you will properly undergo this biological union of fidelity and safety." Slowly, but gradually, one by one the spectators advanced toward the platform. The bishop was drenched with sweat. He fell on the chair and watched the people coming. The success of that initiative was the prelude to the fight against a disease that has been plaguing Africa and the world in the last decades. It was the beginning of a new era, the union of morality and physical preservation.

Bishop Mitango's picture appeared in all African newspapers. He was enjoying every moment of his glory. It was short lived, since a news story took him by surprise. He was in his office studying some documents related to the bracelet project, when his secretary handed him a letter from the Holy Sea. He thought that his rights were finally vindicated. Eagerly, he opened the envelope and unfolded the letter. He read a few lines of the letter with concern. He read it again to make sure he had understood it well. His eyes closed. He opened them slowly and looked straight ahead through the window. The letter slipped off his fingers and fell on the rug. The secretary inquired about the contents. "Your Excellency has something to worry about?"

"No, not really ..." he responded with indifference.

"Your face contradicts your words."

The Bishop decided to reveal the content, "I have been assigned to China."

"What? I can hardly believe it! You have not been here that long!"

"Priests are like merchants. Today, they are here, and tomorrow there."

"This isn't fair."

The Bishop dodged the statement, "The second news is that I have to travel to Rome next week."

"What for?

The Bishop remained pensive. He picked up the letter and said, "They want to relate to me the information personally without relying on telephones or fax."

"Couldn't they achieve the same through an emissary?"

"Rome knows best."

"I still believe that it's all bureaucracy. They are incapable of dealing even with the simplest issues in a normal manner."

"*Roma caput mundi est.*"

"As you wish, Your Excellency!"

The Bishop attempted a half smile. He followed the secretary with his eyes as far as he could, before she disappeared behind the door. He closed his eyes and took a nap.

# Jiudiu, the Mlolongo of China

The New Millennium was celebrated with great fanfare by Christians and non-Christians alike. After all, how many millennia can a human being welcome? The past and present generations are blessed. They bid "goodbye" to one millennium, and opened their arms to the next. Not many people have sufficiently reflected upon this divine favor. Everywhere, a euphoric wave invaded all social strata. The economic boom, the hope of seeing once and for all the wiping up of poverty, the promise of remunerative jobs for every able working man and woman recurred on everybody's tongue and heart.

From the most prominent politician to the least successful businessman, students and teachers, housewives and farmers, military people and religious devotees came the same feeling. They called the New Millennium an epoch that would make the difference. The scientific community hailed it as the Technology Era. A god, unknown to humanity, had descended from nowhere in the space to make life easier, more comfortable for the whole humanity. This was the impression of a large segment of the human race.

The same people claimed that since the eviction of Adam and Eve from the Garden of Eden, human history was marked with a variety of sufferings and deep pains. Yes, death was unavoidable, but technological progress would eventually reduce immeasurably the agony of terrible diseases and even spare sick people from their daily tribulations.

Animal cloning was scary, but also promising. Man and woman would stretch longevity beyond human imagination and be healthy through the use of stem cells.

Robots were already performing precision surgical operations, and would soon be poised for combat action. The conquest of the very formidable human foe, cancer, was within reach. The genome was no longer a mystery and most of the proteins that cause the different types of cancer had been already identified. The moon had been conquered by the Americans and the air was saturated by wonderful expectations. The New Millennium was to pass into history as a millennium of freedom from disease, poverty, injustice, violence and war.

That was the general mood, and in China the Communist Party wasn't alien to this feverish atmosphere of another Renaissance. But the scourge of AIDS was looming everywhere. The government shifted money from urban to rural areas where the pandemic was increasing. To keep it in the city would have added insult to injury. They even consulted with the best medical experts in the word, but in the end resorted to a painful decision. They sent an emissary to the Vatican to invite Bishop Mitango. The few pages of history he left behind in Africa had reached all world embassies; therefore, they were well documented. The Chinese, this time, were facing an invisible enemy, AIDS, that had infiltrated their frontiers. They felt impotent, but didn't give up before it became epidemic.

Bishop Mitango didn't respond promptly to Rome. He hesitated a while. He wanted to be certain that the Chinese invitation wasn't a trap. He consulted the Vatican which confirmed the content of the letter and gave its approval. He was determined to grasp the moment. His aim was to renew the contacts with the isolated and fragmented Catholic Church in China and see if it could gain political recognition and acceptance. With Rome's blessing, he felt inspired; yet, he couldn't comprehend how a country that ejected him from its soil years ago now was on its knees begging him to come back.

The Southern tip of Sichuan, near Xicheng, China, is a "no man's land." The government is particularly sensitive to any foreign intrusion or tourist curiosity there. There is an intercontinental missile base and a base for future interplanetary voyages. The authorities are so secretive that no official or unofficial mention of the bases is ever made. No one is allowed to speak or write about them. There is no doubt that the rigid restrictions on the area are of deep concern to Western powers, even though the satellites provide good intelligence material.

The Chinese are worried about another secret unrelated to the military projects that lies on a mountain nearby. They want to decipher the code that holds a village hostage and that can spread with dangerous rapidity to the rest of the country.

Nature offers the best in vegetation and water. The people are called Norsu and migrated here centuries ago. They still carry on their tradition and culture. They still speak their original language. Somehow, they have not learned Mandarin, the official Chinese language and, understandably so, it causes them difficulties in finding jobs elsewhere.

The utter attachment to their past is an impediment to progress. The only jobs available are in the rice paddies where they work long hours and their backs get curved by the end of the day. It takes an effort to stand erect and greet one another, looking in each other's faces. This community, known for its ancient courteous values, seems to be pursued by a monstrous phantom that pushes them toward the brink of desperation. Good manners don't seem spontaneous. People are distracted, absorbed in heavy thoughts.. Everyone runs for his business. There is no time to waste. It's a matter of survival. It's not religion or politics that creates a distinct social character. There is a big anomaly in this community. Only old people and children walk the streets. AIDS has wiped out an entire generation of youth.

The population consists of poorly dressed and malnourished children, most of them orphans. Their parents didn't die in war but by that terrible disease. Others are locked up in the one-way trip of drugs. They are in jail for offenses they committed against either neighbors or the state.

Xicheng is the land of AIDS. It's the Mlolongo of China. Young people and adults have paid a heavy toll against the scourge of modern times. These people have lost their Tibetan purity and engaged in the mountains of Sichuan in a *carpe diem* that caused the extinction of their youth. The newcomers are trapped in the same cage. Without a job, their dream for a better future evaporates daily and succumbs easily to the temptation of drugs and sex. Heroin gives them what society is unable to provide: ecstasy, the temporary sensation of a terrestrial paradise. To escape this social, economical and human malaise, some girls dress up in miniskirts and take another road. It's a vicious circle. In fact, they are aware that someday they will pay the ultimate price, but at least for the moment, they prefer to join "enemy ranks."

Not all children are destined to be sacrificial lambs on the altar of AIDS. Some of them, already mature, raise a pig or a goat, the only family resource, or they try to get an education. Someday, in proximity of the lunar landing pad, they dream of launching the greatest challenge to the major killer of the 21st century.

With this scenario as the background, Bishop Mitango arrived to Xicheng. Obviously, the government couldn't rest idle and wait for the spreading of the disease and brought him as soon as possible. His reputation had traveled all over the world. His success in Africa in the war against AIDS, with his personal methods, had gained him respect and fame. The scientific community was distant from him, but the statistics were incontrovertible. He had saved ten million lives.

In his first contact with the population, the Bishop observed their condition. Xicheng looked like a place where phantoms come and go. He saw it in the eyes of the children and the old folks.

The Chinese government, in an unusual gesture of appreciation and friendship to the Bishop, granted freedom to a thousand drug addicts. A teenager muttered, "Where am I going to place my father when he comes back? What will I give him to eat? In jail, at least, he had food."

An old woman added, "They also provide some drug-related services, so I hear. Who knows? I only know that no one ever comes back healed."

Bishop Mitango refused the best apartment in town. He took up residence in a poor shed, which was made up of a bathroom and a bedroom. The first had only a hole dug into the ground with no running water. It was so tight that he barely managed to get through it. The latter had a mattress filled with bamboo sticks covered with animal skin. The dirty and black walls were stained with blood. Mice ran freely and lice infested the mattress.

The Bishop went immediately to work to clean, remodel and enlarge his abode. The local authorities provided manual support from the military compound nearby. In about two weeks, he transformed it into a habitable place, even with some comforts.

With the assistance of the interpreter, the Bishop began to visit the districts where the AIDS population was significantly high. He held conferences and private talks with patients and doctors. He revamped the "Chastity Ring" with teenagers and adults alike. It wasn't a novel idea, but he injected into it the concept of blood mixture. He would draw a couple of drops of blood from the those who planned to get engaged, mixed them and put a drop in a tiny crystal cubical attached on top of the ring. They would wear it even after the exchange of vows.

The bold initiative soon shaped up into a vast project to which every day men and women adhered without questioning. Lines of participants were blocks long in front of the hospital where the Bishop had established his general headquarters. The cost was a dollar. Those who couldn't afford it had the option of having a dove picture stenciled on their forehead. It lasted only five years; therefore, they had to renew the ritual. The project even pumped some oxygen into the local economy. Craftsmen's shops mushroomed in a matter of weeks.

The interpreter couldn't believe the change that was taking place around him. He said to an army captain, "One simple idea is moving mountains. The Bishop has not done anything extraordinary. He has not built anything. He has made no clamor. He has not discovered any medicine. I'll have a hard time explaining to my superiors in Beijing that young and old are following him as if attracted by a magic music."

"He is a revolutionary."

"Or a counterrevolutionary?"

"Sh ... sh ..." cautioned the officer. "Don't use that word around here."

"What should I say, a reformist?"

"Not even ... Only the state can utter those words."

"O.K.! Don't you see that people revere him? They look at him as a model. He has given them hope and joy and work ..."

"That's a better word ... Maybe he is a reincarnated Lenin."

"Comrade, captain, you are missing the point. First of all, there is no such thing as reincarnation. Secondly, he has no weapon. He doesn't preach in the streets a new political ideology. I'm short of words. It's a miracle."

"Comrade, be careful! I could put you in jail and discredit you. Remember that in our society there is no such thing as a "miracle.""

"Comrade, captain, I'm not critical of the regime. I'm talking about a single man who has launched a preemptive strike against future AIDS cases."

"How is he able to accomplish it? What weapon is he using?"

The interpreter looked around to ascertain that no one was listening. He brought his mouth close to the captain's ear and whispered, "Prayer."

"What's that? to whom?"

"Christians pray to their God. They call him the God of Abraham, Isaac and Jacob."

"Who are they? Unless they are Communist, they have no place in our conversation."

"It's a long story! I'll explain it to you on another occasion."

"With so many religions around, how do you know that his is the right God? There can be more than one."

"In a multiple choice question, you are confronted with many answers and they are all plausible, but only one is the correct answer."

The captain felt more disturbed than ever. He looked sternly at his companion and said, "How come he has not come here yet?"

"He has, but we throw his emissaries in jail or bar them from entering our country."

The captain remained pensive. He rubbed his eyes slightly, turned on his heels and left without saying a word.

The Bishop was savoring the fruit of his tireless work. One evening, he appeared unusually tired. He had worked all day without a break. The sun had already disappeared behind the horizon when he returned home. On his way, he met with villagers who had spent the whole day in the rice paddies. For each of them, he had kind words.

A few blocks away from his house, he spotted a girl with her thumb in her mouth in front of a decrepit shed. She covered her face. He offered her a bar of chocolate. "Take it! You will like it!" She snatched the chocolate from his hands and ran inside. She reappeared shortly after, as if she was taken by remorse. "Here, take back your chocolate! My parents forbid me to accept anything from foreigners."

"They won't reprimand you for accepting something from me. You can eat it after supper."

"What supper?" She responded spontaneously.

The Bishop got suspicious. He bent over her and queried, "Don't you have parents?"

"Yes, and no," she answered in a low voice."

"Either you have them or you don't."

"I said, yes and no" she hollered, and she smacked him on the face.

The clergyman started to laugh after assuring himself that she had made no damage to his chin. "I wasn't aware that you were so strong."

She observed him closely without taking a step back. She cleaned her nose with the back of her hand and said, "They are both in jail."

"On what charges?"

"Drug trafficking … I heard that tomorrow they will be released."

"I'm glad for all three of you."

"I'm not!"

"Why is it? Don't you love them?"

"How can I help them? I need food myself. I have to beg to survive."

The Bishop was visibly moved. He was unable to continue the conversation.

A few days passed and the girl received a bountiful food supply for a month.

It was early in the morning when the Bishop rose. Among his daily activities, he added one. He wanted to visit a hospital between two shoulders of mountains rarely visited by people. That was the residence of the outcasts, those who had lost every hope and waited impatiently for the last day of their earthly life.

The compound was reminiscent of a medieval castle, isolated in a no man's land, forgotten from human tenderness and love. It was divided into big halls occupied according to gender. There was no internal or external facility. The patients were living robots, each living the drama of their existence in an asphyxiating silence. Life had already emitted the verdict against them. The few who could still think rationally welcomed the rare visitor with a dim ray of hope in their heart. A Black man, such as the Bishop, carried a double feeling of curiosity.

Escorted by the ward supervisor and in the company of the interpreter, the Bishop entered the woman's section. In a bed in a corner lay a woman in her sixties, but who looked much older, with her eyes half closed. She spoke in an undecipherable monologue. When she noticed the visitor, she stopped talking and her mouth remained open. She whined intermittently. When she resumed her talking, she spoke freely without any reverence to the regime.

The Bishop noted her skeletal body and noticed a cross on her neck. He got close to her and whispered, "May the Lord give you back your health and peace."

The patient suddenly experienced a surge of mental clarity and vigor. "You sound like a priest," she said in a soft voice.

"Yes, I am, my dear."

She tried to find her strength to assume an erect position. He helped her. She said, "Oh, father, you walk through the streets of death, tell me, who are you? Your accent is like that of a person who failed me in the prime of my love."

"Surely he wasn't a priest!"

"Yes, he was! My present condition is the nemesis of a relation I had with him."

The Bishop got anxious. "Where did it happen?"

"Shanghai, my dear ..."

The Bishop trembled. Those eyes, that voice.... He began to make connections. "What did you do for living?"

"I was his secretary."

"What was his name," asked the priest.

"Mitango, Mitango Africanus! I had a son from him. I don't know where he is anymore."

"Ahi! Ahi! Ahi!" screamed the Bishop and brought his right hand to his heart. The interpreter quickly helped him sit on an old straw chair. The woman reclined her head on the pillow and spoke no more.

A doctor was rushed on the scene to ascertain the Bishop's condition and assisted him until a helicopter flew him to the nearest hospital.

A week later, Bishop Mitango left China. The doctor told him to go back to Africa. His heart had become very weak. Before he left, he got a written statement from the authorities that the lady would be treated with respect and humanity for the rest of her days.

Bishop Mitango had started a process of sexual education that saved millions of lives and set up a model for future generations to escape the curse of AIDS. China was eternally grateful to him. Throngs lined the streets and chanted, "Wan Sui, Mitango, Wan Sui"—Long live Mitango!

# CARDINAL MITANGO
## AFRICANUS

It took about a month and with great care for the Bishop to recover from the Chinese hospital experience. He healed slowly but steadily. Whenever or wherever he went, he was welcomed with extreme warmth and honor. He had conquered the heart of millions of people. He wasn't content yet. He was concerned about AIDS, the main killer of Africa, and wanted to put a stop to it.

The weeks went by and the Vatican again invited Bishop Mitango to Rome. Africa gained him enormous recognition, but at the same time, he realized that carries responsibilities.

It was a crispy morning when the plane landed at Leonardo da Vinci Airport, where a limousine was waiting for Bishop Mitango. A Vatican representative was at hand to welcome him and whisk him away.

At St. Peter's Square, a Franciscan priest was waiting for the guest of honor. As the Bishop stepped out of the car, he led him to a building across the Vatican Museums for his lodging accommodations.

The following day, everything was ready on the Church steps for the nomination of the new Cardinals. Bishop Mitango took a seat on the first row on the east side reserved for the clergy. The Franciscan priest approached Bishop Mitango and whispered something into his ear. The Bishop blushed and showed signs of incredulity. The priest accompanied him to the Cardinals' section. The Bishop whispered to his guide, "Are you sure this isn't an error?"

"Rome doesn't err," responded his guide.

"Will the Holy Father mention my transfer during a solemn and pompous ceremony? I don't see the significance of it."

"It's not up to you to judge."

The Bishop's comments were not in line with the Church's doctrine. He recognized his mistake and added, "Father, I apologize. I'm very sorry. Rome talks and I obey."

"Good!"

"If I'm not indiscreet, may I ask the reason why Mercurius, the first Roman pope whose name is well documented, changed his name into that of John II? Also, who was the one who reigned the least?"

"As far as I know, it was Zachariah. He was pope for only four days."

"Before the ceremony was held inside the church, right?"

"Right! John Paul II changed the inauguration ceremony location in 1978. Why did you ask that question?"

"Thirst of knowledge, Father."

"I see."

The Pope arrived on foot and sat on the throne. His assistant placed the tiara on his head. In an unprecedented action, the camerlengo explained the significance of its three crowns: the holding of the spiritual and temporal power. "This means" he said, "that he is the Vicar of Christ, the world guide and the kings' supervisor. He also has three functions. He acts as a priest, prophet and king and, lastly, as Christ."

The camerlengo withdrew to his seat and the Pope's secretary handed him a booklet from which he read the formula of the creation and the nomination of the cardinals. The secretary began to call the new Cardinals. Each one humbly proceeded toward the Pope's throne, genuflected, kissed the Ring of the Fisherman, which is the sign of primacy in the Church, and made the oath of fidelity. He placed the red biretta on their heads and with the Creation Bull assigned them a church in Rome. They exchanged the hug with the sign of peace and returned to their seats.

Bishop Mitango was watching the ceremony with an enormous interest. Suddenly, he heard his name. He didn't move nor respond. The speaker repeated his name a second time. The Bishop turned his head in all directions. The Franciscan priest motioned to him to move. He didn't understand the meaning. This time, the priest gestured to him to get up and go to the Pope. The Bishop felt disoriented. The Pope was patiently waiting. The silence was oppressive. The guide hastened to the Bishop and urged him to meet the Holy Father. The Bishop struggled to get up and proceeded unsteadily toward the Pontiff. He genuflected and kissed his ring, "Your Holiness, your servant is here."

The Pope smiled, "We have heard a lot about you, Bishop Mitango. Your great work has reached the steps of St. Peter's Church. As a Vicar of Christ on earth, I declare you Cardinal."

The Bishop was stunned. He was waiting to hear about his new assignment and instead, he got a promotion. He was visibly confused. The Pope placed the biretta on his head and said, "Cardinal Mitango Africanus you may go now. Many challenges are waiting for you."

The newly elected Cardinal attempted to speak, but his lips trembled. The Holy Father asked him, "Did the Cardinal wish to speak?"

"Your Holiness, I am not worthy of this high honor."

"No one is, my dear Cardinal, but by the grace of Jesus, we must continue his work. Go, now! The African Church and the whole world need you. In fact, they are expecting a lot from you. Your next assignment is San Peter in Fiuggi, a few miles from Rome."

Cardinal Mitango kissed his ring again, struggled to get up and returned unsteadily to his seat. The crowd gave him a standing ovation that lasted five minutes.

The Pope had changed his mind about the Bishop's new location. He is going to hold his residence only a few miles from the Vatican.

# FIUGGI

After he was raised to the rank of cardinal, the Pope appointed him head of the powerful African Evangelization Church. The newly elected Cardinal was occupied most of his time in the Vatican, but didn't forget his previous church, Fiuggi, where he celebrated the Mass on Sunday.

Fiuggi is a resort town just south of Rome and is famous for its spring and thermal waters. Public records, based on clinical studies, claim that it has healing properties on gastrointestinal and urinary tracts and, most importantly, on kidneys. The water is considered to be some of the best in the world and is shipped daily in glass bottles. The town residents used to fetch it freely at specific public locations, but now they have to pay a fraction of the regular price. A political party, "Ecology to the People," purports that water belongs to everybody and it should not be sold. The residents have not protested so far and the issue has become dormant.

The thermal water is an additional bonanza for the local economy. Patients afflicted with arthritis and rheumatism spend two weeks a year in those waters for mud baths and massages. The sand mixed with the water is kept at a moderate temperature. When it's applied to the body, it frees it from epidermal impurities. Later, the mud is rinsed off and reapplied.

At the new parish, Cardinal Mitango became the sweetheart of the parents and children alike. Every Sunday, after Mass, he walked out of the church and offered candies and chocolates to children. In the summer evenings, he became accustomed to strolling down the streets. As soon as they saw him, young people would surround him with affection. He reciprocated by telling stories of the African continent. They sat on the stairs or on the ground and listened to him with a great attention. On hot days, he bought them ice cream from a passing vendor.

Within a healthy and serene environment, the Cardinal moved freely among the local residents. His popularity was on the increase. The thaumaturgic gift he bragged to have brought from Africa, increased even more his public figure. He received every month a shipment of herbs that he claimed possessed healing properties and he used them during religious rites.

Cardinal Mitango delivered his healing gift every Sunday. His methods were always controversial. There were times when he appeared on the altar with a lion at his side. The frightened parishioners fled at the beginning, but returned when he reassured them that it was inoffensive. "Why do you flee from a friendly beast? After all, he is the king of the jungle," he shouted. The people didn't hear his words. Their eyes were fixed on the animal.

A skinny older man yelled, "He won't have much to eat out me if His Excellency lets him loose." His neighbor whispered to him, "No, but he would have a feast on that fat lady." The lady heard and ran out screaming.

"People of little faith!" exclaimed the prelate halfway between the serious and the facetious. He commanded the beast to lie on the altar, and proceeded with the Eucharistic liturgy.

He turned around and said, "*Orate fraters!*" To his dismay, the pews were empty. His face got pale. He stopped the sermon and called the lion. The beast quickly came to him and sat by his side. The parishioners were dispersed in front of the church beating their chests. When they saw the Cardinal and the lion, they were about to flee, but he called them back. They stopped, but didn't obey. They were waiting for the cardinal's next step. He knew that it was a very important moment for him. He ordered the animal to dance, and he did. Afterward, he told him to kneel before St. Peter's statue and he obeyed. The people watched amused and in awe.

From the crowd, an old man decided to act. He had a son on a wheelchair paralyzed from the waist down. As he pushed the chair, the people pushed back to make room and looked at him with pity. When they arrived at a close distance to the Cardinal, the boy began to cry. Cardinal Mitango, realizing that the presence of the beast was creating an obstacle to his plans, ordered the lion to withdraw in the sacristy, which he did. A chorus of 'Alleluia' rose from the crowd. At that point, the boy ceased crying and the parishioners took courage and timidly came closer.

The Cardinal put a mask on his face, burned some herbs and inhaled the fumes. Within a minute, he started to dance on the steps of the church. The tension rose. No one was talking. The attention was focused on the priest and the boy. The Cardinal was perspiring profusely. Drops of sweat fell on the hot stone and sizzled. The boy watched them bubble and disappear. The Cardinal shouted, "Come, my friend, come! " The boy was confused. The Cardinal threw away the mask. His face was completely wet. His shirt was drenched. He rejected the impulse of grabbing a towel and wiping himself. Instead, he cried out, "I got rid of my mask. I want you to get rid of your past, of your sickness. In the name of the Lord, walk!"

The paralyzed boy never took his eyes from the Cardinal, and when the prelate repeated the same rite, he slowly stretched his feet and legs. A ticklish feeling made its way from the upper legs to the feet. His father stepped forward to help him, but the Cardinal stopped him. The parishioners surrounded the boy. The Cardinal shouted again, "I'm waiting for you. Come, come to me!" The young man held both arms on the wheelchair and made an effort to obtain an erect position. His father was watching him motionless. The boy took a step, two three and reached the arms of the Cardinal. "It's a miracle! A miracle! The miracle of the mineral water," shouted the crowd and in a few minutes the whole church was filled. The police had to intervene to rescue the boy from suffocation and the Cardinal from being carried on the shoulders through the town.

People testified that "the miracle of the mineral water" was actually the prelude to further miracles. The Vatican displayed cautious reservations and refused to comment. The Cardinal boasted of possessing a healing gift. One fact remained undisputed. The church was always packed on Sunday.

The Vatican's vigilance increased and sent its watchdogs to the area. The Cardinal's image began to suffer. Rumors of an intimate relationship with his secretary started to fly around until they became insistent. The parishioners' esteem for him never vacillated. The purported miracles he carried out were sufficient to eliminate any doubt from their minds.

The Cardinal either ignored the rumors or simply didn't care because he went ahead helping the secretary to get the annulment of her first marriage from the Sacra Rota. As that wasn't enough, the Curia was concerned about the high stipend he paid her. "What you don't do, you don't see," murmured the "bad tongues." A Vatican private investigator reported that the lady left her children at home and spent vacations with the Cardinal in a remote area of the Dolomites. Cardinal Connelly disclosed in a closed session that Cardinal Mitango was part of the obsessed sexual culture and needed therapeutic help.

Father Mitango responded in his own way. He stated that he didn't take any lesson from someone who came from the most immoral nation on earth. He accused his colleague of having been discredited as a young seminarian, and went to work as a manager in a company whose president was a close friend of the Cardinal since his childhood. He was reinstated in the priesthood later, mainly for the scarcity of priestly vocations. The townfolks sided with Cardinal Mitango for he was immensely popular among them. The Vatican was displeased by the bickering and cautioned both prelates to moderate their tone and avoid any language conducive to misunderstanding and internal strife.

Eventually, what cast some doubts on the Cardinal's gift to heal was also his social behavior. He was present at wedding receptions or at parties where he danced, ate, and drank. His popularity reached the pinnacle when he accepted an invitation from the organizers of the Moscow Spring Festival where he participated with an African song, "Gubudu, Gubudu." Although he had a fairly good voice, his song didn't win the nomination. Despite the failure to bring home one of the first three prizes, his recognition gained momentum and he sold one million CDs in China alone.

In Africa, every radio station played "Gubudu, Gubudu" and young and old sang the song everywhere: in the streets, in the school halls, in the stadiums and on the beaches.

Some African politicians sent his name for the Nobel Peace Prize. In his hometown, in Accra, in Malawi, in Capetown, the local governments erected statues in the main squares in his honor.

Everything was running smoothly for the Cardinal until a tragic event shook up Fiuggi. A nun accused a priest of sexual molestation. The news rocked the serene atmosphere of the town. The priest reacted angrily to the accusation, "It's absolutely false! I ignore the motivation at the basis of this accusation, but I can prove that it's devoid of even a grain of truth. Obviously, someone is pulling the rope behind the curtain either out of envy or in hope of an easy remuneration settlement."

The townfolks considered the case to be murky. They feared that negative news of their town would damage the spring water business and have a negative impact on the local economy. "Who is going to drink our water now?" they protested.

The prosecution didn't accept the priest's defense and threatened to play a tape of telephone interceptions in which one could hear explicit sexual innuendos.

"Garbage!" replied the priest. I was joking with the nun. Someone, or more than one, is trying to catch and fry me in his pan. It's not that easy. The truth will prevail."

During the deposition, the judge asked the man, "Why didn't you reveal that earlier?"

"Your Honor, they threatened me not to make any charge."

"Did you inform Mother Superior?"

"Yes, I also told other nuns. They were terrorized. They too in different occasions were subjected to verbal and physical provocations."

"And how did they react?"

"Very easily! Some of them threw out the habit and returned to the civilian life."

"Didn't Mother Superior contact Cardinal Mitango?"

"I have no idea, Your Honor."

"When you realized that she didn't take any action, why didn't you get in touch with him?"

"He never returned the call."

"Did you talk it over with their families?"

"They wanted to put their hands on him."

"When did you decide to press charges against him?"

"When I decided to give up the habit."

"You mean you are an ex-priest?"

"Yes, Your Honor!"

The judge showed signs of nervousness. He adjourned the case and ordered the secretary to get hold of Cardinal Mitango. He opened the session and asked, "Cardinal, were you aware of the priestly misconduct behind the scenes?"

"No, Your Honor! The priest is well liked in our community. He has assisted many drug addicts and alcoholics and saved many of their lives."

"Why didn't you respond to the calls?"

"May I remind this court that I do most of my work in Rome."

"So, you disregarded them."

"I didn't say that."

"Have you heard of a letter that the nun sent to Cardinal Ratzinger?"

"I have no knowledge of it, sir."

The judge dismissed any act of the Cardinal for lack of proof. The day before he issued the verdict, a newspaper reported that the priest's body was dangling under the ceiling of the rectory. The nun began psychiatric therapy.

# The Cardinal's Demise

Within the Vatican walls, an anti-Mitango movement brewed with the papal knowledge. The liberal, populist demeanor of the Cardinal ran onto the rocks for many reasons. The last, but not the least, was his purported gift of healing. Private criticism became public. The pope was caught in a crossfire. To please the conservative wing in the Vatican and to prevent any further political and other denominations' criticism, he created a special commission to report by the end of the year. Before the work began, he made a last attempt to avert unnecessary internal bleeding of the Church and ordered the Curia to call for a preliminary meeting in which the Cardinal's participation was assured.

The meeting was free from an inquisition label, but it turned out to be a hot debate.

The president of the commission was Cardinal Sodano. He reminded the commission that the nature of the gathering was informational and had no power to implement any decision. Its only obligation was to refer the content to the pontiff. He also reminded them to use fairness in their judgment.

The first to ask permission to speak was the Australian Cardinal from Canberra. He looked at his notes and said, "Cardinal Mitango, do you realize the gravity of the accusations lodged against your diocese?"

"Your Eminence, I heard about the allegations of a cover up in the case of a priest ..."

"Your position appears factional in the matter. How well did you know the priest and the nuns?"

"Actually, we met sporadically in my office for a drink."

"And the nuns?"

"Casual encounters."

"Were you aware that he was aspiring to be bishop and cultivated close relations with some prelates in the Vatican?"

"I don't deny that possibility."

Jakarta's Cardinal calmly rose to his feet, "Your Excellency should know that the Canadian and the Italian bishops don't approve of the illegal activities being exercised in your diocese."

"For instance?"

"They are highly skeptical of the miracles that happen during your Mass."

"They happen under the sun. What can I say?" He responded calmly.

The Cardinal from Los Angeles interjected, "The exorcism, the religious rites mixed with native witchcrafts may have future deleterious impact on the Church."

"Your Excellency, what you call witchcraft may be different instruments of calling divine intervention. I use them because they have their values."

The Cardinal of Accra was patiently waiting his turn. When it finally arrived, he said, "Brothers, each one of us displays his character, his personality. Cardinal Mitango's *modus operandi* may differ from ours, but it's serving the interests of the church. The number of parishioners has increased and so have the revenues. He is well liked, even loved, by everybody. We should abstain from unleashing premature and harsh criticism on our beloved brother Cardinal."

The Cardinal stood on his feet for a minute or so and none of his brothers rebuked him. At that point, Cardinal Mitango raised his hand and addressed the assembly. "First and foremost, I wish to thank my brother Cardinal from Accra for his wisdom and kind words on my behalf. Secondly, you ought to know that the Vatican manual on exorcism is outdated. You lack the courage and the determination to rectify the past, to revise and to modernize. Yet, if a poor, humble priest from Africa celebrates the Mass with new rituals that contrast with the Church tradition, but revitalizes it, you label him "impostor.'

"Let me be more straightforward. I heal and you accuse me of causing a rift among you and a loss of faith among the parishioners. You call me a progressive man because I mingle with priests, nuns and people. Go around and see if they love me. Walk in the streets and mention my name to the children. Come to my church and see if there is any empty pew …" He waited for a reply which came promptly. He looked at the next speaker and shook his head, but sat and listened.

The Cardinal from Leningrad stood up and exclaimed, "Your Eminence has been very active in raising money for convents that never reaches its destination.

You organize clubs where the presidents have the stench of mafia. The Holy Father is as concerned about your activities as we are."

"There are expenses, Your Eminence," and he opened up a revenue book on the table.

The Cardinals exchanged doubtful looks, but made no remarks. The Cardinal from Viet Nam, Noi Yeng, took off the eyeglasses and set them on the book. Everyone was waiting for him to take the floor, but he wiped his face and put back his glasses without saying anything. Someone laughed and there followed a chain reaction which seemed endless Cardinal Noi Yeng wasn't sure if the humor was directed at him, but to dispel any doubt from his mind, he decided to speak. "My brothers, we are being confronted with the erosion of priestly values that undermine the work of the Church, and present vocations. The focus of our debate isn't just the complaints of a nun and the subsequent suicide of a priest. The majority of the nuns have returned to their families. It's important to remind ourselves of the fundamental role they play within the church and the community. They visit the sick in the hospitals and the detainees in jails. They educate the children and feed the poor. They assist the widows and attend on drug addicts …" He stopped brusquely and sat. Someone made a hilarious remark, but it was too soft to be heard.

The Cardinal of Tokyo, Katenacuru, opened his arms and stated, "The statement made by our brother clearly insinuates that the judiciary approach taken by Cardinal Mitango was a failure, not to say scandalous."

"Not so fast," responded Cardinal Echevarria. "We haven't determined yet if the nuns responded to the sexual provocation of the priest or if they blew the whistle when they realized that there was a lack of reciprocity."

Cardinal Mitango was outraged, He jumped on his feet and shouted, "What's is wrong with falling in love? It's the fire of life. It's part of our human instinct."

The head of the Congregation of Faith fired back, "Your Eminence, let's not forget that we are married to the Church. We took a vow and we must respect it."

"I have a lot to say about that, brother Cardinal. Peter was married, wasn't he?" insisted Cardinal Mitango.

"True, but the Church has the right to make rules and change them as long as they don't impinge on Christ's teaching."

The Vietnamese Cardinal was dissatisfied in the way his intervention ended. He told them that he didn't finish his remarks and asked permission to continue. "I'm sorry that you drew premature conclusions from my unfinished remarks. I support the initiative of debating the change of the priestly celibacy state. Four of our brothers have already separated from us. How far can we go without looking at the signs of the time?"

The participants' reaction was immediate and sarcastic. The debate was getting inflamed. The commission president hit the gavel and said, "We are not called here to reaffirm or deny the validity or invalidity of the chastity vow, neither do we have jurisdiction over Cardinal Mitango's future." He again hit the table with the gavel and said, "The discussion continues."

The Cardinal of Bulgaria raised his hand and said, "Brothers, religious life is a vocation, not a profession. If one withdraws from the vow, he can no longer exercise his priestly functions for he gives up his priestly rights." His remarks were suffocated by complaints from many sides. A hubbub ensued until the president hit the gavel again.

The confusion abated and the Cardinal from Brazil asked permission to speak. The president responded that he would be the last one. "Dear brothers," he exclaimed, "this heated debate is the direct consequence of misbehavior, misjudgment and negligence of duty on the part of those involved in the case. When the dust is settled, you will find out that the losers are not just two or five or them, but all of us. Think about it!"

No one seemed to contest that statement. The president expressed his gratitude for the healthy exchange of ideas. "I heard your input. I'll report to His Holiness. Thank you very much for your contribution. I don't need to remind you to pray for the soul of our brother priest, the nuns, our Eminence Mitango and for our beloved Church. You are dismissed."

In the Curia's office, the president of the commission on celibacy looked frustrated. He opened Cardinal Mitango's dossier and said to his assistant, "The Congregation of Faith is furious with Mitango. They are ready to publish a pamphlet that refutes all his teaching on exorcism." He noticed that the Cardinal from Toronto wished to speak and granted him permission.

"Perhaps we should inform him of how clever he was in hiring people he paid to assist him and how much higher his income was in comparison to other parish priests. Needless to say, he created an affluent society around him that has become an embarrassment to the Church. The Communist newspaper *l'Unita* is about to publish a series of articles that offer evidence of his off-limit life style."

Another member added, "He doesn't conform with the evangelic spirit at all. He is a frustrated man who pursues 'protagonism'. He needs a lesson in humility."

The Cardinal from Calcutta said, "Mitango annulled a marriage of a famous person by twisting this Rota's hand. I'm disappointed that we are revealing these truths in this unofficial gathering and not in the presence of Mitango."

The rest of the group didn't share the same feelings, "Nobody stopped us from talking. I can assure you of that. We are not confronted with one problem, but with a series of endless problems. If we all spoke, the meeting would have lasted a long time. Nonetheless, you can still add our remarks to the previous ones when you hand the file to the Holy Father."

The president closed by saying, "Let's pray that this tempest has quelled, but with Mitango, you never know what his next move is. When you deal with him, there is always a surprise waiting in the corner, Thank you again for your time and wisdom."

It was a Monday morning. Life went on as usual at Fiuggi. A long line of patients waited to be admitted to the clinic for the mud baths. In the streets, the fruit vendors shouted and children played soccer. Cardinal Mitango had just celebrated the Mass and went to the sacristy. His cellular rang. The voice said, "Your Eminence must immediately return to Rome. Report to Cardinal Sodano."

At two o'clock, Cardinal Mitango knocked at the door of the office of Cardinal Sodano. The secretary welcomed him and invited him to sit. She informed him that the Cardinal was temporarily absent, but it didn't matter because he had a letter for him. Cardinal Mitango opened it. The Holy Office was ordering him to take permanent residence in an apartment at Porta Angelica. "Your new assignment is "Overseer of San Peter Basilica. You may not celebrate Mass anymore at Fiuggi. Cardinal Sodano will be available for further elucidation."

The Cardinal slowly refolded the letter, walked out and closed the door behind him.

Outside, his assistant was waiting anxiously. He rushed toward the Cardinal, who said, "We must pack up right away and return to Rome."

# St. Peter's Church

Mitango was empowered to oversee the restoration of the Basilica. He was responsible for the treasury and the archives related to it. His job was awesome!

San Peter Church was built over the Constantine Basilica from 306 to 337. It was so dear to lay people and clergy that no pope dared to either reconstruct or demolish it. Not even Nicholas V in 1451 dared to touch it!

Julius II, the warrior pope, didn't need any advice or consultation from anyone. He was indisputably the most magnanimous pope of all time. He was blessed with being pope during the Renaissance and took advantage of it in all its dimensions. In 1506, he summoned Bramante, a great architect, to reveal his plans for the construction of the new Basilica. Even great artists were victims of demanding popes. Julius II, displeased by the way the project was proceeding, fired him and didn't lose any sleep over the dismissal. He replaced him with Sangallo, a student of Brunelleschi.

The new pontiff was also a warrior. To confirm that fame, in 1507, he went to Bologna to snatch the region away from foreign invaders. He earned the nickname of "Julius Caesar" and boasted of being a pope-emperor. To exemplify his position, he put his effigy on one side of his medal with the famous sentence, 'Veni, vidi, vici,' and on the other side he placed the effigy of the Roman emperor.

In building the new Basilica of San Peter, the pope planned to use the Pantheon as a model and didn't care how much he invested money in art treasures. His love for art was boundless, and he had a voracious desire to make the new construction one of the seven wonders of the world. He purchased the Lacoonte, discovered on the Thermae Bathis, which was considered the best example of sculptural perfection of the antiquity.

Cardinal Mitango looked at the pope's painting and said, "I inherited a tremendous responsibility from you, but I don't have your power."

In his first day in office, the new overseer of the Basilica called a meeting of all his associates and stated, "Today, more than ever, I need your support, guidance and understanding. I rely on your patience, knowledge and experience for the success of the church. Please, help me to carry out my titanic duty." Everyone bowed his head and expressed his full support, commitment and cooperation to the newly appointed supervisor.

# The Shoah and the Vatican

The Israeli Ambassador to the Vatican was getting uneasy. He walked up and down the office while the secretaries were trying to keep up with the unusually high number of calls coming in that morning. The air was saturated with tension. His government ordered him to have a meeting with the Basilica's new supervisor, Cardinal Mitango, at the earliest date. He also coordinated some internal affairs relative to World War II. The Jewish government was concerned about the many complaints lodged against the Vatican by the Shoah's survivors. At the heart of their contention was an issue of enormous financial implications. They claimed that during World War II, the Yugoslavian Jews gave jewels, money and testaments to the Vatican Nunzio to help them escape. They didn't dispute the lives that the Catholic Church saved by providing sanctuaries and, later, escape to America. They express once again their deep gratitude, but refused to renounce their personal wealth despite the fact that half century has passed by.

The telephone rang in Cardinal's Mitango's office, "Hello, the Jewish ambassador wishes to speak with the Cardinal."

On the other line, one could hear the voice of the Cardinal, "Hello, ambassador, so nice to hear from you."

"Your Excellency, if you don't have the time to meet briefly with me, I'll convey my government's most pressing matter to you now. I'm sure that with you we can find a quick and reasonable solution to the issue."

"And what is it?"

"I suppose you are acquainted with the history of the Shoah, the Holocaust."

"Of course, but not the issues with the Vatican. I have just been assigned to this new Ministry."

"Yes, yes, I know it. Forgive me, but it would be better if we could arrange a meeting where there is no danger of telephone interception."

"That's a reasonable request."

"This evening at Trastevere, across the Tiber. Dress in civilian clothes and use a hat. See you at seven."

"At seven."

The Cardinal hung up the receiver and reclined on his armchair. He appeared tired already. He closed his eyes and pretended to rest. He asked for an expresso and called on two attendants to do some research on the Shoah. They made gestures of deference and went to research. Not even a brush of wind was felt around the area.

It was already dark on the bridge, darker than in previous evenings. The air was immobile under a blue sky. It was neither chilly nor humid.

The river's waters had reached the ebb on the left bank, but on the right they still kept murmuring. The grass had grown wild on both sides and some tourists looked in a small mirror of water to see their reflection. The traffic was scarce, scarce as never seen before. Maybe the Romans were gathered at the Flaminio's Stadium for a soccer game. There, there was chaos. The windows in the buildings were closed.

A car arrived on the bridge and stopped. The Cardinal stepped out and looked around with suspicion. As he didn't see anyone, he walked up and down the street. Not even a soul passed by him. It was seven fifteen. He was getting impatient. He turned around. The sound of the heels on the pavement called his attention. He stood frozen and glanced in the stagnant water at the river bank to see if any human silhouette was reflected in it. The sound continued and got closer. With his peripheral vision, he noticed a gentleman, very distinguished in his clothing, with two big rings on his fingers. They resembled emeralds, judging from their brilliance, perceptible even at a distance. The man wasn't alone. He was flanked by two ladies. One was tall and the other short like the man. Jewels were shining everywhere on their bodies. Necklaces of pearls surrounded their necks and fell all the way down to the bosom. The brilliant earrings were round, and long enough to reach almost the top of their shoulders. The wrists were covered with gold bracelets and every finger had a ring.

The Cardinal didn't recognize them. He had never met them before. As they approached, he smelled the perfume of violets and roses. He breathed in deeply and shook his head a bit. The man and his companions stopped and introduced themselves. Good evening Your Excellency. I'm …"

"Yes, I recognize your voice." The Cardinal froze because of how the man had addressed him. The man caught his uneasiness and calmed him down, "Don't worry. These are trustworthy ladies. They are my are my confidants, my personal secretaries, if you know what I mean. Madam X and Madam Y."

"It's so nice to meet Madams X and Y."

"Every man deserves a pretty woman at his side; sometimes two if he can afford them."

The Cardinal smiled.

The man insisted, "Wouldn't you agree, Cardinal?"

They got closer to him. The man wasn't absolutely sure that he had dissipated any doubt in the Cardinal's mind. It meant a lot to him that the guest feel comfortable. So he added, "But if they make you nervous, I'll send them back to the office."

"Oh, no, not at all, ambassador," replied the Cardinal with a gesture of assurance.

The man felt that it was imperative to make a clarification before the situation could get complicated. He said, "Cardinal, I would like to eliminate a misunderstanding."

"Which is?"

"I'm not the ambassador of Israel. I'm acting on his behalf. He had a last minute engagement and couldn't make it."

The Cardinal didn't appreciate it and was ready to leave. He felt embarrassed and feared that he was being used. The gentleman's voice was familiar. How did he confuse his voice? Maybe he heard it on television.

The man thought that his fame had reached the Vatican, therefore he didn't need any introduction. The situation was getting entangled. To ease up the tension, he said with a smile, "Let us start all over again. I'm Lucky Star, head of the Poor Church of Brazil."

The Cardinal's body shook. If he had doubts before, now he was convinced that the ambassador had set up a trap for him. In a moment of pride, he protested, "I beg your pardon, sir. I'm aware of only one universal church, and that is the Catholic Church."

"With all due respect, Your Excellency, we best express the notion of Unified Church because we are a mosaic of religions. We are an umbrella under which nobody gets wet."

"I think I read about you."

"I thought so. My church is the most progressive and powerful."

"So powerful that you ended up in jail."

"Nonsense! That was a fallacious interpretation of the American law. In fact, I regained my freedom as you can very well see."

The girls got a bit closer to the Cardinal. The scent of their perfume engulfed his nostrils and he backed up against the bridge parapet. The Cardinal realized that he was in an unsuitable predicament and made an attempt to get out of it. "I'd better leave. It was nice meeting all three of you."

"Where are you going?" responded the Reverend. "You must stay with us. You have no choice." The girls smiled. The Reverend continued, "Your Excellency was supposed to meet with the Israeli ambassador. Unfortunately, he couldn't make it. I want you to know that I took care of your dispute. He has no reason to bother you anymore."

The Cardinal gave a sigh of relief. The contention with Israel would have caused him a lot of problems. But he wanted equally to defend his cause, "The Church is poor. Where would it get all that money? More than half a century has gone by. People have died."

"They could open the archives," contested Lucky Star.

The Cardinal tried to justify the Vatican's action, but he didn't need to. The Reverend didn't want to spoil the evening and said, "I'm not going to press for it. I repeat once again. I put a big chunk of meat in his mouth and took care of the Shoah."

"And the Israeli government …?"

"You said that most everybody died … As you can see, you have nothing to worry about. As a matter of fact, I'll send news to the newspapers agencies that you were able to resolve amicably a thorny issue with Israel. I give you also permission to use my name to confirm it."

The Cardinal was visibly astonished. He was speechless. The traffic was getting more intense. It was hard to hear well. "Now, we can skip the meeting. I have to return to my office. Tomorrow is a busy day."

"Not so fast," replied the Reverend. "We should have a party worthy of the occasion. Half an hour will do it. Come, the girls are harmless."

"I would not exactly say that," responded the Cardinal looking at the girls.

"I agree with you to a certain extent," the Reverend continued, "wine and women are as old as human history. They have destroyed the lives of millions of men. They have collapsed governments and nations went in disarray and defeat, but they are still the best gift to man."

"What does that have to do with me? I'm a priest."

"Nothing or everything! It depends on you. You are free to move at will, to do as you wish. You can join us for a coffee and cheer for the fortunate event or go back to the Vatican and return to your lonely office within the cold marble walls...."

The girls wore gowns that split at the knee and the bodice formed a deep V. They took the Cardinal by the arm and said, "Won't you come just for a little while? It's only a cup of coffee. You can spare a half hour for us, can't you?"

The Cardinal blushed. He didn't want to answer. The girls massaged his hands and led him with them.

Lucky Star snapped his fingers and the door to the establishment opened. "Don't worry, Excellency, everything is magic around here." Once seated inside, four young ladies, two blonde and two brunette, appeared. Lucky whispered something and they left. They came back two minutes later. Two carried large trays of appetizers and pastries. The others brought bottles of champagne, cognac and red wine.

The Cardinal remarked, "Too bad we don't have Strega. I would make a good drink."

The Reverend didn't bother answering. He snapped his fingers again and a side door opened. A young Asian lady brought in what Mitango had asked. "This place *is* magic," he admitted.

"Whatever you wish is here, my dear Cardinal.

The ladies filled the glasses, One of them was specially marked and the head lady made sure that would be The Cardinal's glass. At the completion of their duty, they withdrew bowing before the prelate.

The Reverend raised his glass and exclaimed, "Cheers to our beloved Eminence who has given us the great honor of sharing with us these moments."

One of the girls added in a sweet voice, "We hope that His Eminence will find happiness."

One of her friends, said, "Only our church can give that happiness."

The Cardinal protested, "Wait a minute!"

The same girl replied, "I didn't mean that. I meant our 'church.'"

The Cardinal laughed and raised his voice, "Cheers!"

The girls responded altogether, "Cheers! Long live the Cardinal!" One by one they hugged and kissed him.

The conversation was proceeding according to the Reverend's plan. The glasses were emptied and filled. He noticed that the Cardinal was sweating and excused himself along with three girls to give him a few minutes of privacy. The

Cardinal appreciated it. The door closed and he drank another glass of Strega, then, he reclined on the sofa. He was feeling sleepy.

The door opened again. A young lady sat next to him and whispered in his ears, "Don't you think that a man needs a woman at his side?"

The prelate made an effort in answering and stammered, "I agree with you."

"I don't see why you should deprive yourself of the sweetest being on earth. It's not fair."

"Yes, but I'm already married to the church," he replied, brokenly.

"Do you have the church next to you when you go to bed?"

"I better go, now." He made an effort to get up, but he was weak, too weak and sleepy.

The girl took a strand of her long her and put it in the Cardinal's ears. The perfume made him feel even more inebriated. He put his hand on the girl's knee, but she withdrew and said, "No, no, no, naughty boy. You said that you are married. Really, I don't believe those who say that priests don't have blood." She took a cigarette and began to smoke. She touched his nose with her long nails and whispered, "Your time will come when you get what you want, not with me but with one of your choice and for a wife."

The Cardinal fell into a deep sleep. The Reverend opened the door and congratulated the lady, "Job well done, my dear. Make sure you get in touch with my assistants in the States to get the ladies ready. This marriage will have such a deleterious impact on the Catholic Church that all religions will join us."

The lady assented. "As long as I'm here, why not sip a cup of tea."

"Great idea!" exclaimed the Reverend.

Lucky Star had accumulated an enormous fortune. He owned property in every corner of the world. One of his buildings was across the bridge. The interior was warmly decorated with paintings of Rembrandt, Picasso, Dali' and Velasquez. On the main wall hung a giant picture of himself. He wore a high turban and a vest that reached the floor. From his neck fell a large medallion in various colors, all gems, with the cosmos under them, symbol of the Poor Church, whose picture sat next to him. On the rest of the walls, there were pictures of beautiful women.

The Reverend gave an order to the ladies to make it as pleasant as possible for the guest when he woke up. They told him to rest assured that his words were their commands.

Cardinal Mitango didn't show up in his office the following morning. The secretary answered "unavailable for the day, but when the Secretary of State looked for him and couldn't find him, the Vatican went into turmoil. The Cardinal had disappeared leaving no message, nothing about his whereabouts. The news secretly spread to Fiuggi, where the townfolks believed he was playing a prank. Of the opposite view was the Curia where a suspicious mood prevailed.

At Saint Patrick's cathedral in New York, a man knelt before the altar. Cardinal Mitango. The church was empty. He bowed his head and said, "Lord, forgive me. The flesh is weak. You created me like this. What can I do?"

Suddenly, he heard a voice. He thought he was dreaming or it came from his conscience. The voice was loud, "My dear son, you need to acquire a sense of equilibrium."

"What equilibrium? I can't live without a woman. She is the fulfillment of all my emotional needs."

"That's all?"

"… Of my aspirations and dreams. Why does the Church deny us this privilege? Are we made of stone? Weren't we made to complement each other?"

"A religious life," answered the voice, "isn't made up of privileges, but of self-denials, deprivations, humility and servility."

"Lord, get someone else in my place. I reached the point of no return. I surrender, but don't hold it against me. I have the religious vocation, but I can't bring it to completion. I want to love a woman like every man."

The wind entered through the glassy windows, slightly open, and jolted the cross on the altar. The noise shook the Cardinal, who got scared and looked upward. He interpreted the event as ominous, and backed up a few feet. "Lord," he continued, "I asked for strength and here I am, as weak as ever. I begged the Archangel Michael to stand by me with his flaming sword, but the temptations have multiplied."

"You must persevere in prayer," the voice insisted.

"How many times have I prayed, Lord? Perhaps I don't know how to pray. Teach me!"

"My dear child, I taught you. You are the type of child that unless he goes through a dramatic experience will never learn the lesson."

"Why don't other men have the same sensitivity to the opposite sex. Some priests are indifferent."

"A woman should not be the object of desire, but to share love and suffering."

"So why does the Church impede me from attaining this goal?"

"The Church is the governing body of Christ on earth and you must submit even when you think that its rules are apparently inconsistent with reality."

"You have created me flesh and bones and you expect me to be wholly spiritual?"

"If you couldn't take the heat, you should have gotten out of the kitchen, I mean the seminary, from the beginning."

"But it was my faith that brought me where I am."

"Why don't you offer your body to Christ instead?"

"Why can't I be a priest and a husband?"

"I can't undo what the church has done."

"Don't we have to renew ourselves?"

"That's true and renewal should occur in every moment of your life. Nonetheless, when you deal with a divine institution, such as the Church, you have to wait until the time is ripe."

"Lord, don't hold it against me. I'm not like others."

In that instant, a noise broke the silence. He turned around and noticed a man with a white collar and black suit dashing out of the back door. "… And all along, I thought the Lord was talking to me …"

# MITANGO'S MARRIAGE

In the meantime, Fiuggi had become a center of pilgrimage. From Moscow to Shanghai, from Capetown to Buenos Aires, sick people flocked Mitango's former church in search of a miracle. They came alone, in groups, by planes and boats unaware of the Cardinal's removal and disappearance.

In China, the ruling party tried to discourage the pilgrimage. Some of them considered him a renegade, a traitor, a counterrevolutionary. For the younger politicians, however, the benefits that he brought to the AIDS population were too vivid in their hearts. Even though their resolution to allow and encourage the pilgrimage didn't pass, they wished to be counted among his friends.

The Russian Politburo didn't pay much attention to the trips made by the faithful. It was too engrossed in the Chechnya war and obsessed with oil profits. The Patriarch of Moscow, Alexis II, remained neutral. Only a few hard core Orthodox second rank leaders tried to cool the enthusiasm, but the pilgrims ignored their pleas, and marched on the trail of hope to Fiuggi.

Pilgrims from the Indian peninsula and Japan were driven by the same desire. They longed to see and touch the great healer and maybe receive a miracle.

Unfortunately for all of those souls, Cardinal Mitango was meeting in a luxurious hotel in the United States with Lucky Star and four ladies from whom he had to pick one for wife. Two of them were from Beijing with Confucius' background. One was from Nagasaki and was Catholic. The fourth came from Thailand and had no religious preference. The secretive meeting laid the ground for the elaborate marriage.

The Cardinal checked for the last time each of the candidates and placed a flower on the head of the chosen one. He took her by hand and walked to an adjacent room to confer about the wedding arrangements. Eventually, they found agreement on all aspects and emerged glittering from the meeting.

The Cardinal's choice fell on the Japanese woman, named Tokina. She was fifty years old with an artistic background. Her stature was short. Her long, black hair fell on her shoulders, and almond eyes sparkled. Besides her native language, she spoke Korean and Chinese. Her demeanor was sweet and so was her voice. She spoke more with her gentle gestures than with the tongue.

The Reverend and his cohort were pleased by the course of the events.

The stage was set for the wedding. The air was still and the sky transparent. The sun had already descended behind the horizon. A lonely dog in front of the Unification Church was chasing flies that flew by. The parking lot was deserted. The whole area appeared to have fallen under a dormant spell. But, as soon as the tower bells rang, the traffic became alive again.

The marriage, which was top secret, had an inside "deep throat." The news traveled by the speed of light, and one hundred thousand pilgrims gathered in Fiuggi before a giant television screen with the hope that the Cardinal would remember them and touch them with his thaumaturgic powers. The images of the Reverend and his assistants flashed on the maxi-video, but the Cardinal never showed up. Despite the disappointment, people remained in the square until the end. Immediately after, the contract specifics were already common knowledge. It called for two months of chastity obligation. The sexual clause made some people twist their nose. One of them remarked, "He is over seventy years old and she is only fifty. How long are they going to wait? What is he going to do with her? The age differential is too great."

He had just finished talking, when a woman from the crowd, shouted, "Miracle! Miracle!" That word, like a magnet, attracted everybody's attention and one by one they fell on their knees. All eyes were concentrated on a man who threw away his crutches and started walking. This event had just taken place when an old man from India, mute since his birth, began to talk. The crowd got ecstatic and ignored the fragmented pictures of the marriage appearing on the screen and whatever was related to it. The important thing was that Cardinal Mitango hadn't forgotten them.

The few policemen at hand had their work cut out to contain the flow of people toward the places where the purported miracles occurred.

The wedding was under way. A man wearing a white smoking jacket with a red flower on the lapel was climbing out from a limousine. He met Tokina on the main entrance and gave her his hand. Cardinal Mitango grew increasingly nervous. Reliable sources, close to him, revealed that he was a man alternating moments of tension with times of joy.

The ceremony began with a Korean priest marrying a dozen couples, who shouted "Mon sie" and left in a hurry.

Cardinal Mitango and Tokina moved toward the altar. There was no place to sit in the church. It was crowded to capacity. Among the guests, there was a vice-president of a South American country, whose name we won't mention to respect his wishes, and a Catholic priest from a nearby diocese.

The Reverend appeared in Oriental robes and announced that an hour earlier he had seen Jesus. The crowd shouted, "Benzai—Ten thousand years of life!"

At the end of the ceremony, young girls, dressed in white, threw rice on the newlyweds. Clusters of reporters were waiting impatiently. They threw a barrage of questions to him, but he released a simple statement, "The union between me and Tokina is a gift from God, therefore this sacrament is valid. After forty years of being a Catholic priest, the Lord has granted me the privilege to fulfill my dream. I refused to be hypocrite,. Many of them, men and women, on the sideline, engage in all sorts of illicit behaviors, which cause so much pain to the Church. I'm Mitango Africanus and stand by my words. Thank you and goodbye." The Reverend's assistants whisked them away and the guests also departed for a reception, whose destination was known only to them.

The news of Mitango's wedding rocked the Vatican's walls. Cardinal Sodano, who had previously ordered him to stop celebrating the Mass, expelled him from the Curia and consulted with Cardinal Ratzinger on the possibility of excommunicating him. The pope cautioned everybody to exercise self-control in their public comments.

The newlyweds disappeared from public view. Reporters were disseminated to every major city. In Africa, instead, some unconfirmed reports indicated that they were moving in the Washington area. A few days later, they were spotted around the capital.

One reporter asked him, "How does it feel to be married, Cardinal?"

"Great!"

"The religious ceremony put a seal on the marriage."

"It was a full sacrament. What else is there to add?"

"What are your expectations from Rome?"

"I expect a blessing."

"A papal blessing?"

"We will see."

"How do you respond to the allegations of abuse of power and violation of the exorcism rules according to the Catholic manual?"

"Absurd!"

"The Curia president has ordered you not celebrate Mass *sine die*."

"I'm still a priest, not a salesman."

"They have accused you of organizing clubs with the specific purpose of helping the poor, but you have manipulated the funds."

"Absolutely false! There was no lucrative purpose in handling the money."

"They also charge you with exploiting your image on television for personal gains and miracles which were a fluke."

"I deny categorically all the charges."

"And the song you sang, "Vundu Vundu?""

"There was nothing scandalous about it. If you want people to come to church you have to identify yourself with them."

"Even at the cost of the truth?"

"Rubbish!"

"Who is Lucky Star?"

"He is the head of the Poor Church."

"Did you, at any time, realize that the Reverend's real aim was to use you to attract disaffected Catholics to his church? Didn't he pursue the goal of dispersing the sheep by controlling the pastor?"

The Cardinal didn't reply. He stood in the midst of the crowd in a pensive mood. Another reporter from Germany insisted, "Do you agree that the Reverend's main and only plan is to create a schism with Rome?" Again, there was no response. The crowd was waiting with their mouth open for a response which the ex-Cardinal never uttered.

A newsman from Congo made a last attempt to get an answer, "Didn't the Reverend create in you a new symbol of rebellion? He didn't cast an arrow at the Vatican. He let you do it."

"Enough!" shouted the prelate and rushed into a limousine nearby that the Reverend's associates had ready for him.

Lucky Star was a powerful man. His abilities surpassed those of the American president.

Initially, he roamed from one church to another. He felt very unstable. He considered the Presbyterian bishop too permissive regarding women, letting them do whatever they wanted.

He also considered Buddhist monks a waste of life. "They spend most of the day in contemplation. They don't do anything except rest."

He depicted the Islamic Ayatollahs as men of power who preached hatred and violence instead of peace. They usurped political authority, but hardly played their primary role of prayer and peace.

During the Viet Nam War, Christian faith diminished. Too much blood, too much suffering too much death catapulted the soldiers and part of the population into an identity crisis. Not many were interested anymore in going to church and following the Commandments. Lucky Star was shrewd. He understood that it was his time to act. His claim that God had revealed a message to him since he was in his teens gained a few followers. He organized a meeting and emerged as the leader of the Unification Church. When his followers grew in number, he made frequent comparisons between himself and the prophet Mohammed. He made a bundle of money by arranging interracial and international marriages and his fame knew no bounds.

From his hotel room, Mitango was watching The Reverend's rally of one million people in the capital and marveled. "This man is powerful and rich," he said to his wife.

According to American authorities, the money that flowed into the Reverend's coffers was not able to be accounted for. The IRS checked his finances and found irregularities. They sent him to jail in a western state for tax evasion.

Mitango read in the newspapers about his friend's misfortune. The man who blessed his ring was no longer free. He remained perplexed and for the first time he began to suspect that he had been defrauded and humiliated.

To most people, the aftermath of Mitango's marriage is shrouded in a blanket of hypotheses. His public appearances were a rarity. To his well-wishers, he responded that he and his wife had agreed to have children after the abstinence period and that he was going to spend the time to write his memoirs.

He was very watchful of the briefcase containing his notes and never left it unattended wherever he went. He made his wife aware of its importance. "Tokina," he whispered to her, "Don't let anyone touch it. You must promise to keep it a secret."

"Do you mean during your lifetime?"

"No, even when I have passed away."

"And if I'm in a dire need and someone offers me a lot of money?"

"You should not be concerned about that. The Reverend will provide you the means for living a comfortable retirement. We both signed a deal to protect you during your the old age."

"What is so secretive about the briefcase and how good is it if nobody will open it?"

Mitango puffed up in a clear show of impatience and walked around the room absorbed in his thoughts. Some drops of sweat appeared on his forehead. He looked back at his wife and burst into a state of rage that mirrored his internal turmoil. "That's my life! All the Vatican's secrets are there! Do you understand now?" he shouted in a progressive crescendo.

Tokina got scared by the tone of his voice. She went to him and said in a sweet voice, "I would never give your suitcase to anyone, anywhere, anytime if this is what you want. I didn't mean to provoke your anger. You know that I would not do anything that could even remotely harm or offend you. I love you, my dear Monsignor." She hugged him and invited him to sit on the couch.

The return trip from the honeymoon brought a change in Mitango's personality. He caressed his wife's face and said, "During my lifetime, the briefcase is a defense against possible troubles. If the pope doesn't want to reach a compromise with me, then I'll publish a book. With its revenue, we will be able to live comfortably without the Reverend's assistance. I thought it over. I don't want to rely on him anymore as soon as the situation stabilizes."

"My dear, whatever you decide, I'll follow you." She took by hand and led him to the bedroom where he dozed off for a while.

In the Vatican, Cardinal Ratzinger was leading a group of conservatives from the Curia to excommunicate Mitango. He argued that Cardinal Mitango broke the chastity vow, left the Vatican without permission and without leaving any information about his destination. According to an insistent rumor among them, he had amassed a fortune he dissipated in part by donating lavish gifts and, on the other hand, by purchasing jewels for himself. As if those charges were not sufficient, along with the purported miracles and broken rules on exorcism, they accused him with sexual harassment of a nun.

The prevailing mood was of consternation and indignation. For most of the members, Mitango was a rebel who was causing havoc in the religious community. Only three Cardinals were level-headed in their intervention. They praised the immense contribution that Mitango brought to the Church and, at the same time, they admitted that he inflicted a serious wound to their institution. The strongest favorable and cautious defense came from his old friend, the Cardinal from Niger, but it was a lonely voice in the desert.

The overwhelming majority of the African bishops didn't share this view. They felt betrayed by Mitango and feared a new plague would soon spread in their continent. These were neophytes in the Vatican with a strong record on conservatism. If the Curia dragged its feet, it was due to their hope that he would repent and come back to the flock. But the stage was being set for public excommunication.

In one of his rare appearances in public, Cardinal Mitango was spotted by reporters while he was going to a concert. A young Canadian newsman in front of the building asked him, "Your Excellency, in the Vatican they are debating about excommunicating you. You have no more supporters."

"First of all, I have a lot to say about my marriage, but I'm afraid to be misunderstood."

"Why did they remove you from the Curia?"

"You should ask them."

"Aren't you embarrassed?"

"Listen! My popularity in Africa is well documented."

"Many prelates claim that you use herbs during exorcisms."

"Enough with this rubbish!"

"Do you feel that you are being singled out because you are black?"

"You mean if a white priest gets married they don't cause such a clamor?"

"Like Jeronimo Podesta' from Argentina."

"I would not equate priests with Cardinals. Remember that it's more than the color of the skin, but let's close the conversation."

"One last question! Are you hoping to have children?"

"How many times must you reporters ask the same question? Abraham was 100 years old when he had Isaac. My wife was born when I became priest. She is still able to bear children. She isn't too young, but still.... Remember that God is also man. There are about eighty features that characterize man. If these characteristics are not fulfilled, man isn't complete."

"Your Eminence, what is the main trait?"

"Love, yes love! Without love, life is incomplete."

"Why, then, did you marry in a strange church and go through the propitiatory ritual of "*mon sie*," and why did you drink from the same cup as the Reverend? Earlier in your life, you were alone to raise the chalice and drink from it. Then, you distributed it to the congregation."

The Cardinal didn't respond. He lowered his head and remained silent. Suddenly, there was an ominous silence. He looked around. People had lost interest momentarily in getting a glimpse of him. An oppressive silence descended on the crowd, broken only by the continuous clicking of the cameras. Mitango brushed his curly hair with his fingers, massaged his face and ears and headed for the entrance of the building.

His entourage provided the necessary assistance to keep the people at a distance.

# THE BRIEFCASE

No one really knew the Cardinal's abode, except Lucky Star and his inner circle of confidants.

On August 15, the Cardinal and his wife were dining when the back door screeched. A man, with his face covered, quietly entered the premises and started to search in the closets, mattresses and drawers. In the living room hung a big oil painting of the Cardinal. He wore glasses and displayed the eternal broad smile. The intruder put his hand on it to ascertain that it was indeed an oil painting and not a fake. His fingers collected some dust. He brushed it with a cloth, stared at him for the last time and moved to the studio. The Cardinal followed him with this smile up to the door. "Life must be good for him. He smiles all the time," he muttered.

On the back of the desk, on the wall, there was an oil painting of the Cardinal's wife in her younger years. She was absolutely charming. The unwanted visitor touched it gently, but he slipped against the desk causing the painting to move. To his surprise, beneath the painting lay a vault. His face brightened. He finally got where he wanted.

The vault hid the secret. But, how to unlock it? He put his index finger on his mouth as if he were in a pensive mood. The combination, where was it? He looked at the painting, detached it from the wall and placed it on the floor against the desk. He went back to the vault and started to turn a few numbers. In that moment, the alarm system went on.

He became frenzied. His mission had failed miserably. He had one worry that gripped his mind. He had to find his way out before the Cardinal arrived.

The Cardinal and his wife dropped their silverware and stared at each other. The telephone rang. The police was rushing over. The Cardinal cautioned his wife to stay calm and not to go anywhere. Their eyes expressed surprise and fear.

The alarm system set in motion by the intruder kept on screaming for about five minutes. The police made an immediate search of the house and found the studio in disarray. They reached the Cardinal and his wife and assured them that nothing had been stolen. The alarm system stopped screaming. A minute later, the Reverend's assistants arrived.

The police captain took out a notebook and a pen and asked the Cardinal, "Your Eminence, do you mind telling me how much money you keep in the vault?"

"What money?" He looked straight across the room and said, "There is no money."

"Do you have jewels?"

"Not even. They were looking for something else, sir."

The officer scratched his head. The Cardinal was still shaken as was his wife. The officer made a phone call, filled out a report, made the Cardinal sign and took off.

# THE PRODIGAL SON

The new day came. The sun woke up early. Mitango's residence was already full of activities. The phone rang intermittently. The Cardinal's wife was still visibly apprehensive. Her husband displayed the usual confidence. In the midst of the confusion, he took the unusual step of picking up the phone and calling the Vatican. He asked to one of his friendly cardinals to arrange a meeting for him with the Holy Father. The reply wasn't favorable, neither it was discouraging. The Pope was getting ready to go to Castelgandolfo for his summer vacations.

Cardinal Ratzinger, the pope's right arm, was inflexible. He reported to his colleague, who had inquired, that "Without abjuring his marriage and stating a *mea culpa*, and if he doesn't repudiate the secret deal with the other church by August 31, Mitango will automatically fall into excommunication."

The news made Mitango sink into his couch. His wife sat next to him and leaned her head on his shoulder. "My angel, I'm going to take the suitcase to a bank vault tomorrow. There it will be safe."

"My head is spinning, my love. It may explode any moment if I don't obtain an audience with the pope."

"What? You are requesting an audience with your pope?" She inquired with dismay.

"I have to. It's a *sine qua non* of all my problems."

His wife understood that it was no time to contradict him and said, "Don't be tense, honey. Don't be a prisoner of the events. I feel very sorry I brought so much sorrow in your life."

"Don't be silly. I know I'm right." He took her hand and placed on his heart. You are the sunshine in my dark days." He looked outside and noticed a flock of swallows resting on a cherry tree branch. They chirped for a while, then flew away. "I resemble them in a way. I'm in a constant movement, activity. Sometimes, I don't know where I'm going or why. Inner forces drive me and I can't stop to search like they for freedom of mind and heart. I wonder if we have anything in common."

"You can't always fly, my angel. At times, everybody needs rest. Yesterday you were young; today you are a bit older."

"I have to see the Pope. I have to explain to him that the Church has an erroneous interpretation about priestly marriage."

"It would be more accurate to state 'tradition,' my dear."

"You are right. I used the wrong word. I have to be more cautious, otherwise I cause ambiguities. He will understand if I talk to him personally without interference."

"My love, don't torture yourself! Give our marriage a chance. Everything will be fine."

"It's not that that bothers me, my dear."

The Cardinal kissed his wife on the forehead and excused himself. He walked to a nearby Catholic church; opened the door slowly and entered. He wore a big black hat. He removed it and genuflected. He headed to a lateral nave and threw furtive glances around to ascertain that no one was following him. The church was empty. He took a seat in a pew and knelt. He did the sign of the cross and fixed his eyes on the crucified Christ.

Ten minutes of contemplation passed by. The Cardinal stared at the cross and said, "Lord, my heart is a boat in a stormy sea. I'm being persecuted by my own ideas. I have betrayed the chastity vow, my church, my people in Africa and my rank.

"*Mea culpa, mea culpa, mea maxima culpa!*" He accompanied the act of contrition by beating his chest three times. He twisted his lips and added, "I should beat my brains as when I beat eggs. The echo of my deeds is reaching your throne and I feel like a tiny ant. I have no place to go." He raised his head, as if he were waiting for a response, and continued, "Lord, you don't even look at me. You are turning your face away. I can see it. I can feel it. Why can't you look straight in my eyes and tell me what you think. I can't carry the burden anymore. I don't want to hurt the church. But these people don't want to accept reality. He paused a few seconds, incapable of discharging his feelings. Twenty minutes had elapsed since he came in. He wanted to go back home. He wife was going to wonder. He raised his head and said, "Oh, Lord, why didn't you kill me before I started this protest. I know, I know. I committed a great sin. I turned to a man who doesn't even share my theology. Why did I do it? But, as for marrying …"

A pigeon flew through an open window and flapped its wings causing the Cardinal to disrupt his monologue. Mitango followed him up to the pillar in the main nave close to the altar. He didn't know what to make of it. He turned his attention back to the cross and said, "You see, Lord, I can't even talk to you in privacy." He heard a noise behind him. A couple ladies came in to pray. The Cardinal hurried to say, "Lord, I beg you, before I leave this temple. Guide me. Show me the way, whatever it may be at whatever price." He got up, turned his back to the two ladies, and left.

The bird flew out and rested on a pope's poster in front of the entrance. The Cardinal observed him motionless until the bird took another direction. The Cardinal said, "This may have a meaning for me. I need to see the Holy Father."

Back home, the Cardinal made repeated attempts to get in touch with his fellow African cardinals in the Vatican. Maybe they could have been capable of arranging meeting with the pope. They all replied that they would look into the matter.

The Cardinal felt more relaxed. In a moment of privacy, he said to his wife, "I want to communicate directly with the Holy Father. I don't need intermediaries, I want to tell him that I intend to spend the rest of my life with you in Africa, a continent still to discover its vast traditions of spiritual and family values."

Tokina stood there listening meekly. Her husband insisted, "Let's not forget that AIDS is the "*flagellum hominids*" in Africa and I want to continue working to prevent its spread. I also wish to use my healing power and exorcism capabilities to bring people back to my faith."

His wife was receptive to that idea and gave her consent. Her husband jumped to his feet and improvised an African folkloric dance taking two steps forward, one lateral, and one backward. The sweat started to flow down the cheeks and he thought it prudent to take a pause. Mitango said in exhilaration, "I don't want to break away from Mother Church."

"Your mind is still on it, isn't it?" inquired his wife. He didn't respond, He took a towel and wiped his face. "Why don't you change religion?" she suggested.

"None of that! Obviously, you forgot that I'm a Cardinal of the Catholic Church."

"Yes, Monsignor."

"The last word has not been uttered yet," he said in a firm tone of voice.

"They are going to give you an ultimatum, my love. Do you foresee the implications for us?"

"I already know what they are up to, but I'm going to prevent them from carrying out their plan."

"I'm not a Christian. To me it's taboo, but I don't understand, how you will be able to avoid excommunication?"

"That's why I'm trying to arrange a meeting with the Pope. I would like to reach a compromise. I stay married and he can banish me to Africa where I can exercise my priestly functions as an exorcist and healer."

"Your Pope will never give in. He has always been opposed to that status. Stop with these grandiose illusions about yourself, my dear."

"He must accept this compromise; otherwise, the consequences will be catastrophic."

The Cardinal was getting excited. The sweat reappeared on the forehead. Tokina took her handkerchief and wiped it. "Don't get nervous, honey. Stay calm. Somehow, the tempest will abate and the sun will rise for us."

"Do you realize that Orthodox priests are allowed to marry, and ministers from different denominations have been accepted with their wives without causing any scandal? This is what will shake up the Canonical Law and irritate those who have demanded my head."

The Cardinal's last argument appeared plausible and convinced Tokina that after all it was worthwhile to pursue the fight. "You can't imagine how much I love you," she said. He looked at her, brought her head to his heart and caressed her hair.

The time was running out and the Cardinal kept pressure on the Vatican with overtures. The deacon of the Cardinals' College restated that a meeting with the Pope was possible only if the Cardinal made a public act of contrition, abjured his marriage, rejected the Reverend's friendship and submitted to the papal authority without preconditions. The deacon's words, once again, demonstrated the determination that prevailed on this matter in the Vatican. A new directive was issued to the clergy. No one was allowed to comment on Cardinal Mitango's case. The result was positive. Less talk contributed to the lessening of the tension and, finally, to a papal meeting prior to the excommunication deadline.

The Reverend, although was opposed in principle to the meeting, didn't do anything to obstruct it. His assistants worked behind the scenes to provide bodyguards up to Castelgandolfo's papal summer residence. They insisted that the Cardinal needed protection. The reader may remember Pope Paul's warning that Satan was present in the Vatican.

# THE POPE AND MITANGO

The meeting with the Holy Father was emotional. The Cardinal arrived at the papal residence in civilian garments, fine slacks, a black short sleeved shirt and a pair of sandals.

As he was presented to the Pope, the Cardinal fell on his knees, kissed Peter's ring and bowed waiting for the blessing. "Brother Mitango, why do you wish to leave us?" asked the Pontiff.

The Cardinal broke down in tears. Mitango waited to regain his composure and said in a soft voice, "Vicar of Christ, I never wanted, neither do I wish now to leave the Church. I beg you to allow me to carry on my activity as an exorcist and as a healer in my country."

"My dear son, it's the Holy Sea's tradition to set the chastity vow. I, Peter's descendent, have no authority, neither do I wish to change it."

"This is an exceptional case, Holy Father. Let me go to my people. I beg you."

"I can't change this set of rules, brother Mitango, on an individual basis. It would create a chaotic situation and signal the end of the tradition."

"Holy Father, the Church can bend these rules because we made them, not Christ."

"Would my brother be more explicit?" gently asked the pontiff.

"You allowed ministers from other denominations to maintain their marital status when they chose to be Catholic."

"But, you are not a convert! Take time to reflect on your actions. We want you to come back to the flock."

"I never renounced it, Your Holiness."

"You must repent before *urbi et orbi*. If you are observing the forty days of chastity vow, you are still in time to annul the marriage and be reinstated without penalties.

"Holy Father, she is my w ..."

The Pope placed his right hand on the Cardinal's head and blessed him, "*Ite in pace, frater.*"

The Cardinal remained in a genuflected position hoping for an absolution or some kind of help. When he realized that the Pope had finished, he kissed again the ring and, in a slow motion, joined his assistants in the waiting hall.

Outside, Rome was as bright as usual. A crowd of reporters was waiting on the front steps of the Basilica. Streams of pilgrims were heading into the main square. It was an immense colony of moving souls in search of forgiveness and peace. Suddenly, they noticed the media pressing toward a man and speeded their pace to see what was going on.

The reporters asked the Cardinal the outcome of the meeting. He responded, "I'll make my decision in a couple of days." They pressed for more information, but the bodyguards kept them at a distance.

The Vatican's press secretary didn't make any comment on the meeting and this added more ammunition for suspicion of a secret deal.

The night came too soon for Mitango. He looked exhausted. Evidently, he had in mind to gain the Pope's approval, but the scenario remained more enigmatic than before.

The only encouraging note was that he had been able to obtain a second meeting in two days. He called his wife and announced to her the outcome. "How are you, my dear?"

"Apprehensive, as you may surmise."

"Imagine! I told him that many people lied about me."

"You did?"

"Why not? I'm sure of it."

"What was his reaction?"

"He didn't reply to that statement, but I came out with the perception that he believed me."

"Did you reach any compromise?"

"Not yet! In a couple of days, we will meet again. So, be patient, my dear. I love you."

"I love you too."

Two days later, Cardinal Mitango was back at the papal summer residence in Castelgandolfo. He smiled at the Swiss guards, as they stood at attention.

The pope's secretary accompanied him upstairs and led him to the pope's private studio.

The preliminaries lasted about a minute. The secretary withdrew and closed the door.

The Pope opened the conversation, "Brother Mitango, I'm concerned about the Curia's pressing for excommunication unless you are willing to publicly denounce your error."

"Your Holiness, I reflected on my behavior and I'm ready to make a step backward. I submit in all humility and unconditionally, to the Mother Church's authority. I'm Catholic, and Catholic I wish to be. I implore you to keep my rank and recognize my marital status. I reiterate my wish. I want to live in my country for the rest of my life."

"Brother Mitango, your marriage is null. You profess being a staunch Catholic and yet you contracted your marriage in a sect which is distant light years from the Catholic beliefs. That marriage constitutes an apostasy. You got the blessing from another faith that doesn't share common values with us. Do you realize this?"

"Your Holiness, with all due respect, I wish to insist that obligatory celibacy doesn't help the priests nor the Church. The Church has to renew if it wants to strengthen itself."

"If marriage is the issue, why did you marry at the age of 80?"

"Holy Father, I have been trying to reform the Church within my parameters. Now, I'm old and I can't fight anymore. I just want to retire and live peacefully."

"Brother Mitango, reflect seriously on the damage you have done to yourself and to the Church. Remember that if you persevere in your request, there is nothing I can do for you. Once you leave these walls, the door will shut forever behind you. The Commission on the Propagation of Faith is meeting right now in a special session. They are waiting for your decision."

The Cardinal genuflected, kissed Peter's ring and headed for the door.

"I'll pray for you Mitango."

The Cardinal stopped for a moment to hear the pope's words and passed through the door. Instead of leaving the building, he headed for the room where the Commission was meeting.

It was a stormy session. Cardinal Mitango expressed all his disappointment to the clergymen who spread lies on his account. Not one of them accepted the charges and told him flatly that he was a frustrated man and needed help. He responded indignantly, "At the present pace, the Church is going to be stagnant pretty soon. Obviously, you love this status quo."

The president replied, "Bishop Mitango, may I remind you that tradition is an important part of the Church. How many times should I reiterate this point? Don't come to us to accuse. It would help if you explained the reason for breaking the chastity vow allying yourself with a religious sect that's seeking world dominance."

Mitango lost his habitual coolness. "Mr. President, you are all responsible for my marriage. All these years, you have exasperated me and others who share my philosophy. Renewal isn't in your dictionary. It never prevailed on your rigidity. You don't wish the Church to grow."

The members of the Commission were losing their patience. The president stated, "Cardinal Mitango, time is no longer on your side. You have until August 27 to decide. Only two days and a half are left."

An African cardinal recommended a softer approach. "Brothers, I propose that Cardinal Mitango undergo detoxification therapy along with a period of contemplative study."

The suggestion appeared to satisfy the whole assembly. Cardinal Mitango didn't protest. An Italian Cardinal, a close friend of his, asked for a pause. He called Mitango for a private conversation. At the end of it, he convinced him to accept the resolution.

The news of Mitango's decision made the round of the world in a matter of seconds.

The press sought to find out the place of his confinement, but the destination was kept secret.

Back at home, Tokina was disturbed by the brusque turn of the events and awaited a call from her husband. The hours passed, and so, the days. Each time she called the Vatican, she got a busy signal. Finally, she decided to go public. Assisted by the Reverend's entourage, she called a press conference, accusing the Vatican of human rights violations. She accused them of having drugged her husband. A reporter reminded her that, according to Vatican sources, her husband was undergoing a period of contemplation. She didn't believe it, claiming that her husband always called her when he was out of town. Considering the stall and the lack of cooperation from Rome, she decided to go on a hunger strike at St. Peter's Square. Needless to say, the Vatican got apprehensive about it.

Cardinal Mitango never got in touch with his wife again, nor did she get the chance to visit him or talk to him on the phone. One evening, he appeared on national television and made the following announcement, "I came back to my

Catholic Church. I submit totally to the papal authority. I repent of my insubordination and subsequent marriage. I took this decision freely without coercion from anyone. I have regained my full ecclesiastic status and I intend to serve the Church in anyway I can."

The television appearance, instead of quelling criticism, created more doubts. His ex-wife refuted his statement, claiming that he had changed completely. In her view, he was completely unrecognizable and insisted on her fear that he had been drugged. She concluded that only a meeting with him would dissipate her suspicions. "It can't be my husband. He isn't the one I know. I'll believe him when I see him alone. Mitango has to tell me those things in my presence," she protested.

The days dragged on with no solution in sight. During the short appearance, he reaffirmed his intentions of submitting to the will of the Church and that he considered his ex-wife a sister.

Tokina's efforts to locate Mitango proved fruitless. The world press made some concerted searches, but it too failed. Rumors that had the Cardinal in a monastery in Africa were due to the plan of someone to divert his wife's attention elsewhere.

Some reporters succeeded in tracing down a monsignor who supposedly had contacts with the Cardinal. "Did you see Cardinal Mitango recently?" Asked one of them.

"I saw him and talked to him, as good friends do, but that was a couple of days ago."

"Did you discuss his situation?" inquired the newsman.

"Of course, we did! We spent a great amount of time discussing the temporary flight from the Church and the consequences."

"Did he admit his errors?"

"Absolutely! He also swore that he never left the Church."

"Did you give him any advice?"

"He doesn't need my advice. We try to help each other."

"Did the Curia accept his act of contrition?"

"Listen! He made a public statement in which he expressed sorrow. What else can he say? Now, he is immersed in a contemplative series of spiritual exercises."

"Do you think he needs them?"

"From time to time, we all do. We should recognize our finiteness and the infinite love of God."

"In our first inquiry, they told us that he was in the vicinity of Rome. Later, we heard that he is in Africa. We called all the monasteries, but found no truth in the rumors."

The monsignor laughed and said, "Reporters are constantly in search of sensationalism. If you try to find his residence, you never will. They are constantly moving him."

"It looks like he is under house arrest," asked a newsman from India."

"Now, wait a minute! This is a media fabrication. The Inquisition is dead."

"According to his wife ..."

"You mean, his sister," corrected the priest.

"Choose any word you wish to characterize their relation, but according to her, he is in a state of detention," added the reporter.

"If he maintains the anonymity of his residence, we should respect his wish for solitude."

"Let's change the words," asked a young journalist from Peru, "He is being forced to stay where he is."

"The Bishop is an octogenarian. He made up his mind."

"Why don't you allow us to see him?"

"Me? Are you joking? I'm not a Curia member. We would better serve his plans if we pray for him."

"And his wife? And his marriage?"

"It's invalid. It's not recognized by the Church. The marriage was contracted outside of it and with an unbeliever. The case is complex, my friends."

"Was the Bishop excommunicated?"

"The excommunication was suspended. He is back in the flock."

It was humid. People sought shelter under the portico. The monsignor couldn't breathe well, surrounded by the swelling members of the press. He excused himself and turned away from the microphones. One reporter stubbornly followed him although many people complained about his pushing and shoving. When he reached him, he said, "The Reverend claims that he met Jesus as a teenager, and he is a terrific publicity manager."

The monsignor thought he had gotten rid of the press. He looked back and had to admit that he was wrong. "You people never quit. Let me tell you. That man made a business out of arranging marriages and made a fortune out of it. It has been on newspapers and television. Is that the type of person you want to follow?"

The crowd followed. The newsman lost balance and stumbled. The microphone fell on the ground and the somebody stepped on it. He recovered it and, when he got up, he stretched his arm holding a broken phone. He looked around with anxiety, but it was late. He had lost his prey. Waves of people around him swallowed the monsignor.

Tokina, in the meantime, was getting exhausted by the Vatican's determination to hush the whole issue. She hoped that at least an epistolary channel could open with him. She wrote the following letter to him:

My dearest,

I have been spending horrible days and sleepless nights. I'm a candle whose flame is getting dimmer and dimmer. I look at myself in the mirror and I see a shadow of myself, a ghost. I feel empty inside. The time passes and I don't see you. I'm losing hope to get you back. I strongly suspect that they have abducted you and placed you under strict surveillance. You can't communicate with the outside world. I hear a secret rumor from the Reverend's folks that you are at a hermitage, but I wonder if the news is credible. I see you in on the screen of my computer confined among high, cold walls and I fear for your life.

Tomorrow, I'm going to stage a hunger strike. There is no other alternative. Either they release you, or my death is near. The world is watching. I hope I can raise the media's interest.

Don't worry about my financial assistance. The Reverend has been providing me with all necessary needs. He has assigned four bodyguards for my protection. I appreciate it, but I don't care anymore about my safety. I have only one objective, to have you in my arms.

If they won't deliver this letter, I'm going to take legal action against the Church.

Remember, you are always in my heart.

Your wife,
Tokina

# The Hunger Strike and Escape from the Monastery

The days repeated their routine in New York. Heavy traffic and financial transactions were the two most visible activities. The temperature dropped for a week, very unusual for the Big Apple. Then, it got warm again and in the evening people felt relieved. The sun sprawled on the big sheet of the river and prepared to go to bed. The tourists were impressed by nature's spectacle. Someone suggested that it was a phantasmagoric view of the sun's sunbathing before it withdrew. Whatever it was, it seemed to be a surreal picture of beauty. Tokina watched fascinated, but with sadness. Her man lived in another continent, under vigilance, and she had no way to see him. The sun's hue lost its luster and she went home with the intention of taking action.

At St. Peter's square, oblivious of the media presence, Tokina sat on the front steps and began her hunger strike. A newspaperman placed a microphone close to her mouth. She looked at it and turned away. The sun was covering the apostles' statues before withdrawing behind Michelangelo's dome. Tokina closed her eyes.

A guard closed the central door. The noise made Tokina return to reality. She looked back and saw a priest. She got up and ran after him. She stretched her arm to attract his attention and said, "The video is a fluke." The clergyman looked surprised at the woman. The reporters quickly arrived at the scene, but the priest proceeded straight ahead.

Tokina began a monologue, which was interrupted only by an aggressive reporter, who brushed everyone out of his way to address the lady, "You claim that your ex-husband ..."

"I beg your pardon, sir. He *is* my husband."

"I apologize, madam. You have stated that your husband is drugged."

She paused a few seconds to ponder her reply, then, she answered, "He has changed too much. My heart breaks at seeing him in that condition. I guess I had a wrong perception of the causes and impact of the drugs on people. Now, it's much clearer to me."

A middle aged woman reporter asked her, "Bishop Mitango stated that you are an adult and he is sure you will understand."

She raised her head as if someone touched a vital nerve of her body and said, "You are absolutely right! I do understand that the religious authority forced him to make those statements."

"There is some speculation that the Vatican would be willing to allow you to see him, but only in the presence of an interpreter."

"What for ...? Husband and wife don't need interpreters."

"A rumor is flying around the Eternal City according to which Lucky Star's agents are manipulating your life."

"First of all, let's make this clear. Nobody tells me what to do except my husband. He is currently in prison and I don't accept any video as credible. Even his letters have been edited. Can you imagine that? Nothing is original. Furthermore, what can I say about the Reverend. His people have been very helpful in these times of trial. They have not abandoned me for an instant. I have words of appreciation for them and their leader. If he got rich, it doesn't concern me. I'm worried about my darling's fate."

"Madam, your husband is a reformer, therefore ..."

Tokina looked perplexed. That word sounded strange to her ears. She hesitated a while before she answered, "My husband is exasperated by decades of conservatism. He is an innovator, a promoter of fresh and new ideas. But, this is the triumph of traditionalism."

A girl, who wasn't part of the media, shouted, "He knocked at the pagan door to give vent to his frustrations and, when he realized the harm he caused to the Church, he stopped."

Tokina didn't have the chance to reply because a bodyguard stepped in and prevented any further questions. A brawl ensued among reporters and bodyguards. The prompt intervention of the local police restored the order.

Tokina had a restless night. On her way to St. Peter's square, she was waiting for the traffic light to change, when a reporter approached her in her native tongue. She looked at him somewhat disoriented. She wanted to reply, but she felt exhausted. Restless days and sleepless nights were leaving signs of bodily and mental exhaustion. The man insisted and she, in a thin, almost imperceptible voice said, "He isn't the type who remains indifferent for a long time to this situation. Early or later, he will explode. He is my man, I know him. I would do the same. We oriental women would die for our men rather than suffer these humiliations. It's inculcated in our culture, tradition, history and in our DNA. A person, as he stated many times, will never be complete by himself. Why do you think we were created man and woman?"

"You keep on stating that he is your man ..."

"Well, he is," she interrupted him in an elegant manner.

"Yes, we hear you. The question is another. Did he break the Church rules? The Curia considers him a rebel."

"Nonsense! Call him whatever you want. For the world, he is a reformer."

"Forgive me for being personal. Did you take any pregnancy test?"

"You are violating my privacy now. At the opportune time, I'll release a statement."

Suddenly, she cried out, "Poor Monsignor, dearest husband, they have been destroying you little by little."

The newsman was shocked by the outburst, but pressed on, "As I understand it, he is at a spiritual retreat, not a prison."

"Sir, please, call it jail!" She searched for something in her pocket and pulled out a picture. "Look at it. He is emaciated and unshaven. During our married life, he always shaved. He was extremely conscientious about his personal appearance."

The man tried to ask additional questions, but the guards told him that it was enough.

Cardinal Mitango's retreat location was the object of assiduous speculations and research, as we mentioned earlier. Many names were flying around, but none were accurate. The Vatican resorted to a strategy of removing the Cardinal from his dwelling whenever there was evidence of media presence. The Reverend, too, made efforts to locate the Cardinal, but each time he got close, the prey would slip away. Exasperated, he offered a million dollars to whomever provided information leading to the identification of the location. On at least two occasions, a private investigator identified the retreat, but the religious authorities smuggled the Cardinal in the trunk of a car and dispatched him to another unknown destination.

The monastery of St. Benedict in Aosta lies between the French and Italian borders. It was erected in medieval times on the tip of a gorge accessible only by a narrow path dug in the rocky shoulders of the mountain. The monastery hung on a platform naturally excavated over the course of millennia. There was still no electricity, not because it wasn't available, but it was a choice of the abbot, in order to keep the monks focused on work and prayer. They used torches and candles to illuminate the interior of the mammoth structure.

The monks' rules were rigid. They had frugal meals and attended to frequent fasting, study, work and prayer. No one weighed more than 140 pounds, except the gate's guardians. The meals were basically composed of vegetables and dairy products that they produced. They were economically self-sustaining.

No visitor ever ventured to climb the impassible rocks. The only path to the monastery terminated a mile or so away and was secured by German shepherds and steel gates.

The abbot introduced Mitango to the monastic community one evening at sunset. He could hardly see anyone's face. Long hoods almost covered their eyes. There was no welcoming ceremony befitting a dignitary. Each one pronounced the word "*Pax*" and went about his activities.

After the evening meal and prayers, Mitango got to know his cell. A small bed, a chest to use for personal clothes, and a desk were the only pieces of furniture. He read the rules set on the desk and remained silent. It was cold during the night and he couldn't close his eyes. The gloomy faces of the monks were stamped in his mind.

A few weeks passed by and he looked at his waist. He had lost a lot of weight. He felt weak and haggard, too weak for the hearty man he used to be.

Every activity followed the same ritual. One morning, after a frugal breakfast, he joined the monks in prayer. A brief study period followed. During this time, he stared at the gate locked with double chains. Two men operated the opening and closing of it. The only monk allowed to enter and leave was the one in charge of the garbage. He passed through every Monday to get rid of the trash he carried on a cart, as quickly as possible so as not to disturb the brothers in prayer. It wasn't hard for him to go down the hill with the load. On the way back, he sweated, although the cart was empty. The dumping area was a deep, round well.

The monk in charge of the garbage had a stone face. When he raised his hood under the scorching sun or when the weight required extra efforts, one could see how deep his wrinkles were. He was in his fifties, but looked older. Besides taking care of the trash, he also worked on the farm adjacent to the monastery. That explained in part his dark complexion. He had a bell attached to the rope around his waist. It served to alert his co-friars in case of emergency.

The monks' lives was severe and simple. Their motto was *"ora et labora."* The monks were divided into groups. One group took care of the kitchen, a second the liturgy, a third the field, and a fourth, charity. I should add that a fifth group was occupied in the production of liquors. No one was allowed to leave the monastery without permission or a strict search at the main gate. Hardly any visitors arrived, but whatever his rank, he was subject to the same rule.

We left the garbage monk on his way out, so let us catch up with him.

The sun was about to rise. A dense mist hung deep in the valley. The animals were beginning to wake up. The monk rested the cart on the pavement of the corridor and went to his cell for a couple of minutes to pick up his gloves. On the way out, he found the cart full and heavy. "I don't understand why they don't wait for me to pick up the bags," he complained. He placed a mask on his mouth, tightened his jaw muscles, bent his legs slightly, got a firm grip on the wooden handles, and, with an unusual effort, pushed the cart to the gate.

At the exit, one guard raised his hood, checked his ID, searched his body. Another took a spear and darted it in the garbage. He pulled it out and signaled to the one attending the gate to raise the chain. Two small mice fell from the cart and the guards ran after them. The abbot was terribly afraid of them and he gave strict orders to keep them off the premises.

The monk, with strenuous efforts, passed through the gate and followed the path downward.

The hole where the monk dumped the trash was located about a mile from the monastery and was about fifty feet deep. At the end of the day, he would burn the garbage.

The monk rested the cart, took a deep breath and discharged his cargo. The power he used to lift made him lose his balance and he fell. He implored help from a few saints. The intense pain kept him on the ground for a few seconds and didn't see the big load falling into the well. He heard only the tremendous impact, and felt relieved. "I could swear I had two tons on that cart," he complained, grinding his teeth. His hood came off. He was completely bald. He got up and searched for matches in his pockets. They had fallen to the bottom of the ditch. He made a gesture of discomfort and headed back to the monastery with the empty cart.

Under the papers and debris, something unusually big was moving. A head showed up. The eyes searched for the monk. Two rats bit him on the legs. He pulled out the knife and staved off a second attack. He struggled to stand and lost balance three times, sinking in the trash on all sides. He almost got swollen by the mountain of garbage. He heard the sound of footsteps nearby and his heart pumped furiously. His face was covered with black marks and his eyes were swollen. The rest of the body was smeared with all sorts of garbage. The man cautiously and with great fatigue climbed out of the deep hole. He limped and the grimace on his face was symptomatic of the great pain he was enduring. He touched parts of his back and chest to ascertain that he hadn't fractured any ribs. He was aware that he was running out of time. He had to leave before the arrival of the monk. He threw on top of the pile a couple of bones he got from the kitchen and took a deep breath. Slowly, he dragged himself up the ditch and rolled down until he hit a bush. He was too exhausted to move on.

The garbage monk arrived and lit a match. The garbage started burning. The heavy smoke rose high for a while and descended in the valley below blackening everything in its way. The stench was unbearable and the ash slowly settled down covering the head of the man under the bush. From the mountain pass a second monk was running and puffing toward the incinerating hole. He arrived breathless at the scene and said, "The Cardinal … the Cardinal has fled."

"No, it's not possible! How did he escape? He has to be in his cell. Maybe he's washing himself at the well, praying, eating, something. He must be somewhere. Search for him," the garbage man responded with apprehension.

The other monk stopped talking. Drops of sweat fell on the stones. He looked at them and his eyes moved to the ditch. He noticed some bones. He panicked and started to scream. He was scared to the point that he took a pocket knife and was ready to slash his throat. The garbage monk grabbed his arm and said in a firm voice, "You fool! What do you think you are doing? No one commits suicide in this monastery."

"The Cardinal died. Look at the bones!"

"Those are not the Cardinal's bones, you fat head. Those are from the kitchen. They were supposed to be used for the soup, instead, someone used them to scare you. Pray San Francis that you have not lost your habit today." He shook him and said, "Now, calm down before you end up below alongside the bones."

"What are we going to tell the abbot?"

"Tell him whatever you want. If no one can find him, neither can you." He set the last pile on fire and rats scrambled away, running for their lives.

A third friar showed up. He too was short of breath. He began to beat his chest, "Brothers, the Cardinal is no longer at the monastery. We searched all over. We are in deep trouble."

"Escaped where? The monastery is a fortress," responded the garbage man.

"Not as impregnable as you may think. The abbot sounded the alarm. Our brothers screened every corner of the monastery. They found two mice, but not a trace of the Cardinal. Do you realize the ramifications? We will all end in the hole, burning for our sin."

The garbage man said calmly, "Oh no, I'm out of this mess. I'm going to run away if he accuses me."

"Brother," answered the monk who just came, "Everybody is pointing the finger at you."

The garbage monk's hands and voice began to tremble.

The third monk said, "You have no place to run. The abbot can find you anywhere. The best thing to do is to report to him that he escaped from the roof. He didn't place any guards there, so it's his fault." The other two monks were listening and scratching their heads.

The flames rose upward and the smoke pursued them. The stench stretched for miles around the area. The friars covered their mouths with masks. They paused a long time. The garbage monk, who appeared the most aggressive, broke the silence and said, "Brothers, your arrival speaks an eloquent language." The other two looked at each other, but didn't reply. "The abbot may think that I'm an accomplice of the Cardinal," he added, "but he is mistaken. The truth is that I didn't even seen him. But if somehow, he became part of the garbage, the flames have incinerated him."

"The abbot expects you to provide hard evidence of your innocence," explained the monk who arrived last.

"I will not. Indeed, you will. Tell him you saw them," and pointed out at some bones in the hole."

"You fish head! How can you be so naïve?"

"How am I supposed to know where the Cardinal is? Was I his bodyguard," yelled the friar.

"No, but the Vatican will be at your heels soon."

"There is no peace, no peace for me, no peace not even in these desolate mountains, no peace for any of us," he said and broke into tears.

About two hundred yards away, the Cardinal rolled down the slopes and ended up against a tree. He lay there immobilized and out of his senses until a shepherd passed by and took him to his house at the border of the village.

A second story relates that a woman, affected by a rare pulmonary disease, was confined in the woods. During her morning walks, she noticed a man with bruises on his face lying with his arms wide open. After the initial scare, she touched him to see if he were dead. He woke up, but couldn't move. He was aching all over. She grabbed his hand to help him stand up. In that moment she felt a warm feeling running throughout her body. All the pains stopped. She looked at him and said, "You are a holy man. You should have told me that before. I would have treated you more gently." He didn't answer. She continued, "Can't you talk? What happened to you?" She turned his face upward and realized that he was wounded. She didn't know what move to take, go to town and shout to the world that she was cured by a saint or stay there and help him. She opted for the second thought. She dragged him to her hut to give him the proper care.

The Cardinal moved his lids and fingers step by step. His mouth was dry. She offered a glass of water he drank eagerly. He tried to talk, but he was in deep pain. He made a gesture to her not to reveal his presence to anyone. She assented. That same evening the Cardinal started to open his mouth. Once again he reiterated the same request. The lady assured him that no harm would be done to him.

Early in the morning, two monks knocked at her hut. "Good morning, wonderful lady."

"Good morning brothers. How can I help you?" she replied with a timid voice.

"We would appreciate if we could enter and take a short rest inside."

"No one told you that I'm affected by a rare disease and that it's contagious? Unless, you want to die like me, day by day …" she warned them.

The two monks exchanged inquisitive looks between themselves. One of them whispered in the other's ear, "We are all dying day by day, but I don't want to die that fast." His brother told him that he had heard about the lady's disease and suggested they leave immediately.

Whether the Cardinal was able to make contacts with the American embassy through the Reverend's emissaries or whether the counsel himself was instrumental in providing assistance for the flight to New York, we are not absolutely sure. An anonymous source close to a high ranking official claimed that the first version was more accurate. We are not sure either if the shepherd or the lady's account is the most credible. We leave it to the imagination of the reader. We can report, however, what transpired from the a member of the staff of the American embassy, "The Cardinal's daring adventure resembled one from television's *Mission Impossible.*

The news that the Cardinal had escaped from a maximum-security monastery caused tidal waves inside the Vatican. The Secretary of State removed the abbot on the spot and whisked him away to a remote location stripped of his authority. It seems that at the bottom of his misfortune lay the iron hand he used to govern the monks, submitting them to restricted movement, long periods of prayer and food deprivation, as it was reported by the monks.

The map was getting smaller for Cardinal Mitango. He appeared before the press in San Francisco announcing to the world his regained freedom and his intention never to go to jail again. Before he closed the news conference, he called for the creation of an organization called "Married Priesthood."

Tokina, the Cardinal's wife, stood next to him and her face radiated with joy. It had been a long time since they held each other's hands. She looked emaciated, had lost much weight, and her eyes, although they sparkled like trembling stars, were exhausted.

The Cardinal was center stage. All the cameras focused on him. Once in a while they zoomed in on his consort. The photographers' lights flashed incessantly. The Cardinal was accustomed to the limelight. His wife pressed her body against his.

One reporter raised the microphone and asked him, "Article 1382 of the Canonical Code explicitly inflicts excommunication 'sentential latae' without papal approval. It's automatic, particularly when dealing with a controversial issue of this magnitude."

"Not at all," the prelate responded calmly. Those threats are devoid of any significance."

"Would you be willing to sit down with the Curia and discuss the issue?"

"At this stage, I'm willing to talk only with the Holy Father, who should assure my safety and freedom to come back."

"Do you realize that you are shaking the system from its foundations. How can you reasonably expect that the Pope validate your marriage and give you carte blanche for the ordination of a married priest while you are excommunicated."

"It's only a document signed by the Pope."

"But even ordinary laws are written on paper," rebutted another reporter.

Tokina, who hadn't spoken a word during the news conference, whispered something in her husband's ear. The Cardinal pointed to a tall, slender man close by and said, "Ask him. He founded an American Catholic Club in the eighties. He can tell you if I'm concerned."

The press shifted attention to the ex-priest and, as soon as the microphones were close to him, he stated, "Cardinal Mitango has nothing to fear. He is acting within the legality of the Canon Law. Since he escaped from the monastery, he has regained his identity and he has no intention of losing it again."

"Who helped him to escape? Your men or the Reverend's assistants?"

The ex-priest tried to dodge the question. He looked hesitantly at the Cardinal and, after receiving a nod, stated that the issue was very sensitive and he was going to observe maximum discretion. "I can tell you this, we are in constant contact with the Cardinal and we will continue to work to strengthen our relationship."

"Did you or didn't you provide any assistance to the Cardinal while he was in the monastery?" shouted another reporter.

"You mean 'jail'?"

Everybody laughed. The same reporter insisted, "Are you excommunicated too?"

"I'm like Lazarus. The Pope, my friends, has to stop politicizing his position. When he can't subdue an honest opposition, he threatens excommunication. You will see that our movement will acquire respect and admiration because we are open to dialogue. We are the church of the future."

People looked at each other with skepticism. They shook their heads and expressed dissent. Tokina pulled her husband's arm and suggested they leave. She was tired and needed rest.

The press conference didn't please the Vatican. Behind the marble walls the atmosphere was sober and lips were tight. Everybody was expecting a reaction from Rome, which came without delay. A note from the Curia said, "If Cardinal Mitango's public ally repents for his actions and submits to the ecclesiastic authorities, Mother Church will, as always, forgive."

The Vatican personnel was tightlipped, but a monsignor talked to his brother, "He has firecrackers in his pocket."

"I agree," responded the other with a clear air of preoccupation. There should be a firm rebuttal to his situation and his future plans, otherwise the boat will rock and water will seep all over. If he follows up with his plan to ordain married priests, the *latae sententiae* will be automatic."

# MITANGO, WIDOWER TWICE

Mitango was relaxing with his wife in the living room. He picked up a book on saints from the shelf and opened to the index page. He opened the book half way and got immersed in reading. Fifteen minutes later, he shelved it. He took a pen and a paper, wrote a few lines and stopped. He got up and looked out of the window. In the distance, the Statue of Liberty reminded people from every corner of the globe that no one will ever extinguish the torch of freedom.

His wife Tokina joined him in the contemplation. She sensed an unusual uneasiness in him. She put her left hand on his shoulder and said in a sweet voice, "In Japan, we say that a lonely person is unhappy when he is alone. What's bothering you?"

"Nothing, nothing," he responded rather quickly without pondering his response.

"What do you mean by that? Aren't you happy with me, my dear?"

"It's not that. You are a super woman, baby. You are a rare species of wife. You enclose in your character everything a husband could dream of. You are the oasis of my desert, the star of my nights, and the sun of my winter."

"But …"

"I have dreams."

"I guess so. Lately, you have been talking in your sleep."

"Do I proffer stupidities?"

"I couldn't say. You speak Latin and I don't understand it. Incidentally, did you read that Cardinal Verzine advocates the Mass in Latin at least once a month?"

"*Lingua Latina mater linguarum est.*"

"What does that mean, my dear?"

Mitango turned around and staring at her said, "Bones of my bones, flesh of my flesh, a higher call, an urgent feeling, an indescribable attraction, a powerful voice like the roaring shouts of the waves against the cliffs are streaming through my veins, seeping in my bloodstream and anaesthetizing my brain. It's a fireball that's melting the ice in my heart. I feel powerless."

"What ice, my dear? Don't you love me anymore?"

"I repeat. It's not that. I betrayed the expectations, the fidelity vow of my first wife."

"Oh, no!" exclaimed Tokina. She brought her right hand to the heart and collapsed in her husband's arms. Vain were the efforts of Lucky Star and his attendants to revive her.

Mitango became distressed. He quickly ran for the Holy Oil and gave her the Extreme Unction.

Tokina had a royal funeral. 150 ministers of the Poor Church lined up in front of the church. They were dressed in white with black hoods. Around their waists were ropes, the symbol of poverty and humility. A carriage with six horses bore the casket. After an hour of delay, the procession finally moved. It was headed by the Reverend and accompanied by a multitude of girls dressed in transparent veils. The band, composed of fifty musicians, played a funeral march. The ministers were lined up on both sides of the road. Many heads of state rode in bulletproof cars, surrounded by a police motorcade. The Cardinal was sitting on the carriage.

# Mitango's Second Repentance

After his wife's death, Mitango began to court Rome again. Through the intercession of Asian and African Cardinals, he obtained another private audience with the Pope. Considering Mitango's state of celibacy, his repentance and his wish to be reinstated as a full fledged priest in the previous Cardinal rank, the Pope forgave the prodigal son.

The Curia didn't forget Mitango's escape from the monastery and the criticism it was subjected to, especially from the left wing of the European government. This time, the toll they demanded from Mitango was high. They pressed the Pope to ban him from conducting exorcisms and celebrating the Mass, except in dire situations. Cardinal Sodano, with the entire Curia, strongly suggested he be relegated to St. Lazarus, in Canada, in secret, guarded 24 hours a day by four bodyguards, far away from public scrutiny. They argued that among senile and patients in a vegetative state, Mitango would have ample time to spend his last years in meditation and prayer. Never again he would be allowed to walk in the street.

The Pope had his reservations about the new confinement, but pressed by all sides, he gave in and signed the document that would empower the Curia to dispatch Mitango to the Canadian sanatorium. From then on, the Cardinal became only a number, a name, relegated to a land close to the North Pole, forgotten by everybody. His dream of having a permanent assignment in Africa vanished forever.

Massimo stopped the VCR, bowed his head and sadly stated, "So this is how Mitango came to be here. Unbelievable! His stamina, his fighting spirit and his determination are legendary. He is a myth. Yet, I don't believe this is the last word on him. Like the phoenix, some day, he will rise from his ashes to climb again onto the world stage. With him, anything can happen."

# THE INVITATION

Arian arrived at her office at 9:00 sharp. She was always punctual and demanded punctuality from her subordinates. She reviewed the day's schedule with her secretary, put on her uniform and began her routine activities.

At noon, before going for lunch, she picked up her mail and quickly reviewed it. One anonymous card attracted her attention. She sat and opened it. She read:

> Dear Arian,
>
> I regret not having been in contact with you in recent months. My words will never compensate the help that you, so generously, gave me, especially in my time of need.
>
> I would like to take this opportunity to extend an invitation this weekend for a dinner in a famous restaurant in downtown Montreal. I have something to reveal to you.
>
> Please accept my invitation. I'd be eternally grateful.
>
> Don't use your office phone, for I fear that my calls may be intercepted. Use your home or a public phone and a pseudonym, for instance, "flower."
>
> With great respect,
> Massimo

Arian was intrigued by Massimo's invitation. It wasn't that she mistrusted him. She felt that two months of oblivion were too many. Her pride had been humiliated. Her dreams had been dimmed. She looked at the phone over and over. To call him or not to call him? She moved nervously around her bed. Her mind appeared in a state of turmoil. She couldn't make up her mind. She picked up the phone, but hesitated to dial the number for a while, until a recorded voice said, "Please, hang up and try again." She heard that voice *ad absurdum*, then she dropped the receiver. She had been raised in a family where politeness was highly cultivated. She picked the phone up again. Her hand was trembling and her heart was beating nervously. She brushed her hair backward with the tips of her fingers, looked at the numbers and dialed. It was the wrong number and she had to redial. She sank on her bed. A gigantic mirror covered almost one side of the room.

The phone rang on the other end. No one was answering. The answering machine was activated. She said, "Flower calling. Everything is fine." She dropped the phone and felt exhausted. She looked in the mirror at her hair growth. It had grown an inch!

She needed a dye job.

Massimo decided that it was time to act, to find out if all his suspicions, his dreams, his expectations had a reason to exist. He had insisted and won. Arian, finally, had accepted an invitation to dine with him. He was so excited that he wasn't sure what to buy for her on the first date. After much debate, he opted for flowers. He passed by a nursery and thought that it was the best place to buy them.

The outside display of plants and flowers was overwhelming to his eyes and knowledge. He passed by vases of dahlia and ostisperum, but they didn't attract his attention. He glanced at the tea shrubs. They resembled violets and appealed to him, yet in the midst of a sea of flowers, he thought it better to wait for a better selection.

"Patience is a virtue" he said loudly, and chuckled when he stumbled against a pot of impatiens. "I wasn't aware that flowers can be impatient. No wonder it's not flanked by any other flower," he muttered facetiously. The owner, who was standing behind him, said gently, "'Impatiens' is the name of the flower." He laughed again. He asked her if gardenias belong to the rose family.

She twisted her lips in a gesture of denial and added, "Don't get deceived by the petals that are open on top. She pointed to the zinnias with the white and red petals, and suggested that they could make a nice gift.

Massimo looked more confused than ever. He explained to her that he wanted to look around and then decide. He touched a geranium to feel the texture and admired its pretty brown leaves.

A group of children suddenly dashed in front of him and started to put their hands on everything they saw. They broke the stems of some marigolds and terenia with blue flowers that had already made their way around the pole. Massimo cautioned them to be kind. They looked at him with curiosity and headed toward the barn where they found better things to play with.

Massimo continued to peruse all sorts of flowers. Before the exit, he read aloud, like a child, "supertuna." A voice behind him corrected him, "No, it's 'supertunia.'"

"I'm sorry!" Massimo responded in a distracted mood. He left the area without reporting to the owner. "I wasn't impressed much," he sighed. "I'm going to a flower shop. I'm confident I'll find a better selection."

Massimo hadn't communicated with Arian for a long time. Father Mitango had provided him once with a metaphor of the sun and the moon. Massimo smiled, but didn't pay too much heed to it. He had a more specific plan in his mind. He stretched his legs on the armchair and reminisced about the old times, when Arian voluntarily offered him her assistance, the warnings about Elixir and the key that allowed him to open her office door to dub the tape. He looked at her picture and couldn't believe the striking resemblance she had with the girl he met in Lugano. He locked himself in his room, took a pen and an invitation card and wrote a few lines. He stamped it and rushed to the street to mail it. The rest of the evening he spent it thinking, planning and dreaming. He didn't sleep much during the night. His mission was getting close to the end and he didn't wish to leave without settling a case.

# Le Cheval Blanc

In the aftermath of Lugano's disappointment, Arian was deeply hurt. She was very attractive and the courtship was intense, but refused to go out with any young man aspiring to her hand. The scar in her heart suggested to her that men are, by nature, basically unfaithful.

In the succeeding months, a head nurse position was open at San Lazarus in one of the departments. She accepted it and was committed to it wholeheartedly. She was determined to forget, to forget and to live. She ate frugally and lost thirty pounds. The doctor warned her not to lose any more.

The sight of Massimo at the health institution sent shock waves through her spinal chord and revived old memories. She wasn't sure who he really was. The voice was extraordinarily the same as was the demeanor. So she played the game of "wait and see." The invitation came as a surprise due to previous couple of months' lack of communication.

On the evening of the date, she wore a lavender dress that just reached the bottom of her knees. It was made of silk and swayed at will especially when she moved or a breeze passed by, emphasizing her body's sinuous silhouette. She purchased the dress in a stylish boutique in Montreal. The shoes were, as the dress, Italian style, with high heels that added a few inches to her height.

On the job, she wore her hair in a French twist, but for that special occasion, she let it flow loosely on the shoulders, rich in fragrance. Her makeup was subtle, almost nonexistent. She looked in the mirror and smiled. Her lips opened and showed a line of white teeth that shone like gems. She turned off the light and got ready to leave.

Massimo, too, resorted to an Italian boutique for his clothes. He wore a blue suit with a white shirt and red tie. In the jacket's breast pocket, he placed a red handkerchief that matched the tie. His shoes were black and lustrous and belonged to the latest fashion.

At the Cheval Blanc everything had been organized. Only the protagonists were missing.

It was 7:45 in the evening when Massimo arrived at the restaurant.

"*Bon soir, monsieur.*"

"*Bon soir.*"

"*Comment allez-vous?*

"*Bien, merci. Et vous-meme?*"

"*Pas mal, merci.*"

Massimo launched a glance all over the room, but didn't see his date. He asked for a cognac and waited. As the time went by, he started to get visibly nervous. He kept on moving in all directions and gave occasional glances to his watch. He got up and visited the bathroom. He was afraid she would not show up. His stomach was having pangs. He went out to check if she had arrived.

The main door opened and a waiter, in white gloves, welcomed a lady. "Bon soir, mademoiselle."

"*Bon soir, monsieur.*"

"*Entrez-vous s'il vous plait.*"

"*Je vous merci bien.*"

He escorted Arian to the private room. "*Asseyez-vous, mademoiselle.*"

"*Merci, monsieur.*"

"*Voulez-vous boire quelque chose maintenant?*"

"*Pas du tout pour ce moment. Merci.*"

"*D'accord,*" and he left.

Massimo was started to get impatient outside. He waited five minutes. No one was parked in the adjacent lot. He came in and went directly to the private room.

Arian heard the squeaking of the door. She felt someone's fingers on her eyes. At first, she thought it was a dream, but when she heard a familiar voice whispering sweet words in her ears, she felt relieved. He withdrew his fingers and hugged her. "*Bon soir, mademoiselle Arian. Vous-êtes tres charmante, une femme fatale.*" She smiled.

The waiters knocked at the door and asked, "*Voulez-vous du vin blanc ou du vin rouge?*"

"*Du vin blanc et rouge, s'il vous plait.*"

"*Qu'est-ce que vous voulez comme plat de viande?*"

Massimo told him to wait a while. The waiter returned shortly after and placed the bottles of wine and a box on the adjacent table. He excused himself and closed the door behind them.

Massimo took his handkerchief and covered her eyes. "Don't open them until I tell you." He unwrapped the paper from the big box on the next table and said, "Now, you can open them." She untied the cloth and opened her eyes. In front of her, there was an arch of one-hundred fresh red roses. She was overwhelmed by their sight and scent, took a deep breath and muttered, "Thank you, but ... but ... why all this ...?"

"This is the least I can do for you," and kissed her on her forehead.

Arian felt confused, but did her best to conceal her emotions. She started to perspire. He took his handkerchief and wiped her face with gentle touches. He couldn't find the proper words to express his happiness. He rushed to the next table to open the bottles of wine, but stumbled against a chair and almost toppled the silverware. He regained his composure and did his best to be calm.

He asked her, *"voulez-vous du vin blanc ou du vin rouge?"*

*"Ça m'est egal."* He poured the white wine in her glass and handed it to her. He filled his, raised it and said, "To your happiness."

"To yours," she replied in a soft voice.

"To your future."

"To our future."

As soon as he took the first sip, Massimo tried to sing:

*"Chevaliers de la table ronde,*
*Goutons voir si le vi nest bon.*
*Goutons voir, oui, oui, oui,*
*Goutons voir non, non, non,*
*Goutons voir si le vi nest bon."*

Arian smirked and said, "You'll never make it as a singer, but I appreciate your effort."

He held her hands and kissed them. She blushed. The color of her cheeks matched that of the wine. He whispered in her ears, *"Vous-êtes tres charmante."* She smiled faintly.

Massimo raised his glass again and said, "Cheers! To your health and to our happiness."

She raised hers and repeated the same wish.

Massimo took a seat in front of her and began to sip his drink. He was so happy that he had hard time talking. She looked in his eyes and told him to slow down. He looked at her hair and took a step backward in a clear sign of surprise.

Her hair color was different from when he saw her the last time. A cold feeling ran through his spine. She resembled the girl he met long ago in Lugano.

Arian acknowledged the uncomfortable moment and asked, "Is there something bothering you?"

"No, no, I want to apologize for the long silence that fell between us in the past couple months and the way I approached the whole matter." His hands caressed her hair, "I'm indebted to you for all the guidance you gave me from the beginning. I didn't know how to reciprocate, so I decided to invite you to dinner. It's only a small token of appreciation."

Arian smiled and with a flare of vanity in her voice, replied, "Is that the only reason? Usually, gratitude lies at the bottom of the list in people's relations." She smirked and turned her eyes toward him in an inquisitive manner.

"How else could I have expressed better my gratitude if not in person?" he asked.

She lowered her eyes and became serious. "Do you realize that I'm risking my job right now? If someone sees me here with you, it's all over for me at San Lazarus."

The sudden subject change shook Massimo, but he dominated his feelings and answered, "You don't have to be concerned. Downtown Montreal is safe. We traveled in separate cars. I made the reservation under a false name."

"You are absolutely insane!" responded Arian a bit resentful.

Massimo lowered his voice and said, "Last night, I hardly slept. You can't imagine with what trepidation I was waiting for this moment."

"And why is that?"

"Ah, I forgot. You didn't read the card on the roses. He picked it up and handed it to her, "*Pour vous.*"

Arian remained perplexed. She took the card and read it. The fragrance inundated her lungs. She felt inebriated. "Red roses for you, forever … The real Massimo."

As she finished reading the last word, Arian got mixed emotions. She stared at him and inquired, "Who are you?"

"I came here to ask you the same question."

Arian rose to her feet and was ready to leave. Massimo invited her to sit down and stay calm. "I don't know where I met you before. Since I saw you the first time, I have not been able to be in peace with myself. I have to find out. Your eyes, your hair are too unique. They can never be confused with others."

Arian became pale like wax. She covered her mouth with her right hand and was unable to speak for a while. When she recomposed herself, she said, "Your voice, your manners remind me of someone I met a long time ago. One day in Lugano, we went our separate ways, but I never forgot his voice."

"That day, she gave me only her name, the color of her eyes, her smile and a goodbye. I could never find her."

Arian was in a complete state of mental turmoil at this point. She lowered her head and her necklace came out of her shirt. Massimo became speechless! He recognized the effigy of the Blessed Mother and the letters he engraved on it. He had no more doubts.

He said, "It's high time to take off our masks. He rubbed his face and fell backward on the chair. Then, he pulled his gloves off. Arian looked at them and recognized the birthmark. Her heart rate rose dramatically. She started to sweat profusely. He shook his head with incredulity while she remained with her mouth half open. Massimo too was perspiring. In the immediate silence, each was trying to find an answer, each was looking in the mirror of the past. He took off his jacket and placed it on another chair. Arian looked at him with her eyes half closed, and noticed a gold heart with a cross next to it. It shimmered under the light. The events were traveling at the light speed. The game was over. She had no more doubts.

Arian screamed. In that scream, both saw their past. Massimo hugged her immediately. She turned her head to the side and remained still. Massimo realized that she fainted and quickly placed under her nose the small bottle of vinegar from the table. Slowly, Arian regained her consciousness. She laid her head on his shoulders while he held her tightly. Suddenly, he felt his upper arm wet. He touched it. He took the handkerchief and wiped her tears. She sobbed, "It's not possible! It's not right that we wasted all this time."

Massimo hugged her and said, "I'll never let you go again."

"Why didn't you search for me, my darling?"

He sounded surprised, "What? Didn't your mother tell you?"

"Tell me what?"

"I called day and night. After a month of inquiries, she flatly informed me that my insistence was unwelcome and strongly suggested me to give up. She told me … that you were in a convent."

Arian started to cry again, "How could my mother be so insensitive to my feelings."

Massimo tried to calm her down, "Maybe she was being overprotective."

"In what sense?"

Massimo took a deep breath. Again, he wiped her tears and didn't respond. He didn't wish to open a wound whose pains were hard to bear. She was waiting.

So as not to disappoint her, Massimo gave his last explanation, "The bare truth is that I was a Catholic and you are a Muslim. She mentioned the '*disparitas cultus*,' as Mitango said, and talked about the Shaada that invalidates marriages between a Catholic and a newly baptized person. But, I'm no longer a believer, so it doesn't apply to me."

Arian looked at him with surprise, "You mean you are not a Christian?"

"I don't belong to any religious creed anymore. I'm out."

"I can't believe it."

"Well, to conclude my assessment of the contacts I had with your mother, I remember that at one point she suggested that a dispensation could be obtained, etc., etc., but they were all excuses. She made me understand that it was advisable to extinguish my hopes and dreams at the beginning rather than when they got inflamed."

Arian covered her face with both hands, "I feel ashamed." She burst into tears again, "What a waste of time.... What a waste of love.... What a waste of life."

Massimo tried to console her. He plucked a rose from the bunch and put in his mouth. Then, he offered it to her, "You will always be my queen."

She hugged him tenderly and leaned on his shoulder for a long while during which they exchanged smiles, sweets words and future plans. They had forgotten dinner and decided to eat a bite.

They didn't chew the food. They gulped it. Arian wiped her lips and said, "Sweetheart, you must leave San Lazarus as soon as possible. It's too dangerous for you."

"Darling, I can't run away now. I have to honor my commitment. The stakes are high."

"What commitment? What are you talking about? Venus is a terror."

"I have to finish a book ..."

"I don't understand."

"I'm a journalist and I have embarked on a mission. I have to complete it."

"I suspected it all along, but I wasn't completely sure."

"But, darling, did you feel anything when you met me the first time?"

"There was something unique in you. I couldn't spell it out. I was victim of a grand illusion. And you?"

"I had the same feelings. I searched for you all the time. This was another reason why I have been staying at San Lazarus."

"Of one thing I was certain. I noticed that you falsified information on the questionnaire, but I kept quiet."

Massimo bowed his head and said, "Did you discover it? I'm at your mercy."

"My love, why do you use this language? I risked my job and my life for you even before I fully recognized you. But, darling, leave that volunteer job. I beg you."

"I will do my best to make you happy."

Massimo didn't intend to finish the evening on a sour note and talked about his profession at length. Arian was getting tired and leaned her head on his chest. In a soft voice, she said, "Darling, I'm sweating. I feel dizzy," and closed her eyes."

"You drank too fast, my dear," he replied.

Arian had her eyes still closed. Massimo got up, opened the door silently and made a gesture to someone. Two vocalists, a man and a woman, entered and started to sing "Vive la Canadienne!"

*"Vole, mon Coeur, vole! ..."*

Arian slowly opened her eyes. She thought she was dreaming and held onto Massimo's arm. She smiled, but she couldn't get up to dance. She lost her balance and fell into his arms. Her face reddened and she started to perspire profusely. "I can't take it anymore, my darling." Massimo paid the singers and asked them to withdraw.

They were alone again. Arian hung with both arms on his neck and whispered, "Honey, I'm so sorry! I don't feel well. I'm not accustomed to queenly receptions. The contrast between here and San Lazarus is abysmal. I ... I didn't expect the first evening to be so splendid, so full of surprises and so ... painful. I feel overpowered by your kindness."

"And love," he added.

"And love," she muttered.

The two hugged each other. Arian looked through the window and said, "It's a full moon. Let us hope it will always be full of happiness for us."

Massimo didn't hear her last words. He was immersed in deep dreams. She said, "Are you sleeping on me? I understand. We ought to leave now. It's getting late." Massimo, to show her that he wasn't sleepy, said, "I won't leave unless you promise me that the dream born in Lugano is still alive in you and that someday, despite your mother's opposition, we will carry it to the end."

Arian made an effort to smile. She was well aware that it was repetitious, but to please him said, "I promise, *'Chevalier de la table ronde.'*" They both laughed. Arian asked him to go out for some fresh air. He consented and asked the bellboy to carry the roses to Arian's car.

The night breeze woke Arian up more than Massimo. In a matter of a few minutes, she felt refreshed and began talking again with great vitality. They walked down the street hand-in-hand. Occasionally, he put his arm around her waist. The traffic light turned red. At that point, she asked him about Mitango. Massimo recounted how he first met his son and, later, him. "After Ching's death, we got very well acquainted."

Arian thought she didn't hear well and asked a second time about Ching. She was unaware of their relationship. Massimo kindly repeated it. She couldn't believe it! "Can you imagine that? She said. "Even priests have children. This is a bombshell!"

"They are human."

"Excuses, excuses!"

"He was a remarkable man and journalist."

"So I heard. Where did you meet him?"

"At a party ... Why didn't you know it?"

"I wasn't absolutely positive. San Lazarus has become a spy nest."

"You have hit the nail right on the head!"

"The worst is yet to come. There is a secret war being waged. It won't end until the end comes."

"You are being very enigmatic."

"You have gained enough knowledge not to ask me that question."

"Don't you have a file on Ching, Mitango ...?"

"No, Venus is the central office collector in connivance with the main bureau."

"That's how Ching died ..."

"If you are a volunteer, how have you been able to find this secret information?"

"Through my friendship with Mitango ... I have reached a respectable degree of confidentiality since I told him that I met Ching, and that we shared the same profession."

"That's interesting. Be careful! The guards keep a constant watch on him."

"The Vatican keeps him locked up. If he escapes, the walls around San Peter will shake."

"How did you find out about his prelate status?"

"I related to him that I was in the process of completing Ching's dream. How else could I have gained his trust?"

"I still caution you, my darling."

"That he is a high-ranking official, I have no doubts. A couple of years ago, I interviewed him before he was confined here by the Vatican."

"You did recognize him, then?"

"Not really. You must be aware that he too had some facial changes. Remember that the Church changed his name before he was institutionalized, but for obvious reasons we still call him Mitango. We don't want to create confusion."

They stopped before the red light. Arian shook her head and the fragrance of the perfume reached Massimo's nostrils. He pulled her close to him. "Be careful, we are in the street, darling," she said smiling at him.

The light changed to green. They crossed the street and stopped at an ice cream parlor. "The French ice cream is delicious," she said.

"But the Italian is supreme," he remarked."

"That's because you lived in Italy for some years."

"O.K., now you'll see for yourself what I mean."

Arian took a small cone with nuts. After testing the first bite, she exclaimed, "This is absolutely divine."

Massimo laughed. "I had a premonition that you would issue an exuberant comment."

"You read my mind. Now, let me see if I can read yours. You mentioned to Mitango our experience in Lugano. Isn't it true?"

"I did it while we were conversing about faith. I confessed to him that I'm an unbeliever."

"You mentioned that before. What happened?" She asked with interest.

"Well, I told him that I was depressed. I felt alone, terribly alone after your mother's hostility towards me. God rested in his universe, ignoring my troubles."

Arian breathed deeply and exclaimed, "Oh, no, now we have to deal with religion too."

"Not really. I don't have any religious issues. I have nothing to change. I feel serene, tranquil, happy."

Arian didn't respond. She was thinking. The temperature was dropping. The sky, as in every summer, was the stage for dancing stars. They trembled, shone, moved with heavenly music. A meteor decided to leave the pack and fell into space and, finally, somewhere in the frigid waters of the Atlantic Ocean. The wind was gathering in the surrounding areas of Montreal ready to visit the city later in the night, but for the moment the air was still. Only the motors of the passing cars rumbled and spoiled a peaceful evening.

Arian pulled closer to Massimo and put her arm around him. "It's chilly, darling. I'm getting cold." Massimo took off his jacket and placed it on her shoulders, "You are too sensitive to mother nature," he said.

The parking lot was mostly deserted. Massimo smelled the rose in Arian's hair and said, "This scent is simply fabulous. It invades my lungs with joy."

Across the street, someone was taking snapshots of them.

# ARIAN AND THE TAPE

Arian invited Massimo to her house for supper. It was a Saturday evening. Massimo bought a dish of Italian pastries. Arian couldn't resist the temptation and ate a cannolo.

"Irresistible!"

"Aren't you going to eat?"

"I just did."

Massimo kissed her. She said, "Darling, didn't you come here to eat?"

"I'm going to."

"I prepared for you a special Arabic dish."

"It sounds terrific!"

Both laughed and sat at the table for everything was ready.

After dinner, the two sat on the couch. Arian's face expressed a serious look. "Is something bothering you, *mon amour?*" queried Massimo.

"I was thinking about Mitango. He is such a mysterious man."

"Is that all? I thought it was a simple matter." Arian smirked. "It's serious. But first, we have to dance. I brought a disk."

"*Je regrette mon amour.* We dance in public, not here."

"What's wrong dancing here, my darling," Massimo protested jokingly. "Don't be grumpy!"

"Never mind! You know why."

"Oh, darling, it's just a dance. We should begin to practice a few steps."

"*Mon amour, je t'adore, mais* … dancing is dangerous when we are alone."

"If somebody has a dirty mind …"

"Sometimes, we say that we are in control of ourselves but then passion plays its tricks."

"Are all dancers 'lost souls?'"

"Not at all! It depends on various components, age, marital status and self-control. Many people dance because they consider it a physical and mental exercise."

"Darling, even Mitango is a super dancer."

"Good observation, *mon amour*! I would be interested to know who he is and what he did prior to San Lazarus."

"First, you have to give me a kiss."

Arian blew a kiss to him. Massimo protested, "No, no, I don't like that."

"*Mon amour*, you are quite flirty today. Here's the best kiss, right on your cheek. Are you happy now?"

"Almost." He pulled her close to him and kissed her.

"Arian stretched all the way on the couch and said, "Let's hear."

Massimo ruffled his hair and said, "It's on a tape."

"Great! Put it on and let's begin."

"Hold your horses, darling. I already saw it, as you know."

"But, I didn't. I'm awfully curious, *mon amour*."

Massimo attention fell on her wrist. He asked her, "What is that?"

"You mean the bracelet?"

"Yes. What is written on it?"

"'Chastity 'til marriage.' It's a vow that some of us have made. It works. Every young girl and man should carry it."

"Where did you get that idea from?"

"I'm not too sure, but it was a Catholic priest who promote the idea. I hear that it's having great success in Africa." Massimo stood motionless thinking about who it could have been. He frowned and dropped the subject. Arian reminded him that he had to put on the tape and spoiled his thoughts.

When the tape was over, Arian exclaimed, "What a man! I don't believe what he did!"

"It's not over yet, my darling."

"What?"

"That's what I said."

They had an espresso. Massimo complained that it was bitter. She promised that she would learn to make it better in the future. Massimo smiled. She grabbed his nose and pulled it down. "Ouch! You are hurting me."

"You hurt my feelings."

"I was kidding, my darling."

Arian became serious again, "I have to find a job, when we get there."

"You are absolutely right!" He touched his temples and added, "Didn't we discuss this before?"

"I don't care if we did it. Can't you act with more sensitivity when I talk about my future employment?"

Massimo smiled, "If it makes you happy to go over the same subject, go right ahead. Objectively, I don't question your concern, but I assure you that you already have a job."

"I do?" replied Arian ignoring his information.

"At home."

"Which home?"

"Ours ... You will take care of the children, when we get married. I don't want you to work anymore. After all, the income from the book will be sufficient to get us financially secure for the rest of our life."

When Arian heard that, she jumped on her feet and screamed with joy. She surrounded his neck with her arms and started to swing from left to right. "Oh, darling, I love you so much!" she shouted excitedly.

"Easy on me ..." he protested.

"And the government's money?" she inquired.

"That too! It will help us to purchase a house."

Arian was elated. She grabbed a pen and a piece of paper and started to write an agenda for the marriage. Massimo tried to calm her down. "I'm just ecstatic, darling. Can you imagine? We are going to be husband and wife. Don't you love it?"

Massimo remained silent. He didn't wish to spoil the happy mood. At the end, he said, "How are we going to get married?"

"What do you mean?" she replied with worry in her voice.

"You are a Muslim and I'm an atheist. We can marry by the Justice of Peace, not in church."

"I'm not opposed to that prospect. Mosque or church for me it's O.K." she tried to assure him.

Massimo was in an evident state of tension and began to walk up and down the room. He leaned his right shoulder against the wall. He showed concern for something. He released the necktie knot and stared at the floor. Inside his shirt pocket, he had a small calendar. He stood erect and opened it. She followed him with worried eyes, waiting for his next action. He didn't say anything. She walked on her tiptoes until she reached him. She looked on his calendar and noticed Mitango's name. "The Bishop keeps on talking to you even when he isn't around," she inquired with a touch of resentment.

"He is part of my life for good or for evil."

"If that's the case, why don't we discuss the matter with him? I'm sure he will give us good advice."

"He knows where I stand."

"Listen, darling, if it pleases you, I'm willing to make a change."

Massimo felt horrified at the idea that Arian had to compromise her beliefs, "We live in a civilized society. I would never accept it. Faith isn't on sale. It's a gift. I don't want to change and I don't wish you change on my account. One has to change when he or she really believes in the nature of the change and not just for the sake of it ... because it serves a cause."

"We believe in the same God of Abraham, in Jesus as a prophet and in the Blessed Mother."

"In Jesus as a prophet, not a Redeemer."

"Well, that's different. God can't have sons."

"But, your religion teaches you that there was something mysterious in the birth of Jesus."

"It's true. We do know that Mary was Virgin and that she had no husband. That's the crux of the matter. We don't have any explanation."

"What a paradox! The Koran teaches that Jesus had a mysterious birth, that he was a Prophet and that he did miracles, etc., etc., but it doesn't accept what he says about his relationship with His Father."

Arian didn't have an answer, but to continue the conversation, she said, "Why don't you find out?"

"Don't say that! I told you that I'm an atheist. It's a waste of time. I'm just pointing out the contradictions of your religion."

"It's fine with me. When the pear is mature, it will be ready to fall."

"In that case, two pears must get ripe. But, I have my doubts. Maybe, we should live together."

"Darling, I could never accept it. I refuse to live like two irresponsible human beings under the same roof. Either we act as one, or we don't. I don't want to be an anonymous wife, without rights. If we love each other, we face problems together, as a single entity."

Massimo realized that he was walking on a tightrope. He took her hand and led her to the couch. They sat next to each other. They were staring at each other, neither one making any comment. Arian opened her mouth in the act of talking, but he placed his hand on it. "Even if I hypothetically went back to church, it would not solve the issue," he stated.

"Are you concerned about me?"

"That too …"

"I told you already that I have been reading the Gospel and I'm more and more attracted to it. The scene that mostly impresses me is when Peter answers to Jesus, "Where shall we go? You have words of eternal life. You are the Way, the Truth, the Life."

Massimo didn't wish to embark on a theological debate. It was the least thing on his mind. He kissed her on the forehead and said that he would call her later. She accompanied him to the door with chagrin. No word was spoken.

# THE NEWS

Venus dialed a number. On the other line, a polite voice answered, "Hello."

"Hi, I need your assistance."

"Could you elaborate?"

"A professional man of your caliber never asks such a question on the phone."

"I'm sorry! I could be in your office at 11:00 sharp if you give me easy directions."

"Now, you are being too inquisitive," she replied in a fastidious tone, "You got it!"

An hour later, the unnamed man, we will call Mr. A. to protect his identity, arrived at Venus's office. Before he sat, he scouted every inch of the office with his eyes. He bent a few times to ascertain that no microphone was present. Venus watched with amusement. As the investigation came to a close, Mr. A sat in the chair and propped his legs wide apart on the desk. He pulled a pen and a notebook from his shirt pocket and got ready to jot down any information he deemed important for his mission.

Venus observed an ulterior exhibitionistic act and exclaimed, "Is Mr. A satisfied?

"Absolutely!"

"And now what?"

"That's why I'm here for."

"Did you ever meet or hear about a young man by the name of Massimo?"

"Massimo what?"

"Campbell."

"Not a clue."

"Well, I'll help you to find it out. First, I suppose you can guess what I'm looking for."

Mr. A smiled, "I wish I was the object of your inquiry!"

Venus smacked him on the face, "You are being flippant on a serious matter, my friend. You ought to know I have no intention of wasting any more time."

The man checked the side of his face where he had been slapped and slowly brought his hand down until he opened it and perused the fingertips. "It's evident that you can't take a joke," he said.

"I'm not paying you to crack jokes."

"You're right. Let's get down to the business."

"Good! Do you know what to do?"

"I imagine." He opened his right hand and started to press against each other the thumb and the index fingers. Venus gave him a dirty look and said, "Don't worry! Do the job and in the shortest possible time. I'll reward you according to the quality of your performance."

Mr. A jumped out of the chair like a gorilla and exclaimed, "Leave it up to me."

Venus briefed him up on Massimo's physical traits and other generalities and escorted him out of the building. "Don't forget! I want to know everything about him," she reminded him. He assured her with a hand gesture and walked into the parking lot. The car shook a few times and coughed terribly leaving behind a cloud of black smoke. It stopped, spit again a few more times and sped away. The guard was about to close the gate, but Venus signaled him not to bother. The residents didn't appreciate breathing the exhaust fumes and complained to her.

It took Mr. A about two weeks to report back to St. Lazarus. He knocked at Venus's office door. She was having a meeting. He started to walk up and down the hall hoping that she would catch a glimpse of him. She did and dismissed the nurses ahead of time.

Mr. A surveyed the office for professional precautions and sat. She fixed her eyes in his. He pulled a white handkerchief from his back pocket and wiped his brows. Venus didn't loosen her eye grip on him. He realized her impatience was getting oppressive and said, "The man, whose name you gave me, isn't what he professes to be. He is here under false identity."

The statement prompted a confusion of emotions and ideas in Venus's mind and heart. Her pupils dilated; her mouth remained in a semi-open position and her arms dropped to each side of the chair. She covered her eyes with both hands in a sign of disbelief and rolled a couple of feet backward in her chair. "What did you say?" she inquired doubtfully.

"I said what I said and stand behind my information."

"How did you find it out?"

Mr. A got slightly uneasy at that challenge. He scratched his head and, turning his face toward her, said, "It's part of my job."

"How reliable is your source?"

"Highly accurate! By the way, I have been in this business for a number of years. I'm an A student."

Venus disregarded his last words. She looked troubled. Mr. A was waiting for further instructions. When she finally recovered from the shock, she queried, "Is he a spy?"

"It's hard to speculate at this moment. Suit yourself."

"Is there anything else I must be aware of?"

"He is a journalist by profession."

As if she didn't grasp the sound of the word, she shouted, "What?"

"Yes, miss, he is."

"Oh, my gosh! I'm astonished." She exclaimed.

Mr. A waited until she regained her composure and continued. "The face that you see isn't his real one."

"What is this, a word game? Could you be more explicit?"

Mr. A scratched his beard and replied, "He underwent some kind of plastic surgery procedures and tinted his hair."

"He is an impostor, to say the least."

"More than that, madam ..."

Venus got enraged. "Now, what else is there?"

"He works for the Canadian government."

"Doing what? He is scum."

"Would you like to hear more, miss?" inquired Mr. A in a very phlegmatic manner.

She shook her head in a sign of denial and embarked on monosyllabic utterances, "This is suf-fi-cient. He is a spy."

"I only know one way to deal with spies. But if you want me to muzzle him ... it costs you a lot more."

Mr. A waited a while longer for orders. He had given Venus all the information she wanted. She was confused and furious that she let Massimo get that far. He interrupted her pensive mood, "Well, I guess my mission is accomplished."

Venus didn't reply. She took out her checkbook and wrote him a check. He got up and thanked her. "If you need any further assistance, I'm always at your service."

"As a matter of fact, I do." The man was listening.

"I want you to report to me his private life."

"As I said, I'm here to serve you." He placed his right hand on his heart and took off.

The weekend passed by without a hitch at St. Lazarus. On Monday, Venus was holding a meeting with her staff when a tall man with a black hat and blue sunglasses showed up at the office. Venus spotted him and adjourned the meeting. Mr. A entered. First he took off his hat, then he bowed to waist height. She offered him a cup of coffee, which he accepted with delight. "Take off those glasses," she said. "They bother me." The man obeyed and sat. She locked the door with a remote control, and sat in front of him. She kept an eye on the monitor from which she controlled the crucial sections of the building. The man observed every move she made. Venus cut it short, "You are not here to investigate me, but to report on a special mission. Do you understand?"

The man didn't respond, instead, turned back to the door, smirked and said, "I have a gift for you, miss."

"Spit it out!"

"I struck gold last night in Montreal."

"Let's hear! You ought to know by now that I detest paraphrases."

"I have something to say about that, miss!"

"Imbecile, quit talking to me like that or I'll smack your ugly face."

The man felt somewhat humiliated by the word choice and the rough tone. He stood silent for ten seconds. The adrenalin was flowing in her blood. The man didn't wish to let their business relation take a dive. He realized that the information meant a great deal to her and replied, "Last night, downtown Montreal, I was browsing around, as you know …"

"O.K., O.K., get to the point."

"Guess who I saw?"

"Who?"

"A young man whom you know very well."

"Who? Massimo?"

"Exactly!"

"Was he alone?"

The man started to laugh. "Did you say alone?"

"O.K., who was he with?"

"If my information is insignificant, I don't expect to be compensated. Conversely, if it turns out to be extremely valuable, I want the proper remuneration."

Venus showed symptoms of impatience. "And the results?"

"I was lucky to have spotted the right girl."

"Congratulations!"

"Don't be facetious! It all happened outside of a famous restaurant."

"Then, speak, otherwise I crack this bottle on your head." She grabbed a bottle from the desk and was poised to strike.

"Wait a minute!" replied the man, more serious than ever. He took the threat literally and got up to take some distance from her.

Venus got visibly disturbed by his behavior and exclaimed, "Sit down and don't act like a clown. My patience has reached its end."

The man came back to his sitting position and stretched his legs on the desk. He looked at her and said, "I have thrilling news."

"Spell it out! My time is precious."

"Last night, you would not believe it."

"Believe what?"

"I saw two birds very close to you."

"What do you mean by two birds, animals?"

"Not quite! I mean the ones with two legs."

"Do you know how many people move around me? And why would I be interested in their love life?"

"Yes, but these are special people."

"Who?" shouted Venus ready to hit him.

"Massimo and Arian."

Venus remained speechless for a while. The color of her face became wax-like. She was in an evident state of confusion. "It's not possible," she muttered. "Were they alone or with a group?"

"In a private room and in a romantic mood …"

"That Massimo was a…. I had my suspicions, but Arian?"

The man put on his sunglasses and stretched his hand. Venus was about to attack him with a tempest of threats, but decided to keep her temper under control. She let herself recline on the chair. Her face became as gloomy as a dark cloud. In fact, she looked petrified. The man moved his hand back and forth in front of her eyes, but she didn't budge. He was debating on the next step to take. He tried to shake her up. She was staring at the wall. He waited ten more minutes and was relieved when he saw her breathing normally again. "For Pete's sake! You scared me. Are the two birds in your nest?" asked the man in an agitated state.

"Never mind," she answered in a feeble voice.

"If I knew that they would have such a negative impact on you, I would have withheld the information."

"No, you acted wisely. Now, I have to determine how to deal with those who eat in your same dish and ..."

"Worry about your health!" said the man in an alarmed tone.

"I must confess to you that I felt the blood rushing to the brains and my heart stopped temporarily." She stretched her arm forward and added, "There is no need for any concern."

"I hope that your temporary condition is unrelated to them."

Venus didn't respond. She showed symptoms of debility and fatigue. Occasionally, she took deep breaths and massaged her neck. She got up to resume her routine activities, but her legs were wobbling. The man shook his head and said, "Miss, you need rest, a lot of rest. I'll come back in a couple of days to pick up the check. If you need me for additional investigations, I'm at your service."

Venus nodded, sank in the armchair and fell asleep.

Outside of San Lazarus, Massimo couldn't sleep that night. He was on the verge of getting up to call her, but resisted the impulse. He didn't want to scare her in the middle of the night. He turned on the TV, but didn't watch it. He walked from room to room until daylight came.

Arian, too, had difficulty sleeping. After various futile attempts to fall asleep with chamomile, she decided to lie on the couch. The last stars were bidding goodbye to mother earth and a bunch of clouds were traveling at a fast speed toward the west, clearing the way to the sun, which was about to show up in the East. Even the birds appeared restless and squabbled among themselves before they reached a truce and welcomed the new day with their chirping.

At San Lazarus, Massimo and Arian returned to their separate buildings. Many disabled people caught a glimpse of Arian and noticed a metamorphosis. The nurses were the first to notice it. One of them whispered to a colleague's ear, "Someone seems to be in love."

The other responded, "How do you know?"

"The demeanor, my friend ..."

"Can you imagine the power that love has? It can move mountains. It can light a light in the heart of a cold person. It's like the sun that melts the polar ice."

"Yea, it can raise dead people from their tombs," she replied in a joking mood.

The rumor of Arian's transformation traveled at the speed of light and everyone speculated on the possible Romeo. Some nurses ventured in making bets about her sweetheart. Arian dismissed any question relating to her private life.

At Elixir, the atmosphere was leaden. It looked like the iron curtain of the Soviet Union. The nursing department was tightlipped. Even the patients felt victims of the depressing mood.

# Party at San Lazarus

Venus and her confidant, Joseline, decided to throw a party for bachelors, and invite a select number of guests. Massimo and Arian were at the top of the list. The two agreed to work on it, but were in disagreement where to have it. Venus proposed the Cheval Blanc, while Joseline was in favor of San Lazarus. "Dear, this is a private business. Everything can be hushed up under the rug here. The restaurant has a nicer atmosphere, but is a public place."

"You are right, but that restaurant has a special meaning if you know what I mean. But, all in all, I go along with you."

"What should we write in the invitation?"

"This health institution wishes to honor all unmarried people with a dinner, in honor of the superb job they perform in their respective buildings."

"No, it doesn't work. Let's make it for nurses and volunteers."

"Brilliant idea!"

"Do you think they are going to be receptive to this idea?"

"Why not? We have to make a list of guests and 'voila.'"

"And what about the drink?"

"I'll take care of it."

Joseline wasn't too fond of Mitango and tried to exclude him from the list. On other occasions, at a testimonial dinner, it would have been a terrific idea, but a bishop mingled with partygoers didn't please her. "He could be an obstacle to your plan, dear."

322 THE LAST CHAPTER

"We won't invite him as a speaker. He doesn't need the limelight. We'll keep him in oblivion as much as possible. Nobody knows who he is. So what is the concern?"

"As you wish," responded Joseline, absent-mindedly.

"It has to be the most sumptuous banquet ever seen in this region."

Venus announced her plan to the rest of the nurses and all assured their participation and cooperation. Venus assigned each of them a task, setting the organizing machine in motion. Later, Venus made an accurate list of quests. There were fifty altogether. Claudette was responsible for mailing the invitations.

Massimo visited Arian and showed her the invitation. She did the same. They looked at each other for a while without making any comment. Massimo was the first to express his doubts about attending the party, "I fear she has sinister designs."

"There is no question about it, but if we don't attend, it may have different repercussions. Let us pretend that everything is normal and our relationship is as before, nurse and volunteer."

"Splendid!. Nobody knows anything about us. If she wants to honor us, nurses and volunteers, for our independent work, that's fine with us."

"Does she ever throw parties for people like me?" Massimo inquired with curiosity.

"Oh, yes, it's a tradition."

"If that's the case, we have nothing to worry."

"Not quite! I don't trust her. Make sure you switch the drinks at the table."

"What do you mean?"

"You have be shrewd in some occasions. Do you understand now? She is capable of anything."

"You mean ..."

"Just for precautions ..." insisted Arian.

"How can I do it in the presence of a large crowd?"

"I'll cover you up."

Venus and her assistants worked feverishly to organize the party in a building separate from the residents and used exclusively for that purpose. They decorated the dining hall with balloons. A large sign, with the names of the nurses and volunteers, was displayed on the wall. On the long, rectangular table, they placed flowers galore in magnificent center pieces and candles every four feet. The names of the guests appeared in front of each silver plate. Venetian glassware was the main attention on the tables along with bottles of champagne from France.

One wall was decorated with large pictures of Bacchus and Ariadna in the act of pouring wine before a frenzied crowd.

Against the opposite wall, a statue of the same pagan god dispensed incessantly the beverage through his intimate organ. That place was the most crowded.

On the wall next to it, a pleased Cupid was casting an arrow. Girls with white gloves and in splendid attire were moving around with large trays of stuffed mushrooms, small eggplants, covered chocolates, and rings of squash fried in butter.

Against the last wall, another large table had a mountain of Italian pastries. A sign informed the guests that it was reserved for the end.

At 8:00 sharp, the guests began to pour in. They marveled at the hall's splendor and the succulent food available. Everyone lavished praise on Venus's taste, elegance and glamour. Occasionally, some indiscrete guests opened a window, and the stars took a peek inside.

Massimo, Arian and the Bishop arrived fifteen minutes late. Arian was dressed in a violet silk long gown with a plunging neckline. Her pointed leather shoes were of the latest fashion from Milan. Her long blond hair flowed in waves over her narrow shoulders and a fragrance of peach exuded from her.

Massimo wore a blue suit and a red necktie. His hair was lustrous. It looked as if he had applied a translucent cream on it. His shoes were soft moccasins. His after shave lotion was very strong for the occasion.

The Bishop dressed casually, with a brown pair of pants and a striped shirt. He had sandals on his feet—uncommon attire for a first class gala. His companions made no remark, knowing that he had a sound justification behind it. However, when the Bishop saw everybody in elegant clothes, he realized he was going to cause sarcastic comments and criticism. He rushed back to his room to change. The other two patiently waited for him.

The party was in full swing. Massimo and Arian mingled with the guests, while the Bishop maintained a low profile. From time to time, Venus launched a deep look at him.

Half an hour later, people were still talking and drinking informally. The band played first country music, but when someone displayed chagrin, it resorted to Canadian French songs. The most acclaimed were, "Vive la Canadienne" and "Chevaliers de la Table Ronde." Those who remembered the words sang along. The atmosphere assumed an even higher level of joviality when some special outside guests switched to dancing.

Massimo and Arian concluded that it was the moment to act, and proceeded to check the seating arrangement. In their glasses, the color of champagne was slightly different. Arian moved around the table to Venus's and Joseline's glasses. She made sure her arms blocked the action from the other guests. With the speed of lightening, Massimo switched two glasses with his and Arian's. No one saw the move, not even Mr. A., who was munching and drinking next to Bacchus's fountain, throwing occasional glances in the Bishop's direction. A man with a war medal on his chest approached Mr. A and said, "Fill it to the brim, sir, for this evening is party time. You seem to be a serious man. You ought to enjoy yourself."

"I'm like Lamec. For an injury, I kill. No one slaps me. I live by the '*lex talionis*,' vengeance to the brim."

The old man couldn't understand the underlying meaning. However, the last word, "brim," convinced him that the man was eccentric, with a part of his brain someplace else.

Nurses and volunteers danced freely. The older guests got engaged in endless disputes, spilling wine and other liquors on each other's suits. The loud music contributed to more dissonance among them, to the point they could hardly understand each other. It was party time and it didn't matter if most of the faces appeared shiny, like the ice crystals on mountain tops.

At 10:00 on the dot, Venus and Joseline came from behind a curtain and called everyone's attention. They were both dressed in long silky gowns. In that angelic splendor, Venus took the floor and said, "Ladies and gentlemen, nurses and volunteers of this noble hall, please, take your seats. The confusion suddenly stopped. Arian and Massimo, who were on the opposite sides of the hall, went back to their designated chairs. Venus raised her champagne glass for a toast. She smiled sardonically and her glass touched that of Massimo and Arian. Joseline did the same. Venus continued, "*A votre santé.*"

"*A votre santé!*" responded the audience in unison.

Venus, launching long and self-satisfied glances to Massimo and Arian, added, "This evening, we celebrate fidelity and hard work, two qualities that are losing ground day by day. Massimo and Arian, each in their respective roles, like all of you nurses and volunteers, have contributed immensely to the diffusion of these two working characteristics. All of you nurses and volunteers epitomize the true human spirit, the model for the modern generation. We salute you and we bless you on your new residence."

Nobody understood what Venus meant by "residence." "It's too ambiguous," whispered a boy to a nurse. She lowered her head in a sign of agreement.

It was Joseline's turn. She raised her glass even more and stated, "Massimo, you worked with Arian before. You know each other and seem to form the ideal couple."

The audience reacted enthusiastically to the news. Everybody was surprised. Joseline cut it short and said, "Your next happiness will be eternal. To both of you with pleasure! May you bring joy and peace wherever you go. Your contribution will be remembered forever."

Massimo and Arian pretended ignorance in the matter, but accepted in good humor the congratulations of the frantic participants. What followed was just incredible. There was no sipping, but only gulping of champagne and wine. Shortly after, some of the glasses were full, others were empty. The chaos abated. Many of them were snoring. Venus and Joseline's eyes met with those of Massimo and Arian. It was a long, interminable reading of mind. It was the scrutiny of their souls.

Ten minutes passed by and Venus and her friend started to sweat. Venus got up and leaning over Massimo and Arian whispered, "Have a good time on your next fabulous journey."

"I wish I knew you a little better," responded Massimo.

"The same goes with you Mr. False."

"And that is?"

"You played a perfect game until the end. Now, both of you are about to enter an unexplored kingdom from where no one ever came back. Have a terrific trip!"

Massimo pulled back his chair. He held Arian by the arm. He appeared ostensibly concerned about the disclosure of his identity. He turned to Arian and said, "You are a traitor! You were the only one to know about my real name. Goodbye!"

Arian stopped him, "You can't leave me like this," she responded enraged. "Even now that you labeled me "traitor," I would never betray you. You don't know the true meaning of love. And now, I'm the one who is leaving."

Massimo blocked her way. He whispered in her ear, "My love, if you get estranged from my life, I'm lost. If you really love me, stay with me. Together, we will find out who revealed my identity to her. Forgive me. I need you now more than ever. I love you."

Arian dropped her arms, "You make me so mad!"

"I didn't mean it." He placed her arms around him and hugged her. He heard sobbing.

He looked at her and noticed tears flowing down her face. He took his handkerchief and wiped them. "Don't do this to me, my love. I feel worse when you cry. I want you to laugh." He assured her that no one was listening and said, "We are navigating in deep waters. Let's pay attention to what is in store for us." She nodded and kissed him.

Massimo was getting apprehensive. Venus was conducting herself as usual. He started to doubt that whatever she put in the champagne glass had deleterious effects. She wasn't showing any sleepy symptoms. On the contrary, both she and her friend looked absolutely normal for the time being, except for the sweating.

A shiver ran up Massimo's spinal chord. Arian started to breath heavily and tightened her boyfriend's hand. The tension rose when Venus called, for the second time, everyone's attention. Massimo asked Arian if she felt sick. She replied that she was suffering from heat exhaustion and needed fresh air. Massimo invited her to be patient. His fear grew intense. He didn't believe that the liquor had any effect on Venus and started to worry about their own lives. "What if Venus and her friend played a trick on us?" He whispered in Arian's ear.

It wasn't an easy task to revive the audience. They struggled to keep their eyes open. Some of them were half drunk already and took time to return to their seats. Massimo was taken off balance by the course of the events. Venus raised her right hand and the guards locked the doors. Massimo's suspicions grew even more. Venus raised the glass once again and said, "This party's memories will reside in your hearts forever." The guests complacently stretched their ears to hear more. A volunteer tried to stand on his seat, but lost balance and splashed his glass of liquor on a nurse's dress. The glass fell on the floor and broke in a thousand fragments. Those who were a little sober helped to clean the area and restore order.

Massimo's eyes were searching outside of the window. The moon had turned into an orange color. The wind lost its gentle touch and grew increasingly nervous. Massimo dispelled from his mind any doubt about his thinking ability. He hardly exchanged a word with the Bishop the whole evening and Arian was experiencing emotional disarray.

It was Joseline's turn to talk. Her voice shrieked in the air and called for the audience's undivided attention. She smiled half way and announced a spy game. "It's the most sensational that you have ever seen." Her words didn't have much impact on the half sleepy audience, but she continued anyhow. "Each one of you will undergo a series of questions related to the booze." Those who still maintained some mental lucidity laughed so hard that they too lost balance and fell backward. A pandemonium ensued and it took a while before Mr. A took upon himself the responsibility of restoring the order.

Joseline felt weak and sat. Venus struggled to stay on her feet, but fell to the floor just the same. Her voice had already lost its habitual firmness. It sounded weaker, "Tonight, we will disclose the identity of the spy game, as Joseline told you. You'll love it!"

The audience was waiting for instructions when Arian felt suddenly devoid of strength and gave out a whining sound that was interpreted as fainting by Massimo and those close to him. She slid out of her boyfriend's hand, but he was quick to help her regain a standing position. It was hot and she decided to sit. The people created space around her, to let her breathe easier. One of them rushed to a window and opened it. Venus and Joseline received with joy the news that Arian wasn't doing well, but also realized that they, too, were losing control of the situation. Their bodies were weaker in their normal functions. In a last desperate attempt to prevent any escape, they almost simultaneously tried to alert the guards, but their voices fell dead in their throats.

Their aides suggested they take a break in the room adjacent to the hall. Venus seemed to give in to the suggestion and was comforted by the fact that Arian was still surrounded by attention. Her last thought was that both Massimo and his friend were going to collapse soon, fall into a coma, and eventually to die.

Mitango, seeing that Arian wasn't recuperating well, called the ambulance of a nearby hospital.

Venus turned to her friend Joseline and said in a feeble voice, "I want them to cook in their own broth. I hope I can be a witness. The entrance and exit are locked." She waited for a reaction from her friend, but her glassy eyes sought only help. The ambulance arrived and whisked them away to the nearby ward.

Upon their return, they picked up Massimo and Arian.

The guests lost interest in the party and one by one deserted the hall.

# DEATH AT SAN LAZARUS

The dramatic events of the last evening led people to all sorts of speculations. The prevailing belief indicated that all four people who felt dizzy or weak overindulged in the alcohol and therefore they needed a good night of rest.

In the medical ward, the situation spoke a different language. Joseline and Venus were talking less and their voices were fading. From what she could make out, Venus still wanted to be informed about Massimo and Arian's conditions. One of the nurses replied that they were under observation in a local hospital, outside of the compound. Venus wondered if she would ever see them again.

At the hospital, the doctors diagnosed a severe case of mental distress for Massimo and Arian and advised them to stay off the job for a couple of weeks.

At Arian's house, Massimo commented, "Honey, we made it! We came through the ordeal unscathed."

"When I felt sick, I was afraid she pulled a trick on us at the last moment. You could never be absolutely sure what she was capable of doing in the midst of the chaos." She tightened the belt around her waist and added, "Look at the weight I lost, but I'm so happy we got out alive. Now, I have another problem."

"Which one?"

"The job ..."

"Don't even think about it. You are not going to go back anymore to San Lazarus."

"How am I going to support myself?" she replied with concern.

Massimo smiled. He looked straight in her eyes and said, "It's over honey. You will be staying home and I'll go back to my profession."

"That doesn't solve my situation."

"You don't seem to understand."

She hugged him and said, "Darling, I love you so much!" She released he grip and asked, "And, of Mitango, what will become of him? After all, he delivered us from this mess."

Massimo gently squeezed her hands in his and replied, "We can't do anything for him. Cardinal Mitango has his destiny shaped up. He is like a river which has to run its course. He is a man who makes history."

"But he is old now," she responded with apprehension.

"Out of all his mistakes, he has learned the lesson. You will see."

Venus and Joseline's conditions deteriorated. The doctors couldn't make a diagnosis. Their room was guarded around the clock by stout bodyguards. No one was allowed to enter without special permission. Venus made a last, futile attempt to inquire about Massimo and Arian, but her wish never became a comprehensible sound.

The results of the tests finally came. The doctors tentatively concluded that a radioactive material was responsible for the patients' demise. Initially, they theorized the presence of thallium, but further studies discovered traces of polonium 210 in their blood. They were confined to the last room at the end of a long hall and kept under vigilance around the clock. Doctors feared that the radiation was contagious. Only medical staff had access to their room and had to observe strict rules.

In the successive days, the doctors theorized that placing the moribunds in two separate rooms might be conducive to an amelioration of their conditions. The results were disappointing; indeed, they both got even worse. Further tests demonstrated the presence of thallium in Joseline's blood, but there were those from the medical field who disagreed. It was the classical homicide over which judges and lawyers would find it difficult to prognosticate which way would sway the jury. Doctors were confronted with a rare case of nuclear blood contamination and were at the mercy of guessing. They simply had no knowledge of how to treat it. To the residents getting increasingly nervous, the medical team explained that it's very hard to make polonium 210 and that Russia produces only 8 grams annually. The Russians use it to perforate oil fields in the Caucasian region. According to reliable sources in the scientific community, polonium 210 doesn't posses the power to poison. Their claim is substantiated by tests they conducted on mice, but not on humans.

The doctors who consider polonium 210 poisonous remind us that Marie Curie died from being in contact with radioactive material. The opponents taunted them, explaining that the French scientist didn't use the proper protective equipment. They even display astonishment that such a famous physicist was too careless.

At this time, neither side appears to be right because they could never establish the real cause of death of the Nobel Prize winner.

A close associate of Venus asked one of the team doctors how much polonium 210 was sufficient to kill a person.

"0.2 micrograms," responded the doctor without hesitation.

"Why does it take so long to detect it?" queried a nurse.

"It's not that easy. Normally, it gets lost when you go to the bathroom. We discovered it in the urine by pure luck. We were looking elsewhere."

"How can we protect ourselves here?"

"You have to ingest it in order to be contaminated, but the positions are controversial. Some colleagues offer another hypothesis. According to them, the proximity to the patient can be reason for contamination."

The news reached the ears of the Canadian Parliament, and the Secret Service launched an investigation. The citizens of Quebec ridiculed the government for his lax behavior. They pointed out that radioactive material is available on the internet for $69.00. As a matter of fact, they went on record that the three major isotopes are on sale, Polonium 210, Strontium-90 and Cobalt-60. They also underlined that Polonium 210 is one billion times more poisonous than cyanide.

Venus, in writing notes, couldn't understand how she and her friend got contaminated. She hypothesized that it happened during the manipulating time.

She felt that her existence was vanishing like a candle. Each hour that passed by was like a year of her life bidding goodbye. Her body was covered with medical wires and her voice became feeble, almost inaudible. The medical team didn't know how to treat it. It felt impotent with radioactive material.

Realizing that her life was coming to the end, she sent for Mitango. Her aids were disconcerted by such a request. They couldn't understand the meaning that an old man would have in her life.

Mitango was acquainted with the situation and surmised that the request had a religious component. He put in a briefcase the garments for the Last Rite and departed. The guards checked him out and let him in. The assisting nurses handed him special garments to use and gave him specific instructions to observe. Then, they let him in and locked the door behind him.

As Mitango approached the patient, he put the stole on over his shoulders and took a seat next to the bed. Venus made an effort to realign her position. Monsignor helped her to feel comfortable by placing his left arm behind her back. She touched his pulse and then held a firm grip on it. The Bishop looked at it, but made no objection. Their eyes met. A shiver, like an electric current, crossed their bodies. There was a pause that lasted an eternity. An ineffable attraction bound them together. The air was saturated with suspense. Neither one of them was able to utter a single word. Then, Venus's body jolted. In a spur of impellent emotions, her lips slowly moved, "Father, I'm so happy that you came to see me."

"It's O.K. daughter. Rest and you will be fine. Now, let's hear the confession. At the word "daughter," Venus trembled visibly. She raised her head and added, "My life has been a complete disaster. I don't know where to start or finish."

"It's fine, daughter. Don't worry. This suffices."

She whispered haltingly, "I waited a lifetime for this moment."

"Daughter, stay calm. You need rest."

She stammered, "No, father, I can't rest until you know that I'm your bio … logi … cal daughter. You impregnated my mother Brigitte."

The Bishop became pale. The wrinkles on his forehead showed in all their depth. He felt old and decrepit, lonely and sad. He released his hand from her grip. A pain crossed his chest and his head fell downward. Silence reigned undisturbed for a long time. Finally, the Bishop gave signs of momentary relief. He slowly searched in his briefcase for the Holy Water and sprinkled a few drops on her. With evident efforts, he picked up the bottle with Holy Oil, deepened his finger in it, and made a sign of the cross on her forehead. His voice was almost inaudible, "By the power given to me by the Church, I absolve you from all your sins, in the name of the Father, Son and Holy Spirit. Amen. *In Nomine Domini, peccata tua remito.*" He leaned over and kissed her cheeks. They felt like wax. He touched her pulse. He didn't feel any. Her eyes were open, but glass-like. He placed his ear on her chest. The heart had stopped beating. He remained in meditation for a few minutes.

Someone knocked at the door, but he didn't hear it. When he woke up from his deep contemplative mood, he got up and leaned for the last time to kiss her forehead. A couple of tears wetted her cheeks. He did the sign of the cross, picked up the briefcase with struggle and, dragging his feet, headed for the door. The nurses understood that Venus's soul had left her body. They also noticed that Mitango was in great pain.

# Revelation and the Pontiff's Death

Massimo and Arian heard about the Bishop's heart attack and paid him a quick visit at San Lazarus, where he had been reinstated. Mitango was sitting in a big leather armchair. Massimo inquired about his health status, but got no answer. Arian touched her boyfriend's arm and shook her head. Massimo got the message and didn't press the issue. The atmosphere was gloomy and neither one of the visitors knew how to approach the matter or to carry on the conversation. Actually, they had in mind to ask him to dinner, but realized that he couldn't move from San Lazarus, and they dropped the idea.

Ominous clouds gathered aggressively in the sky above. The winds swept the area and lightning lacerated the air. Thunders followed to increase the fear of an imminent storm. It came, but lasted only half an hour.

The air cooled down. The Bishop asked to open the window. He felt refreshed. A minute of movements on the chair helped him to find a comfortable position. The two guests were expecting that he would make an effort to break the stalemate. The telephone rang. Massimo jumped to pick it up, but Mitango motioned him to let it go. The two young people were undecided on what to do. Massimo thought that by inquiring about Venus the conversation might take off. "Do you know by any chance how Venus and Joseline are?"

Upon hearing Venus's name, Mitango turned his head to the side as if he were perturbed by the question. His jaw got tight. The others acknowledged they had touched a sore spot and apologized. Mitango didn't wish to hold back his feelings too long, "Venus is dead," he replied.

"What?" shouted Massimo. A guard took a peek to ascertain that nothing drastic had happened. He was reassured when he saw that everything was normal, and returned to his position outside of the door.

"And Joseline?"

"By now, she is also dead."

"Oh, no!" exclaimed Arian with a horrified look.

"How did they die?" inquired Massimo.

"It appears an act of radiation poisoning. The doctors have issued conflicting reports. Once they claimed it was thallium and a second time, polonium 210."

Massimo felt compelled by the Bishop's somber attitude to ask him, "Were you acquainted with Venus?"

Mitango waited. Massimo and Arian didn't know what to make out of it. The Bishop lowered his head and muttered, "She was my daughter."

"They are all daughters and sons to you," explained Massimo.

The Bishop reclined his head backward and said between his teeth, "She was my biological daughter."

Massimo and Arian looked at each other horrified. "Are you kidding?" asked Massimo.

"No, and I hope that both of you will keep it a secret. You are a son and a daughter to me. I don't have anybody anymore."

Massimo and Arian assured Mitango that their lips would be sealed on that subject. They felt honored that the Bishop held them in high enough esteem to tell them. A long silence followed.

No one was willing or capable of talking anymore. Massimo wanted to go out and breathe some fresh air. He wanted to confess to have committed homicide. He was visibly shaken.

The Bishop's cellular rang. He was unwilling to pick it up. He was tired, sick and sad. He hadn't been sleeping. On the last ring, he decided to answer. He thought that the lawyer was calling him to inform him about Venus testament. "Hello!"

"Hi, Cardinal Mitango?"

"Yes."

"This is the Pope's private secretary."

Mitango inquired again to assure himself to have heard well. He paused a few moments to straighten in his chair and said, "How can I help you?"

The secretary pointed out the voice was unclear and suggested to the Cardinal to speak louder, which he did and the conversation continued. "I'm calling to inform you that our beloved Holy Father passed away last night."

"What happened?" inquired the Cardinal, half in a daze.

"The medical bulletin indicates heart failure. We will hold the funeral next week and we invite you to participate. You had a great rapports with him."

"But, I … I …"

"I know. Cardinal Mitango, the Curia has lifted its restrictions in case of the Holy Father's death."

Cardinal Mitango remained speechless. He didn't have the strength to thank the secretary. The line remained open until Massimo reminded him to turn off the cellular.

Mitango was staring at the wall. Massimo and Arian understood that something serious had occurred and slipped out of the room without saying a word.

# FIRE AND DELUGE

Due to the long weekend, the administrative body opted for the viewing of Venus's body for three more days.

On the date of burial, the funeral director and his assistants draped the casket in a Canadian flag and positioned themselves to take the body for burial. At that moment, sirens screamed and the funeral procession stopped momentarily.

Joseline didn't die at the same time as her boss, as the doctors had predicted. Psychosomatic conditions play a relevant role in determining how long a patient can resist. She put up a valiant fight against the radiation or whatever was the cause of her imminent death. At the end, she too succumbed to the destructive force of the nuclear elements. Shortly after her friend's departure from the earth, she fought desperately for her life. Alone in her room, she jerked her body to the left and knocked an open bottle of alcohol on a candle above the night stand. In a matter of seconds, flames engulfed the whole room. A window was open, it was very windy outside. The fire spread at light speed to Venus's room. Doctors, nurses, assistant administrators and all the personnel were trapped inside. The ball of fire reached the patients' buildings and the administrative underground offices of the Joy of Living complex.

Massimo was completing discharge papers when he heard the sirens and ran directly to Mitango's room. Smoke had already choked many residents to death. What the smoke didn't do, the fire did. The guards were no longer in front of Mitango's room. With the impending danger, they left the room unattended and ran for their safety.

Massimo wetted two towels. He used one to cover his face and the other to protect Mitango, who was laying on the chair, apparently dead. Massimo did what he wasn't supposed to do. He opened the window and allowed the oxygen to come in. There was no other exit available. He threw the screen away and placed Mitango hanging on the window. He jumped out and rolled on the grass because his clothes had caught fire. He ran back to drag Mitango out of the danger. His clothes were burning. Massimo placed the shirt on Mitango's face and squeezed the water out of it to extinguish the small flames on the body. With the remaining strength, Massimo grabbed Mitango under the arms and dragged him toward the exit.

The police arrived, but had to stop at the gate. Inside, the steel doors got automatically closed. It slowed down the burning rage of the flames, but it didn't avoid a monumental and tragic catastrophe. The firemen finally arrived on the scene.

At the main gate, Massimo was applying mouth to mouth resuscitation on Mitango. A paramedic saw him and rushed over to help him. As soon as Mitango showed signs of life, they helped him in the ambulance and took him to the hospital.

The firemen were engaged in a frantic operation to extinguish the fire. Tongues of flames were billowing in the sky and there was no sign of an imminent storm. The firemen fought the fire for hours, before they could begin to extract bodies from metal bars and ashes. No one escaped death.

The rescue operation was going on when the sky got suddenly dark, dark as asphalt. Clouds gathered above the health institution and lined up in battle formation. The vanguard consisted of small, dark and ominous clouds. They had one feature in common. They all looked pregnant, overdue and ready to deliver. The rear guard was made up of monstrous clouds that ran after each other across the area above San Lazarus grumbling and thundering like wild horses. The air cracked and the wind blistered. The meteorological forecast called for a severe rainstorm over the whole region, but it was far from accurate. A few drops of water got swallowed up by the raging fire and bleak smoke. The traffic disappeared like in a magic land. The trees swayed in all directions ready to fracture their backs. Even the bushes and grass trembled for their fate. All of a sudden, the clouds opened their wide mouths. They couldn't hold back anymore the load and split wide open. The rain poured down onto the earth at an alarming speed. It hit the rooftops, the wire poles, the windows, the doors, the streets, the fields. The animals in the barns were restless and the dogs' barking was a premonition of a sinister event. The firemen's sirens continued to scream like jackals. A storm of unprecedented proportion exploded. After a couple of hours of relentless down-pour, the streets were flooded. In a matter of hours, the water level rose to one meter. Carcasses of animals and all sorts of objects floated aimlessly. Cars were no longer visible and people took refuge on the highest floors, in attics, and, finally, on roofs.

The National Reserve rushed to the scene with helicopters to evacuate the sick and the old, but the visibility was terribly low and they had to return to the base. The general in charge had to postpone the rescue operation until the storm abated.

Church bells rang throughout the night. The daylight came, but the rain increased its speed. At the end of the fourth day, the weather forecast called for cautious optimism. The atmospheric conditions ameliorated. The clouds gave signs of exhaustion. By nighttime, one by one, they receded and eventually disappeared.

The deluge of biblical dimensions caused immense losses both on a human and economic level. It shocked not only the local community, but Canada and the world at large.

The sky smiled again with its sun, but people didn't have the strength to reciprocate. Houses were still flooded. Humanitarian aid arrived from different sources. At San Lazarus, people of all ages were busy searching for their loved ones, for their pets, and for objects dear to them. The area was an enormous cemetery without tombs.

The walls of many crumbled houses and buildings were the real testimonies of an apocalyptic tragedy. They seemed to be stretching their arms to heaven and begging for help. It was nature's funeral.

Eventually, the water receded and the gnashing teeth of steam shovels began to scrape and load mountains of debris onto trucks. Hardly anyone spoke. They moved around silently like phantoms. Their backs curved to touch with reverence anything that appeared to be familiar. Children looked for parents and parents searched for children. The government Recovery Teams worked incessantly around the clock to aid and give hope, to clear and rebuild. The world watched. The Vatican sent Catholic relief organizations to help the survivors and to save Cardinal Mitango.

San Lazarus was a massive pile of debris. Everywhere, one could hear the crackling sound of the flames and the howling of the coyotes. The painstaking job of recovering the corpses took weeks. Many were never found. Their bones were later found in fields or at the bottoms of lakes. Gone also were the records that would have incriminated the administrators. San Lazarus disappeared forever from the map. Hundreds of years of history were flushed down the drain.

# MITANGO IN THE
# HOSPITAL

In the aftermath of the great flood, before moving to Montreal, Massimo and Arian paid a brief visit to the Bishop at the hospital.

Mitango appeared in subdued mood, but confident that the course of health would turn for the better. He was recovering from smoke inhalation and minor burns on his hands and face.

Massimo couldn't hold back his feelings. He was a reporter by profession and had witnessed too much suffering and death. He couldn't suppress the voice of his professional conscience. He sat down and remained silent for a time. He placed his fingers in Arian's hair and started to play with it. Mitango inquired with a mixture of curiosity and reproach, "What is the problem with your fingers, my friend. You keep them too busy."

"Massimo replied, "I'm obsessed by the silence of your Church."

The Cardinal first smiled, "It has been doing all it can. It doesn't dominate the elements of nature. It can only pray and help.

Massimo turned his head toward him with a reproachful look. The Cardinal changed his position to be more comfortable and said, "What don't you like?"

"The silence of the Church speaks too loudly."

"Do you mean that it has not doing or saying enough?"

"Exactly!" responded Massimo with a serious countenance.

"You are being philosophical and theological, but unnecessarily critical," replied the Cardinal annoyed by his friend's comment.

"Take it as you wish. I'm not referring to deluge. I have to send a final report to the government and I think about the pro bono philosophy which has characterized the Church's policy since Constantine times. There has been a tug of war between state and religion, but in the end, they helped each other."

"They should cooperate or not? By the way, what brought you to this topic?"

"I just told you that I have to send a detailed report to the government on how doctors write medically unnecessary prescriptions, the insurance corruption, etc., etc. I suppose conspiracies will continue in other health institutions but this report will put an end to them. Aside from that they want to know my reactions. I have seen so much! I'm going to tell them also how your Church talks about euthanasia as an evil, but it doesn't speak against the immoral prices of medicine that the pharmaceutical companies charge, the food being wasted every day by restaurants and school cafeterias. It never raises its voice against air pollution …"

"My dear friend," said the Cardinal adjusting again to the right side, "The Church is always concerned with the existence of evil and the spreading of evil because it affects everyone of us. Evil and nature have destroyed San Lazarus. What could the Church do?"

"Why did it not move before to stop the immorality of Joy of Living?"

"The Vatican isn't an investigative body. It had no influence at all on the Joy of Living administration. It's the government's responsibility to uncover corruption. Likewise, it would be foolish to blame the Church for not doing enough to prevent the tragedy of San Lazarus."

"Then ask your God to justify this catastrophe! I can hardly swallow it. I feel depressed."

"The justification theory excludes the presence of evil in the world. This is a preposterous philosophical view. We affirm that God doesn't support evil; He doesn't sanction it; He would not want it to exist."

"How many people have perished under the rubbles of earthquakes, bomb explosions, in a church? The questions that spring spontaneous from our hearts are, "Where was God? Why did He abandon us?""

"God has his plan. How else can we explain the natural disasters of biblical memories, poverty, incurable diseases, hatred and wars?"

"If you reflect on it more carefully, "added Massimo, "Satan is on a winning streak for eternal dominion."

"Your theory is fallacious," replied the Bishop. "If that were the case, it would make Satan more powerful than God, which is impossible."

"Look at yourself! Doesn't the devil have the upper hand? Your God should overpower him."

The Bishop frowned; he wasn't going to let the argument slip away from his grip. "Don't be so sure!" He replied. The god of evil will never prevail. He may win only small battles and that's because God doesn't intervene. When the eternal time swallows up our chronological time, even the demons will end up in their endless damnation."

Massimo shook is head. He didn't agree with the Bishop. "Yours are mere speculations, pure theories that bounce back in confrontation with reality. This is the difference between evil and good, Lucifer and God. I'm a realist, while you love to theorize."

Mitango responded, "Your logic is earthly-oriented. Your life's paradigm is self-centered, meaningless, wingless, godless. You have no place to go. You are in a human cage. Your god of nothingness is mute, deaf, shapeless. As rational beings, we feel sure that there is a divine entity, an eternal Spirit, who controls the universe and the destiny of mankind."

Massimo laughed. He was going to argue his point, but Arian reminded him that she wanted to arrive in Montreal before dusk. Massimo assented, he turned to Mitango and said, "We are about to leave for Montreal. And you, what is your future?"

The Bishop placed his burned arms on Massimo's hands, but withdrew them quickly. He looked at both of them and said, "The doctor said that I need to stay here at least two more weeks. I deserve a vacation. I would like to visit the Yosemite Falls, which are easily accessible from San Francisco Bay. Did you ever go there?"

"No, I didn't. Right now, that's the last thing in my mind." He paused and said, "Oh, wait a minute! Maybe we will visit it on our honeymoon."

"Oh, it's gorgeous! The massive Yosemite has high and low cascades. According to the geologists, it has the greatest granite monolith on earth. I also want to see Bridal Veil Fall with its 620 foot gorge. The water hits rocks, spins and falls in a turbulent descent."

"How do you get there?"

"Highway 120 is the shortest road from San Francisco."

"If I'm not mistaken, Marshal discovered gold on the American River in 1848."

"Yeah, everything was peaceful until the gold rush began and tent cities sprung up all around it. There is a lot to see.... Afterward, I'll see if I can do some work."

"You always persevere, don't you?"

"I'm like the fish in the ocean. They have no fixed place to live. They are in perpetual movement."

"You never change, my dear friend." He took a professional card and gave it to him.

"If you need anything, you can count on us."

"I know I can. Incidentally, how are you doing with the book?"

"You mean *The Last Chapter*?"

"Yes!" and his face glowed.

"I'm about to finish."

"I'm going to buy it," and he made an effort to get up. Massimo invited him to stay put and hugged him. Arian did the same. Tears appeared in the Bishop's eyes. Massimo and Arian couldn't stand the emotion and ran out.

# THE "SENTENTIAE LATAE"

Massimo and Arian took residence in Montreal in two separate apartments. Massimo resumed his journalistic profession. Arian wasn't working, Massimo wanted her to arrange the wedding. Montreal was a place of recent memories. The balmy climate was conducive to a romantic evening, so, they decided to eat at the Cheval Blanc. They sat at the same table where they dined before. Their minds were flooded with memories. Arian was reminiscing about that date when a bellboy knocked at the door and handed a bunch of red roses to Arian. Massimo gave a tip to the boy, who bowed and withdrew.

Arian smelled the roses. The scent inebriated her nostrils and longs, not to say her heart. She closed her eyes and remained silent for a while. Massimo waited until she opened her eyes again and said, "You look like a goddess, but I'm starting to believe you have a secret admirer."

Arian laughed. She touched his nose with her index finger and said "Don't be silly!"

"Who else would send them to you?" He inquired.

"You are being cruel," she quipped.

"O.K. then, open the card and read it! The note will confirm my position."

Arian read the card and broke down in tears. "Why do you do this to me? You are a sadist," she stated facetiously.

Massimo hugged her and helped her to wipe the tears from her cheeks. "Sweety, you are the air of my lungs. You killed the monster and led me through the labyrinth. You saved my life and my profession. I owe all to you. You gave me your love and the energy to go on. You steered me to the right direction. I would not have been able to accomplish my mission with the government and with Fania without your indispensable contribution."

Arian blushed. For the first time she really felt important. She brushed her hair and checked her face in the mirror. She lifted her head in a gesture of satisfaction and placed her arms around his neck. He was waiting for her to say something. She whispered something in his ear and he smiled. Massimo told her to close her eyes. He took a small box out of his back pants pocket and gave it to her, "This is yours. It goes with the roses. You may open it now."

She looked at the box and asked, "What's this?"

"It's a secret."

"No, tell me!"

"If I tell you, it's no longer a secret."

Arian, by then, expected any surprise from him. She was quite nervous and her attempt to open it failed. She turned to Massimo for help. He took a knife from the table and ripped the paper. Arian opened it. Her face glimmered. "I can't believe it!" she exclaimed. "It's awesome!"

"Put it on!" Massimo invited her.

First, she hugged him over and over until Massimo stated, "This gift deserves a gift."

She nodded. Massimo had just started when the waitress appeared on the threshold of the door with two trays in her hands.

Massimo felt robbed, but Arian assured him, "My darling, someday, you will have all the time in the world. Remember that freedom thrives only under the tutelage of responsibility and discipline, otherwise it becomes violence to freedom.

"I didn't realize you were a moralist."

"There is no alternative to a healthy existence, my dear."

Massimo's cellular rang and she stopped talking. On the screen appeared the Cardinal's number, but Massimo was concerned about the gift and didn't respond.

Arian took Massimo's hands in hers and leaned with her head on his chest. "Darling, real love transcends passionate love. If you really love me, don't get frustrated. Someday, you will be proud of me. Nowadays, girls don't have any concept of true love. Starting from the way they dress, they don't respect any code. It tells you a lot about their behavior. Girls who dress immodestly invite the opposite sex to make all sorts of conjectures. I refuse to be like them. I don't want people to make salacious remarks about your wife. I'm here to honor you and our family. Got it?"

Massimo marveled at the moral lesson that his girlfriend taught him. For the first time, he agreed that modesty is a crown of glory for a girl. He looked at her bracelet and said, "Father Mitango did many good deeds in his life, despite his weakness."

Cardinal Mitango survived the suffocating moments and the burning at San Lazarus and never forgot Massimo for his heroic act. The doctors dismissed him from the hospital after two weeks. He had to make a choice. He refused to make contact with the Vatican. He didn't trust the invitation and believed that it was a trap. He resisted the temptation, and flew to the Pacific coast. San Francisco was much more secure. He visited the Yosemite Falls and the countryside for about a month. He looked rejuvenated and ready to pursue his objectives.

In the subsequent days, he worked body and soul to a long time pet project, a Church free from traditional rules and more in tune with current times. He ordained ten married men to priesthood and called for a conference to defend his action. The news reached the most remote corners of the globe and raised many eyebrows in Rome. It was an act of defiance and insubordination that the Vatican couldn't overlook anymore. It also precluded further possibilities of opening communicative channels with the new Pope. The other denominations applauded Mitango's action because it was consistent with the Gospel's teaching, but the Curia applied the *"Sententiae Latae"*—an automatic excommunication that went into effect immediately. Cardinal Mitango had another thought brewing in his mind. He was ready to talk to the pontiff, but on his own terms, otherwise he was determined to create a schism.

Massimo's failure to respond promptly to the Cardinal didn't please Arian, "Darling, don't you think it was unkind of you not to respond to his call?"

"I will, as long as you are happy."

"No it's not right. He's having more problems and maybe he needs to convey his feelings to you."

"What kind of problems is he having?"

"He is having a final confrontation with Rome. At his venerable age, I don't think it's advisable."

"Oh, yes, I heard of it."

Massimo was playing with his lower lip. Arian passed her hand in front of his eyes. He caught the message and said, "Life is complicated and unpredictable because it's mysterious. A colleague from California called me up this morning and informed me that the Cardinal is still thinking about having a child later on."

Arian twisted her head toward him, "With whom? This is ridiculous! He's out of his mind. This is egoism, plain egocentricity. Who is going to raise him at his death? How long does he expect to live? I'm sorry! This is pure folly! And what about his future wife? How is she going to have a baby at an old age? Is he going to marry a spring chicken?"

"I share your feelings. It doesn't make any sense to me. Do you understand, now, why I'm atheist?"

"What does that have to do with anything? You should state that modern priests want it both ways. They like to get married and serve God. Don't they learn the rules before entering the seminary? Why don't they leave when they find out they can't uphold their chastity vow? I respect those who give up their habit if they fall in love, more than those who complicate their lives and the Church's too. But, no! They have to stay, complain and make a lot of noise like wasps. Obviously, they enjoy generating malcontent among the clergy and, and as a result, they cause a loss of faith in the believers. I suspect that we are also dealing with egocentrism."

"My dear, the whole issue amounts to a loss of values. No one reads the Bible. Nobody wants to talk about it. They fear that by reading it they get bitten. I'm no longer in the Christian flock and that's none of my concern, but this seems to be the truth. People are more interested in the decoration, the outside ..."

"You mean, everything is a façade?

"Exactly! Rarely do you hear a clergyman telling it as it is. One of them is Cardinal Hummes, who the other day, admitted that priestly celibacy isn't a dogma."

"He is right, but did you see how he changed his mind as soon as he reached the Vatican? He tried to mollify his position. He said that Peter was married, but the tradition imposes its restrictions."

"Maybe, others too got married, but we have no direct evidence. Could you explain to me why the Church is adamantly opposed to marriage for its clergy?"

"The Church has solid reasons to maintain her stiff position. Her contention is threefold: although it's not a dogma, the prelates argue that it's a tradition, a discipline which has been standing for seventeen long centuries. It goes back to the year 306."

"That's debatable. And they could change that tradition."

"Of course, but it's inconvenient," rebutted Massimo.

"Why do Protestant and Anglican ministers get married? The vocation has increased in their ranks."

"I'm sorry to disagree with you. Since the Lutheran Reformation of 1532, there has not been any vocation increment. Ask them!"

Arian didn't agree completely with her boyfriend on the priestly rebellion and proposed her own ideas. "I believe that the sexual revolution is undermining the

Church progress. The god of sex is dominating. It's a terrific business and as the Chinese say, "When it comes to business, we don't give any discount."

"Your argument is valid, there is no doubt about it. We are being overwhelmed with sex language and innuendos in magazines, radio, TV, music, newspapers, etc."

"I hope you don't get upset at me, darling, if I ask these questions."

"No, I'm not upset. You are not asking; you are answering, to be accurate," rectified Massimo. "At any rate, I don't belong to any church, why would I get irritated. The basic issue is how to change a law enacted at the Council of Elvira, Toledo, in 306, which prohibits priestly marriage."

"Before that date, didn't the clergy have the freedom to choose the celibacy state or not?" asked Arian.

"They were also lay people who opted for a chaste life. According to the Church, as I understood it from Cardinal Mitango, the first reason for celibacy is Christological. The candidate promises to follow Christ's footsteps, as did Paul.

The second motive is ecclesiological. The candidate priest understands that the Church is going to be his spouse and, therefore, he has to dedicate his life to her.

The third reason is eschatological. What does this mean? The clergy's celibate life is a preannouncement of the future life. I don't think that the American and Canadian clergy should take argument very lightly. The Vatican is dealing with an issue whose roots are deeply embedded into her history, into the apostolic age."

"If you look at it from the Church's perspective, it's a wonderful life," said Arian. She looked out and noticed that the moon was smiling. "And, those who can't make it, but have faith? What are they supposed to do?"

Massimo laughed, "Let's talk about ourselves," he suggested.

"I'm afraid we can't do it without mentioning the Cardinal. He is part of our life," emphasized Arian.

Massimo lowered the tone of his voice and said, "I suppose you are right."

Arian appeared more interested than ever in learning the fundamentals of the Catholic Church. She was fascinated by Church history, the councils, the synods, the saints, and even the temporal power of the pontiff. The internal dissention of high ranking officials, she explained, "was part of the growing process. Islam is much more simple as a religion, but squabbles occur there too." She was a bit tired and leaned with her head on Massimo's shoulder. She confided to him that she felt sorry and concerned about Father Mitango's excommunication.

Massimo had something else going through his mind, but bowed to his girl-friend's request and said, "I share your concern. He is officially excommuni-cated."

"He doesn't seem to care, though?"

"He'd better! When I talk to him, I'll tell him."

"He is a man of courage though."

"There is no doubt that someday he will rewrite part of the history of the Catholic Church. He is a champion of common sense."

"Is that why he is being persecuted?"

"Easy on the words!"

"Well, he has no choice. Incidentally, how strong is his reputation as a healer and exorcist?"

"I don't have the faintest idea! If I'm an atheist, how can I believe in the mira-cles of Father Mitango? I must admit that he still has a reasonable following in Fiuggi. His ex-parishioners swear by his thaumaturgic gift. Although such claims have widespread consensus among the populace, from the Vatican walls only skepticism emerges. And you know how conservative the Church is on miracles? In the Vatican, the main accusations are the use of magic rituals during the Mass and his weakness with the opposite sex."

At that statement, Arian laughed with all her lungs. She couldn't understand the rationale behind it. "Love is the most beautiful gift from Allah. Do you find anything wrong with that? All men are interested in women. If they don't, some-thing is unnatural." She covered her face with both hands and blushed.

# MITANGO'S CRISIS

Mitango lost everything at San Lazarus, even the briefcase. He traveled to San Francisco with absolutely nothing.

In California, he took residence in a five star hotel across from the Golden Gate and, with the assistance of Poverty Church, he organized a conference on Married Priests, his pet project.

As we had the chance of mentioning before, just to remind the reader, Poverty Church was headed by a man who surrounded himself with an aura of Messianic grandeur. In fact, he claimed to be the Second Messiah. He went even further by claiming that he was greater than Christ because he didn't get married, even though he was contradicted by one of his staff who declared that Jesus married Mary Magdalene. The Reverend or Lucky Star masterminded the conference and supported it financially.

The conference wasn't born under a good premise. Cardinal Mitango's association with the Reverend caused an internal friction with other Catholic organizations on Married Priests. Not only did they disdain the relationship, but refused to attend the conference, thus creating mini-schismatic fractures that worked against the Cardinal's main plan. To them, it was repugnant to submit to, not to mention to accept, the sponsorship of a church whose ideals were antithetical to the Catholic Church. Poverty Church advocated the vilification of the cross by trashing it or breaking it as a symbolic gesture of departure by the priest.

The Cardinal's aspirations were soon doomed to failure. Out of 200,000 registered participants, only a few thousand actually attended the conference. The criticism lodged by the small Catholic clubs for Married Priests pierced the heart of the Cardinal.

The following day, sitting in his hotel room, the Cardinal was experiencing a deep depressive mood. He plummeted into an isolationistic state and became unapproachable. In the afternoon, he looked in the mirror and, for the first time, he felt lonely, extremely lonely inside, and nauseated to the point that he ran a couple of times to the bathroom on the verge of vomiting.

Beside the bed, he fell on his knees before a crucified Christ and in the midst of a spiritual crisis cried out "Lord, I repudiate everything I did, even with good intentions, outside of the Church. My conscience is in a state of turmoil. I can't stand it anymore. My association with the Reverend is the greatest crime I committed. It's greater when I think about my silence. I didn't renounce it and didn't denounce it. I placed myself at the mercy of a man who usurped your glory and divinity, a man who pretends to be greater than you. This is the greatest apostasy of our times and I did nothing to disassociate myself from him and his cohorts and didn't do anything to expose his Endemic arrogance to the world.

"I'm at fault Lord for acquiescing to the profanation of the cross, the symbol of our redemption, with my silence, and this weighs like a rock on my heart.

"No, no, it's not so much my desire to get married that bothers me. Look at me! I'm like a candle which is being consumed by the flame of individualism and more individualism. I let those two forces manipulate me. It should not be like that, but '*Vincit Vim Virtus*.' I allowed this arrogant man to enter into the veins of our Church and sew rebellion.

"I'm no longer worthy of being your son. I beg your forgiveness and I vow here and now to be no longer a tool of separation, but of union, not of dissention, but of communication. I won't let you down anymore, my Lord and my Savior. If I don't honor my word, let me die. Life would not be worth living anymore."

He fell forward with his arms widespread and remained in that position the whole night.

# Massimo's Report

Massimo submitted his research material to the Canadian government. As a result of it, the Parliament made a sweeping change in the health care system. Their first priority was to crack down on dishonest insurance companies. To that end, it enacted a law that created a Senior Citizen Institution under the direct supervision of a state authority. This reform allowed, as a first step, the temporary integration of old people in their families' homes. The law provided only certified nurses to assist the patient during the day for medical needs, and a nurse practitioner who attended on the patient's needs until the family members came back from work. Those relatives would be paid for the rest of the night and weekends on hourly basis, if they so chose.

Additionally, the new law provided for a family member to stay home and take care of the parent or relative. The pay would be equitable to the one earned on the job, including the benefits.

Furthermore, the law stated that nurses, attendants and family members would be subject to impromptu daily visitations by federal agents. Private institutions would be the last resort, especially for those old people who longer had relatives. In that case, health care centers would operate under the direct supervision of federally appointed personnel, who in turn, would be under the supervision of another team.

The legislators agreed unanimously that an old person is much happier and healthier living in a home environment than in an institution. Such optimum results could be obtained only under a tight scrutiny of a federal supervision.

Lastly, the report called for the creation of centers reserved exclusively to family clans, relatives and close friends. Such a congregation would be conducive to better health and more productive life. Mentally capable patients, if they so desired, could exercise some working activities. It also suggested the installment of hidden cameras for patients' surveillance. This technological application would reduce the manpower of daily checkups from 30 to 50%.

The Canadian government took the report seriously and has embarked, ever since, on a gigantic project. According to the Finance Ministry, there would be a saving of two billion dollars in the first five years and an improvement of life by 25%. The fabulous initial results are catapulting Canada into the forefront of old age health care, a model to the world.

There was one more obligation for Massimo to complete. He called Fania, the editor, and reported to her that he had complied with federal agreement and he was approaching the final stage of *The Last Chapter*. She felt relieved and asked how many more pages he had to write. "I'm not sure about the number," he replied, "but I'm close to the end."

"What is the holdup?"

"Some events have yet to develop."

"I don't like your short responses."

Massimo smiled. "Darling, my words are roses that I throw on your balcony."

"You better write those words in your book, never mind the roses."

"You are an inspiration to me."

"Quit being silly or I'll hit you on the head when I see you. Give my love to Arian. By the way, will you invite me?"

"You will be the first, my lovely cousin."

"O.K., Valentino, keep me informed as soon as you finish. Great job!"

"Ciao."

"Ciao."

# THE VATICAN'S CALL

Massimo wanted to get in touch with the Cardinal, but his cellular was constantly busy. His private secretary was trying to keep up with the calls coming from everywhere. "This phone doesn't stop ringing. At times, I feel like changing the number," she stated almost perturbed.

The phone rang again.

"*Bon jour*, this is Father La Salles. Is the Cardinal going to Rome?"

"Sorry, Father, I have no information at the moment."

A minute later, the phone rang again, "Hi, this is Father La Fayette. Is the Cardinal available or did he leave already?"

"I'm afraid he is still in town."

A third time within a minute the phone rang, "Hi, I'm Father Forgette, is the Cardinal around or did he leave?"

"Not that I know. If he does, you will be informed."

At eleven o'clock, Father Forgette called again. The secretary told him to wait. She turned to Cardinal Mitango and said, "The Cardinal who is in favor of married priests in on the line."

This time, the Cardinal picked up the phone. "Father Forgette, how are you?"

"Good news for you, my buddy."

The Cardinal attempted a half smile, "Is it? Not really ..."

"What do you mean? You must go. It's your duty."

"You forgot that I'm excommunicated."

"It's trash, Cardinal, pure and simple trash."

"Not with the Church, my old friend. The Pope has already riled that other Christian denominations are either defective or not true churches. Can you imagine the status of Poverty Church?"

"I understand. See if you can arrange a compromise."

"Some in the Curia side with me, but the new secretary of state, Bertone, holds the philosophy of the previous pope. Hummes is malleable and Giordano is hesitant. Paradoxically, the African bishops are firm on the excommunication."

"Their private feelings should not impinge on your right to vote. Incidentally, the Pope wants to revamp the Mass in Latin. Latin is the language of God; its mystery. We have thrown in a few years all that is mystery. For instance, when the priest says, *"Introibo ad altare Dei."* (I will go to the house of the Lord) ..."

"The Orthodox Church has maintained its liturgical mystery even in the gestures."

"Right, the Eucharist has its own language. It's not the same as that of the painter ..."

"Right, how they changed it, I don't know. Latin was the official language of the Church, law and theology. In 1570, it was completely renovated. Everything is regulated. There was nothing spontaneous, emotional, creative. Then, came Vatican II ..."

"My idea is that if they issue obligatory rules on this matter, it's going to follow a disaster. The Church should not rule on every minutia."

"I agree with you. Going back to our previous topic, can you promise me you will travel to Rome. As you know, many things happen at the death of a pontiff."

"An excommunicated priest doesn't stand a chance in a thousand."

"The Reverend can use his leverage to see if you can at least vote."

"Not a chance, my friend. Virtually the whole Curia is against me. Why would they bend my way? That would be a defeat, whose repercussions would make the Church tremble for the next century and beyond."

"I insist. We must carry our cause to Rome. You are the only high ranking prelate in our movement who can cause a jolt to their thinking."

"I have done it, and look what happened to me. And, what happened to Lefebvre? You don't realize that Rome doesn't condescend to compromise on certain issues. It entrenches in a one way street."

"We are a growing church. New priests are swelling our forces."

"I won't give them any satisfaction. I'm not going to humiliate myself. If they wish to open a dialog with me, they have to do so on my terms."

"Be realistic! You have nothing to lose."

"Oh, yes, I do. My freedom and possibly my life."

"Your safety is being assured by the Reverend."

"Listen! I escaped twice. The third time could be fatal for me."

"Don't exaggerate!"

"I'm being realistic. I'm a free man and I'm determined to remain free."

On the other line, Father Forgette was waiting patiently for the Cardinal to change his mind. There was a long pause. Finally, Father Forgette said, "I repeat, we can provide you with an escort."

The Cardinal wasn't interested in continuing the conversation any further and ended it by saying, "I'm going to carry on my battle from here."

# THE CONCLAVE

In the Sistine Chapel, the Cardinals were conducting the election for the new pope.

After the first ballot, there was a deadlock between Cardinal Hummes and Cardinal Mi-Song from China. The next ballot showed a change in preference. This time, it was a battle between Tattamanzi and Hummes. To break the deadlock that had lasted for a month, the Latino and African cardinals initiated a pro-Mitango movement. They invoked his name to break the deadlock. The Canadian representatives voiced opposition. Their contention was that Mitango had forfeited his right to vote by engaging in an activity which was clearly schismatic and that excommunication prevents a cardinal from participating in the voting process. Tension began to rise and some of them were losing their self-control.

The dispute lasted all day. Before breaking ranks for supper, Cardinal Ruini launched a proposal that appeased everybody. If Cardinal Mitango would come to Rome and refute his association with Lucky Star and repent before the world in a timely fashion, the elective body would consider his admission. This suggestion received unanimous consensus and Cardinal Ruini called Cardinal Mitango, but he wasn't in San Francisco. The Cardinal College was in dismay.

Cardinal Mitango remembered the promise he made to Christ after the flood survival, prepared the suitcases and departed.

Lucky Star became furious, for the Cardinal had left without his approval. He claimed that he had made hundreds of thousands of dollars flow into his coffer and now he deserted him. He called that behavior defection and high treason. He immediately withdrew the bodyguards and all financial assistance from him. Then, he announced a reshuffling of his plans and started to work on a secret project.

# THE PILGRIM IN ROME

Even in winter, the Roman climate is tepid, inviting, full of gusto, like a glass of mellow wine. The average temperature is about 70 degrees F. On January 22, the weather conditions worsened dramatically. People scrambled for coats and scarves in the stores. Coffee shops were crowded with sneezing people, who added an extra shot of Sambuca in to their espresso. Nobody challenged the weather, except for dire needs. The sky was gray all around. The sun was sleeping in its empire. The cold spell increased in the following couple of weeks before releasing its grip on the Eternal City.

It was during the freezing days that an old man huddled in a monk habit. He took the sandals off his feet and walked barefoot. He spread ash on his head, took two sacks that he had sewed together and slid them on his shoulders. He didn't have any food or water with him, only a Bible. As he arrived on St. Peter's steps, he sat and bent foreword in a posture of prayer. Occasionally, he took off his glasses and cleared the mist off of them with a rough cloth. He covered his head with a hood, which made him unrecognizable. Tourists and pilgrims launched glances of curiosity at him and soon formed a circle around him. Every hour, he got up and walked around the Vatican. In the evening, he slept under the Bernini colonnades. The Italian police and the Vatican personnel didn't make any attempt to remove him. The man, who used to exorcise, to dance, to sing, to heal, stood there in the freezing night coiled in on himself, devoid of strength and, perhaps, hope, defenseless, impotent. Gone were his charisma, his smile, the sparkle in his eyes. Those eyes that used to stare at evil, to threaten it, to order it out of someone's body, eyes that shone in the spotlight of television interviews, now they were buffeted by blistering winds and cold. That voice that resounded under the vaults of the churches or in the streets to drive out evil spirits, that ordered a maimed patient to stand and walk, that made pronouncements against AIDS, slavery, and injustice, that thundered against prostitution, that sang joyful songs in the festivals before an oceanic TV audience, now languished in the depth of his throat. Those feet that ran and jumped during the religious liturgy or interlaced in African folkloric dances in public or at a party, and that genuflected before the crucifix in deep contemplation, now were motionless, cold and twisted in an awkward position, in a completely dormant position. The man had distanced himself from the world. He didn't hear the bell, the crowd, the police sirens. He appeared to be in a total abandonment of his body and mind.

For three days, the man repeated the rituals. At the end of the third day, he struggled to climb the stairs. He paused a while to regain his breath and composure. He tried again, but he was devoid of strength and plummeted down the steps. A cameraman ran over. He helped him to stand up and reach the top. The newscasters gathered. At that point, he raised his hands to heaven and stated, "I wanted to go back to Mlolongo, build a church and spread the Gospel of Jesus Christ. Instead, I married and ordained married priests, as you all know, in defiance of my Mother Church."

There was silence, a long inexplicable silence interrupted by the sound of heavy feet of the Vatican's gendarmes.

The Swiss guards were formally created by Julius II in 1506. It was a corps of 150 guards that in course of the centuries has decreased slightly, reaching the present level of 130. To be eligible, the young Swiss young people must have completed military service. They are enrolled for two years that can be extended at the discretion of the captain.

At the end of the third day of the hooded man's penance, and with the Conclave still in session, the commander of the Swiss guards, assisted by two lieutenants, came over and conveyed a message to him. They helped him to read it, and led him to the Sistine Chapel. Drowsy and weak, he refused to wash up and change his clothes. He was half dazed and didn't know what was going on.

An African Cardinal got out of his seat and brought a glass of water to Mitango. An oppressive silence hung in the Chapel. It seemed a surreal picture. Father Mitango's eyelids vibrated, opened slightly and closed again. This proceeded for a couple of minutes until he was able to open them all the way. He looked around. The Cardinals' faces were stiff. He recognized most of them. He raised his head to Michelangelo's Last Judgment and stared at His skin dangling down in Purgatory. The Cardinals continued to observe a respectable silence, too heavy for him to bear. He covered he face with both hands and fell forward on the floor. Someone got up with the intent of helping him, but the president motioned to him to stay put.

During the Conclave no cellular is allowed in the Chapel. Cardinal Mitango had one in his pocket. Suddenly, it rang. The Cardinal College froze. How was it possible that the guards had failed to check him out? They were amazed and tried to call the attention of the president who was ready to put a stop to it, but Cardinal Mitango was already talking. "Hi, Father Mitango. I'm happy you followed my suggestion. The Reverend doesn't share my philosophy, but he will get over it."

Cardinal Mitango, finally, responded in a resolute manner, "Father, my involvement with the Married Priest movement is over."

"What?" the Father replied with astonishment.

"That's what I said and I stand by it."

"You mean … you are going to leave us?"

"Father, I'm all done fighting the Vatican. Whatever change we wish to bring, it has to be done from inside in a collegial fashion and without external interferences. The Pope is our leader. We must obey him."

"Are you departing from the Reverend?"

"I'm leaving him, his money, his power, his institution, his way of life, his philosophy and his aid. I don't want to have any part of him anymore. The Church, my Church is a divine and human institution. I messed up in the approach and I'm ready to put en end to this rebellious spirit once and for all. You tell the Reverend that I uphold the crucifix. It's the symbol of resurrection. Tell him that the Messiah came once and will come for the second and last time. Tell him that I repudiate everything he stands for and all of you who don't have the courage to stand for your belief. I don't think Rome will forgive me this time. My sin is too great. I can't undo what I have done. When I was a seminarian, I learned that I had to unite, not divide. The Vatican may not forgive me, but the Lord will. Goodbye, Father."

Father Forgette didn't have the opportunity to answer. His hand remained stiff for a while until his phone fell on the table.

The rebellious Cardinal turned off the cellular and threw it in a corner. "I'm so sorry that had to happen." The Cardinals were speechless. Father Mitango was exhausted and fell again face down on the floor. He made an effort to straighten his back, but failed. With his head down and the arms stretched out, he regrouped his energies and cried out, "Before the world, I repudiate everything I have done with the so called "Poverty Church" and those independent groups that try to create havoc within our Church. All these schismatic mini-movements are a danger to our Catholic faith.

"I take this opportunity also to confess my sins to the Church, to you and to God, and pronounce the Act of Contrition. I come back to where I came from and submit unconditionally to the Church Magisterium and to the papal authority. I'm ready to accept any disciplinary action the Holy Spirit wants you to impose on me. His power is greater than anything else in the universe. He has subjugated me. I have sinned against the Church and against heaven. Although I acted in good faith, it's time to come back home. This is my home, our home. We must be careful neither to generate internal rifts, nor to offer signals of dissent among us. We must obey, be humble and patient in our discussions. Our ultimate goal is to work for the success of our Mother Church for which I'm ready to shed my blood. Treat me as you wish from now on. I'm prostrated before Jesus and I implore forgiveness. I beg an act of clemency to you Princes of the Church to annul the excommunication and accept me as a re-born man. I'm no longer worthy of being a priest or cardinal. I only implore your forgiveness. I can't run away anymore. My race ends here and now."

The entire body of the cardinals disregarded the cellular episode, the excommunication and the marriage. They gave him a standing ovation that lasted for five minutes. The Secretary of State helped him to stand up and exchanged the kiss of peace. The presiding cardinal recommended an hour of pause during which Mitango could wash up and put on the cardinal's garments. The Curia would, in the meantime, ratify a document for the annulment of the excommunication.

Cardinal Mitango came back with full cardinal rank and the election proceeded. The presiding officer counted the ballots and announced the election of the new pope. The crowd in St. Peter saw the green smoke rising in the sky and cheered.

# Habemus Papam!

The election resumed. They counted the ballots and the presiding cardinal ordered to put the paper for the gray smoke in the stove. A shout of jubilation followed his words. This time, the general feeling was that a "dark horse" had been chosen. Many speculated that the new pope was from India, Pakistan or China. And, someone guessed that he would be from Russia. All the attention was focused on the president. He called for order. Once everyone took his seat and observed silence, he said, "*Habemus Papam!*"

Again, the electoral college applauded. The chapel became suddenly silent when the president took a paper in his hands and read, "Cardinal Mitango is His Holiness."

Some hardcore conservatives protested, but it was too late. The president reminded them of the gifts of humility and obedience. The chapel quieted down.

It was an intense emotional moment for the majority of the Cardinal College, but especially for Cardinal Mitango. He protested, tore his garments and cried out, "No, this isn't possible! He begged to rescind the results on the basis of his unworthiness. He looked around and scrutinized each one of them seeking sympathy. He found only smiles. "The Church has spoken, Holy Father," said the president.

"Holy?" repeated the Cardinal with disbelief. "I'm not holy. I'm a sinner. I betrayed my Mother Church."

"So, did Peter with Christ. It's not up to you judge, Your Holiness. Christ chose you through us. You are now the Shepard, the Fisherman, the Vicar of Christ."

The new pope knelt and said, "In the name of Jesus, I obey."

The bells rang. A priest appeared on the balcony of St. Peter's Square and announced, "*Habemus Papam!*" About 3,000 tourists crammed the square up to Via della Conciliazione. Everybody was anxious to see the new pope.

Massimo and Arian were watching the course of the events on TV.

"I bet they elected a French pope," muttered Arian.

"No way, he would cause more problems than Don Quijote. Frenchmen are too liberal."

"It depends. They could have chosen a Canadian. You never know."

"It would not make much sense. I would go for a Russian. He would be able to mend the rift with the Orthodox Patriarch, Bartholomew II."

"How about a pope from Mexico or Argentina?"

"That would be fantastic."

"Sh … sh. The new pope is coming to the balcony," said Arian.

Massimo's eyes widened like a football field. Arian almost fell off her chair. The presiding cardinal announced, "*Habemus Papam.*" A roar rose from the square and spread miles around. "*Mitangus Africanus novum papam est,*" repeated the speaker. The crowd cheered. In a blink of an eye, St. Peter's Square became a show of African flags. Black people began to jump from jubilation; others improvised dances.

The Pope gave his blessing '*urbi et orbi.*' He stood there for five minutes to give the chance to the crowd to discharge their feelings of joy and then withdrew.

Massimo and Arian remained speechless. They hugged each other and shed tears of joy.

# THE POPE'S INVITATION

Arian came to her boyfriend's apartment to prepare the evening meal and then returned to her own. She was in the process of cooking, when the bell rang. Massimo entered and hugged her. She kissed him on the nose. "Tired?" she inquired.

"Not much, but I'm still in dismay for the papal election. My colleagues kept on asking me questions all day long. The editor is exhilarated."

"That was a shock. I can't imagine how he got elected. It's beyond my rational thinking."

The phone rang. Massimo picked it up, "Hello?"

"Hi, this is the Pope's private secretary. May I speak with Massimo Campbell?"

"This is he."

"The Holy Father requests your presence and that of your girlfriend next Sunday in Rome at his inauguration ceremony."

Massimo didn't reply. The secretary was waiting on the other line. Massimo coughed more than once, then, he said, "We are honored ... This is marvelous news. Just a moment, please!" He took the phone and placed it on his heart.

Arian feared something wrong happened. She caressed Massimo's head and asked, "What going on, honey?"

Massimo fumbled, "His Holiness ... Pope Mitangus Africanus has extended ... an invitation to both of us."

"It can't be," she answered in disbelief.

"It's true. His private secretary is on the phone."

"We will be there. Thank you, immensely," said Massimo in a quivering voice.

Arian broke down in tears. Massimo pulled a handkerchief from his pocket and wiped her face. "My love," he said, "Life is so intricate, so complex, so unpredictable.

"I'm so confused.... Somehow," said Arian sobbing, "I felt that he would regain his status. I never doubted that he would not forget us."

"It's unbelievable!"

"Let's take a bottle of champagne and toast Pope Mitangus."

"Grand idea! But can you postpone it to later? Right now, let's eat!"

"No, we have to make travel arrangements, the passports ..."

"We have to pack."

"How long does it take? Half an hour?"

"No, darling, your assumption is inaccurate. Women need a lot more time than that."

Massimo changed his mood and became serious. "Remember that we are attending a papal ceremony. He may very well ask us to sit at the front. What I mean is that we have to bring the best of our wardrobe. He is unpredictable."

She nodded. Her face was glowing. "Did you really think that I would not bring enough clothes?"

"I never doubted it." He touched her hair and said, "Arian, he was born to be free. Someday, he will be greater than Luther, not because of his rebellious spirit, but for the spirit of reformation and unity. History will confirm it."

"You resuscitated him, my darling," objected Arian.

"There is a reason why your God has predestined an African priest to be on the throne of Peter."

"What do you mean, 'your God'?" she replied, joyfully patting him on the face.

"I'm sorry, honey. We went in opposite directions long ago, never to meet again. I got disillusioned with the Church policy on gay marriage, gay priests, celibacy status, ignorance and empty faith, loss of values and pretentious sanctity, those sad faces within the church walls, those false prophets and the opulence so common among them."

"Wait a minute!" responded Arian with grace, but firmness. "I'm a Muslim, but I can't negate that that is art, not opulence. It's because of the Church involvement that we can admire such stupendous art productions. Those paintings and sculptures are in homage to the divinity and his ministers. Those works of art are an instrument of faith. I don't accept your verbosity in this respect, my darling."

"I wish I could be wrong," replied Massimo absorbed in deep thoughts. "But I see disrespect to the Church in everyday life. Priests that walk around without the cross on their chest is a form of disrespect, an affront to the religious institution they represent. Every abnormal aspect of their behavior is sanctioned on the basis that they must mix with the crowd. It's an alibi that doesn't sufficiently justify their position. Not to disclose a sign of belongingness, such as the habit or the cross is a prevarication, a shame."

"As a dissident, why didn't you discuss the differences and work for a change? My faith is based, for instance, on the teaching of the Prophet and not on the political hierarchy. I would never change my faith."

"It's not that, my dear. We are an ocean of people in the desert. You don't know how thirsty we are. We seek springs of pure water, but there are very few. Faith is a fire that burns constantly, that allows the union with God, that gives the opportunity to discover him every day. In this technological world, where man is losing his identity, we feel even more the desire to love and be loved."

"Darling, but don't you think that we are wearing masks? Don't you feel the need to search for Allah? We consider him a problem, but we are the real problem. If we throw out the mask, we will meet Him. We are lonely because we choose to be so. This is the price we are paying for pretending to be gods, to do everything on our own terms. Without God, we are like sparrows in a tempest. We lose our own identity. Our existence doesn't have a meaning anymore. We need faith, the vehicle that makes the connection with God possible."

"And that's what I lack, my dear. I don't believe in anything anymore."

"Faith must be cultivated. It can't be placed in a corner to collect dust. It takes time and good will, unless the light strikes you on the way to Damascus." Arian caressed him and said, "Darling, do you think that I'm talking like a Catholic, although I'm a Muslim?"

Massimo laughed. "I would say so, but I also know your tricks," he said. They hugged each other and decided to take a walk. The course of recent events was amassing a lot of emotions on them.

# The Papal Inauguration
# and Marriage

Since early morning, pilgrims and tourists alike were flowing to St. Peter's Square. By 10:00 even the adjacent streets were flooded with people. It was a human ocean that wanted to show support to an African pope. Black people were united for the first time. The greatest representation was from Africa. They came in flocks by sea and air. They dressed in the most exotic colors and traditional costumes, and carried flags, drums and other native musical instruments. The dignitaries from every continent landed in Rome and took seat in the designated area. The Master of the ceremony assigned a priest, as a guide, to Massimo and Arian to the left wing, in the first row, along with Latin American presidents. The African segment was euphoric. They cheered, sang, danced and played. The whole square was a scenario of fable in choreography and emotions. Television cameras were stationed on the rooftops and newsmen, accredited to the Holy Sea, had their reserved seats.

Arian leaned toward the priests and asked, "What is the Pope's hat?"

"That's called, a tiara. It's a cone covered with a fine cloth with a cross on it."

Why does the Pope wear a tiara? Is this another invention of the Church?"

The guide looked at her with surprise. He took off his glasses and said, "It's a tradition." He put back his glasses back on and smiled, and so did Arian. He felt that the answer had been unsatisfactory and added, "Emperor Constantine, before transferring his imperial court to Constantinople, gave it as a gift to Pope

Silvester I. It was a gesture of good will towards the Christians. The Pope didn't wear it, but placed it in St. Peter's Treasure."

"It was never part of the papal vestment?" asked Arian with obvious curiosity.

"Constantine I, a Syrian, was the first pope to war it in 708. He died in 715. San Gregory II was born in Rome, but he continued the tradition."

"How can you be sure?"

"The paintings show it."

"And the crown?"

"Initially, there was one crown. The French Pope, Benedict XII, put three crosses on it. The tiara reappeared in Rome with Pope Nicolo V."

"Forgive my imprudence, but the tiara doesn't express a terrestrial power?"

"Well, no, it really shifted the power from the pope to the papacy."

"Didn't Pope John Paul refuse to wear it?"

"You are absolutely right! It was called 'The Great Refusal.'"

At 10:00 sharp, the Pope arrived in all pomposity and with the escort of dozens of cardinals, and the conversation came to an end. The Pontiff sat on the throne of Peter and blessed the crowd. He looked around and recognized Massimo and Arian. He whispered something to his secretary's ear, who immediately conveyed the message to Massimo.

Massimo and Arian were confused and thrilled. Their emotions overwhelmed them. Someone noticed tears flowing down Arian's cheeks. With unsteady pace and holding hands, they followed the secretary. When they reached the pontiff's chair, the secretary said, "Kneel before the Holy Father, both of you." Massimo had a moment of hesitation, but Arian tightened her grip on his hand. Arian first and then Massimo knelt and kissed the papal ring.

The Pope invited them to stand up. He got up from the throne and embraced them. He returned to his throne and asked the secretary to accommodate them next to him.

The Pope introduced them to the audience, "Look who's here! Two friends of mine." Arian was visibly shaken by the emotion. Massimo held it together better. At one point, he leaned toward the pope and asked him, "How were you able to get to Peter's Keys?"

The pontiff lowered his head and replied, "Someday, we will elaborate. Right now, I have to say that it was the will of God. The Holy Spirit works in so many mysterious ways. We are instruments of his will. I hope and pray that the Christian wind won't only blow on the African land, but in every corner of the world. I want to dedicate the rest of my life to that end."

Arian wore a white silky dress, blue cotton gloves and a white hat. Massimo wore a black suit with a bow tie and a blue shirt. The Pope looked at them and said, "You are dressed for the occasion." He pushed a button and the carmerlengo showed up. "Take these two doves for confession. I'm going to marry them."

Massimo and Arian were stunned. Each one attempted a protest. Massimo explained, "Holy Father, as you very well know, I don't believe anymore."

"But you believe now. You were a believer and you have been reborn again."

Thrilled with the opportunity of marriage before the world, Arian was at loss for words. She started to perspire profusely, "Holy Father," she said in a thin, soft voice, "I was a Muslim, then I studied Christianity ..."

"I know; I know. Now, you believe in the Resurrected Christ, our Savior." He turned to his assistant and told him to proceed with the preparations because he would marry them.

Massimo and Arian, inebriated by happiness and confused by the sudden switch of events, followed the priest. Massimo stopped and looked at the clergyman, "We don't have the rings."

"The Holy Father is aware of it and offers them to both of you as his gift." Massimo muttered, "He is incredible!"

The sun hits hard even in the morning and many tried to find shelter under Bernini's colonnades. Massimo and Arian arrived with the assistant priest and the Holy Father in person celebrated the marriage ceremony.

During the exchange of wows, Arian was so overwhelmed by emotions that she was unable to answer the pontiff when he asked her if she wanted Massimo for husband. He smiled and repeated it a second time. The crowd cheered and applauded.

The Muslim dignitaries didn't appreciate Arian's change of religion. They displayed their chagrin at the end of the ceremony. One by one they departed without congratulating the newlywed.

The groom kissed the bride and acknowledged the good wishes of the cardinals and foreign dignitaries.

It was almost noon. The Pope's secretary announced that the Holy Father was going to convey the '*urbi et orbi*.' At the end of it, he withdrew to his office where he met briefly with some foreign heads of state.

Massimo and Arian decided to stay in Rome for honeymoon.

Two days later, the pontiff spoke again and stunned the world. He said, "You don't realize how agonizing is for me to address this issue. It has caused profound dissensions within the Church since the Fourth Century. I have reached a compromise between tradition and current reality, a mixture that reflects biblical truth. From now on, priests will have the freedom of choice. They can marry or they can uphold their celibacy."

The Cardinals looked at each other in dismay. Some priests in the audience applauded; others remained petrified.

"The Church," the pontiff continued, "needs the courage to synchronize with the times. It has to change, not for the sake of change, but for the sake of truth. The priest that chooses marriage can't live in the rectory and may have to look for a part-time job to sustain his family, and he can't aspire to the rank of bishop. In the event of divorce, he stops being a priest. Times have changed. The world is more technological, academically based and more demanding than generations ago. A bishop has to maintain a celibate state because his onerous obligations are too compelling to divide time between the Church and his family.

"The Church recognizes the affective needs of each individual priest, but we should also accept the fact that chastity has its advantages. Not everyone is born to be celibate.

"This gift is given only to a few. The imposition of celibacy is a failure. The Church can't impose Christ on any conscience, let alone marriage. The Church has spoken.

*Gloria Tibi Domine.*"

The papal bull exploded like a bombshell throughout the world. Each media instrument gave ample space to the news. On the spur of the moment, the reactions were mixed, but then, they became predominantly favorable even on an ecclesiastic level. The debates on priestly marriage soon lost momentum and the mini-schismatic churches separated from Rome on the marriage issue readily announced their willingness to be immediately reinstated in the Mother Church. Those clergymen who were complaining or acting underground, came into the open to hail the papal bull as the greatest in two millennia.

# DEATH OF THE POPE

When Massimo and Arian were alone on the balcony of the hotel, he placed his arms around her and planted a soft kiss on her forehead. The moon spread her splendor over the eternal city. Arian's face glowed. His too was shining. He took her hands and kissed them. She whispered, "From now on, my life will acquire a new dimension. I already feel an enormous responsibility."

"I, too, went through a metamorphosis," declared Massimo in a contemplative mood.

"Did you ever think that Mitango would become Pope Mitangus Africanus?"

"No, it never passed my mind. He had insurmountable obstacles in his way."

"It has to be divine intervention. How else could it be explained?"

"You are absolutely right!"

"Everything seems to be a dream."

"It's not a dream. It's reality. You mean the dream became reality."

"Something like that." She held him tight and said, "My husband, my love …"

Massimo's cellular rang. On the other end: "Hi, how are you doing?"

"Just fabulous, Fania."

"I hear noise in the background. Where are you?"

"In Rome."

"You are being mendacious."

"I have no reason for it."

"You are a lucky dog!"

"Sometimes …"

"Who's in your company?"

"My wife Arian."

"What? I don't believe it!"

Massimo told her about the past events and Fania couldn't believe it. Everything seemed unreal. She asked about the last part of the book and he said, "Tomorrow, I'll send it to you."

"Great! And what about the wedding party?"

"Don't worry cousin! You will be the first to be invited."

"You better, otherwise I won't talk to you again!"

They both laughed. Fania asked him to pass her to his wife and she congratulated her. "When we come back, there will be a wedding reception like never seen in Montreal."

"I count on it, baby!"

Rome was waking up the following morning. The coffee shops were getting crowded and so the trains and buses. The traffic began to move from all sides of the city and the sun was trying to open its way through a bank of thick clouds.

In the Vatican, the personal secretary of the pope had the order to wake him up at 6:00. He knocked at the door a few times, but didn't hear any response. The long silence made the secretary hypothesize that the pontiff was sick. He took the main key and opened the door. The Pope was in a sleeping position. He touched him, but received no response. He checked his pulse and his heart. The bodily functions had stopped. He said, '*Sic transit gloria mundi.*' Now, we will languish in the dust for a long time." On the night stand next to him, there was a half glass of water and a note. He emptied the glass into a flower vase and unfolded the paper. The only written words were, "*Dominus non sum dignus.*"

The secretary ran to the other offices, unable to speak. The Cardinals saw him in distress and got up. Only one remained in a sitting position. He queried, "Is the Holy Father dead?" The secretary nodded his head and sank on the soft armchair.

## THE END

978-0-595-49856-7
0-595-49856-6

Printed in the United States
203004BV00002B/67-96/P